The Quilters Club Quartet

The Quilters Club Quartet

The First Four
Quilters Club Mysteries

Marjory Sorrell Rockwell

ABSOLUTELY AMAZING eBOOKS

ABSOLUTELY AMAZING eBOOKS

Published by Whiz Bang LLC, 926 Truman Avenue, Key West, Florida 33040, USA

For information contact:
Publisher@AbsolutelyAmazingEbooks.com

ISBN-13: 978-1505670998
ISBN-10: 1505670993

A friend said he finally figured out quilting. You buy perfectly good material, take it home and cut it up into little pieces. Then spend days putting it back together again.

- Fons & Porter's Love of Quilting

The Quilters Club Quartet

Introduction

Welcome to Caruthers Corners, Indiana. No, it's not a real place, but it should be. So let's pretend. With a population of 2,574, all the folks know each other pretty well. The founding families trace their ancestors back to 1829, when a wagon train was stranded in the middle of "Indian Territory." Today, it consists of clusters of Victorian houses and a short Main Street that runs past a grassy town square with a bandstand facing the two-story brick Town Hall. The surrounding countryside is farmland, growing corn, soy … and watermelons.

Caruthers Corners is known for its annual watermelon festival. The Cozy Café on Main Street serves watermelon pie. And the DQ next door offers watermelon ice cream.

In the summer, kids fish along the Wabash. Families picnic at nearby Gruesome Gorge State Park. Holidays are special occasions here.

Who would think that crimes take place in such a placid, friendly, pleasant little town? But they do. And sometimes these bad deeds they trace back to earlier times.And often, as it turns out, quilts figure in. Which is why the Caruthers Corners Quilters Club -- Maddy Madison and her friends Cookie, Bootsie, and Lizzie -- get involved in solving the mystery. These quasi-detectives are often assisted by Maddy's spunky granddaughter Aggie.

The stories in this anthology feature these wonderful members of the Quilters Club. Before you know it, you'll feel like you know them ... and next thing you know you will be quite at home in Caruthers Corners. Maybe you didn't grow up here, but it will sure seem like it.

I hope you'll come to love visiting Caruthers Corners as much as I do.

- Marjory Sorrell Rockwell

The Underhanded Stitch

A Quilters Club Mystery

1

Good friends are like Quilts. They age with you, yet never lose their warmth.

- Anonymous

CHAPTER ONE

No Dogs Allowed in the Boneyard

The first memory Maddy Madison had of her childhood in Caruthers Corners was her father saying that her dog Tige (named after Buster Brown's famous canine) couldn't go with them to Aunt Tilly's funeral. "No dogs allowed in the cemetery," he explained. Then jokingly added, "Folks don't want your puppy running off with a bone."

What a silly thought, she'd told herself at the time. Tige preferred table scraps.

That had been more'n fifty years ago. And Tige had long since joined Aunt Tilly in Heaven. She was sure that dogs joined their masters in a joyful afterlife – although Reverend Copeland was strangely silent on the subject.

Sometimes she and her friends at the Quilter's Club discussed the concept of life after death. It seemed reassuring to Cookie Brown, whose husband Bob had passed a couple of years back. A tractor accident.

Vast farmlands surrounded Caruthers Corners, growing mostly corn and soy, although once the area was known for its watermelon crops. Each year the townsfolk celebrated Watermelon Days, a wonderful event marked by bands playing in the town square, a parade down Main Street, watermelon-eating contests in front of the courthouse, and the famous watermelon pie-making competition. Watermelon pie was always a favorite among visitors to the festival. Most people outside of Caruthers Corners had never even heard of watermelon pie. In fact, posters advertised: "Never heard of watermelon pie? Then you need to join the fine folks of Caruthers Corners for their famous Watermelon Festival!"

Maddy had been born here, met her husband Beauregard Madison at Watermelon Days, raised three fine children in the big Victorian house on Melon Pickers Row. The kids (well, if you could call a trio of thirtysomethings "kids") were now off enjoying their own lives in other places:

Bill – the oldest – and his wife Kathy were running a Youth Center in Chicago.

Freddie – the "baby" of the family before his sister arrived – and his wife Amanda lived in Atlanta, where he was a decorated fireman; something that Maddy's husband Beauregard loved to brag about every chance he got.

Then came Tilda, the darling little girl who was adored and spoiled by her brothers and father. Named after her great aunt, Tilly – despite all the childhood pampering – had turned out to be just like her aunt. Sensitive, yet stubborn she lived over two thousand miles from Caruthers Corners (*way* too far away in Maddy's opinion). She'd married her high-school sweetheart who was now a tax attorney with a big firm in Los Angeles. And while Maddy never trusted big pretentious law firms, she was still taken by surprise this spring when Tilly announced that she and Mark were breaking up!

Now, heartbroken and bitter, Tilly and her daughter were headed back to tiny Caruthers Corners, back to the family homeplace with its familiar bedroom, unchanged since her teenage days, pennants proclaiming *Go Caruthers High!*, and cheerleader's pom-poms still decorating her dressing table.

Oh my. What would it be like, having one of the children back home? Maddy asked herself. Especially one with a broken heart and a ten-year-old daughter? She didn't know what to expect. And what's more, she didn't have the slightest idea how she'd handle incorporating a grown daughter and a precocious ten-year-old that she barely knew into the household she and Beau had had all to themselves for several peaceful years now.

So Maddy posed this very question to the Quilter's Club that Tuesday. The four women always met on Tuesday afternoons to talk and stitch and swap quilt patterns. Besides their love for quilting, these four ladies were best friends and confidants.

The Quilter's Club meetings were usually the highlight of the week. Maddy and her quilt-loving friends also gave each other ideas and suggestions on fabrics and colors for their selected quilt patterns. They often exchanged fabrics, too, because everyone had an abundant supply of fat quarters, scraps from other quilts, and of course a selection of favorite old clothes just waiting their turn to be "re-born" in a quilted masterpiece! And if anyone was really in a pinch to finish her quilt (because it'd been promised to a local charitable auction or planned or a special birthday), they all chipped in.

The gathering this week was no different, except that

this time Maddy had the sad story of Tilly to relate.

"Disruptive," snapped Lizzie Ridenour. Lizzie's divorced daughter had breezed into town a few years back, shocked all the members of the Ladies' Auxiliary with her "big city" ways, then disappeared with Reverend Copeland's son for a Las Vegas wedding. Quite the scandal!

"Takes time," Cookie Brown offered better advice. "Wounds have to heal."

"You'll enjoy spending time with your granddaughter," added Bootsie Purdue. "My son never gets home anymore. We haven't seen our grandchildren since Christmas before last." She heaved a sad sigh at the complicated lives we live today.

"I worry about Tilly," said Maddy Madison. "She was always such a fragile girl."

"Children are tougher than we give them credit for," observed Lizzie with an aura of hard-gained wisdom.

"Did you hear about the robbery?" Bootsie changed the subject before conversation could get too maudlin.

"What robbery?" asked Maddy, looking up from one of the watermelon appliqués she was carefully stitching to one of the corner blocks of her stunning watermelon motif wall quilt.

"Why I'd have thought you would be among the first to hear. After all, it involves your husband's great-great grandfather."

"Beau's great-great granddad?" Col. Beauregard Hollingsworth Madison had been one of the town fathers, establishing the little hamlet back in 1829, when Indiana was still considered "Indian territory."

"Yes," continued Bootsie without looking up from her sewing, "his bust was stolen from the Town Hall last night."

"Do tell," said Cookie, leaning closer so as not to miss a word.

"You mean that bronze likeness of the Colonel that sits outside the meeting room?" Maddy was amazed that anyone would want that tarnished old replica of a War of 1812 veteran. It wasn't a very good likeness when compared to the only known image of Beauregard Madison, a late-in-life portrait taken by none other than Matthew Brady himself.

"The very statue," nodded Bootsie. "Thieves walked out with it sometime after midnight. The time's established because Mayor Caruthers was working late on the town budget. Said he was there 'til eleven-thirty or so."

"Did he see anything suspicious?" inquired Lizzie, always one who enjoyed juicy details.

"Not a thing," answered Bootsie, pleased to be the harbinger of fresh gossip. It wasn't often she delivered a scoop that other members of the Quilter's Club hadn't already picked up on.

"Well, the thieves can keep it for all I care," said Maddy with a degree of finality. "I always hated that ugly old statue. Made the Colonel look like a deranged madman."

"But he's founder of the Madison line," said Cookie, shocked by her friend's callous admission.

"Oh, I'm sure the Colonel had parents. And they had parents before them. He wasn't the first."

"Oh, you know what I mean. He was a town founder."

"Only because his wagon train broke down here." Maddy's husband was technically Beauregard Hollingsworth Madison IV, but she'd just as soon the lineage start with him and their three children. Which brought her thoughts back to Tilly and her granddaughter, arriving tomorrow by bus. There was so much to do. Clean Tilly's old bedroom, lay out fresh linens, fix up the guestroom for her granddaughter, buy a Welcome Home banner down at the Dollar Store, prepare her famous watermelon pie (her daughter's favorite) ... yet here she sat chattering on about some stupid old statue. Probably a high-school prank at that, an initiation into the Fireball Club. Those silly boys were always up to mischief, weren't they? Surely they could find a more interesting prank than taking that heavy old bust.

"I wonder if the thieves will try to ransom the Colonel's statue?" Bootsie nattered on, nearly missing her stitch.

"They'd get more money melting it down for the bronze," opined Lizzie. Now, with her quilt top complete, she was carefully basting the sandwich together, stopping every couple of inches to ensure the batting and backing stayed in place under the quilt top.

"But that's a town heirloom," squeaked Cookie. She was secretary of the local Historical Society.

"Good riddance," said Maddy as she gathered up her quilting materials. "I have to run. Too much to do before Tilly and Agnes arrive."

"Well, I'd think you would care about the robbery," huffed Cookie. "After all, it's your family."

"My husband's family," she corrected her friend. "And

it's not like they stole the Colonel's skeleton from the cemetery. Right?"

CHAPTER TWO

Clueless in Caruthers Corners

Madelyn Agnes Madison (née Taylor) was known merely as "Maddy" to her friends. And she had no closer pals than the other three members of the Quilter's Club. They had grown up together, comprised Caruthers High's chapter of Future Homemakers of America, married local boys, raised their kids together, even took occasional vacations to Disney World with all four families sharing a group tour.

Maddy still had the Mickey Mouse cap with its round ears that Beau had bought her as a souvenir when the kids were still in grade school.

She remembered Cookie's husband Bob – God rest his soul – jumping off the boat in the Pirates of the Caribbean Ride, wading in knee-deep water to retrieve the earring Cookie had dropped overboard. What a gallant act! And his nearly getting thrown out of the park by the security guards had only added to the adventure!

It was still hard to believe that Bob was really gone. The tractor accident was all the more tragic, because Bob had always been a nut on safety, taking all the precautions recommended in the tractor's manual. But no one could have anticipated him getting a necktie caught in the machinery. Because Bob *never* drove the tractor in his church clothes ... except that one time when he wanted to finish the last row of corn before church that fateful Sunday morning so that he and Cookie could get a head start on a long overdue vacation to celebrate their anniversary.

Cookie had let herself go since Bob's death, her hair returning to its natural gray, her makeup sparse, and lipstick non-existence, almost as if she had no reason to ever look pretty again. Believe it or not, Cookie had reined as homecoming queen in high school, with Lizzie her runner up.

Back then Cookie had been a cute pug-nosed blonde and Lizzie a flaming redhead. Lizzie was still a redhead, but the henna-based hair coloring she wore now would never be quite as spectacular as the hair that made everyone's head turn in the twelfth grade when she walked down the hall, flouncing her long red locks over her shoulders.

Bootsie had never been particularly pretty, with her bulbous nose and extra forty pounds, but her outgoing personality more than made up for it. Bootsie was the person everyone seemed to turn to when they wanted to share a secret, celebrate a new love, or cry on a sympathetic shoulder. No wonder she had been voted Most Popular in the senior yearbook. Today, the nose was the same and that forty extra pounds had grown to sixty, but everybody she knew or met loved her.

Besides, Bootsie always had the inside track on everything that happened here in Caruthers Corners, her husband Jim being chief of police. So, of course, she knew all the details about this "crime of the century" − the disappearance of Colonel Beauregard Madison's bronze bust. You'd think it was right up there with the Lindbergh kidnapping to hear her tell it.

Maddy couldn't be bothered with details of the robbery. She had to prepare for Tilly's homecoming. The Trailways bus would pull up in front of the Town Hall at precisely 3 p.m. to disgorge its passengers, usually no more than one or two arriving, often three or four going. The population of Caruthers Corners had been shrinking so steadily over the past few years that the sign outside of town had quit listing the number of citizens. The town budget couldn't afford to keep repainting the number – ever-diminishing from Pop. 3,012 to Pop. 2,976 to (at last count) Pop. 2,574.

Well, the arrival of Tilly and her daughter Agnes would boost the count by two. Did this signal a turning of the tide for the ol' hometown? Probably not, for it was Tilly's plan to "get her bearings," then relocate to a city where she could put her failed marriage behind her and start anew. Not something she looked forward to.

Beauregard phoned at 2:15 to see if Maddy wanted him to pick her up, or simply meet at the Trailways stop.

"Best we meet there," she told her husband. "That way you won't have to close the store so early." Beau owned the Ace Hardware franchise, but lived under the threat of a big Home Depot coming to Caruthers Corners. He bemoaned the changing times: family groceries edged out by the Food Lion chain, stationary shops put out of business by Office Max, department stores eclipsed by the new Wal-Mart in the neighboring town, and local hardware shops unable to compete with encroaching Lowe's and Home Depot megastores.

But Beau hadn't given up yet. He dreamed of days past, when things were not only simpler, but also more genuine. He still believed that the purpose of a hometown business was to provide a valuable service to the residents ... a gentleman's pursuit, not a cutthroat money game. His favorite reading remained historical novels. *Good Old Days* and *American Heritage* were the magazines you found scattered on the family coffee table.

He considered *Somewhere in Time* the best movie ever made, the one where Christopher Reeves goes to Mackinac Island in search of romance back in a kinder, gentler age. The Madisons planned on visiting Mackinac next summer to see where the movie was filmed.

Yes, Maddy had to admit it – Beau was a romantic, always dreaming of a better world. He preferred those old black-and-white comedies on the Turner Classic Movies channel, refusing to watch CNN or those other networks that focused on distant wars and terrorist threats at home. He stuck his head in the sand like an ostrich, hoping the distressing news would simply go away. Unfortunately, life wasn't like that. The new Home Depot was scheduled to break ground in the fall.

But Maddy would not have had him any other way. Her "Pooh Bear" always remembered their anniversary, bought her red roses on Valentine's Day, had cried when each of their children was born. Partly with joy, party with sadness that they would face a world gone awry. The perfect husband when it came to thoughtfulness – which more than made up for his often disorganized ways.

Maddy was the practical one. Paying all the bills,

keeping track of their retirement accounts (zigzagging stocks and slow-growing mutual funds), taking the children to the doctor and making sure their shoes fit. But Beau was first to grab a seat on the front row of every school play, recital, and graduation ceremony.

She had a natural knack for mind games. She was a master sleuth when it came to Clue, a relentless conqueror at Risk, a takeover titan while playing Monopoly. She was also a whiz at Scrabble and remained unbeaten at Chinese checkers. So it was Maddy's secret that she often cheated at cards in order to let her husband win. No need to remind him that she'd beat him out as class valedictorian in high school.

"Okay, meet you in front of the Town Hall at three sharp," Beau was saying. "Can't imagine why somebody would do something like that."

"People grow apart," Maddy replied vaguely. No need to say she'd always considered Tilly's husband a shark in a $2,000 Armani suit.

"No, I mean the bust of the Colonel. Why would someone steal a town heirloom? Not like it's valuable to anyone but the citizens of Caruthers Corners. We'll have to replace it. Yes, replace it."

"Forget that old piece of metal," she said, a little irked that they had been speaking of different things. "Your great-great grandfather may have founded this town, but he did so by chasing away the Native Americans who lived here at the time."

"Indians?" muttered her husband. Still not as PC as she might wish. "That's the way things were back then."

"Things haven't changed all that much. Home Depot's

about to drive you out of business, Pooh Bear."

"*Hmph*, we'll see about that."

"Don't worry," she tried to back away from her harsh words. "I'm sure the Colonel's bust will turn up."

"Maybe sooner than you think," he said. "Chief Purdue has found a clue."

CHAPTER THREE

The Town's Population Increases

The big red-and-yellow bus rolled to a stop in front of the Town Hall at precisely three on the dot. Tilly and her daughter were the first ones off when the door yawned open. And the last, being they were the only passengers. Rumor was that Trailways might discontinue service to Caruthers Corners for lack of traffic.

"Tilly!" shouted Maddy. Beau stood there beaming over his wife's shoulder.

"Mom! Dad!" The slender young woman rushed forward to hug her parents. Then, glancing over her shoulder at the lagging ten-year-old, she motioned her child forward. "Aren't you going to say hello to your grammy and grampy?" she urged.

"Don't wanna," whined Agnes. "I want to go home."

"This is your home for now," her mother snapped. A little to harsh, in Maddy's estimation. But she knew better than interfere between a parent and child, even if they were her own flesh and blood.

"I want my daddy."

"Well, honey, you can't have your daddy right now. So please try to make the best of it," sighed Tilly with a weariness that made it clear she'd been saying this to Agnes over and over to no avail. So she gently pushed her

15

whining daughter forward to greet her grandparents. An awkward moment under any circumstances since the last time Maddy and Beau has seen Agnes she was only six years old.

"You'd best mind your manners, young lady."

Agnes didn't much look the part of a young lady. She wore a baggy sweater and faded blue jeans, her sex only revealed by the length of her hair. And these days that wasn't a reliable measure. The freckles that covered the bridge of her nose reminded Maddy of her husband at a young age. Pale skin that became splattered with brown spots when exposed to the sun. Not that Agnes had seen much sun in smog-laden Los Angeles.

"Hi Grammy, hi Grampy," the young girl offered a perfunctory greeting. Her heart obviously wasn't in it. She fidgeted and tried on a smile, but it had an artificial look, like a Halloween mask that didn't quite fit.

At that moment Maddy regretted they hadn't made a trip to California last summer to see their daughter and her workaholic husband, a chance to have better bonded with this child who was practically a stranger. Instead, they had elected to visit the Grand Canyon with Bootsie and Jim Purdue. With the low crime rate in Caruthers Corners, it was easy for the police chief to take a two-week vacation. And Beau never hesitated to hang a CLOSED sign on the hardware store door and take off.

"We've only got three bags," said Tilly, sounding apologetic that her life had been reduced to a trio of small suitcases.

"I'll get 'em," offered Beau, stepping forward, his meaty palms reaching for the matching Sampsonite luggage. He balanced one in each hand, the third under an arm, like a stevedore aiming for a big tip.

"Thanks, Dad." Tilly gave him a weary smile, one that said it had been a tough year. And sure enough, it had. A dozen years of marriage down the drain. Her dreams of a handsome, doting husband and a home with a white picket fence shattered. Now she and her daughter were adrift, like rudderless boats with no shoreline in sight.

"C'mon, dear," said Maddy, wrapping an arm around her daughter. "Let's go home. Melon Pickers Row is just as you left it."

"Yes," sighed Tilly. "But I'm not."

≈ ≈ ≈

That night Tilly's spirits seemed to pick up as her mother served pot roast, a family favorite. Dinner was mostly small talk, everyone studiously avoiding the subject of Tilly's fractured marriage. Suffice it to say, you never want to divorce a lawyer, even one who specializes in taxes. Tilly thought there must be an elective course in law school called "Hiding Your Assets." And her husband undoubtedly had placed at the top of his class.

Nonetheless, the pot roast was succulent – comfort food stirring up those secure feelings of childhood when the world was a friendly place. The mash potatoes were heaping mounds, "dirty taters" as her mom called them, mashed with the skin intact. The home-grown green beans melted in your mouth. And those fluffy buttermilk biscuits were as large and round as the bread plate itself.

"Yummy," said Tilly, just like she did as a child.

Young Agnes was not so appreciative of the sumptuous meal her grandmother had laid out for their arrival. "May I be excused?" she mumbled.

"Why, dear, you've barely touched your pot roast."

"Don't like it."

"Agnes, don't be rude to your grammy," Tilly reprimanded her daughter. "She went to a lot of trouble to make us this wonderful dinner."

"Is there a Jack In the Box around here? I'd rather have a hamburger."

"Agnes!"

"There, there," said Maddy. "Don't force her to eat. She gets hungry, she'll come around."

"I'd just soon starve to death as be here," frowned the obstinate girl. "I want my daddy and I want to be in my own house!"

"Agnes, we've talked about that. Your father is much too busy to worry about us."

"I want my daddy," the girl repeated, face screwed up as if about to cry.

"Want to go for a ride into town?" asked Beau, ever the peacemaker. "We can get us an ice cream parfait at the DQ."

Agnes pretended not to hear, but her eyes lighted up just a little. Taking that as his cue, Beau stood up and held out his hand. "Come along. We'll leave your mom and Grammy to clean off the table."

"But – " Maddy was about to say she'd baked a watermelon pie, then thought better of it. "Never mind. You two go have some ice cream while we girls catch up on local gossip."

"Okay."

Crisis diverted, Beau and his granddaughter shuffled

out the front door and down the walk to the big blue Buick in the driveway.

"Sorry about that," said Tilly, close to tears.

"Don't be," smiled Maddy, giving her a reassuring pat on the arm. "More watermelon pie for the two of us."

"Yummy," repeated Tilly, a faint smile crossing her pale lips. "You always knew how to offer comfort foods at just the right time."

≈≈≈

Late that night, after everybody was in bed, Beau rolled over to face his wife. "Are you gonna be up for this visit?" he asked quietly, voice little more than a whisper.

"I have to be. She's our daughter."

"It's not Tilly I'm worried about. You think she's delicate, but I'm sure she's tough at the core. I'm more concerned about how you'll do with Aggie."

"Aggie?"

"She says that's what her friends call her."

"And you're already her friend?" A feeling of failure crept over Maddy. Would she ever bond with this rude, damaged child?

"Sure we're friends," said Beau. "I bought her ice cream."

CHAPTER FOUR

A Relaxing Pastime

As her husband was heading out the door that morning, lunch bag in hand, Maddy realized that in the excitement of Tilly's arrival she'd forgotten to ask Beau about the clue he said Chief Purdue had found. Not that she gave a fig about the missing statue. Rather, her precise mind wasn't content to leave questions unanswered.

She stuck her head out the front door, but was too late to catch him. The ancient Buick was already lumbering down Melon Pickers Row, past the stately Victorian homes, headed toward the Ace Hardware building on Main Street. Oh well.

"Mom," came Tilly's voice from the kitchen. "Would you mind watching Agnes this afternoon? I have a conference call with my lawyer. Mark's asking for custody."

"Of Agnes?"

"He's not talking about our parakeet."

"Surely he's not serious. A daughter belongs with her mother."

Tilly shook her head, brown hair brushing her shoulders. "Try telling that to a man with too much money and power for his own good."

"Of course, I'll watch her. Perhaps she'd enjoy going to the Quilter's Club with me. I'm sure all the girls will make a fuss over her."

"Whatever. But don't expect Agnes to take up quilting. She hates crafts – what she calls 'busy work'."

"Busy work indeed. Quilting is a very relaxing hobby. And it taps your creativity."

"Hey, you're preaching to the choir. I made my first quilt at ten. Don't you remember?"

"Your daughter's age," Maddy pointed out.

"Good luck in converting Agnes. She'd rather play video games."

"Nothing wrong with that. But quilting, knitting, crocheting – they're all nice skills to develop."

"Oh mom, who needs to knit when you can buy a sweater from China for a fraction of what your own time's worth?"

Maddy gave her daughter a disapproving glare. "Tsk, tsk. There's a special pride and pleasure in making things yourself. And we can't depend on China for everything. Else we'll wind up with all our money over there."

"Thanks for that lesson on trade deficits. But I still like my new Afghan made in Hong Kong."

"Have it your own way. But I'm taking Agnes to the Quilter's Club this afternoon. Perhaps there's still hope for *her*."

≈≈≈

"Hi, girls. Meet my granddaughter Agnes," said Maddy as she ushered the reluctant youngster into the room at the senior center where the Quilter's Club met every Tuesday. It was a wonderful room. A dozen comfortable chairs scattered around the edges and a large table they used for cutting and measuring fabrics. They did a lot of work on their own, but having a table, cutting mat, cutters, plus iron and ironing board, gave them the option to work on any part of their quilt-making during their informal meetings. One long shelf along the back wall held baskets of fat quarters and scraps available to anyone who wanted them for their own project. They each added fabrics to these baskets on a regular basis.

"Hello, Agnes," chirped Cookie Brown, offering a little wave.

"Welcome, my dear," said Bootsie Purdue, raising a coffee mug. She was the caffeine queen, a ten-cups-a-day addict.

"Aha, a new member," kidded Lizzie Ridenour. The club's attendees had dwindled from eight to four, the last loss being Jennifer Brown, Cookie's sister-in-law when her husband accepted a higher-paying job in Indianapolis.

"I'm not joining your stupid ol' club," said Agnes.

Lizzie ignored the rudeness, having raised two rambunctious daughters (one of whom ran away with the minister's son). "We'll wait to see if you pass the initiation test. Not just anybody can join, y' know."

"Pass the test?"

"Grab a seat over there and we'll get you started on a quilt of your own," Lizzie continued. "The test comes later."

"But I don't wanna take a test – "

"That's okay, my dear. We're not looking for new members right now anyways," Bootsie joined in, a quick study.

"But wait – !"

"Don't beg," said Cookie, catching on to the game. "Just because your grandmother vouches for you doesn't guarantee you membership in the Quilter's Club. We have very high standards."

"What if I wanna join?"

"See that big basket of scraps on the end of the shelf? Pick out nine different pieces of fabric that you would like in your quilt. We'll get you started with a small nine-patch quilt. It'll be easy to make and it'll be your own unique creation. Do you know how to sew?"

"No."

"Here, let me show you," said Lizzie, scooting her chair next to Agnes's. She was the best quilter in the group. "First, we have to thread the needle," she instructed.

A half hour later, Agnes was proudly practicing small stitches on a folded piece of fabric. Her stitches were uneven lengths and too loose and crooked to work well on her quilt. But with practice she'd soon be good enough to start connecting her nine squares.

Maddy spoke up, just to be making conversation. "Bootsie, I heard your husband found a clue in the Missing Bronze Mystery."

"What mystery?" asked her granddaughter, pausing, her needle in the air.

"Someone stole your great-great-great – I'm not sure how many greats – grandfather's bronze bust from its place in the Town Hall building," volunteered Bootsie.

"Two greats," corrected Cookie, the genealogy expert.

"Wow," said Agnes. "Is the Quilter's Club trying to solve the crime?"

"Us? No way," laughed Maddy. "We'll leave that to Bootsie's hubby, the chief of police."

"Wow! Your husband's a policeman? Just like on TV?"

Bootsie suppressed a chuckle. "A policeman, yes. But not exactly like you see on television. Mostly he hands out parking tickets."

"The clue?" reminded Maddy. "What was the clue he found?"

"Oh that. A footprint."

"What?"

"A muddy footprint. At the base of the pedestal the bronze bust sat on."

"What size?" inquired Agnes. Out of the mouth of babes. "What size shoe was it?"

"Lordy, I didn't think to ask," said Bootsie, feeling upstaged by a child.

≈≈≈

"Size fourteen," replied Beau Madison that evening. "Jim said the footprint was a size fourteen shoe."

"Isn't that rather large?" said Maddy. After all, Beau wore a size nine.

"A regular Bigfoot," he agreed.

"There can't be many folks in town with feet that large. It ought to narrow the list of suspects down considerably."

"Maybe," he replied vaguely.

"Do you know anyone with feet that size?"

Beau shrugged the question away. "Not offhand. But I don't look down at everybody's clodhoppers. You'd have to be a shoe salesman to notice something like that."

Agnes tugged on her grandmother's arm. "Didn't I see a shoe store when mommy and I rode into town on that big bus?"

"Yes," Maddy said thoughtfully. "Pic A Pair is located on Main Street. It's been there since your mother was your age. Old Mr. Duncan has been selling footwear for the past forty years."

"Why don't we go ask him about Bigfoot?"

Tilly rolled her eyes. "Agnes dear, you should leave that to Chief Purdue."

"Well, it wouldn't *hurt* to ask," she said.

CHAPTER FIVE

Shoemaker's Children Have Shoes

Arthur Duncan had just opened his doors that morning when Maddy strolled into the shop, her granddaughter in tow. "Ah, Mrs. Madison, a new pair of shoes for the little lady?"

"Not today. But I do need some information."

"We only sell shoes here," he cut her off. "You want information, go to the library."

"You know the library was closed down last fall for lack of funds."

"It's that dab-blasted Internet," the old man complained. "Nobody reads books anymore."

"I do," said Agnes. "I just finished *Anne of Green Gables.*"

"Well now, that's refreshing to hear. A youngster who actually cracks a book. Guess that earns you one question. What's on your mind?"

"Who in Caruthers Corners wears size fourteen shoes?" Maddy blurted.

"Funny you should ask. Chief Purdue wanted to know about my customers with big feet. Called me yesterday afternoon."

"And?"

"And I gave him three names. Tall Paul Johnson, he

27

lives out near the chair factory. Benjamin Bentley, he's got a farm north of town. And my son Denny, he was always big for his age."

"Just three?"

"Maybe there's more hereabout. But them's the only ones I ever sold size fourteen's to. Folk in these parts tend to be small-boned, that Slavic stock in 'em."

"You say your son's a size fourteen?"

"Comes from his mama's side of the family. Basketball teams have been trying to recruit him."

≈ ≈ ≈

"This is fun," said Agnes as they drove out to Tall Paul Johnson's two-story house on Easy Chair Lane. "I like being a detective."

"We're not detectives," responded her grandmother. "We're simply making inquiries."

"Yeah, like detectives."

"Well. Maybe."

Tall Paul was sitting in a lawn chair under a shade tree in his front yard. "I already talked to Chief Purdue," he addressed them without bothering to stand up. "Told him I've never laid eyes on that metal likeness of Colonel Madison. Never had occasion to set foot inside the Town Hall."

"There's a reward for its return," Maddy lied. Well, not really, because she knew her husband would pay one if needed.

"Wouldn't mind claiming the money. But I'd have to have the blasted statue to do that, wouldn't I?"

"Why would anyone steal that old hunk of metal?" she mused aloud.

"Beats me," said Tall Paul. "Can't think anything it'd be good for, other than a doorstop."

≈ ≈ ≈

Next stop was the farmstead of Benjamin Bentley. Tall Paul was said to measure seven feet from toe to crown, but Bentley was shorter and wider, more like a troll from a fairytale book. He raised soybeans on his two thousand acres, a money crop that kept his farmhouse freshly painted and a new Ford pickup parked in his driveway.

"Why me?" he asked them about their visit. "I told Chief Purdue that I didn't steal that bust of your husband's great-great grandpa."

"Well, you're one of the few people around here who wears a size fourteen shoe. And the Chief found a big muddy footprint next to that pedestal where the statue sat."

"*Hmph*, just 'cause I'm a dirt farmer don't mean I don't wipe my feet 'fore coming into a fine building like the Town Hall. My twice-great uncle helped lay the bricks on the Town Hall back in the eighteen hundreds. It's a historic monument deserving of some respect."

"Yes, it's the centerpiece of our lovely little town," Maddy agreed, smiling down at her granddaughter. It wouldn't hurt Agnes to learn some civic pride. Coming from Los Angeles, she didn't have much to latch onto. That city was like the House That Jack Built, a little of this, a little of that, no common heritage like you found in Caruthers Corners.

"Hope you find the Colonel. I know your husband would be heartbroken if it stays missing. T'was him what put up the five hundred dollars to buy that marble pedestal it sat on, y' know."

"Really?" As a matter of fact, she didn't know that. Her husband had been keeping secrets. Was it because he knew she held that old bronze bust in such disdain? Her view of the early forefathers – as scallywags and thieves who stole the land from its rightful owners – was well known. That's why her best friend Cookie Brown had never asked her to join the Caruthers Corners Historical Society.

"Beau takes pride in his ancestry. Guess that's 'cause he's named after one of the town founders."

"Yes, my husband values the past," she admitted.

"We've got one more shoe size to go, Grammy," urged Agnes, getting impatient. It was obvious that Benjamin Bentley wasn't going to confess to stealing the bronze bust.

≈ ≈ ≈

Last stop in their quest was at the Duncan household on the edge of town, a stately abode on Jinks Lane, a shady residential street named after the third town founder. Beauregard Madison, Jacob Caruthers, and Ferdinand Jinks had established this little outpost, but you didn't hear much about Jinks other than this narrow street named after him. He was something of a Black Sheep, having burned down the original Town Hall in a dispute with Madison and Caruthers.

Denny Duncan was sitting in the porch swing waiting for them. His father had called ahead. He was a big fellow, but not quite as tall as Tall Paul. His smile was quick and easy, his eyes twinkling with amusement. "Dad said you think I stole the bronze head of ol' Colonel Madison," he greeted them.

"No, no. We're just asking a few questions," backtracked Maddy. Agnes was standing behind her, somewhat intimidated by this lanky beanpole, much taller than Ben Bentley, although a few inches shorter than Tall Paul Johnson.

"Chief Purdue has cleared me as a suspect," he informed them.

"I figured you'd be innocent, else your father wouldn't have given us your name so willingly."

"Yessum, I've got an ironclad alibi."

"How nice. That saves a lot of questions. Mind telling us about your alibi?"

"Well, it's kinda embarrassing," Denny said shyly. "Of a personal nature."

"We promise to be discreet."

"Well, just to clear my name I'll tell you. I was in jail."

"Jail?" Did he mean that rarely used holding cell in the back of the police office?

"Ask Chief Purdue. He threw me in the hoosegow overnight to teach me a lesson. I'd chalked up four hundred and eighty unpaid parking tickets."

"So you were locked up the night of the robbery?"

"That's right, ma'am. Paying my debt to society. That debt being nearly five thousand dollars in parking tickets. Chief wiped 'em off the books, saying I'd served my time."

"Parking's only ten cents a half hour," she reminded him. "Wouldn't it be cheaper to put a dime in the meter?"

"I never seem to have any change on me," he shrugged.

≈≈≈

"Grammy and I are gonna catch the thief who stole

your statue," said Agnes to her grandfather. The family was gathered around the dinner table, Agnes chowing down on a large helping of meatloaf and mashed potatoes.

"Do tell?" said Beau. Amazed at the transformation from last night's sullen urchin to this hungry Nancy Drew across the table.

Of course it didn't hurt that Maddy had encouraged her to secretly call her father that morning. Being a mother and grandmother made Maddy especially protective of her loved ones. And though she really hated what that pompous man had done to her daughter, she knew that without some sort of contact with her dad Agnes would be a lost and angry child. So she butted in like she always did when she felt she knew best ... but things were stressful enough at the moment, so no need to tell her daughter yet.

"That's right, Grampy. The Quilter's Club is on the case."

"Quilter's Club?" repeated Agnes's mother, fork paused in midair.

"I'm an apprentice member. Grammy and Lizzie and Cookie and Bootsie are teaching me how to sew my very own quilt. It's loads of fun. But nothing like crime solving. I might become a detective when I grow up – like Grammy."

"So Grammy's a detective," said Beauregard Madison, looking quizzically at his wife of forty years. "I learn something new every day."

CHAPTER SIX

History Is Just Old News

Cookie Brown phoned the next morning. "As you know, I'm secretary of the Caruthers Corners Historical Society," she began the conversation.

Maddy sighed. "Cookie, we've been best friends since the third grade. There's very little I don't know about you. Including that time in high school you stole the history exam and passed out copies to the entire class."

"Oh piffle, that was a lame class. It should have covered more local history."

"So what's this about you and the Historical Society?" Maddy tried to stir the conversation back on track.

"That's why I'm calling. All that talk yesterday about Colonel Madison's bust reminded me of something. A document I came across in the society's archives."

"You have archives?"

"Well, it's a filing cabinet filled with old papers, deeds, letters, newspapers, and other historical documents."

"And what was this amazing discovery?"

"Don't be sarcastic. I'm trying to help you find the thief of that old bust. Your granddaughter seems to think we've promised to solve the crime."

Maddy chuckled at the memory of Agnes's excitement at last night's dinner table. "Yes, she seems to have mistaken me for Miss Marple."

"Then she will find this tidbit interesting. I came across an old newspaper account about the relatives of Ferdinand Jinks protesting that their ancestor had been written out of the town's history. They pointed out that the town bears Caruthers' name. And Beauregard Madison's bust sits in the Town Hall. But nary a mention of Jinks."

"There's a street named after him."

"Actually the street was named after his nephew, Jeremiah Jinks. He was a prominent banker at the turn of the century."

"Oh."

"Perhaps one of Ferdinand Jinks' relatives is trying to even the score," postulated her friend. "Stole the bust out of spite."

Maddy stared at the phone, considering this new info. "Does Jinks have any living relatives hereabouts?"

"That's the interesting part. I checked the old genealogy charts and it turns out that Tall Paul Johnson is a direct descendant on his mother's side."

"We just spoke with Tall Paul yesterday. He claimed he's never set foot inside the Town Hall."

"Liar, liar, pants on fire," chanted Cookie's voice, sounding distant over the phone lines. "I have a photograph here in the archives that shows Tall Paul at the ceremony where your husband donated that bronze bust to the town. You can't miss him in the photo. He stands heads above the rest of the crowd."

"You mean he lied straight to my face?"

"Looks like it. Doesn't that make him a likely suspect?"

≈≈≈

"Sure, I recall Paul Johnson being at the dedication ceremony," replied Maddy's husband. She'd dragged Agnes down to Ace Hardware to ask him about Cookie's bombshell.

"Did you know he's a descendant of Ferdinand Jinks?" she continued her inquisition.

"Everybody knows that."

"I didn't."

"Maddy, you could care less about town history."

"True. But this proves Tall Paul stole the statue."

"How so?"

"He wears a size fourteen shoe, just like the footprint found by Chief Purdue. And he's a disgruntled ancestor of a man who didn't get proper credit for helping found this town."

Beau kept stocking his shelves, arranging boxes of wood screws in a straight row. Just as well that Maddy couldn't see the smile on his face. "I'm afraid you've jumped to the wrong conclusion," he said. "Tall Paul couldn't have done it."

"And why not?"

"He broke his big toe last week. Can't walk without crutches. And can't bear any weight on his left foot."

"Left foot?"

"Yep, that muddy footprint was made by a left foot, Jim said."

Darn, why hadn't she noticed that injured toe? Come to think of it, Tall Paul Johnson hadn't bothered to stand up when they dropped by to see him.

"How did he hurt his toe?" Agnes asked.

Beau glanced over his shoulder at his granddaughter.

"Stuck it under a lawnmower, he told Jim."

"Isn't it early in the year to be mowing lawns?" This from a city kid who had never seen many lawns, much less mowed one.

Her grandfather paused, then turned to face her. "Guess it is, at that."

"Aha!" said Maddy, as if they had uncovered another clue.

CHAPTER SEVEN

"I've got a Dog and His Name is Tige"

Maddy was driving home when her granddaughter screamed, "Stop!" Without thinking, she hit the breaks, causing the SUV to fishtail in the middle of Main Street. Luckily, there were no cars in the oncoming lane.

"My goodness, what was that about?" demanded Maddy, her heart beating a staccato rhythm. *Ratty-tat-tat* like Gene Krupa's drums.

"A dog. I saw a dog."

"Dear, there are lots of dogs hereabout. Everybody has one."

"I don't."

"Oh?"

"That dog back there. It was tied to a sign. Said, Give this puppy a good home."

Maddy was about to say that Agnes barely had a home herself, her mother and her having been discarded like an unwanted pair of shoes by that tax shark she called a father. But she caught her tongue in time to say, "Would you like to have that dog?"

"Oh, Grammy! Could I?"

"I don't see why not. If you promise to take care of him. Feed him, brush the tangles out of his fur."

"Yes, I promise!"

Easing the car into reverse, Maddy backed down the block to where a dog of mixed heritage sat next to a sign advertising his availability. A thin woman came out of the modest one-story house that cast its shadow on dog and sign. "May I help you?" she called to her visitors.

"You're giving this dog away?" inquired Maddy, trying to sound casual. No need to appear eager, lest the price might go up.

"To a good home. We're moving to Indy. My husband took a job there. We've rented an apartment what don't allow no pets."

"How much do you want for him?"

The old woman eyed the little girl by Maddy's side. "For her?"

"Yes," said Agnes. "And I'll give him a good home."

"Dogs need a lot of love and care and he will be counting on you to give it to him."

"Oh I'll take really good care of him!" said Agnes with an excited grin on her face. "I'm almost ten and a half and my mom has taught me to be responsible."

"Then you can have him, young missy. He's yours. No charge."

"Thank you, thank you!" Agnes hugged the shaggy dog, causing his tail to wag like a metronome while he covered her face with wet and sloppy dog kisses. It was a case of instant bonding.

"He'll be well cared for," Maddy assured the old woman.

"Oh, I'm sure-a that. I recognize you, Mrs. Beauregard Madison the Fourth. You're one of this town's leading citizens, you are."

"Well, not really – "

"Oh, yes. You live in that big Victorian mansion over on Melon Pickers Row. Reckon this dog's gonna be living better'n me."

"What's his name?" asked Agnes, ignoring the banter between her Grammy and this generous dog-giver.

The woman looked down at the mixed-breed canine. "Guess he ain't got one. He was last of the litter. We didn't get around to naming him."

"Then I'll give him a name. But what?"

Maddy spoke up before she realized it. "I once had a dog named Tige."

"Tige? That's a funny name."

"That was the name of Buster Brown's dog," the thin woman laughed. "I remember the rhyme. He and his master lived in a shoe."

"Lived in a shoe?" said Agnes. "How silly."

"Well, Buster Brown was a brand of shoe," her grandmother explained. "And the advertisements featured him and his dog Tige."

"C'mon, Tige, get in the car," commanded Agnes. "You won't have to live in a shoe no more!"

≈≈≈

"A dog!" shrieked Tilly. "You bought my daughter a dog?"

"Well, we didn't actually buy him," Maddy tried to explain, not sure that she could truly excuse her impulsive act. "He was free."

"Pleeeeease don't be mad, momma." Agnes begged. "Tige is my new best friend," and he needs a good home."

She was rolling on the floor with the yapping animal. They were having great fun, getting to know one another. "Look, he's already trained. He can roll over. And shake. And even play dead."

The dog followed her commands. Ending up on his back, feet in the air.

"Very good," applauded Maddy.

"We can't have a dog," protested Tilly. "I can barely care for Agnes and myself."

"Don't worry, mommy. I'll take really good care of Tige. Feed him and water him and take him for lots of walks. And if Grammy and Grampy will let me earn a little extra money, I'll even help buy his dog food!"

"Mother, how could you do this to me?"

"To you? This was something for my granddaughter."

"Oh, pish." Tilly wasn't very happy about the matter. But Maddy knew her decision had been the right one and it was easier to apologize than ask permission. Her daughter would come around.

"Yes," gushed Agnes, still wallowing with her new pet. "Grammy got me a dog of my very own. And his name is Tige, just like Buster Poindexter's dog."

"Buster Brown," corrected Maddy, having no clue who this Poindexter character might be. Probably some rock 'n roll singer, she'd hazard to guess.

"Yes, Buster Brown. Thank you, Grammy. Thank you."

"You're welcome, Agnes."

"Call me Aggie. All my best-est friends do."

CHAPTER EIGHT

A Visit to the Land of the Dead

Cookie Brown wanted Maddy to accompany her to the cemetery that afternoon. This being the second anniversary of her husband Bob's passing, she wanted to place flowers on the grave. Having her good friend along helped because Maddy had known Bob for as many years as Cookie had.

"Can I go along," begged Agnes. "Please, oh please."

"Yes, if you promise to be quiet. A cemetery is the final resting place for people. And it's respectful to not make unnecessary noise."

"Don't worry, I won't wake the dead."

"Aggie!"

"Just kidding, Grammy."

"Get your coat. It's chilly."

The girl grabbed her Lands End slicker. "C'mon, Tige," she called.

"On no, dear. Tige can't go."

A frown crossed the youngster's face. "Why not? He'll be quiet."

Maddy recalled her father's words. "No dogs allowed in the cemetery," she said. "Folks don't want your puppy running off with a bone."

"Oh, Grammy. Pleas-s-se. Tige won't dig up any bones

41

at Pleasant Glade. I promise he won't."

Briefly, Maddy remembered her own childhood disappointment at having to leave her dog behind. "Oh, okay. But don't tell anybody. We're breaking all the rules."

Cookie was waiting for them near the big iron gate that separated the living from the dead. Pleasant Glade was a rolling expanse of well-manicured grass, spackled with marble headstones and the occasional crypt. The name "Pleasant Glade" had been bestowed back in the '40s when a commercial enterprise took over the town cemetery, but some of the tombstones dated back to the 1800s.

As a child, Maddy had enjoyed reading the engraved epitaphs: "It Was More Than a Tummy Ache" and "Gone But Not Forgotten," with her favorite being "I Enjoyed the Brief Visit!"

"You brought a puppy?" exclaimed Cookie, gesturing toward the sign posted on the iron gate: No Dogs Allowed.

"*Shhhh*, don't tell anybody," replied Maddy. As if the dog's presence was a state secret.

"He's on a leash," Agnes pointed out, as if that constituted an exception.

"Oh well, come along. Bob's waiting."

Agnes glanced nervously at her grandmother. "I thought you said he was dead."

"It's just an expression, my dear," clarified Cookie as she led them down a winding path. "Even I realize my Bob isn't coming back. But when I visit his grave I like to think that I'm visiting his spirit, too. Understand? "

"I think so" Agnes replied tentatively as she picked up her pace, not lagging back now that she'd been reassured a zombie version of Bob Brown wasn't waiting to greet them at the end of the path.

Tige kept stopping to check his smell-mail, leaving messages of his own. Maddy was amazed the little fur ball had that much liquid in him. "Come along, doggy. No dawdling," she urged. But Tige didn't move unless Agnes gave a tiny tug on his leash.

"Here we are," announced Cookie, bending down to place a bouquet of yellow flowers on a plot marked as:

Robert Alfred Brown
Loving Husband and Father
May Angels Fly
You to Heaven
On Golden Wings

"Wow!" said Agnes. "Your husband's in there?"

"No, honey. Just his mortal remains. Bob's in Heaven sitting at the right hand of God."

"You mean he's got a box seat?"

"Something like that," Cookie replied, quickly changing the subject. "Here, help me arrange these flowers in the vase."

Agnes knew what she meant, even though she pronounced vase like "face," while Agnes's father had taught her to say vase like "roz." She knelt down to fluff at the pretty yellow petals, forgetting to hold onto the leash.

"Tige, come back here," called Maddy when she noticed the dog take off after a squirrel, heading down the hill toward an older part of the cemetery.

"Tige!" Agnes took up the call.

Cookie just stood there with her hands on her hips, still exasperated over the dog's presence in the first place. Wasn't that sign on the gate clear enough?

Maddy and her granddaughter gave chase, calling the dog's name as they ran down the hill, dodging tombstones and jumping over graves. "Tige, Tige!"

Before they knew it, the pair found themselves in the oldest section of the cemetery, the dates on the rough-hewn stones predating Pleasant Glade by a hundred years. There were more crypts here, and a scattering of mausoleums that looked like a village for the dead. "Yipes," said Agnes as she scooped up her dog. "We're not in Kansas anymore, Toto." She'd seen a rerun of *Wizard of Oz* just last week on TV.

The dog wriggled free, leaping to the ground and heading toward a stone edifice marked MADISON over the doorway. Time had rotted the wooden doorframe, causing one of the hinges to sag and creating a crack about the size of a doggie door. Tige disappeared inside like a mouse taking to its hole in a baseboard. "Tige – " came Agnes's plaintive cry as she stared into the dark fissure.

"My goodness," said Maddy. "This is my husband's great-great grandfather's mausoleum. I came here with him for a memorial service one Easter. It's a spooky old place."

"I'll say," agreed Agnes, eyes the size of silver dollars.

"We should get back up the hill. Cookie will be unhappy that we upset her visit with Bob."

"But what about my dog?"

"Tige will find his way back up the hill. He won't stray for long."

"Grammy, I don't like him being inside that old stone building. What if a ghost gets him?"

Maddy patted the girl reassuringly on the shoulder. "There's no such thing as ghosts, Aggie."

"What about Cookie's husband Bob? Isn't he a ghost now? Fluttering about up in Heaven like a cloud?"

"I'm not sure where Bob Brown is residing. He had a wild side to him. The man might be vacationing in a hotter climate, for all I know."

Agnes giggled, recognizing her grandmother's words as a joke. "Don't tell Cookie that. She might phone up God to ask Him how her husband's doing."

"That would be a long distance call," laughed Maddy. "Cookie's too tight with a penny to accept that kind of phone bill."

"I'm crawling in there to get Tige," announced the girl. "He might have fallen into a coffin or something."

"No, that's too dangerous."

"I'm not leaving my dog, Grammy. I've lost my daddy, I'm not gonna lose Tige too!"

"Hold on, I'll go fetch him. You stay out here, okay?"

Agnes nodded.

Fishing inside her oversized handbag, Maddy found a tiny Mag-Lite that she used for finding the lock on the front door whenever she and Beau had been out late at the movies. She clicked it on, pointed the bright laser-like beam, and then clamored through the crack at the base of the door. "Heaven help me, this is insane," Agnes heard her grandmother mutter as she disappeared inside the mausoleum.

There was a nervous moment when Maddy feared she

might become stuck, her rump too wide for the narrow opening. Too bad she hadn't been more faithful to that South Beach Diet she'd tried last summer. But with a *plop!* she pushed her way into the dark interior of the mausoleum and scrambled to her feet.

The musty smell made her nose twitch. She thought she heard water dripping. Something scurried in the corner – a rat or the wayward dog? Oh my, was she crazy for doing this? *Indiana Jones* had not been one of her favorite movies, despite the home-state name. She didn't have the adventurous fortitude to be a tomb raider, she assured herself.

"Here, Tige. Nice doggie," she called to the dark. However, her pencil-thin flashlight beam couldn't make out any familiar shapes.

"*Arf!*"

She turned the light toward the bark, spotlighting Tige sitting atop a moldy casket – Colonel Madison's final abode no doubt. But what was that next to the dog? A man's head?

"Oh my," Maddy gasped. There, bronze gleaming in the light of her Mag-Lite, was none other than the missing bust of Colonel Beauregard Hollingsworth Madison.

CHAPTER NINE

Finder of Lost Objects

"**C**ongratulations," said the police chief as he posed for a photograph with Maddy Madison. "You gals found the danged statue." The picture would run on the front page of *Caruthers Corners Gazette*, the town's weekly newspaper. "Who would've thought to look for it in the cemetery?"

Not Maddy – but she wasn't about to give all the glory to a wandering dog. Take credit when you can get it, she told herself.

Agnes and Tige were in the picture too, standing between Maddy and Chief Jim Purdue. Enough credit to go around, she supposed, although the police chief hadn't really had a hand in the bronze bust's recovery.

"How'd you know the thief hid the goods in that tomb?" asked Beau on their way home from the ceremony returning the Colonel's head to its marble pedestal.

"Just a lucky guess," she said, cutting her eyes to Agnes to signal their shared secret.

"Question remains, who stole it?" Beau continued, eyes on the road.

"Why, dear, you did."

"W-what?" Her husband nearly ran the Buick off the road.

"That's right, but it will remain our family secret. Won't it, Aggie?"

"Yes, Grammy. Mum's the word."

"Why would I steal my own forefather's bust?" sputtered Beau, regaining control of the big gas-guzzler.

"Because you wanted to replace it with a full-sized marble statue. A bigger honor for the Colonel."

"Uh, how did you know?" he asked sheepishly.

"Most of it was guesswork. But it was a clue when I found a receipt from a sculptor in Chicago and noticed that you'd withdrawn twelve thousand dollars from our joint savings account."

≈ ≈ ≈

"What about the size fourteen footprint?" asked Agnes. A precocious child, as it turned out. "Who did that belong to?"

"That's still a mystery, my dear. Beau swears he didn't have any help in filching the bronze bust."

"Do you believe him?"

"Well, he is my husband."

"Yes, Grammy. But do you believe him?"

"No, Aggie, I don't. That bronze bust is too heavy for one man to carry. And Beau has a bad back. He can hardly pick up the newspaper. And *Gazette*'s been pretty thin lately."

"Then who?"

"Has to be Ben Bentley. Of the three men with size fourteen feet, Tall Paul and Denny had alibis. That leaves Ben."

"Why do you think Grampy's protecting Mr. Bentley?"

Maddy thought about it for a moment. "Beau's always

been one to stick up for his friends. But I suspect it was something more than that."

"What?" Agnes was leaning forward, hanging onto every word, like someone listening to ghost stories around a campfire.

"Beats me. But there's something else. I haven't told anyone this yet – not Cookie or Bootsie or Lizzie – not even your mom – but I found something inside that bronze bust when I came across it there in the mausoleum. At first I tried to pick up the bust, but it was much too heavy. My efforts only succeeded in making something inside it rattle. So I tilted the ol' thing forward just enough to get my hand inside and there I found it – a ring."

"A ring?"

"This ring," said Maddy, opening her fist to reveal a golden circlet with a ruby-red stone.

"It's pretty," breathed her granddaughter, bending closer to examine the ring. "Does it belong to Grampy?"

"Maybe, by rights of inheritance. I suspect this was Colonel Beauregard Madison the First's ring. I've heard Cookie talk about it, a souvenir taken off his dead body by one Ferdinand Jinks – the outcast town founder."

"But if Mr. Jinks stole the ring, how did it get in the head of that bronze statue?" Young Agnes exhibited a sense of logic that proved beyond any doubt that she and Maddy Madison shared the same DNA structure.

"Hm, good question."

"So the mystery isn't solved!"

"No, not quite yet," said Maddy.

CHAPTER TEN

Just the Man for Heavy Lifting

Maddy Madison was a fine looking woman at 58. Even Lizzie, the most critical of her friends, said she had "aged well." Maddy's hair was still a light brown – thank you, Lady Clairol – and her complexion was smooth. Thankfully she'd never smoked and was careful to get a full eight hours sleep each night.

That's why she wasn't particularly surprised when Benjamin Bentley gave her a compliment: "I always thought Beau married one of the prettiest ladies in the county," he said as he served her a sweaty glass of ice tea along with a slice of gingerbread.

Ben had never married. He shared the sprawling two-story farmhouse with his maiden sister. Looked like the Bentley lineage was coming to a halt with him and Becky.

Becky Bentley had baked the pan of gingerbread just that afternoon and it was as tasty as it was fresh. She could be heard fussing about in the kitchen while Maddy sat on the front porch with Ben.

"What a nice thing to say," she accepted the man's compliment, knowing it wasn't meant to be forward. "But Cookie was the homecoming queen, not me, if you'll recall."

"Yessum, I do. Always had a crush on her, but Bobby

Brown was in line ahead of me."

"Bob's gone," she reminded the huge man. "Maybe you ought to invite Cookie over for dinner some night."

"Aw, it's too late for me and her. I'm just an old bachelor, set in my ways." He nodded toward the house where his sister busied herself in the kitchen. "Besides, Becky's dependent on me. This is the only life she's ever known."

"Becky's a strong woman."

"Well, I s'pose."

"I have to ask you a question, Ben. Don't mean for you to betray any confidences, but I'm aware that you helped my husband carry off that bust of Colonel Madison and hide it in his tomb."

"How come you didn't tell that to Chief Purdue?"

"The statue was returned – no harm, no foul."

"That's true. And it weren't like Beau didn't donate it to the town in the first place." He took a sip of his tea before continuing. "So what's your question, Maddy?"

"I found something inside that old bronze head. Guess I want to know how it got there."

Ben Bentley glanced at Maddy's granddaughter, silently munching on a slice of gingerbread as she listened to the grownup talk. "All right to talk in front of little missy?" he asked cautiously.

"Mr. Bentley, I probably know more about this mystery than you do," responded the girl. Not particularly fond of being referred to as "little missy."

"No offense. I'm just trying to be – what's the word? – discreet."

"That you are, Ben," said Maddy, leaning forward to

pat his massive arm. "But let's not stray from the point."

"You wanna know about the ring, right?"

"Exactly. Last I heard, Ferdinand Jinks had stolen the ring from the Colonel as he lay in his coffin."

"True, as far as the legend goes," nodded the squat man.

"Then how did you come by it?"

"Not me, your husband. Quite frankly, ma'am, I'm surprised you're talking to me instead of him."

That stopped her. "Beau had the ring?"

"That's right. And he stuck it in that old metal head right 'fore we sealed it up in the tomb. Dunno why."

Maddy finished off her tea. "One last question, Ben. Then we'll be on our way. How did my husband get you involved in this little escapade? I don't recall you and him being particularly close friends."

"No, ma'am. I've only come to befriend Beauregard in the last few months, though I attended Caruthers High with both-a you's. As I recall, you and me had algebra together."

"Yes, I remember. You sat behind Cookie."

"That was so I could admire her from afar."

"You really should give her a call."

"Aw, I'm too busy, what with the farm and on the weekends I'm a voluntary ambulance driver with Caruthers Corners Fire and Rescue. Don't have much spare time."

"Be that as it may, Ben. You still haven't answered my question about how you got mixed up in all this."

"Simple answer. Your husband needed some heavy lifting. And when I came into Ace Hardware to buy some wood screws he remembered I'd been weightlifting champion two years in a row back when we were in high school."

"I'd forgotten that. You set a state record, now that I think back."

"Been broken since. But I was a right brawny guy back then."

"Those size fourteen feet certainly prove you're still no lightweight."

"Feel bad about tracking mud into the Town Hall. We'd been down to the Colonel's tomb to pry the door open. Broke one-a the hinges doing it. It's pretty muddy after a rainfall down in that part of the cemetery."

"And you don't know how my husband got the ring?"

"Nary a clue."

CHAPTER ELEVEN

Guilty As Charged

Beauregard Madison IV was not thrilled at having to face his wife that night. She had every reason to be upset with him. He'd fibbed to her, committed a crime (of sorts), and spent $12,000 of their retirement funds without consulting her. All this was totally unlike the Pooh Bear she'd been married to for nearly forty years.

"Honey, I'm home," he called. That line from countless TV sitcoms, *Father Knows Best* to *Leave It to Beaver*. It had been good for many laughs over the years, but Maddy wasn't even smiling when she met him in the living room.

"Sit down, Beau. We need to talk."

"Yes, dear. I know."

"Tilly took Aggie to the movies. A new Disney film about a princess."

"Look, what I did was wrong – " he began weakly.

"You mean stealing the statue? Or lying about it?"

"I didn't exactly lie. I just played dumb when you got caught up in playing *Murder She Wrote*."

That irked her. She looked nothing like Angela Lansbury. The woman was twenty years older than her. "I understand what you were trying to do. You wanted to honor your great-great grandfather with a bigger statue, but you knew Mayor Caruthers wouldn't accept a second one. So you had to get rid of the first statue. You got Ben

Bentley to help you haul it off in the dead of night, stashing it in the family mausoleum. Meanwhile, you had a sculptor in Chicago chipping away on a marble replica of that old hornswoggler as a replacement."

"Guilty as charged."

"Now tell me about the ring." She tossed it onto the coffee table with a *ka-thunk*!

"I wondered what happened to that. It wasn't inside the bronze bust when Chief Purdue hauled it back to the Town Hall."

"No, because I took it. But the question is, how did you come to have it? Cookie says that Ferdinand Jinks stole it back in the eighteen hundreds, his revenge for being kicked out of the town he helped found."

"Well, he did burn down the Town Hall," her husband pointed out.

"Don't evade the question."

"Sorry. I bought it from Tall Paul. You know he was a descendant of Jinks. The ring had been passed down father to son."

"I thought he was related on his mother's side."

"True. They had to make an exception there. His mother was an only child, no brothers to get the ring."

"Why did you hide the ring inside the bust?"

"Stashing it away. I was planning on donating it to the Historical Society when the new statue got erected."

Maddy sighed. "Tell me this, how much did you pay Tall Paul for the ring?"

"A thousand dollars."

"I'm afraid you got gypped, Pooh Bear. This ring is a fake."

CHAPTER TWELVE

History's Mystery

The next day was Tuesday, the regularly scheduled meeting of the Quilter's Club. It was a tossup as to whether Agnes was more excited over starting on her quilt or reporting on their sleuthing.

"Hi, Aggie," waved Cookie.

"Ready to start on your quilt now that you've done so much practicing on your stitches?" asked Lizzie.

"Sure."

"After that, maybe you can solve another mystery," teased Bootsie. She'd seen the picture in the *Gazette* – her husband and Maddy, Aggie and that cute little dog.

"Grammy did most of the work solving the case," Agnes beamed at her grandmother.

Maddy waved away the praise. "My husband turned himself in," she insisted. "Confessed everything to Jim Purdue."

"Yes, after you confronted him." Bootsie pointed out. Being married to the police chief, she had an inside track on such matters.

"I wanna work on my quilt," said Agnes, getting bored, not very interested in the finer points of who did what to whom.

"Come over to the table here with the pieces of fabric

you picked out. I'm going to show you how to measure and cut out your squares so that they will all be exactly the same size," volunteered Lizzie.

"Do I use the lines on this plastic matt?"

"That's right, honey. This is a measuring and cutting mat. Use the inch marks on the mat to lay out your fabric. Then use this ruler and tailor's chalk to draw your cutting lines. Let's make each square six inches on each side. This will be easier to finish and you can hang this on a wall in your bedroom when you're done."

"Neat-o."

"Are you angry with Beau?" Bootsie asked her friend. Unable to let the subject go.

"Not really. Beau's intentions were good, but he got carried away."

"So you're going to forgive and forget?"

"He was just trying to aggrandize that stupid old ancestor of his," Maddy shrugged off her friend's concern. "No big deal."

"Yes, but he committed a crime. Not to mention that he lied to you!"

"Your husband is overlooking the crime, so why shouldn't I forgive the lie?"

"Jim and Beau are buds."

"Well, Beau and I are a bit more than that."

That was logic Bootsie couldn't refute. She zipped her lip and concentrated on stitching a straight seam. Easier said than done.

Cookie was still curious about the details. "How did you know the Colonel's ring was a fake?" she asked.

"Grammy took it to a jeweler," Agnes spoke up. "He

told her the ruby was really a piece of red glass."

"Gems Galore on North Main," amplified Maddy. "I was simply hoping he could confirm that it was old, from the eighteen hundreds. You can imagine my surprise when he asked me if I found it in a Cracker Jack box."

"So is Jim going to arrest Tall Paul for fraud, selling fake rings as family heirlooms?" asked Cookie.

Bootsie shook her head. "Beau refuses to press charges, so Tall Paul gets a free pass – "

" – and gets to keep the thousand dollars," added Lizzie.

"There's that," Maddy admitted.

"Is it true Beau paid twelve grand for a stone statue of Colonel Madison?" asked Cookie. Her quilt was nearing completion, so she could stop to talk without missing a stitch.

Maddy winced. "I'm afraid so. Let's hope it rivals Michelangelo's David."

"What will he do with it?" Lizzie wanted to know. "I heard Mayor Caruthers has turned it down as a gift for the town square."

"So I'm told. My guess is that it will wind up in our backyard overlooking the goldfish pond."

"Really," said Cookie. "What a shame."

"*Hmph*, I'd rather have new kitchen countertops," snorted Bootsie. Not exactly an art afficinado.

"Me, I'd take a new car," said Lizzie. "One of those Japanese SUV's."

"It's not like I get a choice," laughed Maddy. "The money has already been spent. On a marble statue. Not kitchen counters or SUV's or even mink coats."

"Mink coats are out," said her granddaughter. "PETA members would march naked down Main Street if you got one."

"I doubt there are many PETA members in Caruthers Corners," observed Bootsie. "Too many hunters in these parts."

"Don't worry," Maddy assured them. "We will never see the day when my husband coughs up the money it takes to buy a mink coat."

"I haven't priced one lately," said Cookie. "But I'll bet they cost less than twelve grand."

"Touché," said Maddy.

"Can somebody tell me if I cut this square out OK?"

"That looks great, honey. Now start cutting your other eight squares. Then I'll show you how to prepare the seams before you start sewing them together. It takes a little time, but it'll be worth it when your quilt is finished."

"Thanks, Lizzie."

"If Tall Paul sold Beau a fake ring, does that mean he still has the real one?" mused Cookie.

"Who knows," said Maddy.

"Who cares," added Bootsie.

Little Agnes looked up from her cutting. "The Quilter's Club should care," she declared.

That got Maddy's attention. "Why, Aggie?"

"The mystery isn't solved until we find out."

"No, dear," contradicted Bootsie Purdue. "We set out to find who stole the Colonel's bronze bust. Turns out, your grandpa did it."

"Not that he meant anything bad by it," Cookie hastened to amend.

"But we've turned up an even older mystery. What happened to the Colonel's ruby ring that old Mister Jingo stole."

"Jinks, dear. It was Ferdinand Aloysius Jinks."

"So where is it – the ring, that is?"

"Probably in Paul Johnson's sock drawer," Bootsie tried to make light of it.

"I think Aggie's right," Cookie Brown spoke up. "The mystery of what happened to Colonel Beauregard Madison's ring has never been solved. We owe it to history to find it and return it to its rightful owner."

"My husband?" said Maddy. "He's the Colonel's last living descendant."

"No," said a tiny voice – Agnes. "I am."

CHAPTER THIRTEEN

Toe Jam

Tall Pall Johnson was taken aback to find four ladies and a girl at his front door. "I hope you don't mind," smiled Maddy Madison. "We dropped by to see how your toe was healing."

"My toe?" He seemed to have forgotten his "lawnmower accident." No sign of crutches or bandages on his left foot.

"Yes, you told my husband that you'd hurt it while mowing the lawn," said Bootsie.

"Oh, that. Perhaps I exaggerated slightly. More like I stubbed it."

"We brought you this nice pot of soup, thinking you couldn't get around well enough to cook for yourself," said Cookie, holding up a covered aluminum container.

"As you can see, that wasn't necessary. Besides, my wife's pretty handy in the kitchen."

"Here's the soup anyway," said Lizzie. "May we come in?"

It would have been rude to say no, so the giant reluctantly opened the screen door and allowed them to enter. First thing Maddy noticed when they stepped into the living room was the magnificent hand-stitched patchwork quilt hanging over the mantle. The design

63

seemed to be based on Caruthers Corners. She could recognize the familiar landmarks of the town square, the church with its tall spire, the fire station at the end of Main Street, and the old Town Hall.

"How lovely," she admired the handiwork.

"A family heirloom," muttered Tall Paul. "The only thing handed down on the Jinks side of the tree."

"What about the Colonel's ruby ring?" Cookie got straight to the point. "You claimed you had it when you sold a fake to Maddy's husband."

"Wasn't the Colonel's ring in the first place," the man corrected her. "It belonged to my great-great grandpappy."

"Whatever," Maddy brushed his words aside. No point in arguing. "Fact remains, you sold a fake to my husband."

Tall Paul looked embarrassed. "True enough. I never did have that doggone ring. Only heard tales of it when I was a li'l child. My granny used to say the ruby was buried beneath the Town Hall – but she was an old woman, half-crazy at the time. Don't s'pect it'll ever be found."

"So why did you swindle my husband?" Maddy asked point blank.

"Greed, ain't no other word for it. Beauregard wanted that ring real bad. And when he offered me a thousand dollars, I just couldn't turn it down. So I sold him a trinket I'd won at the county fair back in '96. That was the year I met my wife."

Everyone hereabouts knew the story, how Tall Paul fell in love with the sideshow tattooed lady and married her in a ceremony right there on the midway. They had toured for a season or two as a couple, him a 7' giant, and her an example of illustrated skin art. Their traveling came to an end when Emma Johnson developed diabetes and had to retire for health reasons. So she and Tall Paul settled down in this comfortable little house on Easy Chair Lane.

"Buried under the Town Hall?" repeated Lizzie.

"Hm, your great-great grandfather burned down the Town Hall," said Maddy, working on the puzzle. "Maybe he buried the ring on the site before it was rebuilt."

"No, that couldn't be right," interjected Cookie, the historian of the group. "The Colonel didn't pass away until just after the new Town Hall was completed. And legend has it Jinks stole the ring off him while he was laid out at his wake."

"That's right," murmured Bootsie. "The old Town Hall was a wooden structure, but they rebuilt it out of bricks so it wouldn't burn so easily next time."

"But there was never a next time," said Tall Paul Johnson. "Ferdinand Jinks was killed in a freak electrical storm just a few years after the new Town Hall was built."

"God's punishment," said Cookie.

"So what about the ring being buried beneath the Town Hall?" interjected Bootsie.

"A crazy story," said Lizzie, her red hair flaming about her face in the sunlight from the window. "It just proves that Paul's granny was senile like he says."

≈≈≈

At dinner that night Tilly made an announcement: "It's official. Mark's suing for custody of Agnes. He says he has no choice since I won't bring her home. I told him 'why would I bring her home to a father who is too important to ever have a minute to spend with his family!'"

"But I don't wanna go back to California!" the girl

exploded. "I wanna stay here with you and Grammy and Grampy. Why can't daddy come here instead?" Quite a change of opinion transpiring in the past two weeks.

"There, there. You're not going anywhere," said Beauregard. But his promise sounded hollow to everyone at the table.

"We'll get you a good lawyer," said Maddy. "Fight him."

Beau nodded. "I'll call Bartholomew Dingley. He'll take the case."

"No, Bartholomew's closing his law practice next month."

"Why do that?" puzzled Beau. "He has plenty of clients."

"Dear, he's eighty years old. Give him a break."

"Oh."

"Don't worry, Tilly. We'll find you a lawyer. They have plenty of sharks like Mark down in Indianapolis."

"Mom, I already have a good lawyer. Trouble is, Mark's got lots more money than I have to spend on depositions and interrogatories and motions for summary judgment."

"Half of his money is yours," opined Beau. Not quite sure about the legal status of assets in California.

"You once told us he made over two hundred thousand dollars a year," Maddy reminded her daughter. She was confounded by all this legal wrangling. Why couldn't couples split up on friendly terms? Aggie needed a daddy even if he had turned out to be a selfish scoundrel.

"Oh, he makes a lot more than two hundred thousand when you count in all those bonuses the partners get. But his accountant is claiming heavy expenses."

"Mercy, what's this world coming to?" exclaimed Beau. "I only take home forty thousand after expenses at the hardware store and we live well enough on that."

Maddy wasn't about to cite the heavy expenses of hiring a sculptor to create a life-size marble statue of a man who got rich swindling Indians out of their rightful land. "Pass the butter," she said instead.

≈≈≈

The next day while mother and daughter were shopping for the week's provisions at the Food Lion, Maddy casually asked, "What exactly was the trouble between you and Mark? Another woman?"

"No, mom, nothing like that. It was his job. He works all the time, day, nights, weekends. Look up *workaholic* in the dictionary and you'll see his picture."

"Oh my, your uncle Joel was like that. Dead at forty with a heart attack."

"I worry about Mark's health. He has high blood pressure. Not exactly a trait you'd want in a high-pressure job like lawyering."

"Why so concerned about his health if he's dumping you?"

"Mom, I still love the big lug. Just not how he practices his profession. I was patient for a long time. But it never got better. He never had any time for Aggie and me – even when I begged him to consider what should be the most important part of his life."

CHAPTER FOURTEEN

Tall Paul's Granny

A special meeting of the Quilter's Club was called to order. Today's agenda wasn't fat quarters and fancy borders, but instead its members were concentrating on the mystery of the Colonel's ruby ring. Maddy was there, along with Cookie, Bootsie, and Lizzie. And the club's newest member – Agnes – was seated in the big rocking chair.

"Here's what we know," began Maddy, ticking the facts off one-by-one on her fingers. "Three men founded the town of Caruthers Corners: Colonel Beauregard Madison, Jacob Caruthers, and Ferdinand Jinks. Jinks fell out of favor and retaliated by burning down the Town Hall. He was chased out of town, but returned upon the Colonel's death to steal a ruby ring off his body. The ring has never been recovered. My husband tried to buy it from the last living descendant of Jinks, but it turned out to be a fake. Paul Johnson, the said descendant, says he never had the ring. He quotes his grandmother as saying the ring was buried beneath the Town Hall, but that can't be right. The timing's off."

"Pretty well sums it up," nodded Cookie, taking notes. As secretary of the Historical Society, she was an inveterate record keeper.

"Why did the three founders get mad at each other in the first place?" asked Agnes.

"Good question," said Bootsie. "Cookie, do you know?"

"Yes, the Historical Society has Jacob Caruthers' journal in its archives. According to Caruthers, it was a falling out over a woman. Seems that Colonel Madison married Jinks' betrothed."

"I can see why Jinks might have been peeved," said Lizzie. Always a bit of a *femme fatale* herself.

"He was angry enough to burn down the Town Hall," Bootsie agreed.

"Yes, but why did he steal the Colonel's ring?" asked Agnes, her curiosity having the clarity of a ten-year-old mind.

"Hmm, I don't know," admitted Cookie.

"Spite," guessed Lizzie.

"Maybe he was just mean," tried Bootsie.

"No, I think it wasn't his ring to begin with," said Maddy. "Remember, Tall Paul corrected us when we called it the Colonel's ring. Maybe Ferdinand Jinks gave the ring to his sweetheart, but she kept it when she ran off with Beauregard Madison."

"Could be," said Cookie. "Records show that Colonel Madison's wife preceded him. Perhaps he kept the ring in remembrance of her, not knowing it had originally been Jinks' ring."

"So Jinks was merely retrieving the ring he'd given his fiancée before she dumped him for another man," Maddy summed it up.

"Then it's properly Tall Paul's ring, not mine," concluded Agnes, sounding disappointed.

"That aside, where is the blasted ring?" said Lizzie, frustrated by all this speculation.

"The only clue we have are the words of Tall Paul's grandmother," Cookie reminded her.

"But she was senile," Lizzie shot back.

"Maybe, maybe not," said Maddy.

≈≈≈

"Your grandmother – what exactly did she say?"

"Huh?" said Tall Paul. He was surrounded by all the members of the Quilter's Club, having been cornered on his porch as he came home from the Food Lion, his arms filled with groceries.

"What were your grandmother's exact words," Maddy repeated as the women followed him into his living room.

Paul Johnson screwed up his face to give it some thought. "She said that the ring was buried beneath the Town Hall," he replied.

"Are you sure those were her exact words," insisted Maddy.

The man stood two heads taller than the women who surrounded him. He balanced the supermarket shopping bags in his arms and recited: "Your great-great grandpappy's ring lies beneath the Town Hall."

"You said 'buried' before," little Agnes pointed out.

"Just an expression," the big man said as he sat his grocery bags on a table and turned to face this invading army. "Now that I think back on it, I'm pretty sure she said 'lies beneath the Town Hall.'"

"Plenty of lying going on here," huffed Bootsie Purdue. As the police chief's wife, she wasn't a very trusting soul.

"Hey now, I'm trying to help you out here. Make

71

amends for gypping Maddy's husband."

"You could try returning the thousand dollars," said Maddy as she studied the beautiful quilt over the fireplace. She seemed fascinated by the stitching, running her hand over the surface as if tracing the shape of the Town Hall.

"That money's long gone," replied Tall Paul. "My wife needed a gall bladder operation."

"Oh my," said Cookie. "If we'd known, we would have baked her a pie or something."

"Bertha's a private woman. All those years with the carnival, people gawking at her, turned her against folks. She hardly goes outta the house these days."

"Sorry to hear that," said Lizzie. But you couldn't be certain whether the redhead was being sincere or not.

"Best we get home," said Maddy, hand on the latch of the screen door. "Oops."

Crack!

"Dang, you broke my latch," griped the giant.

"Sorry about that, Paul. But my husband owns the hardware store. Go down there this afternoon and he'll give you a replacement – no charge."

"Well, okay. But don't break my front step on your way out."

"Come along, girls. Time to go."

The Quilter's Club marched down the front walk toward Maddy's SUV. The big man called after them: "If you find that ring, remember it's mine."

As she slid behind the wheel of the Ford Explorer, Maddy replied primly, "No, Paul, it's not. You sold it to my husband for a thousand dollars."

CHAPTER FIFTEEN

Dangers of Quilt-Making

Watermelon Days was coming up. That meant the Quilter's Club had to finish their sewing projects. Quilts of local design were always displayed at the Grange Hall during the festival days.

Maddy's watermelon appliqué quilt was nearly completed. Lizzie had finished hers – a design based on rows of corn – and was helping Agnes make her sandwich with the batting and backing now that she had her nine squares all sewn together. It had taken every minute of her spare time since she started. Maddy's granddaughter had picked a mix of solid and printed colors for her nine-patch. The way she put them together didn't exactly coordinate all the colors, but somehow it still worked. Her finished quilt would be really unique.

Bootsie had chosen a complicated design that she'd found on the *freepatterns.com* website, intricate briars and brambles called "Rose Red." It featured a brilliant red rosebud in the very center of the quilt.

Cookie was coming along just fine, taking her own sweet time. Historians don't like to be hurried. Her brick-like design in a variation of a log cabin motif reflected the façade of the local Town Hall, sure to be a crowd-pleaser.

"That looks really cool," ten-year-old Agnes

complimented the older woman, sensitive to Cookie's being a widow and all.

"Thank you, my dear. But it's nowhere near the workmanship we saw on that quilt displayed over Tall Paul Johnson's fireplace. Those old-timey quiltmakers certainly knew how to sew."

"The Town Hall on that quilt looked different than yours."

"Remember, I told you the original Town Hall was wooden. But after Ferdinand Jinks burnt it down, they rebuilt it out of bricks."

"Sounds like The Three Little Pigs," giggled Agnes. "Brick to keep Big Bad Mister Jinks from huffing and puffing and blowing it down."

"Something like that," Cookie admitted. "But he used matches."

"Did they have matches back then?" asked Lizzie, looking up from her stitching. She was a fast sewer, and Agnes's hodgepodge design was starting to look passable.

"Yes, indeed," replied Cookie. "Matches were developed in China in 577 A.D. But modern, self-igniting matches were invented by a Frenchman in 1805."

"You're a font of knowledge," said Bootsie, but it wasn't clear whether this declaration was meant as a compliment or not.

"The point being, it wasn't particularly hard for Jinks to burn down the Town Hall. A few matches and a little kindling, then – *whoosh!* – the rickety old building goes up in flames."

"The fire station's just on the other end of Main Street," noted Maddy. "Wonder why they didn't put out the fire before it engulfed the whole building?"

"The fire engine – it was horse-drawn back in those days – had a broken axel. At least, that's what the newspaper account says."

"Do you think Jinks sabotaged the fire engine?" asked Bootsie, always looking for conspiracies. She was convinced the assassination of Dr. Martin Luther King had been a joint effort of the Ku Klux Klan, the CIA, and the Knights of Columbus.

Cookie shook her head. "There was a mention of the fire engine breaking its axel trying to cross the Wabash River to get to a house fire in Burpyville. So I'd expect it was either just a coincidence or Jinks taking advantage of an existing situation."

"*Ow-w-w*," said Agnes, pricking her finger. She hadn't quite mastered the needlework yet. And the basting of her sandwich was a lot harder than she thought.

"You okay, dear?" asked her grandmother.

"Uh-huh, it doesn't hurt bad." The girl sucked on the tip of her forefinger, tasting the blood.

"We've got Band-Aids over here in the cabinet," said Lizzie. "Let me get you one." She rummaged in a big mahogany breakfront, coming up with a square tin box stamped with a red cross.

"How'd you stick yourself?" asked Cookie, leaning forward to examine the tiny wound.

"My needle hit something hard. Glanced off and jabbed my finger that was holding the middle part together."

"Something hard? That's odd," said Bootsie, running her palm along the surface of Agnes's quilt. "Wait! There is something hard in here."

"Really?" Maddy ran her finger over the fabric, checking it herself. Bootsie was known to exaggerate. But not in this case, for she came to a lump about the size of an unshelled peanut, something solid and unyielding.

"What is it?" asked Lizzie as she finished wrapping the bandage around Agnes's injured finger.

"Dunno," admitted Maddy.

"Hand me that pair of scissors," instructed Lizzie. A take-charge personality to the point of being pushy. "We'll find out what's in there."

Snip, snip!

The determined redhead clipped just enough of the basting to slip her hand into the part with the lump. Her hands as steady as a heart surgeon's. "Here you go," she said, carefully pulling her hand out. "I think I've found the culprit."

"A thimble!" Bootsie declared, staring at the round metal object that had been tucked in the folds of the quilt.

"Why, honey," admonished Cookie, "you sewed up your thimble inside your quilt."

"I wondered where it went," the girl giggled. Showing no apparent embarrassment over her *faux pas*.

"Like a doctor sewing up the patient with a sponge inside," said Bootsie. "I heard of that happening at the Veteran's Hospital over in Indianapolis."

"Never mind that," said Maddy. "I know where the ring is."

CHAPTER SIXTEEN

Martha Ray Takes the Prize

Cookie found the newspaper article in her Historical Society archives. The dateline on the yellowed paper was marked April 12, 1934.

Local Woman Wins
State Quilting Prize

INDIANAPOLIS – Mrs. Martha Ray Johnson of Caruthers Corners placed first in the statewide Quilting Bee. Her design was judged most creative among 112 contenders. Reminiscent of a Currier and Ives scene, the quilt offered a bucolic view of a small Midwestern village. When asked where she got the idea for the design, she replied, "My hometown inspired me. Our Town Hall is a real jewel."

"There you have it," exclaimed Maddy. "The location of the ruby ring, right out of the mouth of Paul Johnson's grandmother."

"You mean – ?"

"That's right," nodded Maddy. "The ring is sewn into that prizewinning quilt hanging over Tall Paul's fireplace."

"Hm," said Bootsie, "maybe the old crone wasn't senile after all when she told her grandson that the ring 'lies beneath the Town Hall.' She wasn't talking about the real brick-and-mortar building – she was referring to the building in the quilt pattern."

"So what do we do?" asked practical-minded Agnes. "Knock on Mister Johnson's door and ask him to let us cut open his grammy's quilt?"

"I doubt he'd simply hand it over," said Cookie, well aware how folks in these parts valued their family heirlooms.

"We have to steal it," declared Lizzie, devious as usual.

"Wait, we can't do that," exclaimed Bootsie. "My husband's the chief of police. How would it look if we got caught?"

"Then don't get caught," snapped Lizzie. Her friend Bootsie was such a wimp, always poo-pooing her brilliant suggestions.

"It's not like we'd really be stealing the quilt," rationalized Cookie. "Tall Paul will get it back once we recover the ring."

"And Maddy's husband is the rightful owner of the ring," said Lizzie. "He paid Tall Paul a thousand dollars for it."

"We need a plan," suggested Maddy's ten-year-old granddaughter with the ease of a professional jewel thief.

"Yes, a plan," repeated Maddy thoughtfully.

≈≈≈

Tall Paul Johnson sighed when he answered the

knock at his front door, finding Cookie Brown standing there dressed in her Sunday finery. "What do you want now? I done told you women everything I know about that blasted ruby ring."

"Oh, I'm not here about that," she lied. "As you know, Watermelon Days is coming up, and every year we display our best quilts at the Grange Hall. This year the committee voted to show not only new designs, but also some of the older quilts in the community. Someone pointed out that your grandmother's quilt there over the fireplace won a state prize, so it would be only right to give it a place of honor in the show."

"Not interested," said the giant, slamming the door in her face.

Darn! Back to square one.

≈ ≈ ≈

Knock, knock!

"Yeah?" Tall Paul answered the door. At first he thought no one was there. The neighborhood kids were always knocking on his door and running, thinking it a fine joke to play on the two carnival freaks who lived on Easy Chair Lane. Then, he dropped his eyes to notice the small girl standing at his doorstep. "Young missy, whattaya want now?"

"I'm selling Girl Scout cookies," Agnes announced brightly, holding up the two boxes her grammy had bought last year but never eaten.

"Girl Scouts! Young girls oughta stay home and learn to cook and clean. Ain't got no business hiking and camping in the woods like wild Injuns."

"Won't you buy a box of cookies? It's for a good cause."

"Them things are filled with preservatives. Might stunt my growth," chuckled the seven-foot-tall man, pleased with his own joke.

Agnes's assignment was to keep him talking while Lizzie slipped in the back door and grabbed Martha Ray Johnson's prizewinning quilt. A criminal act, but Lizzie was a natural-born rule-breaker. Bootsie Purdue had refused to come along, spending the morning with her husband in order to have an alibi.

"You sure are tall," Agnes marveled at Tall Paul's height. "I'll bet your taller than Michael Jordan."

"By six full inches," he said proudly.

"That's neat-o. Were you already big when you were my age?"

"What age's that?"

"Ten."

"No, when I was ten – "

Crash!

"What was that?" the big man looked over his shoulder.

"I didn't hear anything."

"Might-a been Bertha. She could've fallen off the bed. That happens sometime when she has them wild dreams about the circus. I told her to stop taking naps if she can't sleep in peace, but she don't listen to me. Says when she's tired she's tired. S'pose we gotta get her a king-size bed one-a these days."

"Wait!" said Agnes, but it was too late. Tall Paul had disappeared into the interior of his house. He was sure to catch Lizzie in the act of burglarizing his prized patchwork quilt.

Not waiting for the police to come, Agnes raced across the front lawn, jumped the low hedge, and hotfooted it up Easy Chair Lane. Grammy and Cookie were waiting in the parking lot of the old chair factory with the SUV's engine running.

"Where's Lizzie?"

"I think she got caught."

"Oh my," her grandmother said to Cookie. "I told you Plan B would never work."

≈ ≈ ≈

"I can't believe you girls left me behind!" shouted Lizzie as she stepped into Maddy's kitchen where the remnants of the Quilter's Club had gathered to access damage.

"Lizzie!"

"What are you doing here?" said Maddy. "Aggie told us you got caught."

Lizzie Ridenour stood there in the doorway, hands on her angular hips. "Do I look like I've been caught?"

As a matter of fact, the redhead did. She was a complete mess – hair askew, slacks ripped, scratches on her bare arms as if she'd been running through a briar patch. She'd made her escape through the wooded area behind Tall Paul's cottage, an undeveloped section known as No Man's Land. Obviously, it wasn't a land suitable for women either.

"I thought you were a goner," said Agnes, sounding overly dramatic. "He heard you make a noise."

"Yes, I broke the back window trying to raise it. Never got inside the darned house."

"So you ran when you heard him coming," Cookie filled in the pieces.

"Like a bunny. I thought my heart was going to bust out of my chest. Whew!" Lizzie heaved a sigh, reliving the trauma of her escape.

"Well, do we call it off – or go to Plan C?" Maddy put it up for vote.

"Plan C," said Cookie.

"Plan C," echoed Agnes.

"Plan C," agreed Lizzie, shaking her head at her own stupidity.

"By the way," said Agnes, "what is Plan C?"

"Beats me," replied Maddy with a weak smile.

CHAPTER SEVENTEEN

Bad Girls

Beau Madison phoned his wife to say he was working late. Taking inventory at the hardware store. "I've been counting wing nuts all day long. Maybe I should have bought a Burger King franchise instead."

"Don't be too long," Maddy cautioned. "Tomorrow's Sunday and you're leading the church choir for Reverend Copeland."

"Oh right."

Beau had a rich baritone voice. He often sang solos with the choir of Peaceful Meadows Church. And sometimes he led the gospel singers when the choral director was out of town. This weekend Ted Triplett was in Indy visiting his sick mother.

"I'll wait up," she promised.

"Okay, as long as you and those over-aged delinquents you call the Quilter's Club stay out of trouble. Bootsie confessed all to her husband."

"What's Chief Purdue going to do about our mischief?"

"Same thing he did about mine – turn a blind eye. After all, nobody actually went inside Paul Johnson's house. But I can tell you he was pretty steamed when he called me. Called Lizzie's husband too."

"I'm sorry, Beau. I don't know what got into us girls."

"Tilly's going to be mighty upset when she learns you've involved her daughter in criminal acts." His voice was quiet, as if speaking in church.

"We weren't going to actually steal anything. Just retrieve the Colonel's ring."

"You know where it is?"

"Think so."

"That's why you girls were going to burglarize Paul's house?"

"We thought of it as an unannounced visit."

≈ ≈ ≈

"Mom, how could you?"

Maddy had just confessed all to her daughter. Agnes sat there on the couch, looking contrite.

"Guess we got carried away."

"All Mark needs is something like this to claim I'm an unfit mother. Let's not give him any help in this custody fight."

"But we were so-o-o close," wheedled young Agnes. "We almost had the ring."

Tilly threw her hands into the air as if beseeching a higher power. "What is it with this stupid ring? It's making everyone in this family crazy."

"Cookie says it's a piece of history," said Agnes.

"Since when were you interested in history? You got a C- in U.S. History last semester!"

"History is important to Grampy. He spent lots of money on a marble statue of our ancestor, the one who helped found Caruthers Corners."

Agnes's mother gave her the eye. "What do you care about this hick town? You were born in Los Angeles."

"But you were born here, mommy. Caruthers Corners is *your* hometown."

"Yes, but – "

Maddy patted her daughter's hand. "She's got you there, dear."

"Finding this ring is important to you and those crazy old biddies in the Quilter's Club?"

Maddy was taken aback by her daughter's rude outburst. "Hey, those are my friends. Cookie Brown babysat you when you were five. Bootsie Purdue bought you your first bicycle. And Lizzie Ridenour made your prom dress for you."

"Sorry I called them 'old biddies,'" Tilly apologized.

"And crazy?"

"Their actions speak louder than words."

Agnes tugged at her mother's arm. "Hey, I'm a member of the Quilter's Club. And I'm not crazy."

"When did you get inducted in this witch's cabal?"

"Tilly!"

"Sorry, mom. I meant Quilter's Club."

"I've been a member for over two weeks. Lizzie's helping me finish my quilt." She paused before adding, "And we did solve the mystery of the missing bronze bust – even if it did nail Grampy."

"I've never seen you so involved in anything, short of a video game."

"Mommy, Grammy and the ladies of the Quilter's Club are so much fun. I never had friends that let me solve mysteries with them in California. I love Caruthers Corners – except that I want my daddy to come here too. Please mommy. Can't you make daddy move here with us?"

Tilly stared at her daughter as if she'd been replaced by body snatchers. She didn't know what surprised her more. The fact that she wanted to stay in Caruthers Corners or the fact that she still didn't understand that her father didn't want to spend time with them anymore. She'd deal with that later – *again*. But for now at least Aggie liked her new surroundings. "You *really* like it here?" Tilly pressed, amazed at her daughter's change of heart.

"Yes, I like staying with Grammy and Grampy. But I want daddy to be here, too!

"Honey, we've talked about this. We don't always get what you want. But I'm glad you are so happy here."

"I am, mommy."

"And you really think you know where to find that ruby ring?"

"Un-huh. We were about to put Plan C into effect."

Tilly gave a roll of her eyes then answered (much to her *own* surprise) "OK, Count me in, too."

CHAPTER EIGHTEEN

Sunday Morning Coming Down

The Quilter's Club met first thing the next morning while everyone else was in church. "Tall Paul teaches Sunday School, so he'll be tied up 'til noon," Maddy explained to her daughter.

Tilly couldn't believe her ears. "That old crook teaches Sunday School? He cheated Dad out of a thousand bucks selling him that phony ring."

"We'll leave that between Paul Johnson and his Maker," said Lizzie. "The point is, he'll be out of the house."

"What about his wife, that circus tattooed lady?"

"She worked for a carnival, not a circus," corrected Cookie, a stickler for getting facts straight.

"Don't worry about Mrs. Johnson," said little Agnes. "Plan C will take care of her."

≈≈≈

The van pulled up in front of the cottage on Easy Chair Lane. The lettering on the side panel identified it as JIFFY HOUSECLEANING SERVICE.

Maddy had rented the van late yesterday afternoon and Lizzie – having an artistic flair – had lettered it with a soluble non-permanent paint. Bootsie had bought two pair of coveralls and Cookie had rounded up the cleaning supplies.

Maddy made the phone call. "Hello, Mrs. Johnson. This is Myrtle at Jiffy Housecleaning. We're calling to confirm your ten o'clock appointment."

"There must be some mistake," came Bertha Johnson's drawl. She'd been raised in Tennessee. "I didn't order any cleaning."

"Hmm, are you sure? Our records show one hour of housecleaning scheduled for this morning. Paid in advance."

"Paid, you say."

"Yes ma'am. According to our records we owe you a cleaning that you've already paid for."

"Like I say, there must be some mistake – "

"If so, it's your gain. We have a truck on the way."

Larceny crept into Bertha Johnson's heart. "Can you refund the money to me?"

"No ma'am. No refunds. But if you don't want the cleaning, just send our crew back to the office. We're kinda backed up today, plenty of other houses scheduled."

"But it's Sunday – "

"One of our busiest days. Guess folks like to start off the week with a clean house."

"And you say my cleaning's already paid for?"

"That's right, ma'am. But you can send our truck back if you feel there's been some mistake."

"No, no. Send 'em on. If you can't gimme a refund, I'll take the cleaning."

Just then, Bertha heard a knock at the front door. She hung up the phone as she looked out the window. There was the Jiffy Housecleaning van in the driveway. "Hold your horses, I'm coming," she shouted, starting that torturous journey down the stairs to the living room.

Being a recluse, Bertha didn't know many of the town folk. She'd never laid eyes on the two women standing at her front door. "Jiffy Housecleaning," Bootsie introduced herself. "We clean your house in a jiffy." Lizzie was standing behind her friend, wearing identical beige coveralls, red hair tucked under a bandana.

"Come in, come in," Bertha ushered them into the living room.

Lizzie tried not to stare. But this woman was a human canvas, every inch of her skin covered with ink – dragons and swirls and stars and more!

"According to our records, you have an hour's worth of cleaning – already paid in advance. That should cover any room of your choice. Unless you want to pay for additional rooms at seventy-five dollars an hour."

Bertha frowned. "Say, is this some kinda bait and switch? I've got an hour coming. Don't try to wiggle out of it."

"So shall we do your bathroom?"

Bertha bellowed, "You don't get off with a tiny room like that. I want you to clean my living room." That being the largest room in the house.

"No problem, ma'am. Step aside and we'll get to work." Bootsie could sound very officious when she wanted to.

"I'm going to stay right here and make sure you two do a thorough job. No slacking off with a lick and a promise."

"Don't worry, ma'am. You'll get your money's worth."

That sounded all the better to Bertha Johnson, in that

she hadn't paid a nickel. Wasn't her fault if Jiffy Housecleaning couldn't keep its records straight.

Lizzie began vacuuming, while Bootsie polished the coffee table with Pledge. As expected, Bertha hovered over them like a mother hen, pointing out a fleck of dust here, a smudge on a mirror there.

Suddenly, the hum of industry was interrupted by a screech of tires and a child's scream.

"What was that?" muttered Bertha, glancing toward the street.

"Sounded like an accident," said Bootsie. "We'd better go see if anyone's injured."

"But I never go out – "

"Quick, follow me. It sounded like somebody got hit by a car."

As the two women stepped onto the porch, they could see an SUV stopped in the middle of the street, a little dog laying feet up on the asphalt in front of it. A little girl standing on the sidewalk was sobbing, "My doggie, my doggie!"

A carefully staged scene.

Tilly stepped out of the car, shouting, "I couldn't help it. The dog ran right in front of my car."

"Heaven help us," gulped Bertha. "There's hardly ever any traffic on this street."

"Is the dog dead?" enunciated Bootsie, proud of her acting skills. She'd once had the lead in Shakespeare's *Macbeth* in high school, playing the villainous queen.

"No, just injured," replied the driver of the car. "I've already called for an help on my cell phone."

"Thank the Lord," said Bertha.

At that moment an ambulance pulled up, Ben Bentley driving, his huge form filling the cab. Cookie, wearing a jacket that said CARUTHERS CORNERS FIRE AND RESCUE was squeezed in beside him. You could see Ben smiling ear-to-ear, despite the supposed gravity of the situation.

"Over here, the dog," pointed Tilly.

Ben hopped out, scooped Tige into his arms, and hustled the dog into the rear of the ambulance. The girl hopped in too.

"Is the puppy going to be all right?" called Bootsie, ad-libbing.

"If we hurry," rumbled the big ambulance driver.

"I'll follow you to the veterinarian in Burpyville," announced Tilly, getting back into her car.

"Mercy me," exclaimed Bertha Johnson as the vehicles sped away. Not wondering why an ambulance had been called to transport a dog to the vet's.

"Gotta go," announced Bootsie, looking at her Piaget. It was a pretty fancy wristwatch for a housecleaner.

"Go?"

"Hours up, lest you want to pay another seventy-five dollars."

"But you were here on the porch, not working."

"Time is money. We get paid by the hour." Lizzie had appeared on the porch beside them, carrying the vacuum and the bucket of polishing rags.

"That ain't fair," complained the tattoo-covered woman. "I didn't get my money's worth." Not that she'd paid any money in the first place.

"Don't like it, talk to the office." Bootsie was getting

into her role. Giving the words an operatic infliction that had Lizzie rolling her eyes.

"I'll just do that. I'm marching inside and calling Jiffy Housecleaning this very minute."

"See you around," called Bootsie as the two women climbed into the van.

Bertha thundered into the house and grabbed the phone receiver off its cradle, then realized she didn't have a number for the cleaning service. That woman – what was her name, Myrtle? – had called her, not the other way around. She snatched up the thin Caruthers Corners phonebook and thumbed to the J's. Jeffreys, Jillison, Jiggs ... but no Jiffy Housecleaning.

CHAPTER NINETEEN
Armchair Quarterback

"You girls should've stayed longer," Maddy reprimanded her partners in crime as they peeled off their coveralls. "No need to raise suspicions."

"You're one to talk, refusing to be part of the cleaning service," snipped Lizzie.

"Well, I wasn't about to stay another minute," declared Bootsie Purdue. "Tall Pall was due home from church and he would have recognized us for sure."

"Besides," added Lizzie, "I wasn't about to clean her messy living room. The woman's not very neat."

"She a semi-invalid," Maddy pointed out. "I hear she has a really bad case of diabetes."

"Candy wrappers everywhere," grumbled Lizzie, not backing down. "No wonder she's diabetic."

"How did my dog do?" asked Agnes, looking for praise.

"Tige was perfect," said her grandmother. "Laid there as still as a church mouse."

Not that the dog was still at the moment, bouncing up and down and barking with excitement.

"I was glad Ben and Cookie arrived when they did," Agnes said. "Tige doesn't play dead for long."

"Say, where *are* Ben and Cookie?" asked Bootsie, noticing their absence.

"The new lovebirds went for a drive," said Tilly.

"In an ambulance?"

"'Fraid so. I think Cookie has said her final goodbyes to Bob," declared Maddy. "Two years is long enough to grieve."

The newly single Tilly wasn't so sure. "I wish them happiness," she said, just to be polite.

"Let's see the Colonel's ruby ring," trilled Agnes, dancing about, as excited as a kid on Christmas morn.

"You were right about it being in the quilt," said Lizzie. "I've got the ring right here. And Martha Ray Johnson's masterpiece isn't much the worse for wear because the Town Hall building is actually appliquéd on. So snip, snip, a couple of threads and I had it." She held out her palm to reveal a little wad of paper, like the wrapping around a piece of bubblegum.

"Let's see it," said Bootsie. "Find out what all the foofaraw was about."

"Shouldn't we wait 'til Cookie gets back?" asked Tilly. "After all, she's the historian."

"That may be hours," Bootsie complained. "I'm not waiting on those lovebirds."

"What about Beau?" said Maddy. "I think my husband should be here."

"He's still at church rehearsing with the choir," Lizzie pointed out. "We can show him when he gets home." Her fingers were already picking at the wad of paper.

"Oh very well. Let's have a look at this fabulous ring," acquiesced Maddy, not bothering to hide her disdain.

Lizzie peeled away the paper to reveal a shiny gold ring with a brilliant red stone. Despite the years it wasn't the least bit tarnished, as if it had been hidden away in the quilt only yesterday. "Ta da," she said, holding it out for everyone to see.

"Wow! It looks just like pirate's treasure," said Agnes, eyes reflecting the golden ring with the red stone. "And it's all mine."

"Not so fast, young lady," her mother corrected her. "That ring rightfully belongs to your grampy. He paid a thousand dollars for it."

"But I'm the last descendant on the family tree!"

"Yes, but heirlooms and such have to be handed down. It's only yours if Grampy gives it to you. But my guess is it will go on display in the Town Hall."

"Only if Mayor Caruthers agrees," Bootsie noted. "And that old curmudgeon has been pretty jealous over Colonel Madison getting more attention than his forbearer."

"Jacob Caruthers got the town named after him. What more would the mayor want?" said Tilly.

Bootsie laughed. "To hear him tell it, his great-great grandfather founded this town single handedly."

"While fighting off the Indians at the same time," Maddy added, still protesting that Native Americans got a raw deal from the early settlers.

"Maybe so, but I doubt he'll want that ring on display," shrugged Lizzie, a realist.

"Then Grampy can give it to me," said Agnes, still hopeful.

"No dear, he'd likely bestow it to the Caruthers Corners Historical Society in that case," said Maddy. She knew her husband only too well.

"Okay, then Cookie will be in charge of the ring,"

shrugged Agnes, already accepting her fate. "That's almost as good as having it myself."

"Well, at least you can try it on," laughed Lizzie, handing the golden circlet to the girl.

"May I?"

"It's a loose fit. Don't drop it," said Lizzie as she slid it onto Aggie's finger.

"It looks beautiful. But here, take it back."

"Okay, we'll put it away 'til Beau gets home," said Maddy.

"Wait, what's that?" pointed Agnes. "There's writing inside the ring."

"Writing?" said Bootsie.

"Engraving," corrected Lizzie, a connoisseur of fine jewelry. Her own wedding ring was circled with diamonds, but inside it was engraved the date of the marriage.

"Let's see," said Maddy as she held the ring up to the light for a better view. She could make out the words etched into the inner circle of the golden band:

Property of Acme Costume Supplies

"Oh my," she gasped. "This ring's a fake too!"

≈≈≈

Beauregard Madison was clearly puzzled. "Does that mean Tall Paul Johnson's snookered me a second time?" He had just arrived home from choir practice and was completely caught off guard by this new mystery.

"Can't be," Maddy patted his hand as they sat at the kitchen table, phony ring at the center. "How would he have known we'd figured out where to look for the

Colonel's ring?"

"Maybe he planted the clue with you. Led you to looking in the quilt."

"I don't think he's *that* clever," protested his wife.

"Sorry, dad," said Tilly. "We tried to get your ring for you."

"I know, dear. And I thank all of you girls."

Bootsie and Lizzie smiled happily. Tilly and Agnes too. Cookie was still off with Ben Bentley. "Sparking," Beau had termed it.

Maddy wasn't one to give up easily. "Well, our goal is clear. We still have to find the real ruby ring."

"We've got a new clue," said Agnes. "We can start there."

"What clue's that, Aggie?"

"Acme Costume Supplies. Maybe Mr. Johnson didn't plant the ring in the quilt, but somebody did. Let's find out who bought that fake ring."

≈≈≈

The recorded message stated that Acme Costume Supplies was closed for the weekend, but would be open for business 9 to 5 Monday through Friday. They would have to wait until tomorrow.

Locating Acme had been a task in itself. There were no costume shops in Caruthers Corners or nearby Burpyville. But long-distant information turned it up in Indianapolis, the state capital.

"Why didn't he sell you this ring instead of that carnival fake? This costume jewelry looks more authentic than that piece of gold-painted plastic." Tilly was thinking out loud.

"Because he didn't know that the ring was inside the patchwork quilt," said Maddy. The answer was obvious.

"If he didn't know, then who put it there?" asked Bootsie, her brow wrinkled in confusion.

"His grandmother," said Betsey. "Just like we thought all along."

"No, this costume jewelry is too new," Agnes pointed out. "The Acme website says they've only been in business ten years. And the quilt's a lot older."

"That's right," Maddy confirmed. "According to that newspaper article, Martha Ray Johnson won first prize in the state with it back in 1934."

Bootsie shook her head in frustration. "But she told Tall Paul the ring was inside the quilt – or at least hinted as much."

"That's right," said Lizzie. "How could she have known about the ring back when Tall Paul was just a kid if somebody put it inside the quilt only within the past ten years?"

"It's so confusing," sighed Tilly.

Just then Cookie breezed in through the kitchen door. Members of the Quilter's Club didn't bother with knocking at each other's homes, comfortable with an open-door policy. People in Caruthers Corners rarely bothered to lock their doors, the crime rate was so low. Mayor Caruthers joked that Police Chief Purdue barely had a job if it wasn't for parking tickets.

"Hi all," crooned the slender woman. "I'm in love."

"That's awfully sudden, isn't it?" admonished Tilly. She seemed to find the L-word emotion suspect these days.

"Not for Ben. He's had a thing for me since high school. And to think I wasted all those years with Bob Brown."

"You loved Bob," contradicted Maddy.

"Oh, maybe at first. But all the romance had gone out of our marriage by the time ol' Bob kicked the bucket."

"Then why have you been making those pilgrimages to Pleasant Glade?"

"I don't know. Guilt maybe. Or faithfulness. After all, Bob and I were together for more'n forty years."

"So Ben's the one?" said Lizzie, eyes twinkling. She had always been the sucker for romance among the group.

"For now," Cookie declared. "Ask me again tomorrow."

CHAPTER TWENTY

Costume Party

Everybody gathered at the Madison house on Melon Pickers Lane at precisely nine o'clock the next morning. Agnes had printed out Acme Costume Supplies' home page with Maddy's PC. It had the phone number at the top of the page for easy reference.

Beau hadn't bothered going to work, leaving customers standing outside the hardware store looking at their watches. Today, busted water pipes and overflowing toilets would have to wait.

Cookie had brought Ben along, him now conscripted as a crime-solver. Beau didn't say anything, since he was the one who had got the big troll involved in the first place, helping him hide that bust of Colonel Madison in the family mausoleum.

Bootsie said her husband wanted them to keep him in the loop, although he couldn't take an official position, being police chief and all.

Lizzie didn't mention her hubby. Folks knew she and Edgar led somewhat separate lives. He was always off hunting or trout fishing, after retiring from his position as bank president. Caruthers Corners Savings and Loan held most of the mortgages in these parts, but Edgar Ridenour was known to be a lenient man, willing to go the extra mile with a customer during hard times.

Tilly was quiet. She'd talked with her estranged husband late last night, him on California time, and was distressed with his announcement that he was coming to Caruthers Corners to meet with her without any lawyers present. Easier said than done, Mark himself being an attorney with a big L.A. firm.

"Here goes," said Maddy as she dialed the telephone. She had the speaker feature turned on so everyone could hear the conversation.

Rin-n-ng! Rin-n-ng!

"Acme Costume Supplies," answered a chipper voice. "We can accommodate your every party."

"Yes, this is Madelyn Madison over in Caruthers Corners. I'd like to ask you about a previous purchase."

"Yes, ma'am. Satisfaction guaranteed. Did you have a problem with one of our costumes?"

"No, not me. I want to ask who might have bought a ruby ring from you in the past ten years." Even to Maddy it sounded ridiculous, as if the clerk could identify one out of thousands of customers in the past decade. This idea of calling Acme was not such a good one, now that she considered it in the bright light of day.

"A ruby ring, ma'am?"

"Uh, yes. A gold men's ring with a red stone."

"Do you have it with you?"

"Yes, it's right here on the table in front of me."

"Good, now pick it up and look inside the band. Right after our name you will see some tiny numbers. Could you read those off?"

"Oh my, I'll have to put on my reading glasses. Just a

moment. Okay, now I see the numbers. One-ought-seven-seven."

"Ah, yes. I have the stock number right here on my computer. We discontinued that line back in '98. Had a problem with them turning green."

"This one's as shiny as the sun."

"Must have been stored in a warm, dark place."

Sewn into a quilt hanging over a fireplace probably qualified as warm and dark, she thought. But she said, "Do you have a record of any purchasers?"

"We didn't sell very many before getting complains. Here we go, I've got the records up. We sold seventy-two in all."

"Oh."

"But looking at the purchasers, I note that only two have telephone numbers in your area code. We take down the telephone number in case there's any problem in altering a costume to fit. Our tailoring service is very efficient, but sometimes we get backed up."

Bootsie was nudging her. "Ask him who those two were?" she whispered, as if Maddy wasn't about to do just that.

"Can you give me their names?" she politely requested. Prepared for some gobbledygook about customer confidentiality.

But instead he said, "I don't see any harm in that. We're talking nearly ten years ago."

"Yes — ?"

"One was a Martin Wentwhistle in Burpyville. The other was Henry Caruthers in Caruthers Corners. Hm, same name as the town."

"Yes," said Maddy. "That's our mayor."

≈ ≈ ≈

Mayor Henry Caruthers was happy to meet with his constituents, particularly if it was a man whose great-great grandfather had co-founded the town with his own illustrative ancestor, Jacob Abernathy Caruthers.

"Beauregard, so good to see you," the mayor greeted his visitor. He always addressed Beau by his full name in recognition of his family heritage.

"Hello, Lefty."

"Heck, nobody calls me that anymore, Beau. Not since I was a southpaw pitcher on the high school baseball team."

"Guess you'll always be Lefty to me. I was your catcher, remember."

"Them were the good old days."

"Thank you for meeting with me on such short notice."

"I always have time for my friends and supporters," the roly-poly man averred. "Especially if they have a lineage that stretches all way back to my great-great grandpappy's day."

"I'll be brief. Just have a quick question."

"Now, now, no need to hurry. Sit down and I'll have my assistant brew us a cup of tea."

"No thanks. I just had lunch."

"Well then, have it your own way. But before you bother asking, I have to tell you that having a marble statue of Colonel Madison in the town square would be overkill. We already have that fine bronze bust. It's important to keep a balance of recognition when it comes to the town founders."

"That wasn't what I wanted to talk about. I've already made arrangements to donate the new marble statue to the Historical Society. Cookie Brown says it would make a good exhibit in their little museum."

"You have, you say?"

"No need to waste a good statue."

"No, course not," the mayor said. But his tone didn't sound very sincere.

"I came to return this ring." He laid the trinket on the desk blotter.

"W-what's that?"

"A ring you bought from Acme Costume Supplies in Indy back in '98."

"Oh yes, I remember it now. Part of the costume I wore for the town Centennial Celebration that year. You may recall, I came as my ancestor Jacob Caruthers, coonskin cap and all."

"Question I have for you, how did this ring get inside a quilt at Paul Johnson's house?"

"Why, Beauregard, it sounds like you're accusing me of something. I have no idea what happened to the ring. I misplaced it after the Centennial. Haven't seen it in years."

≈≈≈

"Cagey old devil," Beau said of the mayor. "Wouldn't admit to his own name in a court of law. He didn't tell me a darn thing that was useful."

"No, Grampy, that's not so," responded Agnes. "He said he wore the ring as part of his Centennial costume. But why would Jacob Caruthers be wearing a ruby ring. That ring belonged to either Jinks or the Colonel, but not to Caruthers."

"Hm, that's an interesting point," acknowledged her grandfather. "Whattaya make of that, Maddy?"

Agnes's grandmother gave the girl a hug. "You're quite a Dick Tracy Crime Stopper, my dear. You've just opened up a new line of inquiry."

"Who is Dick Tracy?"

"A comic strip detective," said Bootsie. "My husband used to read him all the time."

"Why would Jacob Caruthers be wearing a ruby ring?" repeated Cookie. "There's nothing in the Historical Society's archives that associates him with any such a ring."

"Unless – " said Maddy.

"Unless?" nudged Lizzie.

"Unless it was Jacob Caruthers who stole the ring off Colonel Madison's body, and not Ferdinand Jinks."

"But the legends says – " began Bootsie.

"Legends are just stories, not necessarily true," said Maddy. "What if Caruthers spread that rumor to cover up his own crime?"

"Like they say, history is written by the conquerors," nodded Cookie.

"What's this?" asked Tilly, picking up a scrap of paper from the kitchen floor.

"Oh, that's the paper the fake ring was wrapped in," Lizzie waved it away.

"But there's writing on it," said Tilly.

"What?"

"Writing?"

"Let me see," commanded Maddy Madison, reaching for the crumpled paper. She flattened it onto the surface of the table, studying the handwriting.

Paul Johnson,

When you read this, you will know that the ring your granny hid here is gone. Since you'll never see the real thing, take this $10 imitation with my compliments.

The Rightful Owner

"This is evidence that Mayor Caruthers stole the ring from Tall Paul," said Bootsie. She hadn't been married to a policeman for forty years without picking up a few detecting skills.

"But we just determined that the mayor's ancestor stole the ruby ring, not Tall Paul's," argued Cookie.

"This is so confusing," sighed Lizzie, elbows on the table, head in her hands.

"You gals may as well call it a day," advised Beau Madison. "You're no closer to solving this mystery than when you started. We don't even know who stole the ring, much less where it is now."

"*Au contraire, mon mari*," said his wife, a sly smile on her lips.

"Maddy, we've been married all these years and I never knew that you speak French."

"Pish, dear. I picked up that phrase watching the PBS channel."

"Never mind the French lesson," said Bootsie. "Exactly what are you trying to tell us, Madelyn Agnes Taylor Madison?"

"I know who had the real ring."

CHAPTER TWENTY- ONE

The Arrival of Mark the Shark

Maddy had lived in Caruthers Corners all her life. She'd grown up in that big Victorian house facing the town square, the one with all the gables. The Taylor family had not been as wealthy as the Caruthers or Madisons, but Maddy had not wanted for pretty clothes or trips to a posh summer camp.

She had a great time in high school while still managing to make good grades. And even though she "marched to the tune of her own drummer" so to speak, she was always popular – especially with three of the other in-crowd girls (that being Lizzie, Cookie, and Bootsie). So it came as no surprise when she wound up with the prize catch in the county, Beauregard Madison IV.

They had two fine boys, but Tilly was their only daughter (although Maddy had hoped for more girls). It'd been the happiest day of her life when Tilly married Mark Tidemore, a promising young law student at Ball State University. Little Agnes came a year later, a cute bundle of joy with blue eyes and a quick smile. It was a sad day when Mark moved his family to Los Angeles to accept a junior partnership with a big law firm.

Now here was Mark Tidemore, standing on Maddy's doorstep, hat in hand, asking if Tilly was home – just like he used to do when he was dating Tilly. Only now the jeans and T-shirt he wore were brand new – still creased from the store folds. The baseball hat he held was new, too. Probably didn't have anything besides suites and ties. But he looked like he was happy to be back in clothing that spoke of comfort and home. Seeing him like this again, Maddy could hardly imagine him in those expensive suits that "Mark the Shark" wore.

"I don't know that she will see you," Maddy told him frankly. "Her heart's broken, you know."

"I've handled this badly," he candidly confessed, not able to look his mother-in-law in the eye. "I got wound up with my job, neglected my family. I didn't take Tilly seriously enough when she threatened to leave if I kept ignoring her and Agnes. I figured everything would be okay once I slowed down the next month. But the next month never came and when Tilly walked out, I was devastated. So I tried to bully her into coming back by threatening to take Agnes. But I'd never do that, Mrs. Madison. I'd never separate Aggie from her mommy."

"Come on inside, Mark. No need to stand out here on the doorstep for the neighbors to see. You find a seat in the living room while I go upstairs to see if Tilly's willing to speak with you."

"Mr. Madison's not home, is he?"

"Don't worry about Beau. He's at work. My husband's pretty upset with you, but he will behave as a gentleman. It's part of his breeding."

"Thank you, Maddy." He dared be more familiar, not

having had the front door slammed in his face.

"Don't think you're off the hook with me, young man. I don't share my husband's good breeding. You hurt my daughter and I'll tear your heart out and serve it up as main course at the Fourth of July barbecue."

"Yes, ma'am."

Fifteen minutes later Tilly came down the steps, looking every bit as beautiful as the high school girl Mark Tidemore had married. "Hi, Mark," she said shyly, as if meeting him on a first date.

"Snookums, I've missed you."

"Don't, Mark."

"Look, I've come out here to make things up to you – a new start."

Tilly shook her head, the brown hair brushing her shoulders. "No, Mark, it's too late. You'll never change."

"That's where you're wrong, Snookums. It's never too late. We love each other, you know it."

"I do still love you, but that's not enough. You love your job more."

"Wrong again. I've resigned my partnership at Tatum, Bell and Kaczynski. Cashed out my 401K. Put the townhouse up for sale."

"What? I can't believe you'd ever do that. So are you going to that firm in New York that was calling you all last year?"

"Nope," he said with a mischievous grin.

"Where then?"

"Here. I've going to work here. Caruthers Corners is the perfect place for a new beginning."

"Don't be silly, Mark. What would you do here in

Caruthers Corners? Help Dad run the hardware store? You'd be bored in two days."

"No, I've bought Bartholomew Dingley's law practice. He was planning on retiring. He accepted my offer just this morning."

"You mean – ?"

"Yes – you, me, and Agnes – together here in Caruthers Corners. And I won't get bored. Believe it or not, I was getting really tired of those eighty-hour workweeks. Been there, done that. Now I want my life back. I want you and Aggie back."

CHAPTER TWENTY-TWO

The Evidence Mounts

ogic prevailed. If Jacob Caruthers stole the ring off Colonel Madison's body at his wake, it would likely have been passed down through the family to great-great grandson Henry, the current mayor of Caruthers Corners. And he wouldn't have had to steal it from the quilt.

However, if "The Rightful Owner" stole the ring from Martha Ray Johnson's quilt, replacing it with the $10 costume jewelry, then the culprit had to be the mayor. No one else would have had access to that particular ring marked 1077 inside the band. That meant the real ring had been in the possession of the Jinks family all those years.

Maddy considered this second scenario more likely to be the correct one. No disputing the fact that they'd found the fake ring inside the quilt wrapped in an incriminating note. That mean Ferdinand Jinks did steal the ring, just as the legend suggested!

So far, so good. The mayor had the ruby ring. But knowing *who* had the real ring did not tell you *where* it was.

Nor why Mayor Caruthers considered himself the

rightful owner.

She explained her reasoning to the members of the Quilter's Club, waiting for someone to pick a hole in it. But no one did.

"So what do we do next?" asked Bootsie, unwilling to call it quits.

"Let's divide up the tasks. Bootsie, you see if you can find out how the mayor might have got access to Tall Paul's quilt. Swapping that fake ring for the real one couldn't have been easy."

"And me?" asked Cookie, eager for an assignment.

"You search the Historical Society archives. See if you can find a reason the mayor might consider himself the rightful owner of that ruby ring."

"How about me?" Lizzie raised her hand.

"Lizzie, I want you to figure out where the mayor might keep something valuable – like a ruby ring."

"What can I do, Grammy?" asked Agnes. She'd been left in Maddy's care while her mother and father shopped for a new home somewhere within the town limits.

"You get to assist me. We're going to light a fire under Mayor Caruthers. See if we can smoke out the truth."

≈≈≈

Cookie was the first to report back. She'd found a passage in Jacob Caruthers' journal that shed some light on original ownership of the ruby ring. "Listen to this," she said, then read the entry for May 12, 1829:

The Red Indians attacked again last night. We sustained heavy losses. I thought myself a goner when my flintlock misfired and I found myself facing a warrior brandishing a tomahawk. The quick thinking of Ferdinand Jinks saved my life. He struck the assailant with the butt of his rifle, even though it too was empty of powder, rendering the bugger unconscious. As a token of thankfulness, I awarded Ferdinand my most valued possession.

"It has to be the ring," Cookie tapped the page to make the point. "It was originally Caruthers ring, but he gave it to Jinks."

"And Jinks gave it to his fiancée," Maddy completed the thought. "But she dumped him for Colonel Madison taking the ring with her."

"That's why everybody wanted the ring," squealed Agnes, unable to contain her excitement. "Mister Jinks wanted his ring back from his girlfriend. And Mayor Caruthers considers himself the rightful owner since it had belonged to his ancestor to begin with."

≈≈≈

Lizzie was next to come up with information. "My husband Edgar says Henry Caruthers has a safety deposit box at Caruthers Corners Saving and Loan. Edgar remembers the mayor renting the box back in '98, shortly after the Centennial festivities,"

"In other words, around the time he bought that fake ring and swapped it for the real one in Tall Paul's quilt," surmised Maddy. All the pieces falling into place.

"I'm surprised he would tell you that much about bank customers," said Cookie.

"Edgar will tell me anything when I put on that red

negligee that matches my hair and crook my little finger."

Maddy laughed. "More likely, you agreed to let him take you on a fishing trip to Canada."

"How'd you know that?"

"Your husband invited Beau and me to go along."

≈ ≈ ≈

"Got it," announced Bootsie.

"What?" said Lizzie. "A case of poison ivy?"

"No, silly. I've found out how the mayor pulled the ol' switcheroo with Tall Paul's quilt."

"And – " prodded Maddy.

"It seems the mayor borrowed the quilt to display in the Town Hall during the Centennial celebration. Not only was the quilt an award-winner, it depicted the town of Caruthers Corners. Well, at least its main buildings."

"Why would Paul loan him a quilt with a ruby ring in it?" asked Lizzie.

"Remember, Paul didn't know about the ring being in the quilt. When his granny told him the ring was beneath the Town Hall, he thought she was talking about the real building."

"But how did the mayor know the ring was hidden in the quilt?" asked Agnes, trying to follow the details.

"He didn't," said her grandmother. "He really did borrow the quilt for the Centennial, but he felt a lump inside it when hanging it in the Town Hall. Opening it up, he found the ruby ring."

"Why did he put the fake in the quilt?" Cookie wanted to know.

"He couldn't be sure that Paul didn't know the ring was there, so he took the one he'd bought for his Jacob

Caruthers costume and swapped it for the real thing."

"And the note?" asked Tilly. She and her husband had just put a down payment on that old Victorian on the town square where her mother had grown up.

"Mayor Caruthers has always been jealous of descendants of the other founders, afraid they would steal his limelight. He refused to let Beau put up a statue in honor of the Colonel. And he preferred Paul's ancestor to remain in obscurity. Ferdinand Jinks has practically been erased from the history books. You see, the mayor's a bitter man who couldn't pass up the chance to taunt Jinks' descendant that he had retrieved the ring. But as it turns out, Paul never found the note. We did."

"All that theorizing is well and good," said Ben Bentley who had accompanied Cookie to this meeting of the Quilter's Club. "But how are you gonna get your hands on that ring in his safe deposit box?"

"That's where Agnes and I come in," said Maddy.

CHAPTER TWENTY-THREE

A Return Engagement

"You again," said Tall Paul Johnson, not happy to see her.

Maddy stood her ground. "Oh I think you will want to hear what I have to say this time."

"What makes you think that? I'm pretty busy here. My wife had a bad day on Sunday. Some kind of cleaning service showed up, but left before they finished. Then a dog got bumped by a car right in front of the house. Taken away by a real ambulance and everything. She's not used to so much excitement. She's in frail health, you know."

"I know where the real ruby ring is."

"Do tell?" His interest immediately captured. "Does your husband have it?"

"No, the man who stole it from you has it."

"Stole it from me? I never really had it."

"Yes, Paul, you did. It was right where your granny said it was – under the Town Hall – in you r quilt."

He glanced over his shoulder at the patchwork quilt hanging over his mantle. "It's in there?"

"It was."

"Where is it now?" His eyes were squinted, studying

119

her carefully to ascertain whether she was telling him the truth or not.

"Like I told you, in the possession of the man who stole it. But you can get it back."

"How?"

"First, you have to hire a lawyer," she instructed.

"I don't know any lawyers," said Paul. "Old man Dingley used to handle my matters, but he retired."

"A new attorney is taking over his practice."

"Oh, is he any good?"

Agnes couldn't hold back. "My daddy's the best lawyer in the whole wide world. Grammy says he's a shark."

"Well, now. Drumming up a little family business, are we?"

"Do you want to recover the ring?" said Maddy with an air of finality.

"Okay, what've I gotta do?"

≈≈≈

"One more thing," said Maddy to her granddaughter. "Let's go sit in on the town selectmen's meeting. It should be just getting started."

"Why, Grammy?"

"We want to see the mayor in action."

"That sounds boring."

"Maybe, but detective work takes patience. Just like quilt-making."

They took a seat on the front row, a clear view of the podium. The small auditorium in the Town Hall was filled with long benches, deliberately uncomfortable so no one would be inclined to prolong the meetings.

"I'd like to call this session to order," said Mayor

Henry Caruthers, pounding the gavel with his left hand. "Today, we have a large agenda to cover. First up, a vote on whether the DQ's sign is too large per town ordinance. Who's going to speak on behalf of the Dairy Queen?"

"Time to go," whispered Maddy, slipping out of her seat with the stealth of a ninja.

"Go? We just sat down," hissed Agnes. "I wanna hear 'bout the Dairy Queen sign."

"Come along, young lady. We got what we came to see."

≈≈≈

"Henry Caruthers may be a weasel, but that doesn't make him a thief," observed Maddy's husband. "What makes you so sure he stole the ring?"

"Trust me on this, Beau. I have my reasons."

"Proof?"

"Sort of."

"You can't convict a man on 'sort of' proof. Ask your son-in-law if you don't believe me."

"Mark the Shark is going to help me nail Henry Caruthers," she said matter-of-factly.

"So what proof do you have that the mayor's guilty?"

"He's bad at sewing."

CHAPTER TWENTY-FOUR

Red Letter Day

Mayor Henry Caruthers had been surprised to receive the letter. The letterhead had a Caruthers Corners address, but he'd never heard of the firm.

Mark Tidemore
Attorney at Law

Attention: Henry Jacob Caruthers,

You are hereby notified of a legal proceeding against you by Paul Ferdinand Johnson ("Complainant"), wherein it is alleged and sworn that you did willfully steal one valuable object, a ring set with a ruby stone ("Property"), on or about May of 1998 from said Complainant, and in addition to filing criminal charges with the Caruthers Corners Police Department, you are hereby being notified of a civil proceeding against you demanding return of said Property. Et cetera, etc.

Sincerely yours,
Mark Tidemore, Esq.

"Well, jerk my chain and call me stupid," cursed the mayor. He stormed out of his office, yelling to his assistant that he would be gone for the rest of the day, to cancel all his appointment. He headed straight to Caruthers Corners Savings and Loan on the south end of Main Street, a one-story brick edifice that looked like a cracker box, but was as sturdy as a maximum-security prison.

Mayor Caruthers asked to visit his safe deposit box, flashing his matching key. He kept it on his key chain at all times, along with his other important keys: home, office, Town Hall, car, gate to the town cemetery.

Spending about ten minutes with his lock box, he emerged from the bank like a man on a mission, walking with a fast stride toward his Cadillac Seville. He never made it to the car, intercepted by Chief Purdue.

"Excuse me, Henry, but I have a sworn warrant for your arrest. I'm sure there's been some mistake, but Paul Johnson claims you possess stolen property belonging to him."

"Why that's preposterous, Jim. You know me better'n that."

Unfortunately, Chief Jim Purdue did know the mayor quite well, having gone to high school with him and worked on his first two election campaigns – before coming to realize the small-town politician was a lying, cheating snake. "I'm gonna have to ask you to show me what's in that manila envelope in your hand, Henry."

"This envelope? Personal papers, that's all."

"I'm afraid I have to insist."

Shamefacedly, the mayor upended the manila packet and a ruby ring tumbled out.

CHAPTER TWENTY-FIVE

Quilter's Club Triumphant

"**I** didn't know you were licensed to practice law in Indiana," said Mark's father-in-law, patting him on the back.

"When I graduated from Ball State, I took the bar exam here. For some reason, I kept it up to date, even when we were living in California."

"You did well, Mark the Shark," said Maddy.

"Don't call me that, mother person, or I'll send you the bill."

"But Paul Johnson's your client, not me."

"Yes, but he never would have come to me – my first client at my new law practice – if you hadn't put a bug in his ear."

"He deserved to know."

Mark turned back to his father-in-law. "Are you going to let Paul Johnson keep that ring? It's pretty valuable."

Beau chuckled. "If he returns my thousand dollars. Otherwise you'll have your second case."

"Sorry, Dad, but I couldn't represent you. It'd be a conflict of interest."

"Well, whattaya know. Back in the family ten minutes,

and you're already working against me."

"Calm down. I promise to have a word with my client. You'll either get the ring or the money."

"Take the thousand dollars," Maddy advised her husband.

"You might want to think twice about that," said Mark. "The ring appraised for twenty thousand dollars."

"It's historic significance?"

"It's ruby," said Mark, his arms around Tilly and Agnes.

≈ ≈ ≈

"We still haven't finished off the mystery," said Agnes as she licked on an ice cream cone. She and her grandmother were sitting at a picnic table at the DQ, a popular gathering place in Caruthers Corners. Lizzie and her husband Edgar were at the next table sharing a banana split. Cookie and Ben Bentley were two tables over, heads together, like that famous scene from *Lady and the Tramp*.

"Whatever do you mean, Aggie? We found the ruby ring."

"Yes, Grammy, but how did you know the mayor was behind all this?"

"Simple my dear," Maddy said, feeding her ice cream cone to Tige. The shaggy puppy was lying next to Agnes's feet, already devoted to his new pal. "Mayor Caruthers is left-handed."

"So what?"

"Well, the stitches in Martha Ray Johnson's handmade quilt were looped right to left. But the section of the appliquéd Town Hall where the fake ring had been inserted was sewn left to right, the way a left-handed person might have done."

"But when did you see the stitching. Lizzie's the one who took the ring from the quilt when she and Bootsie were pretending to be housecleaners."

"That day we first went to Tall Paul's house to ask him about his size fourteen shoes, I noticed a lump in the quilt. That's why I broke the latch on the screen door. I came back alone that same afternoon, when Paul was at the hardware store getting his replacement. Bertha was more than happy to let me look at the quilt. She doesn't get many visitors."

"You deliberately broke that latch?"

"Of course. I had to get him out of the house."

"So why didn't you look inside the quilt when you went back."

"Didn't have a chance. Bertha was hovering all over me, so happy to have a guest."

"That's why you refused to pose as one of the housecleaners. Bertha would have recognized you."

"I was the only one of us she'd seen."

Agnes giggled at her grandmother's duplicity. "So Lizzie was wrong when she said you were too good to get your hands dirty."

"As many a time as I've helped her plant flowers at the garden club, she should know better!"

"I like your friends. I like being a member of the Quilter's Club."

"You still have a quilt to finish, young lady. Watermelon Days is fast approaching. No slacking off allowed."

Agnes giggled. "I can't believe it, Grammy. You solved the mystery because of a stitch. The things you learn when sewing a quilt."

"Yes, dear, the mayor's stitching was quite amateurish, him doing it backward because he was left-handed."

Agnes smiled at the thought. "We could call it an underhanded stitch," she said, her laugher drifting across the town square of Caruthers Corners, her new home.

The
Patchwork
Puzzler

A Quilter's Club Mystery

2

Marjory Sorrell Rockwell

Quilting with a friend will keep you in stitches.
- Anonymous
-

CHAPTER ONE

Quilts On Display

Maddy Madison was jubilant that her husband Beau had been elected mayor of Caruthers Corners. It was a landslide victory, with him running unopposed after the former mayor resigned in disgrace – a little matter of stealing a historic ruby ring. Retrieved, the ring was now on display at the local Historical Society.

"Good thing Beau got the mayor's job," Maddy admitted to her friends at the Quilter's Club. They met every Tuesday at the Community Center. "He would've had to close down the hardware store anyway, what with that big Home Depot opening up on the far side of town."

"The point is, he'll make a good mayor," her friend Lizzie Ridenour said. Lizzie's husband was a retired bank president and wielded a lot of political clout hereabouts.

"I think it was smart of him to run on an 'honesty' campaign," commented Bootsie Purdue, whose hubby was the police chief. The former mayor had left a taint on the office. "Honesty's a good theme, considering the last mayor had to resign due to financial shenanigans."

"Beau could've run on any ol' campaign promise, don't matter what," asserted Cookie Bentley (now having a new last name due to her recent marriage). "His great-great grandpa being a town founder is pedigree enough for local voters."

As testament, a marble statue of Colonel Beauregard Hollingsworth Madison – one of the original patriarchs of the tiny town – stood proudly in the center of the grassy town square. Maddy's husband of nearly forty years was the Colonel's direct descendent. Beau Madison IV was proud of his distinguished family tree.

Caruthers Corners (population 2,577) was indeed a community that placed great value on its heritage. The town's early days as an Indian territory was acted out in a pageant every year during Watermelon Days. A popular festival hereabouts, you could always count on having a traveling carnival with a Ferris wheel, a watermelon-eating contest in front of the courthouse, and a big patchwork quilt display. People dressed in old-timey costumes ranging from coonskin caps and fringed leather shirts to bonnets and hoop skirts.

The Quilter's Club – these days consisting of Maddy, her friends Lizzie, Bootsie, and Cookie, as well as Maddy's granddaughter Agnes – was in charge of the quilt display each year. Made up of local entries, a premium was placed on the relevance of each design to some facet of Caruthers Corners history. However, this year there was a twist: they had arranged for a special showing of works by a legendary quilt-maker, Sarah Connors Pennington.

Sarah Pennington was a turn-of-the-century Amish woman whose handmade quilts were considered masterpieces of the needlecraft art. Thirty-seven were known to exist, discovered by her grandniece while cleaning out the attic of the Pennington homeplace in Pennsylvania.

She had donated them to the Smithsonian with the condition they be placed on a traveling exhibit. As secretary of the Caruthers Corners Historical Society, Cookie Bentley had made arrangements for the display. Surprisingly, given Indiana's large Amish population, the Pennington quilts had never before been shown in this part of the state.

Little did the Quilter's Club suspect that these famous needlework designs included a counterfeit that would threaten Beau's position as town mayor.

≈ ≈ ≈

The Madisons were all a-dither over the news that daughter Tillie was pregnant, a little sister for Agnes. After a troubled patch in their marriage, Tillie and her lawyer husband – "Mark the Shark," Maddy called him – had relocated back home to Caruthers Corners and set about adding to their family.

In addition to expecting a new baby (due any day now), they had adopted Tige, a dog of undetermined heritage. "Heinz 57," was the description applied by Mark Tidemore. He was pleased to see his daughter take responsibility for grooming and feeding the family pet. Tige rarely left his young mistress' side.

Aggie could be seen walking her shaggy little pooch in the town square across from the big Victorian house where she now lived. At 10, she was in Mrs. Shelton's fourth-grade class at Madison Elementary.

That week before the annual Watermelon Days festival Aggie helped the Quilter's Club unpack the Sarah Connors Pennington exhibit: 12 of the 37 known originals. The colors were dazzling, fire-engine reds and canary yellows and cobalt blues. The designs were abstract, yet reminiscent of log cabins and cornfields and sunflowers. "A genius of the needlecraft art," *Quilter's Quarterly* had termed Sarah Pennington's unique motifs.

"Oh my," said Maddy as she unfurled a quilt that practically vibrated with yellow-and-brown dome shapes. "Isn't this truly magnificent!"

"Is that supposed to be a beehive?" asked Aggie, face squinched as she studied the colorful design.

"Here's a clue," teased Lizzie, pointing to a tiny image sewed into the upper left-hand corner: a honeybee in flight.

Aggie squealed with delight, her enthusiasm setting Tige to barking like a fur-covered maniac. *Yip! Yip! Yip!*

"Shush," said Maddy, but it took a word from her granddaughter to actually calm the dog down.

Following instructions from the Smithsonian, the members of the Quilter's Club were wearing white latex gloves like a surgeon might don. A precaution against oily skin and dirty hands damaging the fabrics. Sarah Pennington's quilts had been appraised at $40,000 each.

Any one of these quilts exceeded Beau Madison's annual salary as mayor.

≈≈≈

Maddy was a pleasant-looking woman who at first glance might remind you of that actress Ellen Burstyn, her light brown hair furled around her face in a short efficient bouffant. Maybe she could have done without a pound or two, but no one would dare call her overweight. She maintained a steady-as-you-go 140 pounds – this, despite her habit of cooking three square meals a day for her family.

No matter how much he ate, her husband Beau remained thin as a rail, a tallish man who looked like James Cromwell, the actor who starred in that pig movie called *Babe*.

If you continued to cast the Madison family as movie stars, daughter Tillie could have been played by pretty Diane Lane, and her hubby Mark was a Dylan McDermott type. And Agnes might have been accurately portrayed by Dakota Fanning's younger sister.

As for members of the Quilter's Club, this movie-star game got a bit more difficult. Bootsie would've been a great role for, say, Tyne Daly. Cookie was a Patricia Clarkson wannabe. And Lizzie – well, Rita Moreno could have nailed the role in younger days.

You take it from there. Maddy thought this fantasy casting was a silly exercise, for she knew nobody was going to make a movie about four middle-aged women who solved crimes – the Quilter's Club at your service.

Still she couldn't help but play this game as she watched that new Jack Nicholson comedy at the Majestic in Burpyville.

An 80-mile roundtrip, the Majestic was the closest movie theater to Caruthers Corners, so a night at the cinema was a special treat for the Madisons.

This trip, it was just Beau, Maddy, and their granddaughter Aggie – providing Tillie and Mark a rare evening to themselves. Not that the couple would be out painting the town, what with Tillie pushing the last trimester of her pregnancy. This would likely be one of the last peaceful evenings at home they would enjoy for the next year or two, because Tillie Tidemore believed in hands-on mothering, something she had in common with her own mom.

"Popcorn?" Maddy whispered, offering the bag to her husband. But Beau was caught up in the comedy up there on the silver screen, ol' Jack at his driest wit, as a man unaware of his own shortcomings.

Her husband was a bit like that, thought Maddy with a certain fondness. Not that his faults were large. It's just that he bumbled through life, on a straight course, never glancing right or left, intent on reaching a destination that no one else could see.

He would make a good mayor, for he loved Caruthers Corners, its people, and its heritage. A do-gooder at heart, he was a perfect visage of Christmas Future for their son Bill, himself a man intent on saving the world. So much alike that they had always been slightly at odds.

Their other children – Tillie and Fred – were more like their mother. Clever, daring, imbued with an insatiable curiosity. But not Bill and his dad, two guys who knew all the answers, even if these answers were somewhat simple and moralistic.

Maddy had grown up reading Nancy Drew mysteries – perhaps that's where she got her penchant for crime-solving. A good talent to have, as she was about to find out in these hot summer days preceding the annual Watermelon festival.

CHAPTER TWO

An Antiques Dealer Speaks Up

Ben Bentley was as short and wide as a hay-bailing machine. Even in his late fifties, his physique was mindful of that high-school boy who had twice won the state wrestling championship. He was Cookie's second husband, her first having died in a bizarre tractor accident. With that in mind, Ben foreswore ever wearing a scarf while plowing his fields on chilly mornings. Wasn't this how that famous dancer Isadora Duncan met her fate? Well, not on a tractor, but the result was the same.

Ben's sister Becky had happily taken over Cookie's historic home in the heart of town, while Cookie moved into the Bentley farmhouse. Kind of like an exchange program, with both sides thinking themselves the winner.

To add her personal touch to the old farmhouse, Cookie had been busily shopping for antiques. Daniel Sokolowski – local proprietor of Dan's Den of Antiquity – was enjoying a windfall increase in business as a result.

It was Sokolowski who first raised the alarm about the authenticity of the treasured Pennington quilts.

≈≈≈

Dan's Den of Antiquities had been located on Main Street as long as anyone could remember. Dan, a wizen little man in his 80s, was said to be a Polish refugee who had come over from Europe with his parents just before World War II – one step ahead of those Storm Troopers who were rounding up Jews, Gypsies, the infirm, and anyone else they didn't particularly like. Dan never talked about his family's past.

The antique shop was a repository for both trash and treasures: Plain glass milk jugs sat next to rare carnival glass in pinks and greens. Lone Ranger silver bullet pencil sharpeners resided on shelves beside six-piece sterling silver tea services. Handmade Amish furniture sat next to genuine Chippendale chairs, Queen Anne imitations resided along side Louis XIV originals.

Pathways wandered throughout the tiny shop, 33 1/3 record albums stacked on one side, old *Life* magazines on the other. Oval mirrors with gilt frames stared back at you. Paintings of long-forgotten ancestors crowded the rose-colored walls.

Other than an outlet store at the chair factory, and these dusty items at Dan's Den of Antiquity, the closest furniture store was over in Burpyville.

Burpyville was a slightly larger town just down the Wabash River on the way to Indianapolis. Indy being the state capital, a city of some 800,000 residents – pretty big compared to Caruthers Corners' 2000-plus souls.

≈≈≈

Cookie Bentley had been boasting about the Quilter's Club snagging a big national exhibit like the Pennington quilts. It was the buzz of the town, anticipation building for the exhibit's opening during Watermelon Days. Caruthers Corners had always been a community that valued needlecrafts such as knitting, crocheting, embroidery, and quilt-making.

"How 'bout giving me a sneak peek?" Daniel suggested one day while Cookie browsed his shop for a Tiffany lamp.

They were in the process of dickering over the price of a cut-glass fixture that was perfect for her new kitchen, so she wasn't about to refuse. Yes, she knew the Quilter's Club had voted against any advance showings, but this *was* exactly the Tiffany she'd been looking for.

"About this price – ?" she hesitated.

"Give me that peek and I'll knock twenty percent off the tag price," he countered.

"It's a deal," she said, regretting her words.

≈ ≈ ≈

"Here you go, a dozen Sarah Connors Pennington quilts. Never before seen in this part of the country."

"Amazing," the antique dealer said, leaning close to inspect the fine stitching and interesting textures of the fabrics.

Cookie glanced over her shoulder, giving her fellow Quilter's Club members a weak smile. She knew they were irked with her for breaking the no-show rule. "Yes, like *Quilter's Quarterly* said, Sarah Pennington's a genius."

"Indeed."

Cookie added, "She's even better than Holly Eberhard." That being the state's Quilting Bee champion. Eberhard had won this year's contest with her ingenious Indiana state flag design.

"Holly's good," admitted Maddy, "but nowhere near the talent that's exhibited in the work of this long-dead Amish quilter."

"Sarah Pennington is nine on a scale of ten," agreed Lizzie. Quite an assertion, considering she was a huge Holly Eberhard fan.

Cookie pointed to a quilt on the wall. "This one is my favorite Penningtons, the famous beehive design."

"Yes, it is quite lovely," agreed Daniel Sokolowski. "Too bad they didn't allow you to display the originals."

That got everyone's attention. "What do you mean?" responded Maddy.

"Well, I assume you know this beehive quilt isn't an original Pennington?"

"Not an original?" exploded Lizzie, her face practically matching her flaming red hair.

"That can't be," shouted Bootsie. Looking like she was about to have a stroke.

"I'm sure there's some mistake here," gulped Cookie. "These are genuine Penningtons."

Ten-year-old Aggie was taking this all in with saucer-like eyes.

"My dear ladies, the thread used on this particular quilt is a synthetic blend. It hadn't been invented back in 1924 when Sarah Pennington made her patchwork quilts."

"Oh my," said Maddy. "What's going on here?"

≈≈≈

The Quilter's Club gathered in the mayor's office, a small suite in the Town Hall building, a brick edifice that dated back to the mid-1800s. It was the oldest standing public building in this part of the state.

"Calm down," said Beau Madison to his wife and her friends. "Don't all talk at once."

They were understandably excited. Had someone

duped the Smithsonian? Or had the prestigious institution misrepresented the quilting exhibit? Or – worse yet – had someone actually stolen the original beehive quilt from the Quilter's Club and left a counterfeit?

"This is a disaster!" moaned Bootsie. She'd already phoned her husband and he was on his way over from the police station.

"Our reputations will be ruined," blathered Cookie, convinced she'd have to resign her position with the Historical Society.

"How could something like this have happened?" griped Lizzie. She was known for her tempestuous nature.

"You're sure it's a fake?" asked Beau, confused by all this carrying-on.

"I trust Daniel Sokolowski's judgment," said Maddy. "He's been in the antiques business for more'n forty years. My mother used to take me to his shop when I was just a girl."

"Let's think this through," suggested little Aggie, proving she'd inherited her grandmother's sense of logic. "The Smithsonian's a smart museum. It wouldn't be that easily fooled. It has experts."

"True," Cookie allowed.

"And they wouldn't send us a fake without telling us," Aggie added.

"True," Cookie repeated.

"That means someone pulled a switcheroo," said Aggie. It was simple in her mind.

"But when, where?" responded Lizzie. The redhead was trying hard to hold her famous temper in check.

"Either on its way to us. Or after it got here," said

Maddy, matching her granddaughter's logic. "One or the other."

"Well, there's not much we can do about what might've happened during shipping," commented Beau Madison. "Best we make sure our house is in order, that it didn't get snatched from under our very noses."

"That's impossible," protested Cookie. "The Pennington quilts have been under lock and key in the conference room of the Town Hall. Just a few steps from here."

"Only Beau has the key," said Bootsie.

Perhaps it sounded too much like an accusation. His response was defensive. "Hey, that's not true. My assistant has a set of all the keys to this building. And so does your husband, Bootsie. Jim keeps a master set down at the police department in case of emergencies."

"Do you still have your key on you?" asked Maddy, eliminating suspects.

"Sure, right here." He dangled a key ring on his index finger, the metal clanging as he wiggled it for effect.

Just then Jim Purdue burst into the office. He was wearing his blue uniform and a badge with CHIEF engraved on it. At six-foot-two and 260 pounds, he took up much of the tiny office. "What's this about a major art theft?" he demanded, glancing from his wife to the other women and back again. "Do I need to call in the FBI?"

"Oh, I hope not," replied Bootsie to her husband. "That could be very embarrassing to the town."

"I'll say," groaned Beau. As new mayor, the responsibility for this disaster would fall squarely at his feet. He'd be impeached for sure. "You've got to recover the missing quilt, Jim."

"A quilt?"

"That's right, dear. One of the Pennington quilts has been replaced with a forgery."

"Didn't you tell me those patchwork quilts were worth forty grand each?"

"The Smithsonian had them appraised for that amount," said Cookie. "But in some ways they're priceless. After all, Sarah Connors Pennington is long dead and can't make any more. I looked her up on Wikipedia. It says she died during a diphtheria epidemic in 1926."

"Maybe I'd better call the FBI. My department's not up to this kind of crime-solving."

"Don't worry, Chief Purdue," said little Aggie. "The Quilter's Club will solve the crime for you."

CHAPTER THREE

An Unexpected Luncheon Date

Nancy Ann Beanie – "Nan" to her friends – had been administrative assistant to the Caruthers Corners mayor through three administrations, counting Beau Madison's. She was said to be more married to her job than to Jasper Beanie, caretaker of Pleasant Glade Cemetery and town ne'er-do-well. It was through the good graces of the mayor's office that her husband didn't spend every Saturday night in the hoosegow sleeping off a binge.

There were no bars in Caruthers Corners, but there were several in nearby Burpyville. The police in that larger burg were more unforgiving and Jasper didn't always make it home for Sunday morning church.

"Nan, do you have your set of keys handy?" asked Beau, leaning his head out of his door to make himself heard in her outer office. The mayor's office couldn't afford a fancy intercom system.

Nan Beanie was a slender woman of indeterminate age, her mousy-brown hair pulled back in an old-fashioned bun. Her hazel eyes were squinty, as if she needed to visit Lenscrafters. "Yes, Beauregard. Right here in my desk drawer," she replied, sliding open the upper right-hand drawer to prove her words.

"Where?" asked Beau, stepping closer to examine the

145

drawer. He saw nothing but pencils, paper clips, and rolls of Scotch tape. No key ring.

"Mercy me!" Mrs. Beanie exclaimed. "My keys are gone. I could've sworn they were here when I opened up the storeroom last Monday morning. I had to get you a new ream of typing paper, you'll remember."

Beau nodded, recalling running low on paper earlier in the week. "You haven't seen 'em since then?" he asked.

"No, mayor. You always open up the building in the morning. And you've been letting the ladies into the conference room each day since those scrap quilts arrived."

"Hm, who could have stolen your keys?" Chief Purdue put the question to Nan. "You rarely leave your desk."

"True enough," she said. "Other than to go to the restroom, but I have the keys with me when I do that. We keep them locked, y' know."

"Don't you go to lunch?" asked little Aggie. Ever the prescient one.

"I bring a brown bag."

"What about Monday?" said Beau. "Didn't you have lunch with Dizzy Duncan?"

"Why yes, I did," the woman recalled. "She wanted to talk about her son Denny. He's up for a basketball scholarship." Nancy Beanie was related to Dizzy by marriage. Arthur Duncan owned the Pic A Pair shoe store on Main Street.

"So somebody could've walked in here and snatched them out of your drawer while you were at lunch?" reasoned the police chief.

"Oh my," said Nan. "I suppose that's possible."

≈≈≈

Nobody would accuse Maddy of being nosey, but she was known to have a curious nature. Her husband wasn't surprised to learn that she'd called on Dizzy Duncan to verify his assistant's story.

"Well, hello there, Maddy Madison," said the shoemaker's wife. "What brings you over here to Jinks Lane?" The Duncans had lived here for years. Their modest cottage was set back from the street, the broad expanse of yard as neatly mown as a tee on a golf course.

"I heard your son Denny's up for a basketball scholarship."

"True. He's got their attention, him being so dang tall. Takes after my side of the family. My dad was even taller than Denny."

"Well, I wish him luck. It's a good thing to play your favorite sport and get a college education at the same time."

Dizzy Duncan smiled. "He'd be the first in our family to get a higher education."

"Is he getting a higher education because he's so tall?" Aggie spoke up. All this talk about college and scholarships was confusing to the youngster.

"This your granddaughter? I heard Tillie had come back home."

"Yes, her husband Mark has set up his law practice here."

"Do tell?"

"He took over Bartholomew Dingley's clients when the old man retired."

"'Bout time. Bart Dingley must be two hundred years

old by now."

"Just about," Maddy chuckled.

Dizzy Duncan focused her gaze on Aggie. "That your dog, young lady?" she nodded at Tige.

"Uh-huh. He's my best-est friend."

"Nice mutt."

"Thank you, Mrs. Duncan." She paused, then said, "Could I ask you a question?"

"Of course, my dear."

"Why do they call you Dizzy?"

"Aggie!" chided her grandmother.

"Oh, that's alright, Maddy. I don't mind saying. It's 'cause my real name is Desiree. Some folks shortened it, maybe because they think I'm a little foolish at times. You know, dizzy."

"Oh."

"You can call me Dizzy, if you like. Everybody does."

"Dizzy, why did you ask Mrs. Beanie to lunch on Monday?" the girl got right to the point.

"That's right, we met for toasted cheese sandwiches down at the DQ. I enjoy getting together with Nan. She's my husband's first cousin. She called, wanting me to tell her about my son's basketball scholarship. Guess she was interested in how the recruitment's going."

"Wait," said Maddy. "She asked *you* to lunch? Not the other way round?"

"Phoned me out of the blue, invited me to the DQ. I truly do love toasted cheese sandwiches with a slice of tomato on them."

CHAPTER FOUR

The World She Knew Has Changed

Founded in 1829 by three fur trappers on their way West, Caruthers Corners is a small town on the Wabash River, tucked away in the northeastern part of the state. In fact, Indiana's state song is "On the Banks of the Wabash, Far Away."

The town's Main Street is as picturesque as a 25¢ scenic postcard, a mile of tree-shaded yards and two-story brick mansions occupied by prominent families. In the exact center you'll see the historic Town Hall, facing a grassy public square complete with a bandstand for warm summer nights and skating pond for cold winter days.

The business district covers only two short blocks of Main Street, not exactly a triumph of commerce – brick-faced storefronts that include a shoe store, the antique shop, two clothing boutiques, and an empty space that used to house a travel agency. Beau's hardware store already had been replaced by a Dollar General franchise.

Just beyond Main you'll find the boxy homes of chair factory workers and other citizenry, cozy but not impressive edifices like those surrounding the town square.

Maddy had grown up in that big Victorian on the square, a house that had been built in 1888 by the founder of the EZ Seat chair factory. Now Tillie and Mark lived there, a proper abode for a successful attorney. She was glad to see it back in the family again.

Maddy's father – Jonathan Bradfield Taylor – had not been of such prestigious lineage as the Caruthers or Madisons or Jinks, but he was accepted among the town's elite. If there had been any question about the Taylor family's social status, Maddy's marriage to Beauregard Hollingsworth Madison IV settled that. Not that the Madisons were highfaluting – they weren't. Back then, Beau was just getting started with his hardware store, a modest establishment catering to local handymen. His name brought him a degree of respect, but being descended from a founding father didn't guarantee wealth.

Money wasn't everything. They had eked along nicely, thank you. Beau had inherited the big house on Melon Pickers Row from his grandfather, a benefit of being last in the family line (until their three children had come along). Now granddaughter Agnes represented the sixth generation since the town was established.

Maddy was happy to have Tillie home again. Maybe she'd have a chance to get to know the little stranger that was her granddaughter. Too bad her sons Bill and Fred lived so far away.

When she was a girl, no one ever considered leaving the hometown. These days, no young people considered staying, often going off to college never to return.

Alas, how things had changed.

Used to be, no one locked their doors in Caruthers Corners. Now a rare Sarah Connors Pennington quilt had been stolen from behind locked doors.

The world was so very different these days.

≈≈≈

Maddy met her daughter Tillie for lunch at the Cozy Café on South Main Street. Aside from the Dairy Queen and a Pizza Hut, this was the only eatery in town. It was one of those silvery cafés constructed from an old school bus. The booths were crowded, but the coffee was good.

"Hi mom. Is it true that one of the Pennington quilts has been stolen?"

"Aggie's been talking. It's supposed to be a secret."

"She's my snuggle-ums. Of course she's going to tell me."

"Well, don't spread it around. We're hoping Chief Purdue can recover the missing quilt before the Smithsonian gets word of this."

"Oh my."

"Your father's afraid he might be impeached before he completes his first term as mayor. The quilts were locked away in the Town Hall's conference room."

When the waitress came over – a girl named Francis that Tillie had gone to high school with – they changed the subject, glanced at their menus, and ordered the soup-and-sandwich special. Today was cucumber bisque and a roast beef with lettuce and tomato.

Waiting until Francis was at the far end of the counter taking another order, Tillie whispered, "Did somebody break into the Town Hall?" Nearly nine months pregnant, she could barely fit in the diner's narrow booth.

"Not exactly. Looks like someone stole Nan Beanie's keys. Your dad has a locksmith over there right now, changing all the locks. Had to pay extra to get him to come

151

out from Burpyville on short notice, but we can't take a chance on more quilts going missing."

"Aggie said the thief left a fake Pennington in place of the original. Pretty clever. It could've been weeks before anyone discovered the switch."

"It was a very good copy," Maddy pointed out between sips of the cucumber bisque. "We'd never have spotted it, except for Dan Sokolowski's eagle eye."

"But who's good enough at quilting to make a near-perfect copy of a Pennington?"

Maddy put down her soupspoon. "That's an excellent question, dear. Answer that, and we might be able to identify the thief."

≈ ≈ ≈

After lunch Maddy stopped by the Historical Society to see Cookie. As usual on Tuesdays, she found her pal in the tiny office, surrounded by a stack of papers, old documents, and faded photographs. Maddy didn't know much about antique photos, but Cookie could tell a tintype from an albumin print at forty paces, so used to researching the history of Caruthers Corners as she was.

"Hi Cookie." The slender woman's real name was Catherine, but nobody called her that.

"Hello, Maddy," she greeted her friend rather despondently. The missing Pennington quilt had put her into a deep funk. The Smithsonian would hold her personally responsible for its disappearance. After all, she'd made the arrangements for the Watermelon Days exhibition.

"Tillie just raised a key question. The answer might help us solve this puzzler."

"That's all this is to you, a puzzle to solve? It might mean my job!"

Maddy waved a hand, dismissing her words. "The only way we're going to save your job – and Beau's – is to find out who stole the quilt."

"Okay, okay. So what's the big question?" Cookie brushed her blonde hair back in a gesture of resolution. The gray mop she'd sported before her recent marriage to Ben Bentley had given way to golden highlights, thanks to Lady Clairol.

"Tillie pointed out that not just anybody could have created such a perfect copy of the Pennington quilt. So the question is, who could've?"

"That's easy. Holly Eberhard. She's the state quilting champion."

"No seriously. Someone with a questionable reputation."

"Hm, that's harder. Maybe one of the runners-up in the state Quilting Bee?"

Maddy frowned. "That's a good suggestion. An also-ran might bear a grudge over losing."

"That's the idea. Someone soured by losing decides to pull off a crime to show how good her quilting skills really are."

"Where can we get a list of the past few year's entrants?"

Cookie swung around to face her computer keyboard, nearly hidden under the scattering of papers. "Simple enough." *Clik! Clik! Clik!* "Here we go, I Googled it."

A nearby printer *whirred* as it spewed out the list. It was short, maybe a dozen names. Many of them duplicates, showing that the same quilters entered the contest year after year. Only the best of the best made it to the finals – so it was a very elite club.

Maddy studied the names. "Holly Eberhard was first runner-up three years ago, but took the top spot this year and last. Sue Ann Morgan is a senator's daughter so it's not likely she would be involved in a crime like this. Christie Thurman died this past winter in a skiing accident. Thelma Wolpner retired due to arthritis. Beatrice Hackleberry married a famous television minister, the one who comes on at nine o'clock Sunday mornings. Hm, I don't recognize this last one, Doris Thornton."

"No, it couldn't be her. I know that name – she signed a big contract with Tiger Brand Yarns. Their spokeswoman. I doubt she'd but that six-figure contract in jeopardy for a forty thousand dollar quilt."

"Drat! A dead end."

"See. I am going to lose my job with the Historical Society. This is a terrible state of affairs."

CHAPTER FIVE

New Member of the Family

That afternoon, Maddy got a phone call from her son Bill. He and his wife ran a Youth Center in Chicago. They loved kids, but Kathy was barren. That's why they had founded Kids 4 U, a nonprofit organization that rescued abandoned children and placed them in good homes.

"Hi, honey," she greeted him. Bill was the eldest son, an idealist through and through. He'd dropped out of college to join the Peace Corps, serving in a small African country called Chad. He'd met Kathy there, another Peace Corps volunteer.

"Hello, mom. How are you and the new mayor doing?"

"Just fine. Your dad loves public service. Y'know, helping people."

"See, I really am a chip off the old block," laughed the voice on the telephone.

"I never doubted it."

"Mom, I'm calling to give you a heads-up. Kathy and I are on our way to Caruthers Corners. Be there tomorrow. Hope you've got a spare bedroom."

"Your old room is waiting for you."

"You haven't turned it into a den or rec room?"

"It's a big old house. We already have a den and rec

room as you well remember."

"Just kidding."

"We've got plenty of room, now that your sister and Mark the Shark have bought a house of their own."

"Good. We'll need an extra bedroom."

"Oh my, you and Kathy aren't sleeping in separate bedrooms, are you?"

The voice chuckled. "No, nothing like that. It's just that we'll need a room for our new son."

"New son?"

"Kathy and I have adopted an eight-year-old Vietnamese boy."

"You mean a kid from the Far East?"

"Not exactly. N'yen's an American, born in Chicago. But he lost his parents."

"And you've adopted him?"

"Yep, figured we oughta practice what we preach. We've been placing needy kids in good homes for more than ten years now. So why not place one in ours. We can provide a good home."

"Bill, that's wonderful. Who in the family knows?"

"You're the first. But maybe you can prepare dad and Tillie."

"Hm, I think I'd better prepare Aggie."

"Agnes?"

"Yes, she's used to being an only grandchild. I hope she'll be willing to share the glory."

≈≈≈

"Adopted a Vietnamese boy!" said Beau, almost at a lost for words.

"That's what he said. And he and Kathy will be here

tomorrow with little N'yen."

"N'yen? That's a strange name?"

"Apparently not in Vietnam."

"Why couldn't they adopt an American child?"

"Beauregard Hollingsworth Madison the Fourth, don't let me hear you talk that way. You sound prejudiced."

"No, just a 'Buy American' kind of guy."

"Well, for your information, N'yen was born in Chicago, which makes him just as American as you and me." She checked the roast into the oven. They were expecting Tillie's crowd for dinner.

Beau shook his head, trying to wrap his mind around this new information. "But the boy's Asian," he said, almost to himself.

"And you're a mixture of English and Irish."

"Don't forget the touch of Czech on my mother's side."

"See, you're a mongrel. More of a mixture than Aggie's Heinz 57 mutt."

"Well – "

"Not another word. Bill and Kathy will be here tomorrow with N'yen. And you're going to be his grandpa."

"Have you told Aggie she's going to have to share us?"

"We'll cross that bridge when we come to it."

"Looks like you're about to cross that bridge sooner than you think. Tillie and Mark just pulled up in the driveway. I can see Aggie and Tige bouncing in the backseat."

Maddy glanced out the window. "Oh my, I still have to bake the biscuits."

"Settle for rolls. You'd better save your energy for telling Aggie she's going to have an Asian cousin."

≈ ≈ ≈

"Pass the potatoes, please," said Aggie. Her manners had improved considerable since coming to live in Caruthers Corners.

"Here you go, dear," said Maddy, handing the bowl across the table. "Help yourself to all you want."

"Thank you."

"I have some news for you. We're getting a little boy in the family."

"No, Grammy. Mommy's expecting a girl."

Maddy glanced at her daughter for help. Tillie's stomach was the size of a watermelon, her delivery date almost here.

"Aggie, I think your grandmother is talking about your Aunt Kathy, not me."

The girl looked up from her helping of potatoes. "Aunt Kathy's expecting a baby too."

"Not exactly. She and Uncle Bill have adopted a little boy. I understand he's eight years old."

"Okay."

Okay? It was that simple?

"He will be your cousin," Tillie continued, making sure her daughter understood.

"Cool."

≈ ≈ ≈

"That went well," said Beau as he prepared for bed.

"Aggie, you mean?"

He nodded. "She took the news without blinking an eye."

"We'll see how it goes when Bill and Kathy get here with little N'yen in tow."

158

"You worry too much."

"I'm more worried about you than Aggie."

"Over N'yen?"

"Well, you did serve in the Vietnam War. Could it be that you have some animosity against Vietnamese as a result?"

Beau climbed under the covers, waited for his wife to turn out the light. "I've got nothing against Vietnamese as long as they're not pointing Kalashnikov AK-47 rifles at me."

"Hush now. N'yen's only eight. It's more likely he'll be pointing a water pistol at you."

"You're right, as always."

Maddy snuggled closer. "Truth told, I'm more worried about that darned Sarah Pennington quilt. That theft took some doing. Somebody had to make an exact copy of that quilt, one that would fool experienced quilters."

"I've been thinking about that. One doesn't stitch up a quilt like that beehive design overnight. This crime took some planning."

"But the exhibit came about rather quickly. Cookie said we got it because another booking fell through."

"That means the crook's nobody local. It has to be someone who was already planning the heist before Caruthers Corners scheduled it for our Watermelon Days festivities."

"Exactly. But the puzzling thing, not just any thief off the street could walk into the Town Hall and snatch Nan's keys."

"Yes, Nan – "

"Go to sleep, dear. We'll talk about her tomorrow."

CHAPTER SIX

Confronting a Culprit

The Quilter's Club met for breakfast at the Cozy Café. Known for its cherry pie, the diner was quite popular. What's more, coffee was only 50¢ a cup and refills were free.

Maddy waited until everyone had placed their orders – an English muffin for Lizzie, poached egg for Cookie, oatmeal for Bootsie, and a bacon-and-tomato omelet for herself – before sharing her suspicions about Nan Beanie.

"I spoke with Dizzy Duncan yesterday about Nan's alibi."

"You didn't mention that," accused Cookie. She didn't like being left out of the loop.

"Sorry," Maddy apologized. "But I had to give what she said a little thought."

"What *did* she say?" Bootsie wanted to know. She loved gossip.

"Remember, Nan said that Dizzy Duncan invited her to lunch last Monday."

"So?" Lizzie was eager to get to the punch line.

"Turns out, it was Nan who invited Dizzy," Maddy informed her friends between nibbles.

"You mean she lied to us?" Bootsie sounded miffed.

"Nan wouldn't do that," argued Cookie. The woman

was a distant cousin.

"Are you saying she stole the Pennington quilt?" asked Lizzie. Blunt as usual.

"Not all by herself. But she apparently helped someone steal it."

"How do you know someone else was involved?" asked Bootsie with the suspicion of a policeman's wife.

Maddy finished off her omelet and patted her mouth with a paper napkin. "Simple. Someone made that counterfeit quilt – and Nan Beanie can't sew. Arthritis. She can't hold a needle."

≈ ≈ ≈

Aggie dropped by later that morning. It was only a few blocks from her home on the square to Melon Pickers Row – a short two-block stroll. Aggie said she had to be home by 2 p.m. to dress up for her Uncle Bill and Aunt Kathy's visit. Oh yes, and to impress her new cousin N'yen.

"C'mon along, we have time to run a few errands," announced her grandmother. "Your mom said you could go with me for the ride."

"Okey-dokey."

Maddy parked in front of the Town Hall in a space marked FOR OFFICIAL USE ONLY. Being the mayor's wife had certain privileges.

"Why are we here?" asked Aggie. "To see Grampy?"

"No, dear. I want to talk with your grandfather's assistant again," Maddy explained as they walked into the redbrick building. "I want to clear up the difference between her story and Dizzy Duncan's."

"One of them is fibbing," Aggie declared, that clear even to a ten-year-old.

"Yes, but which one?" Maddy was trying to keep an open mind, even though her bet was on Nan as the liar. She'd never had a warm feeling about the woman, but had always attributed it to Nan's affiliation with the former mayor, a proven scoundrel.

"I think Dizzy's telling the truth," replied the girl. "She's too, uh, dizzy to be part of a big conspiracy."

"Oh?"

"C'mon, Grammy. Would you trust Dizzy with a secret? She'd spill the beans without even knowing it."

"And so you think your grandfather's assistant is part of the plot to steal the quilts?"

"She seems sneaky to me. Didn't you see that address book on her desk?"

"What of it? Everybody has an address book."

"But hers was open to the phone number of Henry Caruthers, the old mayor. I'll bet she's his spy, telling him everything going on in the mayor's office."

"My, you are a clever girl."

"Thank you, Grammy. I'm going to make a great member of the Quilter's Club."

To Maddy's surprise, Nan Beanie wasn't at her desk. Odd, since it was only quarter to twelve, too early for lunch. Her husband's assistant was a punctual woman, some might say a clock-watcher.

Aggie sat in Mrs. Beanie's empty chair and surveyed her desk, eyes settling on an address book. "Dear, it's not polite to snoop," Maddy chided her granddaughter, something of a don't-do-as-I-do-do-as-I-tell-you statement.

"Yes, Grammy."

Maddy stuck her head in the door to the mayor's inner sanctum. "Hi, dear," she called to her husband who was plowing through a stack of papers on his big desk. "Where's Mrs. Beanie?"

"Called in sick. Claims to have a migraine."

"I didn't know she suffered from headaches."

"She's more like a pain in the – " He halted his words when he saw Aggie standing behind her grandmother. "Well, never mind."

"A pain in the butt?" said Aggie, a precocious child to say the least.

"Something like that," he mumbled, embarrassed at his candor.

"I'd like to talk with her," continued Maddy. "Perhaps I could drop by with some cookies."

"She might prefer brandy."

"Brandy? Does Nan have a drinking problem?"

Beau shrugged. "Dunno. I found a bottle in her bottom desk drawer. I was looking for the stapler, but found Johnny Walker instead."

"You know, I'm not sure where she lives."

"Here," he thumbed through his Rolodex. "She lives at 101 Pleasant Avenue."

"That can't be right," said Maddy. "That's the address of the cemetery."

"Remember, Jasper Beanie is the caretaker at Pleasant Glade. The town provides them a house on the grounds."

"That means they can't have a dog," said Aggie. "The sign on the cemetery gate says NO DOGS ALLOWED."

"Have you been walking Tige in the cemetery again?" inquired Aggie's grandfather, giving her the ol' Eagle Eye.

"No, Grampy. He might dig up a bone."

≈≈≈

"This place looks spooky," said young Agnes Millicent Tidemore as she stared up at the tumbledown two-story house at the edge of the cemetery. A porch fronted the house, held up by chipped round columns. The roof seemed to sag in the middle, as if gravity were winning an unseen battle. The windows were dirty and smudged, making it impossible to see inside.

"Don't be silly," replied Maddy. "Jasper and Nan Beanie live here, not the Addams Family."

"Does Tige have to stay in the car?"

"Yes, dear. Those are the cemetery rules."

"But before – "

"The rules," her grandmother repeated.

"Oh, okay. Tige, you wait right here. I'll leave the window down so you don't get hot."

"Come along before I decide to leave *you* in the car."

"You're just teasing me, Grammy. I have to help you interrogate Mrs. Beanie, because I'm a member of the Quilter's Club."

"Dear, I keep telling you, the Quilter's Club makes patchwork quilts – not solve crimes."

"Have it your way," said Aggie, giving her grandmother a little we-both-know-the-truth wink.

"Let's deliver these cookies," sighed Maddy as she knocked on the big front door. "Remember to stand up straight and mind your manners."

"Yes, Grammy." She curtsied, but that was simply being a smart aleck.

Thump, thump!

"Just a minute," came a voice from inside. A few seconds later, the double wooden doors swung open to reveal a short man with a large wart spotting his chin. "Yeah, whattaya want?"

"Jasper Beanie? I'm Maddy Madison. Your wife works with my husband in the mayor's office."

"So?" Not a very polite individual.

"I understand she has a migraine, so I stopped by with these cookies for her." She held out the box of chocolate chip cookies, left over from yesterday's baking.

"She has a what – ?"

"A bad headache."

"Hmph, she seems fine to me."

"May we come in?" said Aggie.

"If you insist," the man with the wart grumbled. He stepped aside to allow the visitors to pass.

"Nice place you have," said Maddy, ignoring the depressing atmosphere of the dark curtain-shrouded rooms. The furniture was worn and shabby. The pictures on the wall depicted Biblical scenes – the Last Supper, Sermon on the Mount, and Garden of Gethsemane.

"House comes with the job. Pay's lousy, but things are gonna be looking up soon."

"Looking up?"

"Nan's coming into some money. An inheritance, she says."

"You don't say?"

"I do. As a matter of fact – "

"Jasper!" Nan Beanie's shrill voice cut him off. "Don't bore our guests with family business."

Maddy smiled at her husband's administrative

assistant. "That's all right, I'm interested in your good fortune. An inheritance, you say?"

The woman frowned. "Never mind. I try to keep my business life and personal life separate."

Maddy offered a disarming smile. "That's probably more difficult, now that there's been a change of administration."

"What's that s'posed to mean?"

"Simply that it's harder to keep in touch with Mayor Caruthers now that he's out of office."

"It's no problem," she replied. "He calls me all the time." Realizing what she'd just said, her mouth snapped shut, like the closing of a steel trap.

"Too bad you missed him when he dropped by to see you on Monday," Maddy said casually.

Jasper was taking this in. "Nan, you didn't mention getting together with Henry Caruthers." Was that a touch of jealousy in his voice? His wife had worked closely with the old mayor for more than twenty years.

"I wasn't there when Henry came by," she responded defensively. "I was having lunch with Dizzy Duncan. I got me an alibi."

"An alibi?" Her husband was confused.

"Dizzy can confirm it. I wasn't even there when Henry took the keys," blurted Nan Beanie.

"Aha," shouted Aggie. She knew a confession when she heard one.

"Nan, I told you to stay away from Henry Caruthers," growled the woman's husband. Big hands balled into gnarly fists, you could tell he was a man whose temper simmered close to the surface.

"Henry Caruthers is a very fine man. And this woman's husband stole his job as mayor!"

"That's not true," said Maddy.

Nan Beanie raised her chin defiantly. "Well, I won't have to work for him no more when I get that money from Henry."

Maddy said, "Aggie dear, why don't you go wait in the car with your dog. I have to call Chief Purdue."

"Oh no, you're not gonna put me in jail," screeched the pinch-faced woman. Shoving Maddy aside, she dashed out of the room like The Flash. Everyone stood there in a state of shock, only snapping out of it when they heard the back door slam.

"Y-you mean there's no inheritance," Jasper Beanie stammered. "The money was coming from Henry Caruthers?"

"Looks like it," said Maddy. However, she was still trying to put the pieces together.

"Grammy, she's getting away," shouted Aggie, tugging at her grandmother's arm. "Hurry up – or we'll lose her."

The trio raced to the back door, just off the kitchen, and burst out into the backyard. Well, it was actually a long expanse of greenery punctuated by marble headstones – the Pleasant Glades cemetery.

Nan Beanie was nowhere to be seen.

"We lost her," muttered Maddy.

"Tige! Here, boy," called Aggie. The dog hopped out of the open car window and came tearing around the corner of the ramshackle house, yapping like a hound after a hare. "Go get her, boy! Go sic!"

The brownish mutt didn't slow down, cutting across

the cemetery with the speed of a greyhound. *Yip! Yip! Yip!*

"C'mon, Grammy. Tige will catch her. He's a hunting dog."

The cute little mutt looked more like Benjy than a beagle. But he was fast, that much was obvious as he weaved among the tombstones like a show dog running an obstacle course. Maddy and her granddaughter gave chase too, but Tige was over the ridge of the hill before they had covered half the distance.

"Wait, wait!" shouted Jasper Beanie as he brought up the rear. "That's my wife you're after."

They could hear the dog barking, the sound coming from down the hill near the older section of Pleasant Glades. "This way," waved Aggie, leading the charge.

Maddy was huffing and puffing, having trouble keeping up with her ten-year-old granddaughter. Jasper was faring even worse, about to blow a blood vessel with his unaccustomed exertion. "Slow down, slow down," he wheezed. "I'm gonna have a coronary if I keep this up."

Aggie found herself in front of a large mausoleum with impressive Doric columns and marble steps leading up to a padlocked door. She could hear Tige barking inside. But how could that be? The padlock was in place, as thick and foreboding as an iron fist.

"Tige?"

Yip! Yip!

She pushed on the door and to her surprise it swung open with the ease of a revolving door. The phony padlock was merely a prop, designed to act as a deterrent to nosey intruders.

"Tige!" shouted Aggie. And then, like Alice, tumbled down the rabbit hole into Wonderland.

CHAPTER SEVEN

A Railroad Station?

Agnes Tidemore rolled head-over-heels down a steep incline, much like a slide in a playground. She landed with an *oomph!* that would leave a purple bruise on her left buttock. Everybody would be all a-tizzy because the school nurse would report it as potential abuse. Good thing Police Chief Jim Purdue was her grampy's best friend.

"Tige?" she called to the shadows.

Yip! Yip!

She inched forward, engulfed in total darkness, as sightless as a bat in a cave. "Tige?" she called again.

The *Yip!* was closer this time. Then she felt a rough tongue licking her hand. At least she'd recovered her dog. That mean ol' Mrs. Beanie could make her getaway for all she cared. Chief Purdue would catch her and lock her away behind bars. That'd teach her to help some crook steal that valuable Pennington quilt.

Now how to get out? The incline she'd tumbled down was too steep and slick to climb. She clutched her dog's leather collar and whispered, "Lead me outta here, boy."

The dog surged forward, practically dragging her along. She had to shuffle along at double-time to keep up. The smooth marble flooring made it difficult to maintain her footing.

After a few minutes she could make out a faint glow in the distance, a fluorescent light as it turned out. She found herself in a large chamber, like a medieval dungeon with a domed ceiling. Only the artificiality of the fluorescent lighting reminded her that this was the Twenty-First Century. And that she and her dog had been chasing a dastardly art thief, one Mrs. Nancy Ann Beanie.

There had to be some way out of this underground hideaway. She looked around for an exit. In the far corner of the chamber she could see stone steps leading upward, a likely egress. "C'mon, Tige," she said. "Let's go find Grammy."

"Not so fast!" came a voice.

Aggie stopped in her tracks. Even her dog hesitated. She looked around for a source of the male voice. It obviously wasn't Mrs. Beanie speaking, but rather a hoarse baritone belonging to an unseen man.

A spook?

After all, she was wandering about in a hidden recess under a cemetery. She halfway expected to see a bony skeleton come clattering from a side tunnel, a hatchet in hand, just like in that movie *Horrifying Creature from the Haunted House* her babysitter had let her watch that time her mom and dad attended a dance at the VFW Hall.

But no skeletons or ghouls made their appearance. Not even any deranged mole men. She and Tige were all alone in this underground chamber.

"Stay where you are!" ordered the disembodied voice.

"Where are you?"

"Never you mind, young lady. The important thing is, I

know where *you* are. And you're trespassing!"

"Trespassing? I'm inside a grave."

"Not exactly. This chamber was built in the mid-eighteen hundreds as a way station of the Underground Railroad. Escaping slaves were hidden away here as they traveled to freedom in Canada."

"This doesn't look like a railroad station," said Aggie.

"Not the kind with trains," the voice corrected.

"What other kinds of railroads are there?"

"Look, this is a historic monument. Listed with the National Registry."

"And who are you? A ghost?"

"Of course not."

"Then why can't I see you?"

"Look up over the stairway. You'll see the speaker box. I'm with an alarm company in Indianapolis. We have the contract to monitor this facility."

"Oh. So can I get out of this hole? It's cold and damp down here."

"You have to wait for the police. They've been notified of a forcible entry."

"I didn't force anything. I just fell down a hole."

"Tell it to the cops."

≈≈≈

She did.

Chief Purdue bought her an ice cream cone at DQ on the way back to headquarters. "So you and Maddy were chasing Nan Beanie?" he said in a bemused manner. The image of Beauregard Madison's wife and granddaughter galloping through the cemetery in hot pursuit of a suspected quilt-napper would have been quite a sight to see!

"I almost caught her, but she ducked into that railroad station. Maybe she escaped on a train."

"No, I don't think so," he chuckled. "More likely she'll try to catch this afternoon's bus out of town. I'll send my deputy down to pick her up."

"Am I going to jail for trespassing?"

"Don't worry about that. I'm releasing you into your mother's custody. She's on her way down to pick you up."

"What about Grammy?"

"Maddy's in the next room swearing out a warrant for Nan Beanie's arrest. Mrs. Beanie's husband backs up what you and Maddy have told me about her admission she let Henry Caruthers take her keys. We'll be picking up Caruthers for questioning. It's time he gets nailed for his criminal behavior."

"But what about the missing quilt?"

"Still missing."

"Don't worry, Chief Purdue. The Quilter's Club is still on the case."

CHAPTER EIGHT

Arrival of a New Cousin

That afternoon an ancient green Subaru lumbered up Melon Pickers Row and eased into the driveway fronting the Madison household. Before it stopped working, the car's odometer had registered 167,412 miles on it. Bill and Kathy bought the car used ten years ago in Chicago and it was still running fine. Today, the vehicle was piled full of suitcases and backpacks, not to mention three occupants. The kid in the backseat had to be N'yen, the newest member of the Madison clan. As if his eyes with epicanthic folds and yellow skin pigmentation weren't evidence enough, the way his adoptive parents fussed over him was the clincher.

"Bill, Kathy!" came the greeting from the assemblage on the front porch. Beauregard and Maddy looked like the subjects of a Grant Wood painting, while rotund Tillie and Mark the Shark could have passed as a couple on the cover of *Pregnancy Today*. Aggie was wearing a dress for a change, a pretty little pinafore that made her look like an American Girl doll.

"Hi all," called Bill as he ushered his family up the walkway, grinning ear-to-ear, like a guy who'd just won the Lottery.

Kathy presented the young boy in a striped T-shirt and

baggy blue jeans. "This is N'yen, our new son."

Everyone *ooo*'ed and *ahh*'ed, introducing themselves in a confusing Babel. No way N'yen would have caught all the names, but fortunately Bill and Kathy had rehearsed him in advance. "Happy to meet all of you," he said, trying to suppress a giggle.

"He speaks English," blurted Beau.

"Of course, he does, dad. N'yen was born in Chicago, not Hanoi."

"Oh right."

"Sorry, but I do not speak a single word of Vietnamese," said the small boy.

"Don't worry, I'll teach you the two words I know," offered Aggie. "*Bun cha* and *pho*."

"What's that mean?"

"*Bun cha* is grilled pork cop with noodles. And *pho* means a rice noodle soup. My mom and dad used to take me to a restaurant in Little Saigon when we lived in L.A."

"Cool," said N'yen. "But I prefer Big Macs."

≈≈≈

After a sumptuous dinner of baked ham and candied yams – no Big Macs – they were having watermelon pie for dessert. It was Tillie's favorite, Bill's too. But N'yen and Aggie were the ones begging for second helpings.

As Maddy was pulling a backup pie out of the fridge, the phone rang. It was Bootsie, calling to report that Nan Beanie had been sighted in Burpyville trying to rent a car at the Avis office in that big shopping center.

"Did Jim speak with Henry Caruthers?"

"Nope. The former mayor is out of town, according to his neighbors. But he has to come home sometime, right?"

"I suppose he can't afford to skip the country by selling a forty thousand dollar quilt."

"If he stole it."

"I think it's clear he was involved. Nan set up an alibi lunch with Dizzy Duncan so Henry could steal the keys out of her desk, the keys to the conference room where we've been storing the Pennington quilts."

"Why didn't she just hand the keys to Henry?"

"Plausible deniability."

"What's that?"

"A term I heard on a TV show. It means Nan set it up so she could claim she didn't know who took the keys."

"Didn't work very well."

"Aggie tripped her up with a question."

"That kid's going to grow up to be chief of police."

Maddy chuckled at the idea. "Tell Jim to move over."

≈ ≈ ≈

N'yen was outside playing with Aggie and Tige, chasing fireflies in the backyard. It was a beautiful summer evening, the silver-dollar moon combining with porch lights to transform the neighborhood into a magical fairyland. Fireflies twinkled in the night sky like the dancing embers from a campfire.

The grownups were ensconced inside the house, enjoying a family reunion – everybody here, other than middle-son Fred who's a fireman in Atlanta. Maddy had just served an after-dinner brandy and Beau was offering the men an imported Dominican cigar.

"No smoking around me," Tillie warned. A health nut when it came to her unborn child.

"When are you due?" Kathy asked her sister-in-law.

"Imminently," laughed Tillie, patting her oversized tummy. "A girl, they tell me."

"Goodness, I wish I could experience what you're going through. But no luck there."

"You've skipped the hard part. N'yen's going to be a great son."

"He's a wonderful kid," confirmed Bill.

Beau began awkwardly. "What made you decide to adopt a kid who isn't– "

" – white?" Bill finished his father's sentence.

"What I meant to say was – "

"Dad, you're so obvious. You live here in a little town that's ninety-nine percent Caucasian. Minorities scare you."

"Asians aren't a minority," mumbled Beau. "There are more of them in the world than anybody."

"Well, there's one in the family now. I hope you can accept that."

"Bill, don't be so hard on your father," interceded Maddy. "Give him a chance to get used to it. You caught us all by surprise, adopting a child. Nonetheless, we're very happy for you."

"Sorry, mom. Guess we're overly protective of N'yen."

"And well you should be. N'yen's a treasure."

"Thanks."

Kathy changed the subject, trying to avoid any further tension between her husband and his father. "Tillie says the Quilter's Club has lost a valuable quilt."

"True," admitted Maddy. So much for secrets. "Someone substituted a phony for a genuine Pennington."

"A Pennington? Isn't that the Amish woman whose

fantastic quilts were found hidden away in an attic?"

"Exactly. They are considered to be among the world's great quilt designs."

"And you lost one? What does the Smithsonian say about that?"

Maddy cleared her throat, a nervous habit. "They, uh, don't know yet. We're hoping to recover it."

"How, pray tell?" asked Bill. "You have to admit, Jim Purdue's no Hercule Poirot."

Maddy glanced at her husband for support. After all, it was his assistant who had let the thief have the keys. "Oh, we have a few clues."

"Mom, the Quilter's Club isn't trying to solve this on its own, is it?" exclaimed Tillie.

"Well, you might say we're looking into it. The quilt was stolen on our watch, so we have a certain responsibility."

"Maddy," interjected Mark, "we've already had to bail our daughter out of jail today for trespassing. This is not what we had in mind when we allowed her to join your silly quilting club."

"Mark the Shark, as a lawyer you know very well that there was no bail involved. And no charges of trespassing. Aggie simply wandered off the beaten path."

"Quilter's Club? Are you still involved in all that needlecraft stuff?" asked Bill. He remembered his mother's many knitting, crocheting, and quilt-making projects. He still had that turtleneck sweater she'd knitted for him as a Christmas present back when he was in the Peace Corps.

"Knitting and crocheting are relaxing pastimes. And

designing quilts can be very creative," argued Maddy.

"How does crime-solving fit in with that?" asked Tillie. Like a prosecuting attorney going for a confession on the witness stand.

"I think we're making too much of your mother's sleuthing," interjected Beau Madison. "She just dabbles."

"She – and all the members of the Quilter's Club," muttered Mark, not very happy at being called a shark.

"Bootsie, Lizzie, and Cookie are not exactly Charlie's Angels," remarked Beau, a lopsided grin on his face.

"Beauregard Madison the Fourth! Are you implying my friends are not as pretty and charming as those movie stars?"

"Now, Maddy, you know I think highly of all your girlfriends. But Bootsie Purdue is no Carmen Diaz." He wiggled his eyebrows to show that he thought the blonde actress was hot stuff.

"Oh you."

"Mom, dad – you have to take this seriously," insisted Tillie. "You're dealing with real crooks. My daughter could have been injured chasing after bad guys in a cemetery."

"Bad guys!" snorted Beau. "They were chasing Nan Beanie, my administrative assistant. She's about as dangerous as a parakeet."

"I got bit by a parakeet once," said Tillie.

"Okay, your point's well taken," said Maddy, holding up her hands to stave off further comments. "We won't include Aggie on any more of our sleuthing."

"Not include me?" came a wail from the back door. Aggie and N'yen had grown tired of chasing fireflies, returning to the house for another slice of watermelon pie.

"You mean I'm kicked out of the Quilter's Club?"

"Of course not, honey," soothed her grandmother. "You can still sew quilts with us. Just ixnay on the detective work."

"Grammy, that's not fair. I was the one – with the help of Tige – who tracked Mrs. Beanie to her lair!"

"Lair?" laughed Aggie's father. "That was just a historic structure left over from Civil War days."

"It was Mrs. Beanie's underground headquarters," insisted the girl. "I'll bet there are more clues down there. And I would have found them if it wasn't for that man in the box."

"Man in the box?" repeated her father.

"She means the alarm company monitor, a speaker over the stairwell," explained Maddy. She had gone down into the cavern with Chief Purdue to retrieve her granddaughter.

"So where's this woman you were chasing?" asked Bill's wife Kathy.

"Dunno. She escaped. I'll bet there's a secret tunnel."

"Enough of this fantasy stuff," said Aggie's father. "Time we took you home and put you to. bed. It's nearly ten o'clock."

"Good idea," said Tillie. "I tire so easily carrying this little bundle of joy." She patted her pregnant tummy.

"N'yen, I'll bet you're ready to hit the hay too," suggested the boy's new dad. "It's been a long day, driving from Chicago."

"Yes, we were up at dawn," added his also-new mom. "I think we're all tired."

"But I wanna help Aggie catch the crooks," said young

N'yen Madison.

"You mean help her catch more fireflies, don't you?" Bill offered a wide smile, amused by the boy's earnest enthusiasm.

"No, crooks. Aggie thinks she knows where they're hiding – in their underground headquarters!"

CHAPTER NINE

Gently Down the Stream

After retiring from the bank, Lizzie Ridenour's husband spent most of his time hunting and fishing. He held the record for the biggest catfish caught in this part of the state. Some days he would go down to a favorite spot on the banks of the Wabash and dip a hook, bringing with him a good book. Today he was reading *Death of an Expert Witness*, an English murder mystery by P. D. James.

Edgar Ridenour considered himself a bit of an Anglophile, always fascinated by British customs and manners of speech. Sure, they spoke the same language as folks hereabout, but they did it with such style!

Sometimes Edgar himself would say "lorry" instead or "truck." Or "flat" instead of "apartment." It sounded so ... sophisticated.

The Ridenour family came from Germany a couple of generations back. The original name was Reitenauer, but it was handily Anglicized to help his grandparents assimilate into this small town in Indiana. Truth was, Edgar would have preferred an English heritage, and so he downplayed his forbearers. Leave that to the founding families like the Madison, Caruthers, and Jinks.

Edgar was sitting on the riverbank, immersed in the

clever detective work of Adam Dalgliesh, one of P. D. James' favorite characters. He was willing to overlook the fact that the author was actually a woman – Phyllis Dorothy James, despite her non-descriptive initials. Didn't Harry Potter author T. K. Rowling take that same genderless approach, her publishers fearful that a woman wouldn't sell as well as a male storyteller?

Truth was, he actually liked P. D. James' female detective Cordelia Gray better than Dalgliesh. Women were naturally inquisitive, he felt, making them good at ferreting out facts.

His wife was like that, a nosy parker who liked to help her quilting group solve crimes. Maybe he should have put his foot down on these activities, but it occupied her enough that she didn't complain about his solitary fishing and hunting trips. Edgar was a natural loner, content to spend time with himself.

Since retiring from the bank, he'd swapped his clean-cut visage for a hoary beard, Chester A. Arthur muttonchops, and longish hair. Few banking customers would have recognized him at first glance, looking more like a rugged mountain man than a former bank executive.

As he read his mystery book, he became aware of a small aluminum boat floating down the river with the current. He noted a man hunched in the bow, unmoving, like a fisherman, but there was no rod in his hands. The boater looked familiar, yet it took him a few glances to recognize Henry Caruthers, the former mayor of Caruthers Corners. Henry had been a bank customer, but his fortunes had undergone a major reversal after being caught up in a scandal and forced from office. What was

Caruthers doing out here?

"Hello there!" he shouted to the ex-mayor. "That you, Henry?"

The man didn't respond, in fact hunching lower and turning his head away. Was he trying to ignore the greeting?

"Hello!" he called again. And again no response.

Edgar watched as the aluminum boat floated silently past. The man he'd placed as Henry Caruthers continued to ignore him. Perhaps he didn't respond because he failed to recognize this bearded fisherman as the former president of Caruthers Corners Savings and Loan.

Hm, where could Henry be going? There weren't any houses downriver for miles. He'd have to go almost all way to Burpyville before coming to a bridge or place to put ashore.

Strange, he thought.

≈≈≈

"You saw who?" said Lizzie.

"Henry Caruthers, I'm sure it was him."

"Fishing on the Wabash?"

Lizzie's husband shook his head. "No, not fishing. Just floating downstream in a boat."

"What do you make of this?" Lizzie turned to Cookie Bentley. The Bentleys and the Ridenours were having dinner at Bob's Best Bar-B-Q over on State Road 21, just outside Burpyville. Edgar was particularly fond of the ribs, always ordering a full rack. And oversized Ben Bentley could eat two of them at one sitting.

"Chief Purdue needs to hear about this. He's got an ABP out on Henry Caruthers."

"APB – All Points Bulletin," Ben politely corrected his wife. Working as a volunteer ambulance driver on weekends, he knew all the police scanner lingo.

"Whatever," Cookie waved his words away. They had that kind of relationship, where neither could do any wrong in the other's view. "Point is, Jim's looking for that old scalawag."

"Did Henry Caruthers really mastermind the quilt theft?" asked Ben. A trusting man, he found it difficult to believe the worst about people.

"Sure looks like it," said Lizzie.

"I'm not sure Henry's smart enough to be a criminal mastermind," opined Edgar, rubbing his beard thoughtfully. "Take a kickback or accept a bribe – yes. But mastermind the theft of a forty thousand dollar quilt, I dunno."

"Remind me to tell Maddy about the sighting," said Lizzie, knowing she would be hot on the telephone with her friend before the night was over. Liz loved juicy gossip.

"Yes," said Cookie. "Maddy's very clever about these things. Maybe she can figure out where Henry Caruthers was headed in that boat."

"Downstream," said her husband, stating the obvious.

≈≈≈

Maddy Madison was bending over a topographical map of Caruthers County, a leftover from when her sons had been in the Scouts. They used to camp along the Wabash, in an area known as the Never Ending Swamp, a large marshy area down toward Burpyville.

"Whatcha doing, Grammy?" asked Aggie as she burst into the kitchen, her new cousin N'yen in tow. They were looking for gingerbread and milk, knowing that Maddy had been baking all morning.

"Trying to figure out where Henry Caruthers was headed."

Aggie had heard her mom talking about Edgar Ridenour's sighting. "Bet he was going to meet up with his partner in crime, that mean ol' Mrs. Beanie," she offered.

"Beats me," her grandmother threw up her hands, "You kids ready for some freshly baked gingerbread?"

"Yeah!" shouted Aggie. Rubbing her belly in a pantomime of hunger.

"Yes, ma'am," mumbled N'yen, careful to be polite around his brand-new grandmother.

"Here you go, you two hooligans," said Maddy, dishing out generous slices of warm gingerbread.

"Yummy!"

"Yes, yummy!"

"Aggie, what were you saying the other night about a secret tunnel?"

"Just that I bet the Underground Railroad has an escape tunnel."

"Interesting. If you look at this map, you'll see that Pleasant Glades is not far from the river. Here's where Lizzie's husband was fishing. It's just upstream from the shortest point between the cemetery and the river."

Aggie grinned, her face covered in frosting that topped the gingerbread. "So *you* think there's a tunnel too!"

"Well, Mrs. Beanie had to get out of that hidden room somehow."

"I tried to tell everybody she was hiding in a secret tunnel, but nobody believed me," she said poutily.

"Maybe we ought to go look for a tunnel. See what we find," suggested young N'yen. Out of the mouths of babes.

CHAPTER TEN

A Mouse Ran Out and About the House

Aggie was the one who reminded them that the historic Underground Railway site was monitored by a security company. "There's a man inside a black box over the stairs," she said. Not literally meaning that there was a person inside the speaker.

"Hm, that may be a problem," replied her grandmother. "We don't want him calling Chief Purdue about intruders."

"How did Mrs. Beanie get inside without setting off the alarm?" asked N'yen.

"Good question. Perhaps she knew how to disable the system. Had an alarm code or found a turn-off switch."

They were standing outside the mausoleum that served as entrance to the cellar where runaway slaves had been hidden during the mid-1800s. It was an imposing stone structure, the ribbed columns giving off a Greco-Roman aura. A Latin inscription over the portal read MUS UNI NON FIDIT ANTRO. The old padlock had been replaced by an even bigger one. And this one really locked.

"Let's look for a way to turn off the man in the box," suggested Aggie.

"Don't bother. We're locked out." Maddy was kicking herself that they hadn't checked out the hidden chamber before the security company installed this new padlock.

"Grammy, we can't give up. Mrs. Beanie will get away."

"Oh, I expect she's long gone by now. If my theory's right, Edgar spotted Henry Caruthers boating down the river to pick her up at the other end of your secret tunnel."

"Then why did you want to get inside the underground hideout?"

"They had to stash the quilt somewhere."

N'yen pointed at the Latin inscription over the mausoleum's portal. "What's that say, Mrs. Madison?"

"Call me Grammy, dear. Aggie does."

"Okay, Grammy."

Maddy studied the phrase. "My high school Latin is pretty rusty. I think it says something about a mouse."

≈≈≈

Back home, the trio of explorers had another helping of gingerbread and milk, the idea being that brain cells need nourishment. Aggie was studying the topographical map, which was still spread out on the kitchen table, anchored by their glasses of milk.

Maddy phoned Lizzie to report their failure in gaining entrance to the underground chamber where Mrs. Beanie had disappeared. "I'm so frustrated I could spit," she told her friend in an exaggerated whisper.

"I've never been to that part of the cemetery," said Lizzie. "It's icky down there among those old crypts and mausoleums." She was the fashion plate among the Quilter's Club members, always hesitant to do anything that might muss her hair or break a nail.

"Yes, I know what you mean. I kept expecting to be

attacked by rats and spiders." She took another nibble of gingerbread. "Oh, that reminds me. There was a Latin phrase carved over the entrance to that Underground Railway hidey-hole – something about a rat. No, a mouse."

"Whatever are you talking about, Maddy Madison?"

"A Latin phrase. *Mus uni non fidit astro*, or something like that."

"Goodness, Maddy honey, you know I flunked Latin. Had to switch to French. I was better at that." The redhead made it sound like a confession.

"Strange that a mausoleum would have an inscription about a mouse," mused Maddy, taking another bite of gingerbread. She became a compulsive eater when agitated.

"Ask Cookie. She got an A+ in Latin."

≈≈≈

Cookie Bentley answered on the first ring. "Caruthers Corners Historical Society. Sorry, but the museum's closed today. We're only open on Tuesdays and Wednesdays."

"It's me," said Maddy.

"Hi, dear. It's good to hear your voice. I'm worried sick about that missing Pennington quilt. I'm going to have to tell the Smithsonian about it sooner or later, then all heck is going to break loose."

"I'm worried too. Chief Purdue still hasn't found Henry Caruthers. Nan Beanie escaped from that hidden chamber. And still no sign of the stolen quilt."

"Thanks for calling to cheer me up." The sarcasm was evident in Cookie's voice.

"I have a quick question," Maddy changed the direction of the conversation. "It may not have anything to do with anything, but I saw a strange Latin phrase there in the cemetery. Maybe you can tell me what it means."

"I'll try."

"*Mus uni non fidit astro.*"

"Say that again."

Maddy repeated the words.

"It's something about a mouse and a star."

"A star?"

"A mouse doesn't have a star."

"That doesn't make sense."

"Are you sure you got the words right?"

"Not totally," Maddy admitted.

"Let me check. I think I've got a Latin dictionary here on the shelf somewhere. It comes in handy when dealing with old documents."

Maddy served another slice of gingerbread to Aggie and N'yen, then took one for herself. "*Mus uni non fidit astro,*" she spoke the words out loud. "I think that's right."

Cookie came back on the line. "Could that have been *antro* rather than *astro*?"

"Perhaps."

"It's an old saying by a Roman playwright named Plautus: 'A mouse does not rely on just one hole."

CHAPTER ELEVEN

On the Trail

Aggie found out more about this strange "railroad" in the cemetery by checking Wikipedia, the source of all knowledge for the computer generation.

It read:

> The **Underground Railroad** was an informal network of secret routes and safe houses used by 19th Century black slaves in the United States to escape to free states and Canada with the aid of abolitionists who were sympathetic to their cause.

She wasn't sure what an "abolitionists" was, but her mom had told her about slavery. She had been shocked that people treated other people like ... uh, pets. That was as close as she could come to the concept. But even her dog Tige had a better life than those long-ago slaves.

She supposed these local abol-whatchamacallums had built those underground chambers in the Pleasant Glade Cemetery, along with a tunnel leading to the river where black people could sail away to freedom. Good for those tunnel-builders. Nobody should have to be a slave, in her opinion.

According to Wikipedia, more than 30,000 people had escaped slavery by using this so-called Railroad. Only a small number had likely been routed through Caruthers Corners, but who knew? Records were sketchy during that 1810 to 1950 period, noted the Wiki entry.

She asked Cookie Bentley about this strange history of the United States. Wasn't America supposed to be the "land of the free"?

As head of the Caruthers Corners Historical Society, Cookie was a bit embarrassed that she hadn't known about these National Registry sites right here in the town cemetery. "Forgotten history," she explained this lapse. "People don't like to remember bad things."

She'd done some research since the discovery of the underground chambers. The National Park Service listed three Underground Railroad sites in Indiana, but there had been many more.

Jeffersonville was an important station. One route had stations at Charlestown, Lexington, Marble Hill, and Bethlehem, making connection with Hanover. Another route started at Graysville and ran through Wirt and College Hill before ending at Butlersville. Corruption in this route made a change necessary and this led to the formation of Tibbett's route in 1845. Eventually, three grand trunk lines converged at the Levi Coffin residence in Newport, leading from Cincinnati, Madison, and Jeffersonville.

Getting a site listed on the National Historic Registry took some doing. Apparently that had happened under Mayor Caruthers' regime and received no publicity. Turns out, the preservation of the Pleasant Glade chambers and tunnel had been backed by the Indiana Division of Historic Preservation and Archaeology.

All that was before Cookie took over managing the local Historical Society. She could only assume the records were buried in those boxes of files stored in the basement of the Town Hall.

"Bad things? Our town helped save people," Aggie pointed out with a child's simplicity. "That's a good thing."

≈ ≈ ≈

Based on the inscription over the door, Maddy prevailed on Chief Purdue to contact the alarm company to learn more details about this way station on the Underground Railroad. A supervisor checked the records and a survey map before confirming that not only was there another entrance in the cemetery, but that a mile-long tunnel ran from the chambers to an exit near the Wabash. "It's all been closed off for safety sake," he told the police chief. "Our firm monitors it for the National Registry folks, just to make sure nobody gets hurt going down there."

"Hate to ask you to do this, but we're searching for a fugitive. Could you send somebody down here to open up that second cemetery entrance so we can take a peek inside?"

"As long as it's police business, no problem. We generally don't encourage visitors – even researchers – due to liability issues. Those old structures are dangerous. Ready to crumble down around your head."

≈ ≈ ≈

"Who would have thought the Quilter's Club would be investigating a crime that involves a hidden way station on the old Underground Railroad," gushed Bootsie. They were in the Town Hall conference room, putting finishing touches on the Pennington exhibit.

"Actually there's a connection between quilting and runaway slaves," offered Cookie. She'd been doing her homework.

"How's that?" asked Maddy.

"Some people claim that quilt designs were used to send signals to the slaves, directing them to specific escape routes on the Underground Railway."

"Do tell?" said Lizzie, her attention focused on this interest facet of quilting history.

"According to some theories, there were ten different quilt patterns used to convey messages. A particular quilt would be draped over a fence for all to see. But only the slaves knew the code. Plantation owners didn't have a clue."

"How cool," whistled Aggie. Fascinated by these tales of derring-do in olden days – back even before her grammy and grampy were born.

"What's for lunch?" asked N'yen. Thinking with his stomach as usual.

CHAPTER TWELVE

On the Trail

"I'll be danged," said Chief Purdue as the man from the security company raised the lid of a nearby crypt to reveal stone steps leading downward into the darkness. "Another chamber."

"This secret passage hasn't been opened in years. The folks at the National Register thought the tunnel was structurally unsound. I brought the survey map with me if you want to see it, but I don't advise going down there."

Maddy peered down the steps. "You say this has been closed off for years?"

"That's right ma'am."

"Then what's that chewing gum wrapper doing there on the third step down?"

The security guard leaned in to pick it up. "Double Bang," he identified the brand.

"That's a brand-new bubble gum that bangs as you chew it," said eight-year-old N'yen, an expert on candy and such.

"Yes, I've seen it advertised on TV," confirmed Maddy's son Bill, who had accompanied them to the cemetery. "It's the latest rage."

"It tastes like strawberries," added Aggie. "All the kids like it."

"Looks like somebody has been using this passage not so long ago," the police chief stated the obvious.

"Must be neighborhood kids," posited the security guard. "That would explain a bubble gum wrapper."

"Wouldn't you know it if someone entered this passage?" asked the police chief.

"No, this entrance was closed off, so it wasn't wired with an alarm."

"Maybe somebody other than neighborhood kids has been using this tunnel," said Maddy. "I think this is how Nan Beanie escaped. Not through the other chamber."

"The one you were in before was just a holding chamber. This is the one with a tunnel."

"And this tunnel leads to the river?" Chief Purdue studied the survey map.

"That's right," nodded the security guard. "I'm told that slaves were led down this tunnel to the river where they were taken by boat to the next way station on the Underground Railway."

"Should I close off the other end of this tunnel?" asked Chief Purdue.

"No need," replied Maddy. "The mouse has already escaped the hole."

≈≈≈

"This is crazy," said Bootsie. "The police department has a skiff it uses for dragging the river in drowning cases. Jim could have motored us down here in style."

Maddy and her friend were crowded into a rubber raft, a remnant of her sons' Scouting days. She'd used an old bicycle pump in the garage to blow it up, but even so it sagged in the middle from their combined weight. Bootsie had packed on a few extra pounds over the summer, not that she was a lightweight to begin with.

The raft was floating down the Wabash, being kept on course by a few licks of their paddles. They had launched it at the exact spot where Lizzie's husband had spotted Henry Caruthers.

"Wabash" is an Anglicization of "Ouabache," the French's original name for the river. Early traders took that from a Miami Indian word, *waapaahsiiki*, meaning "it shines white." Ironically, the clarity of this longest northern tributary feeding into the Ohio River has been diminished by pollution and silt.

Maddy paddled steadily. She noted that the water was a muddy color, like coffee heavily laced with cream. Dragonflies skittered on its surface. The canopy of sycamore trees dabbled the scene with shadows, giving it the appearance of an Impressionist painting.

"Let's call Jim to come get us. I've got my cell phone here."

"Just paddle," repeated Maddy for the tenth time. Bootsie was always carping about anything that resembled exercise. She was not an outdoors gal at heart.

"But the police boat has a motor."

"Your husband would call out the National Guard. And Henry and Nan would see us coming a mile away."

"Don't be silly. Those two are long gone, the Pennington quilt with them. I'll bet they had a car waiting for them at the Burpyville Bridge."

"Maybe, maybe not."

They paddled along, Bootsie slapping at an occasional horsefly, Maddy surveying the shoreline for signs of a boat landing. So far, the thick foliage looked untrampled.

"There, what's that?" pointed Bootsie.

"A deer path."

"Oh."

The sun flickered through the lattice of the overhanging trees. An occasional fish broke the surface of the water. Once they saw a beaver or a muskrat in the weeds along the bank. But no sign of Henry and Nan.

This stretch of river wasn't near the highway, like where Edgar Ridenour had been fishing, so they didn't encounter any anglers along the banks. The world was silent as they drifted along – *merrily, merrily, merrily, life is but a dream!*

They came to a stretch where trees blocked out the overhead sun. Even so, Maddy felt a bit overheated, perhaps the exertion of all the paddling. Her friend was leaning against the inflated rim of the rubber raft, paddle across her knees, taking in the passing scenery.

"I could use a little help here," grumbled Maddy.

"Wait! I think I saw something flash over there in those bushes," said Bootsie.

Maddy squinted. "I don't see anything."

"Go back, you'll see."

But the current was too strong at this bend in the river to reverse their course.

"Pull over to the bank. We'll walk back."

"Now who's crazy?"

With a Herculean effort, the two adventuresses maneuvered the sagging raft to the riverbank and tied it to a dead sapling. Pushing through the brambles, they worked their way back up the shoreline.

They came to a break in the trees. "There," pointed the police chief's wife. "I told you I saw something."

The aluminum surface of a flat-bottomed boat flashed in the bright afternoon sunlight, marking the spot among the reeds where it had been abandoned. A path led up an incline and into the woods. Muddy footprints offered proof of human passage.

"This is where Henry Caruthers came ashore. He was alone."

"Well, aren't you the Last of the Mohicans. Since when did you get an Indian Scout merit badge?"

"C'mon, Bootsie. It's as plain as the nose on your face."

"Hey, leave my nose out of this!" She was fairy sensitive about her prominent beak.

"I mean, look at these tracks. There's only one set of footprints leading up this deer trail."

"Okay, I'll grant you that Henry Caruthers passed this way. Now let's go home. I've had enough of Mother Nature for one day." She slapped at a horsefly to make her point.

"No, we have to follow him," insisted Maddy.

"Dear, he's long gone. It's been two days since Lizzie's husband saw Henry on the river."

"I know, but we might come across a clue as to where he and Nan went."

≈≈≈

About a half hour later they came to a tumbledown stone structure in a clearing. There was no sign of life, no answer to their calls of *hello*. Peeking through a dirty window, they could see peeling wallpaper and broken floorboards. The door was locked, but they broke the window with a rock and pried the sash up enough for

Maddy to wiggle through. She toppled inside with a loud *thump!* – followed by a painful "*Owww!*"

"See anything?" called Bootsie to her advance scout.

"Nothing yet." Then, after a pause, the voice said, "Wait a minute, I think I've found something here."

"A letter confessing their crimes?"

"More like a map."

"A treasure map? Did they bury the quilt in a chest?"

"No, silly. An Exxon road map showing Caruthers County. There's a route traced with a Magic Marker. If I'm reading this correctly, we're on the south side of Burpyville – just off Highway 31."

"Great! Let's go to the highway and thumb a ride home. I'm getting hungry."

"You and your stomach."

"Hey, are you suggesting I should go on a diet?"

"No, dear. Just that you're not going to starve to death in the next hour." She unlatched the ramshackle door from the inside and swung it open to let Bootsie enter the stone building.

"Hmph," her friend said as she stepped through the threshold of the one-room structure. She glanced nervously at the ceiling to make certain there were no bats. Mice and snakes she could endure, but not fluttery things like bats and bees.

"Here's something else I found," said Maddy, holding up a scrap of paper. "I think it was written by Nan Beanie."

Bootsie bent over the lined yellow paper as Maddy spread it flat on the table. The words were written in a precise script that she recognized as Nan's.

Things to Do :

1. *Call Dizzy about lunch*
2. *Leave drawer unlocked*
3. *Buy bus tickets*
4. *Reserve hotel room in Indy*
5. *Meet Kramer*

"Nan's such a list-maker," commented Maddy.

"This is practically as good as a confession," gushed Bootsie, ever the policeman's wife.

"She already confessed," Maddy reminded her. "That's why she ran away."

"Oh right."

"But here is the outline of their plan. She and Henry Caruthers are taking a bus to Indianapolis to meet with someone named Kramer."

CHAPTER THIRTEEN
Tunnel Vision

Maddy began walking around the tiny room, looking in the closet and opening cabinet doors. "What are you doing?" demanded Bootsie, confused by her friend's bizarre behavior.

"Looking for the tunnel," she said matter-of-factly.

"Here?"

"We know the secret passage at the cemetery leads to the river. The National Registry survey shows that. That means it comes out somewhere near here."

"At this old stone shed?"

"We found this roadmap and Nan's note in this shed. That proves she was here. And the tracks leading from the boat belong to a man, presumably Henry Caruthers. I think he and his partner in crime met up here, planning to make their way to the bus station in Burpyville, and go from there to Indianapolis to see a guy named Kramer."

"Okay, Miss Smarty Pants, suppose you're right. But if I wanted to find a tunnel entrance I'd look for a trapdoor in the floor."

"Bootsie Purdue, you're a genius!" Maddy peeled back the dusty rug to reveal a squarish board with recessed hinges. "Here it is, right where you said it'd be."

"Now can we go home?"

"Yes, but we have a choice of how to get there."

"A choice?"

"We can try paddling back upstream. Or we can try to find our way out of these woods to the highway. Or we can take this tunnel back to Pleasant Glades Cemetery."

"You mean go down in that dark hole? No way!" They had pried open the trapdoor to discover a yawning black passageway.

"Nan came through it, so it must be safe."

"That ol' woman is crazy as a loon. Why else would she get mixed up in criminal activities? I'm not nutty enough to go into that rat-infested tunnel."

"What rats?"

"There are always rats in tunnels."

"Yes, dear. But you said you're not afraid of rats and mice. Matter of fact, I recall that you raised white rats as your high-school science project."

"Romulus and Remus. But it turned out they were Romulus and Rita. I had more baby rats than I knew what to do with."

"You mean your First Prize in the Science Fair was an accident?"

"I'm still not sure how to tell a boy rat from a girl rat."

"C'mon, Indiana Jones. Into the tunnel."

"But we don't have a light. We'll get lost in there."

"It's a tunnel, leading from Point A to Point B. We can't get lost. Besides, I have this." Maddy flicked on the tiny Mag-Light she carried on her keychain. "As the Good Book says, 'Let there be light!'"

≈≈≈

The two women bumbled their way along the narrow

passageway, unsure of their footing due to the uneven stones lining the floor and walls. A lot of work had gone into creating this escape route for runaway slaves.

"Stay close," advised Maddy.

"Close! – I couldn't get very far from you even if I tried. This is like crawling through a storm drain."

They weren't actually crawling, but the low ceiling did force them to walk slightly hunched over. Perhaps people in the 1860s were shorter than their counterparts today, mused Maddy. She'd have to remember to ask Cookie about that. Her shoulders were starting to ache from this awkward bent-over position, but darned if she was going to admit that to Miss I-Told-You-So Bootsie Purdue.

The tunnel was dank, a musty smell that reminded Maddy of her grandmother's root cellar. They were still near the river, she reminded herself. Her flashlight played on the vertical stonewalls, braced with wooden beams. The floor was paved with flat rocks, like cobblestones. Muddy earth oozed between them like orangish grout. She was careful where she stepped.

"Maybe a quarter-mile more," predicted Maddy. She estimated they had traveled about 3/4 of the distance between river and the cemetery.

Her friend was not to be mollified. "My hair's a total mess, Maddy Madison. I'm going to send you the bill from my next hairdresser appointment."

"Keep walking. It can't be far."

"Says you," groused her friend. "For all I know, we're going in the wrong direction."

"There's only one direction."

"Yes, but – "

"Hold on," shushed Maddy. "I think I see a light up ahead. That's strange. I'd think the security company would've turned off the fluorescents in the main chamber."

Bootsie squinted toward the light. "That's not the chamber. That light's moving. It's somebody coming this way!"

≈ ≈ ≈

Maddy's first thought was that the light belonged to a rescue team, volunteers searching the rickety tunnel for her and Bootsie. But when she heard a voice call out, "Who goes there?" she recognized it as belonging to Henry Caruthers. Uh-oh.

She felt Bootsie poke her, a signal not to answer. Her friend had recognized the former mayor's voice also.

Instinctively, Maddy clicked off her Mag-Light. There was no place to hide, but at least Henry Caruthers wouldn't be able to judge their distance from him.

"That you, Nan? Did you forget something?"

The two women held their tongues (some say that was a triumph of willpower over natural proclivities). Maddy felt Bootsie's hand squeezing her arm like a vise.

"Nan?" The man's light grew closer, less than twenty feet away now.

Thinking fast, Maddy shouted, "This way, Chief Purdue! Tell your deputies he's up ahead!"

The light bobbed, then flicked out. They could hear feet clattering on the cobblestones, heading in the other direction.

Bootsie tugged on Maddy's arm. "Come on, Nancy Drew. Let's get out of here the way we came."

They hurried through the tunnel, banging their heads

on the low ceiling, stubbing their toes on protruding rocks, scraping their shoulders on the sidewalls. You'd think the Headless Horseman was pursuing them. But, fact was, Henry Caruthers was racing pell-mell in the other direction – back toward the cemetery!

"Whew! That's was close," breathed Bootsie as they climbed up into the one-room outpost. "Let's go find the highway and thumb a ride back home."

"We almost had him," Maddy said dazedly, as if talking to herself.

"Or vice versa," replied Bootsie.

CHAPTER FOURTEEN

Home Again, Home Again

They got home around midnight, having caught a ride with a UPS driver outside of Burpyville. All the lights were blazing in the Madison household where everyone had gathered, thinking Maddy and Bootsie had been kidnapped. Jim Purdue had organized a search party, but thankfully the two women returned just in time for him to call it off.

Boy, was the police chief steamed! "You what?" he shouted. "I oughta arrest the two of you!"

"For what?" challenged his wife.

"Obstructing justice. Interfering with an ongoing investigation. Worrying the heck outta me."

"Oh, sweetie, I'm sorry we worried you."

"Yeah, well – "

"Sorry, Jim," apologized Maddy. "We were only reconnoitering. We didn't expect to run into Henry Caruthers. I thought he and Nan would be long gone."

"What's this you were saying about a list?" interjected Mark the Shark. Exhibiting a lawyer's instinct for getting at the facts.

"We found a to-do list written by Nan Beanie. It suggests they are heading for Indianapolis to meet someone."

Beau looked over his wife's shoulder at the yellow foolscap. "Yep, that's Nan's handwriting. I'd know it anywhere."

"Who's this guy Kramer?" asked Bill, not to be outdone by his lawyer brother-in-law.

"He was on the *Seinfeld Show*," announced little N'yen, a devotee of television sitcoms.

"No, silly. This is a different Kramer," whispered Aggie, her new cousin's self-appointed protector.

"Oh."

"I suspect he's a fence," opined Chief Purdue. "Someone Henry and Nan are planning to sell the quilt to."

"I can't get over Nan and Henry Caruthers," said Lizzie Ridenour, a woman who loved juicy gossip. "Do you think they're an item? Or merely partners in crime?"

"Dunno," said Cookie. "But I hear Nan's husband Jasper is not particularly happy about this turn of events."

"Do you think Jasper will take matters into his own hands?" asked Tillie, belly as big as a basketball. You could see her delivery date was eminent.

"If he does, he's going to need a good lawyer," said Mark, almost as if thinking out loud.

"Ambulance chaser," teased Bill's wife Kathy.

"Hey, nobody's chasing me," rumbled Ben Bentley, who drove an ambulance on weekends for Caruthers Corners Fire and Rescue. You could tell by his joking remark that he was a good-natured guy, a gentle giant.

"Don't worry about Jasper. He reacted in his usual manner, with a bit of the barley. He's sleeping it off in my holding cell at this very moment."

"Do I need to serve a writ of habeas corpus?" said

Mark, just to show that lawyers had a sense of humor too.

"A what?" asked little N'yen.

"It's Latin for 'You must have the body,'" explained Cookie. She'd been perusing her dictionary again.

"A body! Is somebody dead?" Aggie wanted to know.

"No, no," laughed her father. "It's just lawyer talk, saying 'You can't hold someone in jail without a body of evidence justifying their arrest.'"

"Henry Caruthers is going to wish he was dead if I get my hands on him," growled Cookie. "Tomorrow I'm going to have to call the Smithsonian and tell them one of their valuable quilts is missing."

"Honey, calm down," soothed Ben Bentley, patting his wife's hand. A bearded behemoth, he reminded you of Hagrid from the *Harry Potter* movies. "Don't get so upset over this. It's just a patchwork quilt."

That's when all four members of the Quilter's Club – five counting Aggie – went berserk.

"Just a quilt," huffed Lizzie. "That's like saying the Mona Lisa is just a painting."

"Don't you realize these quilts have been valued at forty grand each?" asked Bootsie.

"They're irreplaceable," declared Maddy. "Sarah Connors Pennington was a master craftsman, perhaps the best quilt designer ever!"

"What'd I say?" moaned Ben, cowering at this onslaught by his wife's friends.

"Dear, you've put your foot in it now," said Cookie, amused at her new husband's bewilderment. "You'll have to learn that we members of the Caruthers Corners Quilter's Club take our stitching pretty seriously."

"Ease up, girls," said Edgar Ridenour, looking almost as fierce with his briar-patch beard as Cookie's muscle-bound husband. "Ben didn't mean anything by his remark."

"Yeah, you girls should be worrying about catching Henry Caruthers and Nan Beanie," added Maddy's husband.

"No," she replied. "We'll leave that up to Chief Purdue. Wouldn't want to be thrown in jail for worrying him."

"Yes, we'd have to call Mark for a habeas corpus," smiled the policeman's wife.

"Don't worry," said Jim Purdue. "I'm gonna stake out the Burpyville Trailways station. We'll pick up Henry and Nan when they try to board the bus for Indy."

"You'll get Nan, but it might be someone other than Henry," murmured Maddy, almost a throwaway comment.

"S-someone other than Henry?" sputtered the police chief.

"You do realize Henry and Nan have an accomplice, don't you?"

"Just how do you figure that, Maddy Madison?"

"We all know it took someone with great sewing skills to make that fake Pennington. Except for using synthetic thread, you can't tell it from the real thing. Neither Henry nor Nan can sew that well. So they had to have a third partner, someone who's a master quilt-maker."

CHAPTER FIFTEEN

A New Suspect

Aggie put it into perspective for them. "It's really quite simple," she said as everyone polished off the last of the watermelon pies. "Who d'you know that's good enough at quilting to make a fake you can't tell from the original?"

"I don't know anyone *that* good," admitted Lizzie. "Even I couldn't do it." The nimble-fingered redhead was considered to be the best quilter in Caruthers Corners, having won First Prize in the Watermelon Days competition three years in a row.

"*Some*body did it," Bootsie pointed out.

"It couldn't be anyone we know," insisted Cookie. "Maddy and I already went down that road."

"How about Holly Eberhard," said Bootsie. "I'll bet she could do it."

"Well, of course, *she* could," shrugged Lizzie. "After all, she's the statewide champion."

"Yes, but who else?" asked Cookie.

"Why not Holly Everlast?" asked Aggie.

"Eberhard," corrected her grandmother. "Holly Eberhard."

"Don't be silly, Aggie," her mother spoke up. "Holly Eberhard's a famous quilt designer written up in all the magazines. I once saw a profile of her in *Quilter's Quarterly*. That magazine features the very best quilters in the universe."

"Okay, but who else could make a perfect copy?" persisted the ten-year-old girl.

"Lots of people I'm sure," said Cookie. "Just not anyone we'd know."

"Besides," added Lizzie, "it wasn't a perfect copy. Daniel Sokolowski spotted the synthetic thread, proving it wasn't made back in the 1920s."

"Close enough it fooled us," said Maddy. "We would have never spotted that modern thread."

"That's true," said Cookie, "but the Smithsonian would've when we tried to return a fake instead of the genuine article." She was dreading tomorrow's phone call to the famous museum.

"You know, Holly Eberhard grew up here in Caruthers Corners," said Beau. "Her mother was a Caruthers."

"I didn't know that," said Cookie, obviously miffed. She prided herself in being an authority on the town's genealogy.

"Beau's right. She was raised over on Melon Hill," said Edgar Ridenour. "The Savings and Loan held the family's mortgage. As I recall, her mother was Henry Caruthers' aunt. That makes her Henry's first cousin."

"No kidding?" said Tillie, chair pulled back from the kitchen table to make room for her tummy. "She's related to our criminal mastermind?"

"Well, that certainly adds her to our suspicious characters list," said Maddy, speaking for the Quilter's Club.

"I'll say," intoned Bootsie.

"Hey now, don't get carried away," said her policeman husband. "Being Lefty's cousin isn't a crime."

"Lefty?" said Bill.

"A nickname from high school," explained his dad. "Henry's left-handed. He used to be a great pitcher. Had a winning season senior year."

"Don't feel bad, Cookie," said Edgar. "Eberhard's Holly's married name. If we'd said Holly Lazynski, you would have placed her."

"Lydia Lazynski's daughter?"

"The same."

"Well, I'll be a ring-tail raccoon."

Her husband Ben patted her arm. "You're my little raccoon," he said affectionately.

"Thanks, Big Bear."

"Big Bear?" repeated little N'yen.

"Just a term of endearment," Cookie said. "But he's as big and powerful as a bear."

"A Teddy Bear?"

"More like a grizzly," said Aggie as she assayed the squat brawny man.

"*Gr-r-r-r-r!*" Ben gave his imitation of a bear, hands raised like giant paws, lumbering toward the wide-eyed children.

"Oo-o-o," said N'yen.

"You're funny," said Aggie.

"We need to take a closer look at Holly Lazynski Eberhard," concluded Maddy Madison as she began to clear away the dishes.

≈≈≈

217

"How are you adjusting to having a Vietnamese grandson?" Maddy asked her husband as she brushed her hair, preparing for bed. The brown sheen of her hair looked fairly natural, nary a sign of gray strands.

"Fine."

"No, really?"

"Really. He's a nice kid. Bright, funny."

"And Asian."

Beau looked up as his wife from the big double bed. "Just because I served in Nam doesn't mean I've got anything against Asians."

"You seemed upset when you first learned that Bill and Kathy had adopted N'yen."

"It wasn't that the kid was Asian. More that the Madisons are a proud bloodline going back to the early 1800s. We've never had an adoption in the family before."

CHAPTER SIXTEEN

A Trip to Indianapolis

"**W**hy are we going to Indianapolis?" asked Lizzie. She'd had a dental appointment before Maddy shanghaied her on this idiotic mission.

"To find Kramer."

"Who?"

"The name on Nan's list. You know, the one Bootsie and I found in the old shack."

"The funny man on Seinfeld," said N'yen, sitting in the backseat with Aggie. Maddy was babysitting the children today. Little did their parents know they were on a road trip to the state capital, a three-hour drive each way.

"Can we stop for a milkshake?" pressed Aggie.

"Yeah, at MacDonald's," chimed the boy.

"How are we going to find this guy Kramer?" said Lizzie, a bit put out by her friend's cavalier attitude. Expecting her to drop everything and flit off to Indy.

"I'm not sure. But we know Nan's planning to meet him."

"But where?"

"Jim thinks the guy might be – what did he call it? – a fence. So we could check out the pawnshops. I've heard they sometimes buy stolen goods."

"You've heard?"

"Well, I saw it in a movie once."

"Great. For a minute there, I was worried you didn't have a sound plan."

≈≈≈

Maddy and Lizzie were thumbing through the Yellow Pages at the pay phone back near the restrooms, while the kids sipped on vanilla milkshakes and ate Big Macs – a gourmet lunch, American-style.

"Here we are, the P's. Pawnshops. Wait, wait, I don't see any Kramer Pawnshops," said the redhead.

"Maybe that's not the name of the shop. He might only work in one."

"There must be a dozen listed here. Do you intend to phone every one of them?"

"Why not?"

"We could have done that from Caruthers Corners."

Maddy glanced up at her friend. "Didn't have an Indianapolis telephone book," she said smugly.

Twenty minutes later they had completed the list of pawnshops, none claiming an employee named Kramer. Maddy and Lizzie were barely speaking. The two kids were on their second Big Macs.

"Now what?"

Maddy shrugged meekly. "We could go to the bus station and look for Nan Beanie."

"We'd just be in the way. Chief Purdue has that covered."

"I love Jim Purdue, but he's not exactly Elliot Ness."

Lizzie glanced to the front of the fast-food restaurant to check on the kids. "Don't be so hard on Jim," she said to Maddy. "He's working closely with the Indianapolis police.

If Nan shows up, they will get her."

"I suppose you're right."

The two women gathered up the kids. "Ready to go home?" Lizzie said to them as they polished off their French fries.

"Sure," said Aggie. "But don't you want to find that Kramer guy?"

"Of course," replied her grandmother. "But looks like we've struck out."

"Did you look in the phone book?"

Maddy smiled patiently. "Yes, we checked all the pawnshop listings in the Yellow Pages."

"But did you look him up in the regular listings – the white pages?"

≈≈≈

Maddy found dozens of Kramers listed in the white pages of the telephone book, too many to sort through. But one business listing caught her eye: Kramer Sewing Notions & Quilting Supplies.

Bingo!

"Aggie, you're a genius!" declare her grandmother.

"What'd I do?"

"Never mind, dear. Just give us another hour and we'll head home."

"Good. My dog misses me."

"Grammy, may I have another milkshake?" wheedled little N'yen.

"Enough for you, young man. Your mother will kill me if I bring you home with a tummy ache."

"My mom was having tummy aches this morning," said Aggie matter-of-factly.

"Tummy aches? Do you mean labor contractions?" Maddy could feel her pulse rate increase. She'd never forgive herself if she weren't by Tillie's side when she gave birth to her second child.

"Dunno. She was timing them with her watch."

"Oh my."

"Should we start home?" Lizzie asked her anxious friend.

"Absolutely," said Maddy, glancing down at the phone book. "But we might stop by this quilt shop for two minutes. This address is just down the street from here."

≈ ≈ ≈

Kramer's Sewing Notions was a small shop that tried to aggrandize itself with a sign in the window claiming *"Indy's Largest Source of Quilting Supplies."*

True or not, the corner windows featured an array of patchwork quilts, sewing machines designed for making quilts, and bolts of colorful fabrics. A sign on the door advised Back in 10 Minutes.

"Rats!" said Maddy. They couldn't afford to wait, not if Tillie was having contractions back in Caruthers Corners.

"Sorry," said Lizzie. "Bad timing."

"Look," pointed N'yen. "I see somebody moving around inside."

Aggie put her face to the door, shading out the glare of sunlight with a hand over her eyes. "I see him too. There behind the counter."

Maddy pecked on the glass door. "Hello in there," she called. But the shadowy figure did not acknowledge her greeting.

Lizzie joined in, pounding her palm against the door.

"Yoo-hoo, hello!"

The cacophony of their banging couldn't be ignored. The man finally made his way to the front door and waved them away. "We're closed, can't you see?" she shouted through the glass. He was a tall fellow with heavy brows and a thick beak-like nose. The perfect candidate for rhinoplasty. "Go away or I'll call the police."

"Call them if you like, Mr. Kramer."

"I'm not Kramer. I'm just the janitor service."

"Where's Mr. Kramer?" pressed Maddy.

"Outta town. Left this morning."

But the sign here on the doors says 'Back in 10 Minutes.'"

"Don't reckon he has a sign that says 'Back in 10 Years.' He's closing the shop and moving to Canada."

"Canada?"

"He has a brother up there. Think that's where the family's from." The man turned back to his work, pushing a mop lazily around the tile floor, wet streaks marking his effort.

"Wait," said Lizzie. "Did Mr. Kramer go alone?"

The man paused and looked over his shoulder. "He had a woman with him. I'd never seen her before. He called her 'String Bean' or 'Butter Bean,' something like that."

"Mrs. Beanie?"

"That might be it." He went back to his mopping.

CHAPTER SEVENTEEN

An Intruder in the House

That afternoon at 4:08 p.m. Tillie Tidemore gave birth to a 6 pound, 7 ounce baby girl. She named her Madelyn Taylor after her mother. Maddy made it to the Burpyville General Hospital just in the nick of time. Mark was a basket case, pacing in the waiting room, while Bill and Kathy brought him coffee and donuts, as well as words of encouragement.

Over protests of the nurses, Maddy insisted on joining her daughter in the delivery room. Ten minutes later, the doctor was spanking the newborn baby.

"Congratulations, little lady," said Aggie's grandfather when she walked into the waiting room. "You have a sister."

"Wow! What a week," she smiled at N'yen. "A new cousin and a new sister. This family sure is growing."

"I got you beat," the boy bragged. "I got a new mom and dad, plus grandparents and aunts and uncles."

"And me," Aggie beamed.

"And you," he agreed.

≈≈≈

"So did you solve the Mystery of the Missing Quilt?" Beauregard Madison asked his wife as they drove home from the hospital. Burpyville was about 40 miles from

Caruthers Corners, but the road was straight and well paved.

"Not quite," she admitted. "But we made progress."

"Any sighting of my former assistant?"

"Almost. We learned that she met up with the owner of a sewing notions shop, a man named Kramer. But it looks like they've skipped the country, off to Canada."

"Well, you still have Henry Caruthers running around here. And what about Holly Eberhard – do you really think she's involved?"

"Difficult to tell. But it might be worth paying her a visit."

"I hear she lives down in Bloomington. That's quite a drive."

"You and I have been talking about a road trip."

"Can't do it right now. As mayor, I've got a lot of work to do preparing for Watermelon Days. The traveling carnival is trying to raise its fees this year. We don't have it in the town budget, but the children will be disappointed if there's not a Ferris wheel and a merry-go-round."

"I understand, dear. Duty calls. If you're going to be mayor, you have to do mayor's work."

Beau turned the big Buick onto Melon Pickers Row, their white Victorian house visible at the end of the street. "I'm sure your cronies at the Quilter's Club would be happy to drive down to Bloomie with you."

Maddy gazed at their house as her husband turned into the driveway. "Beau, you must have been in quite a hurry to get to the hospital. You left the front door standing wide open."

"No, I remember closing it." Years ago, folks in

Caruthers Corners rarely bothered to lock their doors, but it was unusual – then or now – to leave them standing open when away from home.

"You must have been discombobulated by Tillie's need to get to the hospital." She patted him on the shoulder, a reassuring gesture to let him know that this wasn't the onset of senility.

"Hm, I think I oughta call Jim Purdue. I'm sure I closed it. Might be a burglar inside."

She couldn't help but chuckle. "Burglars – here in Caruthers Corners?"

"Somebody stole your quilt," he pointed out. That certainly ended her objections.

Maddy pulled out her cell phone. "Hi, Bootsie. Yes, it was a girl. The doctors are pretty good about getting that right. Six pounds, seven ounces. Madelyn Taylor. That was a sweet gesture, naming her after me."

"Chief Purdue," her husband hissed, reminding her of the purpose of the call.

"I'll tell you more later, Bootsie. Is Jim home? Could you ask him to come over to the house? Beau thinks we may have had an intruder. Thanks, dear." Snapping the tiny phone shut, she turned to her husband. "Jim says he'll be here in five minutes."

≈≈≈

Police Chief Jim Purdue wasn't in uniform, but he was wearing his utility belt, complete with holster and billy club. He carried a .38 Smith & Wesson when on duty, but he'd never actually used it. Caruthers Corners was a peaceful community, not much criminal activity to require SWAT teams and homicide departments like in big cities.

He entered the house, pistol in hand, calling out: "Police. Come out with your hands up."

No response.

Slowly he worked his way room to room, checking closets, showers stalls, and other hiding places, but the house seemed empty. He called for the Madisons to come inside, putting his gun away. "False alarm," he said with a smile. "Looks like Beau's just getting forgetful. You been checked for Alzheimer's, old buddy?"

"I'm telling you I shut that door," Beauregard Madison insisted. "I'm not *that* forgetful."

"House is clear. I checked every room. Even looked in the refrigerator, he said, holding up a turkey drumstick. "Hope you don't mind I have a little snack. You did interrupt my dinner."

"Sorry," said Maddy. "Let me fix you a plate. But we don't have any watermelon pie left. Those vultures we call a family ate every last slice."

"Hold on here," interjected her husband. "There's a scrap of paper taped to the back of the front door."

Chief Purdue quickly said, "Don't touch it. Fingerprints, y' know." He bent closer to read the words printed on the lined notepaper.

I didn't steal your stinking quilt.
- Henry Caruthers

"That's Henry's handwriting alright," confirmed Beau. "I've seen it a thousand times on correspondence in the mayor's office."

"I'm gonna throw the book at him," fumed Jim.

"Breaking and entering. Trespassing. Spitting on the sidewalk."

"What's he mean, he didn't steal the quilt?" said Maddy. "Nan Beanie admitted she let him take the keys to the conference room."

"Can't trust Henry," muttered the policeman. "He was a lying weasel even in high school."

"Aw, Jim, he pitched you out fair and square in that last game of the season."

"No way. That ball wasn't good. Lefty was trying to hit me in the head."

"The umpire called it in the zone."

"You know ol' man Brown was half-blind." The father of Cookie's late husband had been the high school coach, as well as driver's ed instructor. Both were jobs his 40-40 vision should have disqualified him for, but in a small town allowances are made.

"I don't like Henry being in my house," declared Maddy Madison. "He's creepy. That's why I turned down his invitation to senior year prom."

Beau looked up from the note. "Maddy, you never told me Henry asked you out."

"Pish. That was nearly forty years ago. It doesn't matter now."

"Heck it doesn't. You were going steady with me back then. I can't believe he asked my girlfriend out behind my back."

"I told you he was a weasel," repeated Jim Purdue.

"The important thing to keep in mind is recovering that Pennington quilt," Maddy reminded them.

"And the fact that he broke into our house."

"If we don't recover that quilt, the town may be liable," Maddy pointed out. "As mayor, you signed the agreement booking the exhibit for Watermelon Days."

"What'd you say that quilt worth?" inquired Jim.

"Forty thousand dollars. But the museum might sue us for negligence and collect damages."

"Negligence?"

"Dear, it was your assistance who helped steal it."

"Oh."

"Bet this could cost a hundred grand," surmised the police chief.

Beau rolled his eyes in horror. "The town doesn't have that kind of money in its budget."

"Then we'd better find that quilt," said Maddy.

CHAPTER EIGHTEEN

Taking on the State Champ

Turns out, the Quilter's Club didn't have to drive to Bloomington. Holly Eberhard came to them.

"Have you heard?" Cookie Bentley gushed into the phone. "The state's Quilting Bee committee is coming here tomorrow. They want to talk about the Watermelon Days competition, make it a first round for the statewide contest."

"That's great," replied Maddy, fixing breakfast for Aggie and N'yen as she cradled the princess telephone between head and shoulder. "That could put the Quilter's Club on the map."

"Guess who's coming with them?"

Maddy didn't feel up for guessing games. She was still bummed over Henry Caruthers breaking into their house. Not to mention her excitement over her daughter giving birth. She had a new granddaughter to think about, not-quite-one-day-old Madelyn Taylor Tidemore. "Not a clue," she sighed.

"Well, I'll tell you. Holly Eberhard!"

"Really? That'll give us a chance to ask her if she's forged any Sarah Connors Pennington quilts lately."

"Now Maddy, we have to handle this carefully. We don't want to blow this opportunity."

"Have you told Bootsie and Lizzie yet?"

"No, you're my first call."

"Okay, let's meet at the Cozy Café to figure out a strategy."

"Sure. That will give you a chance to tell us about Holly's cousin breaking into your house." Word had spread among the members of the Quilter's Club, thanks to Chief Purdue's wife Bootsie.

"He didn't actually break in. The door was unlocked."

"But he came in uninvited and left you a threatening note."

"I wouldn't call it threatening. Mainly, it denied that he stole the quilt."

"Ha! We know better than that."

"Do we?"

"Of course. Nan Beanie confessed."

"Well, not quite."

"Then why did she run? Isn't that proof of guilt?"

"I suppose so," said Maddy, serving the ham and eggs to the kids. "But I have to tell you, something doesn't feel right about this."

"Oh, Maddy, you're such a worrier."

≈≈≈

The Cozy Café was always crowded. Not surprising, in that it was the only restaurant in town unless you counted the DQ or the Pizza Hut out on Route 21. The Quilter's Club squeezed into a booth at the far end of the converted bus. Bootsie hated coming here because the booth space was so tight.

"Perhaps the Quilter's Club shouldn't confront Holly Eberhard," said Lizzie, worry wrinkling her brow. Her red hair was tied back in a ponytail, a youthful look. With a skillful application of makeup, she looked a decade younger than her 58 years.

"We can't let her get away with this if she's guilty," exclaimed Cookie. "The Smithsonian is going to have a fit."

"Maybe we should let Jim speak with her, keep the issue away from us," urged Lizzie. "I'd hate to see us lose the opportunity to be part of the statewide Quilting Bee competition."

"What if I confronted her?" volunteered Maddy. "I could temporarily resign from the Quilter's Club, so you won't be connected with my putting her on the spot."

"Resign? No way," said Cookie. "You're our fearless leader."

"Not so fearless as you might think. But I'm certainly not afraid to take on Mrs. Holly Lazynski Eberhard, now that I know she's just a local girl like you and me."

"I don't like this plan," said Bootsie. "Your resigning is totally unacceptable."

"Plausible deniability," said Maddy, repeating the term she'd used with Bootsie just the other day. "That means you girls don't have to take the heat if I screw up."

"Screw up? In what way?"

"What if Holly's innocent? She may not like being accused of a crime she didn't commit."

"That's true," Lizzie agreed. "And she obviously has a lot of pull with the state Quilting Bee committee."

"Okay, but your resignation is only temporary," Bootsie caved in.

"A leave of absence," amended Cookie. She was a stickler for proper procedure, an obsessive rule follower.

"Oh my. I hope I can get Holly to confess."

"If anybody can, it's you," encouraged Bootsie. "You're better at grilling suspects than Perry Mason."

"Yes, you should have gone to law school," said Lizzie, adding her own positive reinforcement to the plan. Better to sacrifice Maddy than see the Quilter's Club go down in flames, she told herself.

"Law school? You mean be a lawyer like Mark the Shark? No thank you!"

"Why are you always putting Mark down?" asked Cookie. "He seems like a good son-in-law. Aggie adores him. And Tillie just had another child by him."

"Edgar recommended him to the Savings and Loan. He's now the bank's attorney of record," said Lizzie.

"And he helped Jim with that frivolous lawsuit against the police department. Got the man to drop the whole thing."

"The man who claimed Jim towed his car from the handicap spot at the courthouse, despite a handicap sticker in the window?"

Bootsie nodded. "That's the one. Mark pointed out that the man himself wasn't handicapped. He'd bought the car from Peg-Leg McGinty and thought the sticker went with the vehicle."

"And he's been hired as the town's attorney," Cookie added. "They needed a new one after old Bart Dingley retired."

"Wait up!" Maddy halted this runaway praise for her son-in-law's legal prowess. "If I gave the impression I'm denigrating Mark Tidemore, I apologize. I like to tease him, but that's out of affection. Now that he and Tillie got over that rough spot in their marriage, I couldn't be happier with having Mark as part of the family."

"Excellent," said Cookie. "Why don't you take him with you to confront Holly Eberhard. After all, two heads are better than one."

CHAPTER NINETEEN
A Fateful Interview with a Suspect

Mark and his mother-in-law drove out to Melon Hill the next day, looking for a mailbox marked *Lazynski*. It took them two times circling the block before Maddy commanded, "Stop here!"

She was pointing at a small brick-front cottage set back from the road. There was no name on the mailbox, but a Pontiac parked in the driveway had a bumper sticker that announced QUILTERS ARE NOT SQUARES.

"Yep, this has to be the place," agreed Mark. "That license-plate holder displays the name of a Pontiac dealership in Bloomington."

They parked behind the Grand Prix and walked up to the front door. Before they could press the bell, the door swung open and an elderly woman said, "We don't buy nothing from door-to-door salespeople."

"Oh, we're not salespeople," replied Maddy in his politest tone. "We're here to speak with your daughter, Mrs. Lazynski."

"Holly's not here."

"Isn't that her car in the driveway?" Mark nodded at the Pontiac Grand Prix.

"She went for a stroll."

A voice from inside the house put a lie to her words.

"Mom, who is it?"

"Solicitors," shouted the cranky woman.

"No, I'm the wife of the mayor. And this is the town's attorney."

"Let them in, mom."

The gray-haired woman stepped aside, granting them entrance to a cluttered living room. The couch was covered with protective plastic. Newspapers covered the coffee table, abandoned where they were read. The paintings on the walls were black velvet, a portrait of Elvis displayed prominently over the mantle. "Forgive the mess," the woman muttered as they searched for places to sit.

Holly Eberhard strided in from the kitchen. The state quilting champion looked as chic as her mother looked frumpy. Her short blonde hair was a $200 styling job. Her makeup was picture-perfect, as if she was on her way to a high-society party. "Hi, I'm Holly," she introduced herself, not the least self-conscious about the clutter of her family's living room.

"Holly, my name is Maddy Madison. And this is Mark Tidemore. We're here on a very sensitive inquiry. I hope you will allow us to ask you a few questions."

"What? About my divorce. It's getting quite nasty, I'll admit that. My husband's a jerk. It was him caught with a chorus girl, not the other way round."

"No, nothing about that," said Mark, his voice as reassuring as a priest's. Maddy was impressed. "It's about your quilting activities."

"Oh that. Yes, I'm the state champion. Would you like to see my trophy? Mom has it sitting on top of the sideboard in the dining room."

"Thanks, but that's not necessary," he replied politely. "We'd like to ask you about some of your recent work."

"Ask away."

Mark glanced at Maddy, a signal for her to take over the questioning. She had to admit he was very smooth, more like a porpoise than a shark.

"Forgive me, but I have to ask you this," apologized Maddy. "Did you recently make an exact copy of Sarah Connors Pennington's beehive quilt design?"

"Why yes," Holly Eberhard replied, "I did."

≈≈≈

In all his years as a lawyer, this was the easiest confession Mark Tidemore had ever encountered. Holly Eberhard batted her mascaraed eyelashes and stared at them as if waiting for the next question.

"You freely admit you made a fake Pennington quilt?" Mark repeated carefully.

"I wouldn't call it a fake. I'd say duplicate or replica." She waited for him to continue.

"Do you realize you may be subject to arrest?" Mark said.

"What for? I was commissioned to make an exact replica of three Pennington quilts by the Smithsonian."

"By the Smithsonian – ?" blurted Maddy.

"Yes," smiled Holly. "It's their collection. They can do whatever they choose with it."

"Why would they want copies?"

"So they can maintain a display back at the museum while the originals are on the road tour. It's done all the time, I'm told."

"And what happened with the three replica quilts?"

asked Maddy.

"Two are finished, I'm working on the third. So all are still in my possession. Why do you ask?"

Mark took over. "We have evidence of a crime involving a fake Pennington quilt."

"Well it can't be mine. My quilts are in my quilt-carrying trunk. It's sitting in mom's guest bedroom at this very moment."

"Here?"

"Yes, I brought them with me. As I said, I'm still working on the third."

"Would you mind showing them to us, ma'am?"

"I suppose so. Right now?"

"Could you give us a half hour?" Maddy interjected. "I want to invite a colleague over to inspect them."

Holly Eberhard frowned. "Say, what's this all about?"

"A crime," said Mark. "We told you that."

≈≈≈

Daniel Sokolowski bent over the quilt, a jeweler's glass screwed to his eye. "Hmm," he said as he examined it inch-by-inch. The antique dealer wasn't about to be hurried, determined to make an accurate assessment.

"Well?" said Maddy, getting impatient.

"Just a moment."

After a few more minutes, Maddy carefully cleared her throat and repeated "Well?"

Sokolowski looked up. "Excellent copies," he said.

"Thank you," said Holly Eberhard. "But I *am* quite good at quilting. That why I'm the state champion, for goodness sakes."

"I might mistake them for originals, except for this red

thread. As I suspect you know it's a synthetic blend, not available in 1924 when Sarah Pennington made her famous quilts."

"Yes, but the original thread is no longer available. I was forced to use a substitute. Most people wouldn't notice."

"True," he agreed. "It's a wonder I did. Perhaps it was the way the light refracted on it."

"I'm sure the Smithsonian will be satisfied. Everything else is authentic. It was quite a challenge finding original materials – fabric, threads, batting."

"Yes, it would be," agreed the antique dealer. "Some of these fabrics aren't made anymore.

"These three quilts are excellent copies," said Maddy. "How do we know she didn't create a fourth?"

"Oh, I'd say she did," opined the antique dealer. "Because the fake quilt you have was made with the same synthetic red thread as these three. That's four in all."

"Wait a minute," growled Holly Eberhard. "Are you accusing me of a crime?"

"That's not for me to say. All I can do is tell you that the same person who made these three quilts likely made the fourth that is hanging in the Town Hall."

"That can't be true," she shrieked angrily. "I know how many faux Pennington quilts I made – three, not four."

"That's quite impossible."

Mark held up his hand to silence them. "Mr. Sokolowski, could I ask you to look at this beehive design again. Are you certain it has the same synthetic thread as the others?"

"Well – " the antique dealer hesitated.

"Humor me, please."

"Alright, if you insist." He returned the jeweler's glass to his eye. Everyone waited while he inspected the beehive quilt with even greater care than before. "No way!" he said suddenly. "This can't be right."

"What?" demanded Maddy.

Mark smiled grimly, as if he already knew the answer.

"Should I call my attorney?" asked Holly Eberhard.

"Oh, I knew this sewing stuff would lead to no good," wailed her mother, swaying back and forth on the plastic-covered couch.

"This quilt," pronounced Daniel Sokolowski, "is authentic, not a copy!"

CHAPTER TWENTY

A Culprit Behind Bars

Aggie was sitting there listening to the women's excited chatter. With all the excitement of a new baby, her mother had relented on her ban of Aggie's participation in the Quilter's Club.

"It doesn't make sense," Lizzie was saying. "Why would Holly Eberhard have allowed you to examine her quilts if she knew one of them was the stolen Pennington?"

"Beats me," replied Bootsie. "But Jim has taken her into custody. Now if he can find that rascally cousin of hers."

"Henry Caruthers can't be far," opined Maddy. "But Nan and Robert Kramer are likely in Canada by now."

"Doesn't Canada have an extradition treaty with the US?" asked Lizzie.

"Sure," answered Bootsie, "if you can find them to arrest them."

"I'm just relieved the stolen quilt has been recovered. If we can keep this quiet, the Smithsonian need never know it was missing."

"Forget that," said Maddy. "When they learn Holly Eberhard's been arrested, everything will come out."

"Oh fiddle."

"Lizzie has a point," continued Maddy. "I was there.

243

And I think Holly was as surprised as we were when Daniel announced that her beehive quilt was authentic."

"Maybe she's a good actress," postulated Bootsie. "The fact that Holly had the real quilt and we had the copy proves she's guilty as sin. Case closed."

"What if somebody else switched them," Aggie spoke up.

"That's not very likely, honey." Cookie patted her on the arm, placating the girl for trying to be helpful. "The copies were in Holly's possession. Who could have switched them?"

"Somebody stole yours and it was under lock and key. Hers were in an unlocked trunk."

"Yes, but – "

"Aggie has a point," interceded Maddy. "Like I say, I think Holly Eberhard was as surprised as we were."

"Are you saying Jim has an innocent woman locked up in the police department holding cell?" Bootsie looked like she was ready to pop a blood vessel.

"To tell the truth, I'm not sure. But we ought to figure out exactly what happened, else we might not be able to sleep at night."

Lizzie gave her a stern gaze. "Because we may have accused an innocent person? Or because you can't rest until you've solved the puzzle?"

"Both, I guess."

"Okay, if Holly is innocent, who could have pulled the old switcheroo?" Cookie posed the question. She was almost as compulsive about solving puzzles as Maddy Madison. Every day she tackled *The New York Times* crosswords, unable to go to bed at night until she'd completed every square.

"Henry Caruthers," said Aggie.

"What makes you say that?" Lizzie played along, amused by the girl's tenacity.

"He took Mrs. Beanie's keys, so he probably stole your quilt. And Holly Everlast – "

"Eberhard," Cookie corrected.

" – Eberhard was his cousin, so he could have paid her a visit and switched the two."

"But Henry Caruthers left a note in your grandmother's house claiming he didn't steal the quilt," Bootsie reminded the girl. Not that the police chief's wife actually believed the former mayor to be innocent.

"Maybe he was telling a fib," offered eight-year-old N'yen. Maddy had both kids again today. "I sometimes tell fibs when I don't wanna get caught."

"Now there's a theory I can buy into," said Lizzie. She'd never truly liked Lefty Caruthers. He'd acted like a total jerk back in high school, when they sat next to each other in English class. She remembered him passing her notes with obscene suggestions. Just because he was the hotshot pitcher on the baseball team, he thought he could get away with murder. The nerve of that guy!

"Let's think through this logically," suggested Maddy. "We know Nan Beanie arranged for Henry Caruthers to take her office keys. She admitted as much. We know the beehive quilt disappeared from the locked conference room. There were only three sets of keys – Nan's, Beau's, and Jim's. If we agree that neither my husband nor Bootsie's stole the quilt, that leaves Henry because he had Nan's keys."

"So Henry's a crook. But what about Holly?" Liz was still having trouble believing her quilting idol could have been involved in a heist.

"Holly was commissioned to sew three replica quilts. One of them – we can tell by the matching thread – was substituted for our quilt. Not just anyone would have known about her assignment to create duplicates or had access to them. But Henry Caruthers, who was Holly's cousin, might have."

"So either she was in league with Mr. Caruthers or he stole her fake quilt on his own, then substituted the real one," said Aggie. Seemed a simple one-or-the-other to her.

"Where does this guy Kramer fit in?" asked Cookie. It was all so confusing.

"We know about him because of that to-do list of Nan's we found. He ran a quilting store in Indianapolis. Maybe he was going to help them sell the quilt or planned to buy it for himself."

"I figured Nan was going to run off with Henry," said Bootsie. "She worked for him all those years, maybe fell for him. But it looks like she left the country with this Kramer guy instead."

"I don't get that part either," nodded Cookie.

"If we found Henry, we could ask him," said Maddy.

CHAPTER TWENTY-ONE

Stakeout at the Rooming House

Cookie checked the town's property records. Henry Caruthers had owned a home on Field Hand Road for twenty-seven years. Never having married, he lived alone. The records showed he also owned a tract of farmland east of town that he leased to a farmer named Cassidy for growing corn. And he also had a part interest in a rooming house over on Fourth Street.

"Jim has already checked out Henry's house," said Bootsie. "He's definitely not there."

"I drove out to that big cornfield," reported Lizzie. "There's no house there, just stalks of corn."

"What about the rooming house?" asked Maddy.

"He co-owns it with Holly's mother." Cookie held up a copy of the deed.

"Must not be a very profitable operation," mused Maddy. "Mrs. Lazynski doesn't seem to have two nickels to rub together."

"Her daughter isn't doing so bad," noted Cookie. "I read in the paper she's getting a two-million dollar settlement in her divorce."

"Apparently she married well," commented Bootsie,

an edge of sarcasm in her remark.

"What's the name of that rooming house on Fourth Street?" asked Maddy.

"Mrs. Fogerty's," Cookie read off the name.

"Who's this Mrs. Fogerty?" Bootsie wanted to know.

"Deceased. Apparently Henry bought the property from her estate about ten years ago."

"Maybe Henry keeps a room there," Maddy speculated. "What say we go pay Mrs. Fogerty a visit?"

≈ ≈ ≈

The rooming house was an old pre-war brick home that had been subdivided into four apartments. The names on the mailboxes identified the residents as T. Kelly, D. Birmingham, M. Martin, and N. Jacz, all neatly typed.

"Wait a minute," said Cookie as she studied the mailboxes. "Jacz was Nancy Beanie's maiden name."

"How do you know that?" asked Bootsie, impressed.

"I recall when she married Jasper Beanie, people joked that she'd gone from Jack's to the Beanstalk – a play on her names."

"Are you saying Nan Beanie has an apartment here?" Lizzie asked.

"Maybe it's a love nest," said Bootsie, back to her theory that Nan Beanie and the former mayor had something romantic going.

"Henry owns the building," Maddy agreed. "It would've been simple to set aside a room for himself and his lady friend."

"We think Nan's in Canada," Cookie mused. "But are you saying Henry could be hiding up there in Apartment 4?"

"Let's go look," suggested Lizzie. This was almost as good as reading about Britney Spears in a supermarket tabloid.

"Maybe we should be cautious," Maddy said. "Stake the place out until we see him come in or go out."

"Why not just call Jim and have him come over with all his deputies?" Bootsie offered another approach.

"He only has two deputies," Lizzie pointed out. "Not exactly an army."

"That's three counting Jim, How many is it going to take to arrest a puny little guy like Henry Caruthers."

"We should make sure he's here before we call Jim and his deputies," advised Maddy. "It would be embarrassing if it turned out to be a false alarm."

"I think Maddy's right," said Cookie. "Henry may not be in there right now. If Jim pulls up with siren blaring, it could scare him away. We might never see that little weasel again."

"Good riddance," offered Lizzie.

"Yes, but Henry's the one who can explain this mystery to us."

"Okay, but I'm not going to hide in the bushes waiting for Henry to show up. I don't even go camping with Edgar if I can avoid it."

"We'll park the car up the street," suggested Maddy. "We can keep an eye on the front door from there."

"What if I have to go to the bathroom," Lizzie hesitated. She had a weak bladder, all her friends knew that.

"The Exxon station's one block over," Maddy reassured her. "They keep their restrooms nice and clean."

"I hope this doesn't take all day," grumbled Cookie. "I have a hair appointment at three-thirty." Now that she was married to Ben Bentley, she'd been paying more attention to her looks. Her naturally gray locks looked good in a frosty shade of blonde.

"You hair looks fine."

"I can't cancel my appointment. My hairdresser was supposed to have today off, but I talked her into coming in this afternoon."

"Okay," capitulated Maddy. "We'll keep watch 'til three o'clock. If he doesn't show up by then, we'll turn the matter over to Chief Purdue."

≈ ≈ ≈

At precisely 3 p.m. Henry Caruthers strolled down the sidewalk and entered the rooming house. Maddy had her hand on the ignition, ready to call it a day when Cookie pointed and said, "There he is!"

"Goodness, you were right," Bootsie admitted. "Now let's call Jim to come arrest him."

"Why don't we go talk with him first," proposed Maddy. "I'd like to hear what he has to say."

"What if he tries to get away?"

"Or gets violent?"

"There are four of us," said Maddy. "I don't think he'll try anything with all of us there."

"Let's hope you're right," muttered Lizzie. "I haven't been in a fight since high school."

"You were in a fight?"

"A girl said my red hair made me look like Bozo the Clown. I decked her."

"No kidding? You knocked her down?"

Lizzie giggled. "Knocked her down and poured a bottle of ink over her head. I got two days suspension. I'm surprised you don't remember."

Bootsie said, "I once got suspended for turning on the gas in the Bunsen burner before chemistry class began. When ol' Mr. Pinkus struck a match to light it, there was this explosion that took off his eyebrows."

"I remember that," Cookie laughed. "You got kicked out for two weeks. And your mother wouldn't let you go to the prom."

"Just as well. I didn't have a date. Jim took Judy Jankowitz, as I recall."

"Didn't Judy marry a doctor?"

"A veterinarian. Almost the same thing."

Maddy glared at her friends. "Are we going to talk with Henry Caruthers, or sit here and reminisce about high school?" She knew they were stalling, probably nervous about confronting a criminal on the lam.

"Oh piffle, I guess we're going to go nab ol' Henry," sighed Cookie Bentley, knowing she was likely to miss her hair appointment.

CHAPTER TWENTY-TWO

Henry on the Spot

Knock! Knock!

"Who's there?" came the former mayor's squeaky voice.

"It's Maddy Madison. Don't bother climbing out the window, Henry. The building's surrounded by cops," she lied.

"Dang."

"Open up. It's not polite to keep guests standing in the hallway."

She heard the deadbolt lock turning. "Come on in, if you insist," the voice invited. "I want to hear how you found me."

"Nan told me," she responded blithely. *Liar, liar, pants on fire!*

"Dang," he repeated. "I can't believe she turned me in after all we've meant to each other."

The door swung open. Henry Caruthers stared at the four women standing on his doorstep. "See you didn't come alone. Where are the cops?"

"Outside."

"Oh well, I knew this wasn't going to work out. This

town's too small to hide out here forever. Somebody was bound to spot me sooner or later."

"As it turned out, sooner."

"I left you a note saying I didn't steal that quilt," he frowned at Maddy. "That's the Lord's truth. It was all Lydia Lazynski's doing."

"Holly Eberhard's mother?" Maddy threw Holly's name out there to gauge his reaction. He didn't blink.

"Yeah, Lydia's my aunt. That ol' witch is the one who snatched that stupid quilt and substituted her daughter's handiwork."

That made some sense, Maddy thought. Lydia Lazynski had access to her daughter's quilt trunk, stored there in her guest bedroom. "That's your story?" replied Maddy as if she didn't believe a word of it. "Surely you can do better than that."

"It's the truth. Didn't I tell you so in that note?"

Maddy sat down in an easy chair. She recognized it as the brand made at the chair factory on the other side of town. "Your note wasn't long on detail."

"Like I say, Lydia did it. She saw those copies Holly was doing, then read in the *Gazette* about them Pennington quilts being exhibited during Watermelon Days. All she had to do was swap 'em."

"That's a pretty story. But how did she get the keys?"

"From me. But it wasn't like you think. Nan let me snatch those keys so I could get into Beau's office. There were some papers in the filing cabinet I needed to get my hands on. A few contributions from land developers that might have been embarrassing."

"Proof of your kickbacks," translated Cookie.

"Call it what you like. I went over to Lydia's for dinner one night. I think she stole the keys outta my coat pocket. Or maybe I dropped 'em. Them keys were tagged, didn't take a genius to figure out which doors they opened."

"If you and Nan Beanie weren't in this together, why did she run?" pressed Bootsie. You could tell she wasn't buying his story easily.

"Guess you've figured out she was my girlfriend. This apartment's where we'd meet after hours. She knew about those, uh, contributions from developers. That's why she helped me get the keys. When you found out about her doing that, she was afraid she'd get arrested for being in on those little financial transactions."

"Why didn't she just take those papers out of the files for you?" asked Maddy.

"Your husband didn't let her into that big filing cabinet in his office. No telling what *he* was hiding in there."

"He stores his lunch in there. I pack him a brown bag after day."

Henry glanced at the window. "Are the cops really out there?"

"Don't even think about running," warned Bootsie. "Jim will shoot you down like a dog."

"I was just asking."

Lizzie had a question. "If you and Nan weren't in on the plan to steal the quilt, how come she bought bus tickets to Indy and rented a hotel room there?"

"Surely a woman of the world like you, Lizzie Ridenour, can figure that out. We were going to Indy for a romantic weekend. Can't very well take her out on the town here in Caruthers Corners. Tongues would be wagging."

"Oh yeah?" said Cookie. "How do you explain that fence?"

"What fence? You mean the picket fence I installed at my house on Field Hand Road?"

"No, I mean that man Kramer who was going to help you sell the stolen quilt."

"Robert Kramer? Ha! He's Nan's brother. Changed his name from Jacz so he wouldn't sound so Slavic. Said he got it off some TV show."

"*Seinfeld.*"

"Who?"

"Why did he go to Canada?"

"He accompanied Nan to Vancouver 'cause she was afraid to travel alone."

"I heard he wasn't coming back," said Maddy.

"Who knows? He's been wanting to retire for years. Man's in his late sixties. Nan was the baby in the family."

"They're from Canada?" asked Cookie. "I though Nan grew up in Caruthers Corners."

"Family moved here when she was five. Kramer was fourteen. Another brother, the first-born, stayed behind in Vancouver. Still up there, I'm told."

"All this is a pretty story," challenged Maddy. "But I'd like to see you prove it."

"I don't have to. Send Jim Purdue over to talk with Lydia. Tell her you got the goods on her and she'll crumble quicker'n a granola bar."

CHAPTER TWENTY-THREE

Confession Is Good for the Soul

Lydia Lazynski was a mousy woman, hardly the image you'd expect of a master criminal. And you would be stretching the point to call her that. She was more of a criminal opportunist, someone who stole when the occasion presented itself.

Her biggest score in the past was taking $46.27 from the tithing box at that church with the pointed spire over on Second Street. Another time she'd filched a $10 bill that had been left as a tip at the Cozy Café. So the idea of stealing a $40,000 quilt stitched by Sarah Connors Pennington wasn't included in her master plans. However, the opportunity to do so simply fell into place when her daughter showed up with those replicas.

She knew something about quilts, her daughter being State Quilting Bee Champion and all. But it took her daughter's getting a commission to make duplicates of the Pennington quilts and that old fool of a cousin dropping his keys to the Town Hall to provide her with the unexpected means to pull a switcheroo.

As a matter of fact, she'd intended to switch all three replicas, one by one, giving her a haul totaling better than a hundred grand. Even if she sold them for half that amount, it would provide a nice little nest egg for her retirement. It was becoming clear that spoiled daughter wasn't going to take care of Lydia in her old age.

Holly was much too wrapped up in her own success as Quilting Queen to think about others. Wasn't that why her husband was dumping her? She'd been a selfish child and was now a selfish adult, in her mother's opinion.

Trick would be getting these authentic quilts away from Holly after the switches were made. It'd have to happen before her daughter went back to Bloomington, for once the replicas were completed they would be shipped off to the Smithsonian. With two of the three already finished, the clock was ticking.

Tonight, while her daughter was attending that Watermelon Days meeting, Lydia planned to go down to the Town Hall, keys jangling in her purse, and swap a second quilt, the one with that blue-sky white-cloud design. She carefully took Holly's copycat quilt out of the storage trunk and spread it out on the bed. Looking at it, she had to admit her daughter was talented.

Lydia had already made overtures at finding a buyer for the trio of stolen quilts, having contacted Nan Beanie's brother who ran a sewing notions shop in Indianapolis. He hadn't said *yes*, but he hadn't said *no* either.

Robert Kramer was no fool, Lydia assured herself. He wouldn't walk away from the chance to make a quick fifty grand or more. Dishonest people think like that, assuming that everyone else has the same degree of larceny running in his or her veins.

And now that Maddy Madison and her lawyer son-in-law had discovered the first switch, Lydia didn't have any time left. Having the keys, she could grab the remaining quilts from the Town Hall's conference room and forget about replacing them with replicas.

She was standing there, tracing her fingers along the blue fabric, feeling its texture, admiring the simplicity of the quilt's design, when she heard the doorbell. Darn it, she hated salespeople, missionaries, and kids selling Girl Scout cookies coming uninvited to her door. Privacy was important, she told herself. Especially when you were in the middle of the biggest robbery Caruthers Corners had ever experienced.

Padding to the front door in her bathrobe, she threw it open and shouted her constant mantra: "No solicitors – go away!"

Chief Jim Purdue said, "Don't think you could rightly call me a solicitor, Lydia. May I come in?" Before she could refuse, he added, "Police business, ma'am."

At that moment, Lydia intuited that the jig was up. Instead of her Golden Years spent in a condo in Florida, she would be stuck behind bars at Indiana State Prison up in Michigan City. "How'd you catch me?" she asked. "Did my ungrateful daughter turn me in?"

"No ma'am. It was your cousin Henry."

"That rat! I used to baby-sit him when he was a snotty little boy. I shoulda dropped him on his head back then."

"So you admit you stole the Pennington quilt?"

"May as well. That nosy Madison woman and her lawyer already figured out the real one was here. I 'spect she tipped you off, huh?"

"That's right, ma'am."

"Hmph," Lydia Lazynski grunted. "I never shoulda voted for her husband."

≈ ≈ ≈

"So Henry Caruthers was telling the truth?" said Cookie.

"Apparently so," replied Maddy as she sliced a fresh batch of gingerbread. Aggie and N'yen were hovering nearby, awaiting a helping while it was still warm from the oven.

"First time for everything," commented Lizzie.

Bootsie was pouring milk for the children. "Jim says Henry's getting off scot-free. He did take the keys from Nan's desk drawer, but lost them before he had a chance to break into Beau's office and retrieve those incriminating documents from the file cabinet."

"Yes, but what about those papers?" asked Maddy. "Don't they give Jim enough evidence to arrest him for taking kickbacks?"

Bootsie shook her head. "Seems our husbands have decided to sweep that particular mess under the rug. Bad for the town's image."

"I don't know if I agree with that," said Maddy.

"Don't think our opinion is being solicited. The town council met this morning and took a vote."

"Oh well."

"What's happening with Nan Beanie?" asked Cookie as she passed out colorful carnival plates for the gingerbread.

Maddy used the cake spatula to deliver fat slices to each plate. "I hear she's coming home, subject to Beau's promise he won't file charges against her. And Jasper's taking her back, forgive and forget."

Bootsie added, "Jim says her brother flew back this morning after faxing the police department a letter from Lydia Lazynski offering to sell him the quilts. He claims that he wanted no part of it and has agreed to testify against her."

"How about Holly Eberhard?" inquired Lizzie. "I'll bet she's steamed about being arrested."

Bootsie shrugged. "Oh, she's threatening to sue the town, sue the police department, sue Maddy, sue the next person who looks at her cross-eyed."

"Mark the Shark tells me not to worry," Maddy interjected. By now everyone was nibbling on the warm gingerbread. The Madison family recipe, handed down through the generations, was a closely guarded secret. Even Bootsie hadn't been able to worm it out of Maddy, despite years of trying.

"So will her mother go to jail?" asked Cookie. Surely somebody in this criminal affair was guilty of something.

Maddy understood her friend's frustration. She shared it herself. "Lydia Lazynski will probably do some jail time. But given her age and no prior record, Mark says she'll probably get off with six months plus probation."

"I'd do six months for a hundred thousand dollars in rare quilts," joked Lizzie.

"Keep in mind, Lydia doesn't get to keep the quilt she stole. In fact, Marks says she'll probably lose her house after all the legal bills."

"Why doesn't her daughter help her?" said Lizzie, a little disillusioned with Holly Eberhard. "*Caruthers Corners Gazette* says she's getting two million dollars in her divorce settlement. That should cover quite a few legal bills."

Maddy shrugged. "Unfortunately for Lydia, she raised an ungrateful daughter."

"More please," said N'yen, holding out his plate like the waif in a Charles Dickens story. For an eight-year-old kid, he could certainly pack it away.

"Yes, more," Aggie chimed in, but her first slice wasn't finished. She was just trying to keep up with her new cousin. The Boy with the Bottomless Pit, his new mom called him.

"How do you like having a sister, honey?" asked Cookie.

Aggie grinned, mouth covered with gooey frosting. "She's too little to play with. I like N'yen better for now."

"She'll grow up before you know it," said Lizzie, who still felt competitive with her younger sister who lived in Burpyville. "Enjoy the peace and quiet while you can."

"Quiet?" said Aggie. "She cries all the time."

"A colicky baby," Maddy explained as she sliced a piece of gingerbread for herself. The knife cut through it like butter. The secret was in using buttermilk rather than regular milk.

"Well, at least the mystery is solved," said Bootsie.

"And the Smithsonian will get back all its original quilts," Cookie sighed with relief.

"Plus the State's Quilting Bee Committee has agreed to use our Watermelon Days contest as a First Round in its official competition," Lizzie said proudly. As the likely winner again this year, that meant she'd be going to Indy for the Finals.

"Best of all," said Maddy Madison, "this week my family increased by two!"

CHAPTER TWENTY-FOUR

Wrapping Up the Quilt Mystery

Bill and Kathy were heading back to Chicago today. Tillie and Mark the Shark had come over to Melon Picker Row to say goodbye to them. Aggie was holding the new baby very carefully, as if the tiny entity were a fragile China doll. Beau had wandered off somewhere, but that was par for the course.

"I can't tell you what a great visit this has been," said Bill, hugging his mother.

"Yes, it has," agreed Kathy, lining up for her hug. She liked being a part of this ungainly, something-always-happening family.

"We're so happy for you children, having a child of your own now. I know that's what you've always wanted."

"N'yen is such a wonderful boy," smiled Kathy.

"Where is N'yen?" asked Bill, looking around with a slightly worried expression crossing his chiseled face.

"He was here just a few minutes ago," said Mark.

"Maybe he's in the backyard looking for fireflies," suggested Aggie, still holding her baby sister.

"Fireflies? It's ten o'clock in the morning," said her mother, keeping an eye on the baby.

"N'yen doesn't know they only come out at night," giggled Aggie. Her joke on a new cousin.

"Let me go check," said Maddy. "You guys can be putting your bags in the car."

"Sure, mom." Bill gave her a wink. He knew everything would be under control with his mother on the case.

Maddy walked through the kitchen to the sliding glass doors. You could see the goldfish pond at the far end of the backyard, hints of red and gold swirling beneath the surface. There on the bank was her husband, the small Vietnamese boy at his side. Their words carried across the open expanse of the yard."

"Gee whiz, Grampy, look at the fish."

"Next time you come to visit, the two of us will go fishing. I know a great spot on the river where the catfish are as big as sharks."

"Oh boy, I'd like that, Grampy. You promise?"

"Count on it, young man. I'm going to teach you to hike and camp and fish. We're gonna have us a grand old time."

Maddy slipped back into the house, unseen by the man and boy. She couldn't help but smile, knowing that everything was right with the world.

"Hmm," she said to herself. "Maybe I'll start me a new quilt today." She always liked sewing on a quilt when she was happy.

✿ ✿ ✿

Coming Unraveled

Unraveled

A Quilters Club Mystery

3

A day patched with quilting seldom unravels.

- Anonymous

CHAPTER ONE

The Lost Boys

Maddy Madison had heard the story for years, how three boys disappeared back in 1982 in the Never Ending Swamp, 400 acres of bog, primeval trees, tangled brush, and deadly quicksand, located just north of Caruthers Corners on Highway 102. Parents still told the story to their children as a cautionary tale.

The missing youths – Harry Periwinkle, Jud Watson, and Bobby Ray Purdue – had been 12 at the time, sixth graders at Madison Elementary. They were last seen hiking across Edwin Baumgartner's pasture, a grassy expanse that abuts Never Ending Swamp on its southern perimeter.

Maddy's husband Beauregard Madison was the current mayor of Caruthers Corners. And every time she visited his office at the Town Hall she saw the small bronze plaque that dedicated the building to the memory of that trio commonly referred to as The Lost Boys.

A squib in the *Burpyville Gazette* noting that this was the 30th Anniversary of the disappearance caught Maddy's attention.

At the weekly meeting of the Quilters Club, which took place on Tuesdays in the Hoosier State Senior Recreation

Center, Maddy raised the question to her three BFF's. "What do you suppose happened to those poor boys?"

"Probably stepped in a pool of quicksand," shrugged Liz Ridenour. "Died an agonizing death, no doubt." The redhead tended to be somewhat dramatic.

"Mostly likely they got disoriented in the swamp and died of starvation," posited Cookie Bentley. Being the town historian, she was more practical in her viewpoints.

"Some people think they ran away, went to Indianapolis," shrugged Bootsie Purdue. Her husband Jim was related to one of the boys. "But Bobby Ray's mother hasn't received a single postcard in thirty years so I agree with Cookie."

"The park service ought to drain that ol' swamp," said Maddy as she sorted out her quilting squares. "It's a public nuisance."

"It's a watershed area," Lizzie pointed out. "No one is going to touch it."

Cookie added, "When the first pioneers arrived, more than 80% of Indiana was covered with forest. Now only 17% of the state is considered forested. Nobody's going to cut down those trees."

"Nobody goes in there anymore. Not even hunters," replied Bootsie. "Those boys are the only recorded deaths in fifty years, so the state doesn't consider it much of a hazard." Her husband was the police chief, so she knew about those things.

"Guess it doesn't really matter whether it was quicksand, starvation, or bears," said Maddy, "those poor boys are still dead."

But they weren't. At least, one of them wasn't.

≈ ≈ ≈

The stocky man who presented himself to Chief Jim Purdue at the Caruthers Corners Police Department shook the chief's hand and announced, "I'm your cousin Bobby Ray."

Suspicious by nature, a trait reinforced by twelve years as a lawman, Chief Purdue snorted, "Like hell you are."

But his visitor was adamant. "My daddy's your daddy's brother. Me and your younger brother went to school together. I've been to your family's house for dinner when I was little."

"What's your daddy's middle name," snapped Jim. He'd learned that you could trip crooks up by clever questioning.

"Manfred," the stranger replied without hesitation. Right, as it turned out.

"What was your dog's name?"

"Bowser." The man shrugged. "I s'pect he's long dead after thirty years."

Jim Purdue paused. "Yeah, I remember that old mutt. He was good at digging muskrats out of the river bank."

"That's right," said the stranger. "Me and Harry and Jud used to play along the Wabash. We should've taken Bowser with us on that hike to Never Ending Swamp. It might have turned out different. That dog sure had a good sense of direction."

The police chief decided to take a different tack. "So you boys got lost in the swamp?"

"Did we ever."

"But you obviously found your way out. How come nobody ever heard from you boys again?"

"Oh, we became pirates. Sailing under a black flag."

That's when Bootsie's husband decided that this returned-from-the-dead Lost Boy was totally mad. Pirates? Black flag? They were in the middle of Indiana, for God's sake – not a drop of ocean to be found for 680 miles.

"Hang on. I've got to make a call."

"Sure, I'm not going anywhere."

The police chief dialed the familiar number. "Hello, Beau," he spoke loudly into the phone. "Get your skinny butt over to the police station. I've got somebody you'll sure as heck want to meet."

≈ ≈ ≈

Beauregard Hollingsworth Madison IV was descended from one of the founders of Caruthers Corners, a wily fur trapper who stayed on after his wagon train broke down in "Indiana territory." Even though the state took its name from the Indians, there are fewer than 8,000 Native Americans living here today.

Beau had been elected mayor after the previous officeholder had been run out of town for financial improprieties. He was now in his second term. People said he was doing a good job, which meant he let things coast along without any mishaps.

The mayor was huffing and puffing as he walked into the boxy redbrick building that housed the Caruthers Corners Police Department. He was still in his shirtsleeves, tie askance, looking a bit wild-eyed. "One of the Lost Boys turned up?" he greeted his best friend.

"That's what the fellow claims," responded Jim Purdue. "Of course, he also professes to be a pirate."

"A what –?"

"You know, like Blackbeard. A seafaring buccaneer."

"That's ridiculous," sputtered Beau. "There aren't any pirates these days. Well, maybe over in Somalia. But not here in Indiana. The man must be insane."

"My thoughts exactly," nodded the police chief. "But this thing about being one of the Lost Boys requires some sorting out."

"What's to sort?"

"Well, he knows a lot of stuff that only my cousin Bobby Ray would know. Like his old dog's name."

"Anybody around here might remember that. Boner, I think it was."

"Bowser," corrected the police chief.

"Boner, Bowser, it doesn't make any different. Your cousin's been dead for thirty years."

"Twenty-three," smiled Jim. "The family had to wait seven years to have him declared legally dead."

"So what else does this guy know?"

"He remembers coming to my family's house for Sunday dinner when he was a boy. Described the dining room right down to the mahogany table and the breakfront with its Blue Willow China."

"Plenty of people have been to dinner at your mama and daddy's house out on Melon Rind Road."

"Not lately. That house burnt down in 1988, just six years after them boys went marching off to the Never Ending Swamp."

"So what? He's gotta be a fake. You don't just disappear for thirty years and then turn up like you've been out for a stroll."

"My thoughts exactly. But that raised another question – if he ain't Bobby Ray Purdue, then who the hell is he?"

CHAPTER TWO

Return of the Prodigal Son

Maddy and Beau had three grown children – all happily married, she'd be pleased to report. Bill – the oldest – and his wife Kathy lived in Chicago with adopted son N'yen. Freddie and his wife Amanda lived in Atlanta, where he was a decorated fireman. And Tilly and her lawyer-husband Mark "the Shark" Tidemore had moved back to Caruthers Corners with daughter Agnes two years ago. Then had another, little Taylor.

Twelve-year-old Aggie was an unofficial member of the Quilters Club. She was getting pretty good at making patchwork quilts, having just completed her third.

The Quilters Club was all abuzz about the appearance of Bobby Ray Purdue (or a guy claiming to be the missing hiker). It was a hot topic all over town, especially once the FBI got involved. Never Ending Swamp was close enough to the Ohio border to presume it might have been an interstate kidnapping.

An Associated Press story fuelled the flames:

'Lost Boy' Re-Appears After Three Decades

AP - Thirty years ago three Indiana boys went missing, thought to have been lost in a large marshy expanse known as the Never Ending Swamp. Bobby Ray

Purdue and his two companions Jed Watson and Harry Periwinkle disappeared on August 12, 1982, while hiking near the public land. Despite the posted No Trespassing signs, it is thought the trio wandered into the area known for its quicksand, poisonous snakes, and sightings of bears. But now, someone claiming to be Bobby Ray has turned up. A grown man with a full beard, he says he became "a pirate." Other than that, the mystery man has refused to make any further statements to the FBI ....

Everybody was asking Maddy Madison's opinion on the matter, as her son-in-law Mark had been appointed by Judge Cramer to represent the claimant. Turns out, Bobby Ray Purdue's father had left him half-ownership of the E Z Seat chair factory, the largest single employer in Caruthers Corners. The other half had gone to an older brother, Newcomb Lamont Purdue – commonly known as N.L. And he, of course, was contesting the pretender's identity.

Bootsie got lots of questions too, being a member of the Purdue clan. But she said she couldn't comment due to the impending lawsuit. N.L. was peeved that Mark Tidemore had taken the case, even though it had been by a court appointment.

Liz didn't let that stop her. She loved good gossip. It was she who reported that a DNA test was planned, a move that would scientifically settle the identity question. Her retired banker hubby happened to be on the board of a hospital over in Burpyville, the facility where the test was taking place.

"What's DNA?" asked Aggie. She was a precocious young lady, a straight-A student at Madison Elementary.

"That's deoxyribonucleic acid," answered Cookie, the Brainiac in the group. "It's a material in your body that is unique to you and you alone, what they call a 'genetic marker.' "

"Oh."

"That should settle the matter," nodded Lizzie, red hair bouncing with the energetic motion. She was a gaunt woman, her expression a little pinched, but you could tell she'd been a beauty in her day.

"N.L. is paying for the test," Bootsie broke her silence. Her rounded features made her look like a vintage Baby Huggums doll. "He is convinced the guy's an imposter."

"Why is he so certain?" asked Maddy.

"The eyes. This guy has brown eyes. His brother had blue."

"If he's a fake, will he be in trouble?" Cookie asked the police chief's wife.

Bootsie nodded. "N.L. plans to press charges. Jim will have to arrest him for trying to swindle N.L. out of half of E Z Seat. If he doesn't arrest the guy, we'll never get invited to another Purdue family dinner."

Being the wealthiest man in town, Newcomb Lamont Purdue ruled family members like an Arab potentate overseeing his tribe. He'd hired L. Wainscott Gabney as his lawyer. A senior partner of the Indianapolis law firm of Preston, Whitney & Gabney, he had a reputation for winning cases involving fraud and other white-collar crimes.

Mark Tidemore was going to have a tough time keeping his client out of jail if the DNA backed up N.L.'s accusation.

≈ ≈ ≈

As it turned out, Maddy and Beau Madison didn't learn the results of the DNA test until much later. Their son Freddie was badly burned in an Atlanta apartment house fire while rescuing a two-year-old girl trapped on the third floor. Doctors gave him a fifty-fifty chance of surviving the second-degree burns that covered 30% of his body.

Maddy spent a month at her son's bedside, with Beau commuting back-and-forth to Indiana. The town needed its mayor.

When Freddie was finally released from the Northside Atlanta Burn Center, she brought him and Amanda back to Caruthers Corner to recuperate. It would be a long and painful process.

The Atlanta Fire Rescue Department had pensioned Frederic Hollingsworth Madison out on full disability as well as giving him a medal for his bravery. Founded in 1882, the AFRD protects an area of approximately 132 square miles. Freddie Madison had been assigned to Battalion 6's Engine 27.

Fellow firefighters of Battalion 6 chipped in and bought him a 60" Magnavox HDTV as a retirement present. Maddy had shipped it to Indiana and installed it in his old bedroom in the Victorian home on Mellon Pickers Drive.

"Thanks, Mom," Freddie said as his mother brought another serving of watermelon pie to his room. It had been a favorite of his since childhood. The Caruthers Corners Watermelon Festival had been an annual highlight for him.

"Just lay back and relax till you're feeling better,"

Maddy said. "You and Amanda are welcome to stay as long as you want. Forever would be about right for me and your dad."

"You're going to get sick of living with the Phantom of the Opera. I'll scare the neighborhood children." The fire had left Freddie's face looking like melted wax.

"Don't be silly. You're the same guy that won the regional wrestling championship for Caruthers Corners High. And the winner of the greased pig competition at the 1999 Watermelon Festival."

"Back then they called me Fantastic Freddie. But now it'll likely be Freddie Krueger."

"Oh shush. No feeling sorry for yourself. You're alive. And so is that two-year-old girl."

"Donna Ann Maypole, that's her name. Too bad her mother didn't survive the fire. She handed me her child and said, 'Save her, don't worry about me.' Then she was swallowed by flames."

"What will happen to that little girl. Is there a family?"

"No, her mother was all alone. Her father died in a car accident about a year ago."

"That's a shame."

"Amanda and I are talking about adopting her. She has no one. And we need someone."

"Would the state let you?"

"The fire chief says he can pull some strings. Maybe."

"We'd welcome a granddaughter."

"Amanda plans to go back to teaching. I'd become Mr. Mom. After all, nobody's going to hire a scarred-up goblin like me."

"You're disabled, hon. Your body may never be quite

the same. You can't go back to work for a long time – if ever."

"I know. But it's hard to get used to. I was always the athletic one of the Madisons. Bill was a bookworm. Tilly a dainty little social butterfly."

"Your prowess served its purpose. You saved that little girl's life."

"You should have seen me, Mom. I jumped from that burning apartment building onto the roof of the grocery store next door, that kid in my arms, my hair on fire. The guys on my truck said I looked like a superhero character, the Flaming Skull."

"Oh my."

"And I'd do it over again in a heartbeat."

"Yes, Freddie, I'm sure you would."

CHAPTER THREE

The DNA Test

"**D**on't expect to get invited to the Purdue Family's Labor Day picnic," said Mark Tidemore over dinner that Saturday night. Beau Madison was doing steaks on the backyard grill, complete with his famous sauce made with a secret blend of Tabasco and Jack Daniels.

"Whatever do you mean?" said Maddy. "Jim and Bootsie always ask us over to Purdue Park." A grassy area behind the E Z Seat factory had been donated to the town as a recreation area. The Purdue clan threw a big picnic there on the first Monday of every September. It was a family tradition.

"Guess you haven't heard. The DNA test proved Bobby Ray is who he claims to be. So he's going to wind up owning half of E Z Seat. Ol' N.L. isn't too happy about it."

"What does that have to do with us?" asked Beauregard as he basted the sizzling T-bones.

"N.L. seems to blame me, being Bobby Ray's lawyer. And everyone related to me."

"But you were court-appointed. You didn't have any choice. You had to take the case."

"Tell that to N.L. He's on the warpath."

Maddy had been mixing a summer corn salad, but she

paused at her son-in-law's words. "The DNA test was positive? But how can that be? This stranger's eyes are brown and Bobby Ray's were blue."

"Apparently not. DNA doesn't lie."

"Maybe the family is confused about his eye color," suggested Freddie's wife Amanda. "After all, it'd been thirty years since they last saw him."

"N.L. might get it wrong," said Maddy. "But his mother would remember."

"Not necessarily," interjected Beau as he flipped the steaks. "Everybody knows Maud Purdue's getting senile. Last month she went out to get the mail from her mailbox and wound up at the Dollar General on Main Street."

"So what's this Bobby Ray's story?" asked Freddie. A little out of the loop, he'd been recuperating at the Northside Atlanta Burn Center when the return of the Lost Boy was making headline news.

"Don't know," shrugged Mark the Shark. "He refuses to talk."

"Didn't he claim to have been a pirate?" remembered Tilly. She was setting the patio table with her mother's antique carnival glass plates. Aggie was helping.

"He said something about that before he clammed up," nodded her husband. "What he told Chief Purdue is all we know. He refused to say a word to the FBI. On my advice."

"But what did he tell you?" asked Maddy.

"Privileged conversation," said Mark. "I couldn't tell you what he said ... if he had."

"You mean he didn't give you a hint about what he'd been up to for the past thirty years?" asked Amanda, intrigued by this modern-day mystery.

"Not a clue. Just repeated his claim that he was Bobby Ray Purdue."

"But the DNA showed he was telling the truth," persisted Amanda. "Isn't his family happy to have him back?"

"Apparently they don't believe the test. N.L. says it was obviously contaminated. He's going to bring in another expert to retest the DNA."

"Why doesn't N.L. accept unassailable scientific proof?" Beau shook his head. "Those folks down at the Burpyville hospital know their stuff."

"Because ol' N.L.'s got his head up his –"

"Mark!" his wife stopped him midsentence. "Little ears," she said, nodding toward their daughter Agnes, busily placing silverware on the patio table.

"Oh, sorry," he smiled sheepishly.

"Don't worry, Daddy," grinned little Aggie. "I know where the sun doesn't shine."

≈ ≈ ≈

The next morning after church services, Maddy Madison paused on the steps of Peaceful Meadows to share the conversation about the Lost Boy with her pal Cookie Bentley.

The trim brunette simply rolled her eyes. "Really, hon, that's last week's news," she told her friend. "Everybody in the entire state has heard about the results of the DNA test by now. It was an above-the-fold headline in the *Indianapolis Star* this morning."

"Oh."

"Now if we knew what actually happened to those Lost Boys, that would be Breaking News."

"According to Mark, Bobby Ray refuses to say."

"Then we have to find out."

"Yes," nodded Maddy, "that's a good assignment for the Quilters Club."

≈≈≈

At that very moment the man proven to be Bobby Ray Purdue was meeting with Shorty Yosterman at his house on Jinks Lane. Mad Malcolm Yosterman had passed away last year (an allergic reaction to a bee sting), leaving the house to his only son. Now 42-years-old, Shorty (né Malcolm Jr.) had gone to school with the three Lost Boys.

"Hey there, Shorty. How's it going?" said the bearded man.

"Okay I guess. Whatcha want to see me about?" He eyed his visitor guardedly.

"That ain't no way to greet an old classmate."

"Maybe not. But we're not old classmates. Because you're not Bobby Ray Purdue."

"DNA says otherwise."

Shorty leaned closer as if sharing a secret. "Bobby Ray had blue eyes. I've still got a sixth grade school photo of him. Kept all my annuals and snapshots in a box on my closet shelf. Went through it last week and found a color photo. His eyes were blue."

"Probably the picture faded," shrugged the brown-eyed man.

"Like hell. Now tell me what d'you want from me?"

"Doesn't matter that you don't recognize me. I remember you. Like that time you got in a fight with Roger Moseby and broke his nose. Or the time you shoplifted a Barlow knife from Ace Hardware."

"How'd you know about that pocket knife?"

"I was there, you idiot. I *am* Bobby Ray Purdue."

"Damn. This is so confusing."

"Now listen up, Shorty. I want you to take a message to my mama. She refuses to see me. My brother Newcomb has poisoned her mind about me."

"N.L. doesn't wanna give up half interest in E Z Seat to a stranger claiming to be his brother."

"I told you I ain't no stranger. I'm Bobby Ray."

"If you say so. Now about that note –?"

The bearded man handed him a folded piece of paper. "Here it is. Don't you go reading it. Ain't none of your business. Just see that she gets it. I'll owe you big for this favor."

"If you're Bobby Ray, you still owe me two dollars I loaned you back in 1982. Money to buy a used Schwinn bicycle. I think that bike's still sitting in your mama's barn after all these years."

"Go get it," smirked the man claiming to be Bobby Ray. "You can have it – and we'll call us even."

CHAPTER FOUR

The Man Behind the Mask

"**W**oo," said Aggie, jumping back as she encountered her Uncle Freddie in the hallway at her grandmother's house. "You look scary. Are you always going to wear that mask?"

"It's not a mask," sighed the disfigured man. "I'm always going to look like this. Should be good for Halloween, huh?"

"Does it hurt?"

"Some, but less each day. I have a cream that helps."

"I'm sorry you got hurt, Uncle Freddie."

"Me too, Aggie. But no use crying over split milk."

"I'd cry because my mama would be mad I spilled my milk," she replied innocently. "She doesn't like to clean up after me and the baby too."

"What say you and I go down to the DQ for some custard?" he suggested. "That is if I'm not too scary to be seen with."

"You're scary, but not to me. I'll go ask my mama if it's okay to go. I want a parfait. There's gotta be a cherry on top."

"Sure thing," he grinned, his face feeling like cardboard as the skin tried to wrinkle. He was trying to get used to being seen in public. He couldn't wear a paper bag over his head for the rest of his life. *Here I come, ready or not*, he muttered under his breath.

≈ ≈ ≈

Beau Madison was having a cup of coffee with Chief Purdue at the Cozy Diner. They often met here on weekday afternoons and called it a "Town Council Meeting." Things were slow in this tiny Midwestern hamlet during the summer months. The caffeine got them through the rest of the day.

"What are you going to do about the Lost Boy?" the mayor asked his friend. "Don't like our town being in the national news like this."

"Don't plan to do anything. The DNA test proves he's who he says he is. He hasn't committed any crimes that we know of. So leave him be and the publicity will die down."

"How come he won't tell where he's been for thirty years? Or what happened to his two companions?" Beau added a dollop of sugar to his coffee and stirred it was a slightly-bent spoon.

"His business. Even the FBI has packed up and gone back to Indianapolis."

"D'you think he's covering up something terrible? Like maybe he murdered the other two boys and has been on the run all this time."

"No bodies were ever found. No bones recovered. At the time, volunteers searched Never Ending Swamp pretty thoroughly. I remember my papa telling me the searchers held onto ropes so they wouldn't get separated or lost themselves."

"Hard to do that with all the brambles and trees out there."

"Yes, I expect so. But they didn't turn up a single clue. Not even a footprint."

Beau took a cautious sip. Eunice Miller made the coffee McDonald's-Lawsuit-hot here at the Cozy Café. "How do we know those boys even went into the swamp? Maybe they hopped a freight train to Chicago."

"Ol' man Baumgartner swore that he saw them climbing over the fence that separates his pasture from the swamp. That's all folk had to go on."

"Think he was telling the truth?"

"Why lie about that?" shrugged Jim Purdue, carefully blowing on his coffee. "Besides, that old coot has been dead twenty years now. We'll never know any different."

"So why not just 'fess up, tell us what happened?" He was speaking of Bobby Ray now.

Jim shrugged. "Who knows? Maybe he's planning to write a tell-all book and sell it to some big New York publishing house. He'd make millions."

The mayor nodded. "He just made millions. N.L. signed the papers this morning giving him half ownership of E Z Seat."

"Bet N.L. was gritting his teeth as he did that."

"He wasn't any too happy," said Beau. "My son-in-law was there. Mark said ol' N.L. refused to say one single word to his brother. Just signed the papers, then turned heel and walked out of the room."

"He and his mama – my Aunt Maud – refuse to believe the DNA test. They still think he's a fake."

"Do you?"

"Don't know how you'd fool DNA," said the police chief as he cautiously tasted his coffee. He burned his tongue.

≈≈≈

Bobby Ray – or the guy claiming to be him – phoned Shorty Yosterman that afternoon around 6 p.m. That gave the lanky man time to get home from Pic A Pair, the shoe store on Main Street where he worked as a salesclerk. "Hello?" came Shorty's reedy voice. "Who's calling?"

"It's me, Bobby Ray."

"Says you."

"We've already been through that. Did you deliver the note to my mama?"

"Dropped it off at Sunday night's church service. She wasn't none too happy to get it."

"Did she give you any message?'

"Said she'd be there."

"Thanks."

As he started to hang up, Shorty Yosterman said, "Wait up."

"What?"

"That Schwinn bicycle you said I could have –?"

"Yeah?"

"I went by to look at it on the way to work. Tires are flat."

"That's your problem," the man said as he hung up.

≈≈≈

Aggie and her uncle were seated at the counter inside the DQ. The air conditioning was humming in competition with a Golden Oldie playing on the jukebox – "How Much Is That Doggie In the Window?" by Patti Page.

Aggie was waving a finger like a symphony conductor in time to the music as she spooned her parfait with the other. She liked the song because it reminded her of her dog Tige. She and Tige had great adventures together. Her grandfather was irked because her dog had dug holes in the park across the street from Aggie's house, creating a reseeding project for the City Park Department.

Technically speaking, Caruthers Corners (pop. 2,643) wasn't a city ... and the Park Department consisted of the Gilbert Brothers who had a contract with the mayor's office to look after local parks and trees. Beau Madison had paid for the reseeding out of his own pocket.

Aggie's uncle sat next to her at the counter, slurping on a double cone of strawberry. It was cold to his tongue, a good sign. There had been a period during his recovery when his sense of feeling – particularly temperatures – had been dulled. But the nerves seemed to be healing themselves.

Looking in the mirror that backed the aluminum columns of frozen custard marked VANILLA, STRAWBERRY, CHOCOLATE, and PISTACHIO, Aggie saw a strange reflection. Out in the parking lot was a circus wagon drawn by two white horses. She couldn't read the words printed on the side of the colorful wagon because they were in reverse in the mirror. But she could make out the lion and tiger and bear (oh my!) painted on its side.

"Clown," she said.

"Hey, I don't look that bad," protested Freddie. His medicating cream left his face looking pale and pasty, but that remark was hardly called for.

"I didn't mean you," his niece laughed. "There's a clown coming in the door."

Freddie whirled around on his stool and spotted the

man with white greasepaint and a round red nose – a clown indeed. He'd have to learn to be less sensitive, he reminded himself.

"Hi, Mr. Clown," called Aggie to the new arrival.

"Hello, little girl," he answered. Then called to the teenager behind the counter, "Could I have chocolate sundae to go?"

"Sprinkles?"

"How'd you know my name?"

The counter girl looked embarrassed. "No, I mean do you want sprinkles on your sundae?"

"Oh, no thanks. Just a maraschino cherry will be fine. Matches my nose."

Aggie giggled at his jest. "It does," she agreed.

Sprinkles the Clown tweaked his red rubber nose and it gave off a *honk! honk!* that made Aggie giggle all the more.

"Is a circus coming to town?" asked the counter girl as she handed over the chocolate sundae and made change for a ten-dollar bill.

"No exactly," replied the clown, taking a bite of the creamy frozen custard. "We're holding up at Ben Bentley's farm till a play date opens up in Burpyville. I'm just exercising the horses, Doc and Dopey."

"Aren't Doc and Dopey two of Snow White's dwarfs?" said Aggie, squinting in puzzlement.

"Right you are, young lady. All seven of our animals are named after Snow White's little friends. See that lion on the side of the wagon?" He pointed out the window. "That's Grumpy. He's got a bad temper. And that tiger? We call him Bashful because he's shy. Wants to hide in the corner of his cage all the time. The bear's name is Sleepy. Always wanting to hibernate winter, summer, or spring."

"What other animals do you have?"

"Not many – seven as I said. We're a very small circus. We also have an elephant named Happy and a baboon we call Sneezy. He has allergies."

"Oh boy! I can't wait to see them."

"Sorry, little lady. We're not going to be putting on a show here."

"Doesn't matter," smiled Aggie. "I can come out to Ben Bentley's farm and see them. He's married to my good friend Cookie. She and I are in the Quilters Club together."

CHAPTER FIVE

Risen From the Dead

Bootsie Purdue raised on her tiptoes to kiss her husband goodbye as he left for work. At 6' 2" Jim Purdue towered over her by nearly a foot. He was pulling an extra shift because one of his deputies was sick, a summer cold. She thought he looked handsome in the blue police uniform with the shiny badge with CHIEF engraved on it, not bad for a man in his late 50s.

"Will you be late?" she asked. Bootsie liked to have a hot meal on the table when he came home, so timing was a keystone to her household chores. Other than the Quilters Club meetings every Tuesday and playing bridge on Thursdays, her life revolved around making a good home for Jim.

"Dunno," he grunted. "This Lost Boys case is taking up a lot of time. The State Police have been in my hair all week."

"You don't have any hair," she teased. "Least not since college."

He put on his police cap to hide the shiny dome of his head. "Thanks for reminding me." His male pattern baldness left a ring of dark hair that made him look like Chris Bauer, that actor who plays the cop on *True Blood*. He and Bootsie watched that television show every week, an entertaining vampire soap opera.

"So your cousin Bobby Ray gets half interest in E Z Seat now that he's returned from the dead?"

"That's the way his daddy set up his will, half to Newcomb Lamont and the other half to Bobby Ray once he turned twenty-one."

Bootsie did the calculation in her head. "That would have been back in 1991," she said.

"That's the problem. Bobby Ray had been legally declared dead by then. The DNA test was key to Judge Cramer's setting aside that declaration and giving him his birthright."

"Bet N.L. is none too happy about all this."

"Not very. He didn't like his brother very much when they were boys. And he's none too happy to be sharing the reins with him now."

≈ ≈ ≈

Beauregard Madison IV had a new secretary – Martha Barnswell, a recent graduate of Caruthers High. She was very efficient, even if she was younger than his daughter Tilly.

Tilly could barely hold life together lately, what with the baby now walking and Agnes entering that prepubescent period known as "tweens." Her husband Mark was busy with his law practice, although it would have been more to Beau's liking if he hadn't taken on Bobby Ray Purdue as a client. But business is business.

"Martha, can you find me the Sammy Hankins file?"

"It's on your desk," she called from her post just outside his tiny office.

"Oh, thanks." As mayor, he got entangled in all kind of

disputes, like this property line quarrel between Sad Sammy Hankins and Errol Baumgartner. He'd known Sad Sammy since grade school when he'd got his nickname due to a worrisome nature. Surprisingly, Beau had never met this other guy. According to town scuttlebutt, Errol Baumgartner was something of a recluse. He's inherited the farm from his grandfather, the last man to see the Lost Boys as they crossed his pasture and disappeared into the Never Ending Swamp.

Beau's son-in-law was handling Sad Sammy's case too. But that didn't keep Sammy from petitioning Beau – his old high school chum – to intervene. Friends in high places and all that.

The dispute didn't need his two cents. It would be settled with plat maps and land surveys. But he'd have Martha send Sammy a nice note saying he was looking into the matter. Another problem off his desk.

And now that the DNA test had come back positive, another problem was resolved. The Quilters Club could go back to sewing patchwork quilts instead of playing detective.

CHAPTER SIX

The Wrong Boy

A t 10 o'clock that night the man claiming to be Bobby Ray found Maud Purdue standing just outside the gate of the Pleasant Glade Cemetery. Judging by the scowl on her face, it was not a pleasant reunion for mother and child.

"You showed up," he said, as if surprised.

"I told Shorty Yosterman I would."

The man scratched his beard thoughtfully. "Yeah, but you've refused to see me since I returned to home."

"This is not your home," snapped the old woman. "I don't know who you think you are, but you sure aren't my son Bobby Ray Purdue."

"No, I'm not," he said. "But you can't prove otherwise."

"Why did you get me out here in the middle of the night? You've stolen half the family business, isn't that enough for you?"

The man shuffled his feet. "I told you there's a way you can get the business back – " he began.

That's what your note said. And it's the only reason I'm here, who ever you are."

"I'm Harry Periwinkle, your son's pal. Yeah, one of what they're calling the Lost Boys."

The woman's head snapped up, eyed blazing. "Where's

my son Bobby Ray?"

"Long dead."

She leaned against the gatepost, shoulders heaving with sobs. "H-how did he die?"

"In quicksand, like they thought. The day we disappeared."

"And the other boy?"

"Never you mind. I don't want to talk about that."

The old woman righted herself. "How did you fake the DNA test?"

"That's for me to know and you to find out."

Her angry gaze stared him down, making him lower his eyes as if studying his shoelaces. "So what is it you want from me?" she demanded.

"Nothing much. Just your grandmother's quilt."

≈≈≈

Beauregard Madison was saying to his son-in-law, "Don't get too involved in watching that TV show. You're about to get a phone call."

Mark Tidemore glanced up from a summer rerun of *The Good Wife*. He liked shows about lawyers, not that they ever got it right. "Why's that?"

Mark and Tilly had brought Aggie over to see Freddie. The pair was becoming inseparable, ice cream pals and all. She wanted to talk about the seven-animal circus. She was wheedling for her uncle to take her over to Cookie Bentley's tomorrow to see them.

Beau said, "You'll likely be getting a call from your client."

"Sad Sammy Hankins?"

"Your other client."

Business was slow, so there weren't that many clients it could be. "You mean Bobby Ray Purdue," he said. "Why would he be calling?"

Beau cleared his throat. "I couldn't say anything earlier, but Jim told me your client set up a meeting with Maud Purdue tonight ... and that she asked Jim to be on hand."

"You think Bobby Ray's going to get arrested?"

"Likely. Based on the note he gave Maud, Jim thinks he's trying to pull something shady."

"But –"

Just then the phone rang.

≈ ≈ ≈

"You're under arrest, Harry Periwinkle," Chief Jim Purdue had said, stepping out of the shadows of a mausoleum.

The bearded man turned to run, but Ben Bentley blocked his path. The big bear of a man had been deputized for this occasion. "Hold on, fellow," he rumbled. "You're not going anywhere."

"Crab apples," cursed the cornered man. "You set me up, Maud Purdue!"

"That I did, Harry. You were a lying, thieving little boy. And now you're a lying, thieving man who's going to get his just deserts."

CHAPTER SEVEN

A Ratty Old Quilt

Maddy carefully laid out her quilting squares, making sure they were going to form the design she'd sketched out on a yellow legal pad. Mark the Shark bought legal pads by the ream. She'd been collecting just the right fabric to make this patchwork quilt for weeks.

"Can you believe it?" gushed Lizzie Ridenour, reveling in the juicy gossip. "We've got a Lost Boy. Just not the one we thought."

The four women – Maddy, Liz, Cookie, and Bootsie – had gathered for their weekly quilt-making session at the senior recreation center. Aggie had bowed out to go see the lions and tigers with her Uncle Freddie.

"Harry Periwinkle passing himself off as Bobby Ray Purdue," nodded Cookie Bentley. Her husband Ben had been there at the cemetery to hear the confession. "But why would he do that?"

"A scam," said Bootsie, forever a cop's wife. "He tricked Jim's cousin N.L. out of half the chair factory."

Maddy spoke up. "There, there. Beau says N.L. will get the factory back. That it was a fraudulent conveyance or some such thing."

The women all felt a connection to the day's events. Bootsie was related. Cookie's hubby was in on the capture.

Maddy's son-in-law was the crook's lawyer. And Liz's husband had arranged the DNA testing that proved to be somehow wrong.

"Ben says Harry Periwinkle offered to trade those shares in E Z Seat for Maud's grandmother's quilt," offered Cookie.

"Really?" said Lizzie. That detail had not been reported in the *Burpyville Gazette*.

"I know that quilt," said Bootsie. "It was hand-stitched in 1899 by Amandine Gersbach Purdue, actually her husband's grandmother."

"Wasn't she your husband's great grandmother too?"

"Yes," confirmed Bootsie. "But Jim's side of the family was in disfavor."

"Now why would Harry Periwinkle want that old quilt?" mused Maddy, still sorting her fabric. "I've seen it. Not a particularly interesting design."

"That's a good question," said Lizzie. "If we figure it out, we'll know why Harry Periwinkle put on this charade."

"He still refuses to talk?" asked Cookie, dumping her quilt squares onto the other table in the rec room.

"Clammed up when Jim arrested him," said Bootsie. "Other than asking to call his lawyer."

All eyes turned to Maddy. "Don't look at me," said the pudgy blonde woman. "Client-attorney confidentiality is all Mark said when I asked this morning."

Beau and Maddy had met their daughter and her husband for breakfast at the Cozy Diner. Having been up all night with his incarcerated client, Mark needed a pot of black coffee to stay awake.

"He was preparing a writ of habeas corpus," Maddy

added.

Bootsie rolled her eyes. "Judge Cramer will never grant that," said Bootsie. "Three witnesses heard him confess."

"Well, it's not exactly a full confession," argued Lizzie. "He simply admitted he's not Bobby Ray Purdue."

"But he pretended to be in order to swindle Newcomb Lamont Purdue out of half the chair factory," Cookie pointed out.

"Yes," nodded the police chief's wife. "That's a felony."

"I'm wondering what happened to that other boy," said Lizzie, sunlight reflecting on her Lucille Ball hair.

"Me too," admitted Cookie."

"I'm wondering why he wanted that old quilt," said Maddy.

"Me too," repeated Cookie.

"Surely it's not worth as much as half interest in the chair factory," mused Lizzie, thinking like a banker's wife.

"Yes, why would he be interested in that ratty old quilt?" said Bootsie.

Maddy looked from one to another. "Maybe the Quilters Club should find out."

≈≈≈

Freddie Madison parked his mother's SUV in Ben Bentley's driveway. Aggie's face was pressed against the side window. Beyond the barn, she could see two canvas tents, the colorful circus wagon, a flatbed truck, several large cages, and two white horses grazing in the grassy field.

"The circus!" she cried. "It's here just like Mr. Sprinkles promised."

"Of course it is," replied her uncle. "That's why we came out here. To see the lions and tigers."

"One lion and one tiger," she corrected him. "And a bear and an elephant and a baboon."

"Don't forget the two horses."

"Them too. Seven animals in all. Not a very big circus."

"Your grandfather says it's a kiddy circus. Plays at malls and shopping centers."

"Caruthers Corners doesn't have a shopping center," said Aggie. "I guess that's why they're going to Burpyville."

"C'mon," said her uncle. "Let's go peek in those cages. Maybe I'll feed you to the lion."

"You will not."

"And why not?"

"Because my mother would be very angry if you did."

≈ ≈ ≈

Myrtle Periwinkle had locked her door and pulled down the shades in order to avoid all the reporters gathered outside. Everyone wanted to interview her about her son Harry. Having returned from the dead to pull off a major swindle was news.

There were two television crews from Indianapolis, an investigative reporter from the *Indianapolis Star*, another from the *Burpyville Gazette*, and a freelancer who claimed to be working for the *National Inquirer*. Myrtle's flowerbed had been trampled beyond recovery.

"Go away," she shouted at the knock on her door. Damned reporters.

"Myrtle, it's me – Chief Jim Purdue. Can I come in for a minute?"

"What do you want?" she continued to shout. "You

arrested my son, you pig."

"Myrtle —"

Before he could finish the sentence, the door swung open and he was face-to-face with Harry Periwinkles wild-eyed mother. "Hurry up, before those reporters start taking pictures," she beckoned him inside.

The living room was dark, all the shades pulled down. He could make out the shape of a green Naugahyde couch, an upright piano, and a La-Z-Boy chair. A TV flickered in the corner, tuned to an Indy news station.

"Sorry to barge in," Jim Purdue began politely. "I can understand how you must feel, getting your son back under these circumstances."

"You arrested him, you storm trooper." Myrtle Periwinkle had been a member of the Youth International Party (more commonly known as the Yippies) back in the late '60s. Despite settling down to raise a family, she'd never quite come to terms with trusting the police.

"Myrtle, he's the one who tried to pull one over on ol' N.L., not me."

"Hmph." She crossed her arms, a sign of her refusal to listen to reason.

"Gotta ask you a few questions," the lawman continued doggedly. His smooth head glistened in the flickering light from the TV set.

"Go ahead." Arms still crossed.

"Did you ever hear from your son after he went missing?"

"No."

"So you didn't know he was alive till today?"

She raised her chin as if defying him to doubt her

word. "That's right. I heard it on the morning news. The same station that's on now."

"The weather forecast is looking good for the remainder of this week," a woman standing in front of a large map was saying. Her droning voice was enough to make you wish for a lightning storm to strike her down.

"Got any idea why he might do this?"

"Greed, I suspect. That chair factory's gotta be worth a pretty penny. We Periwinkles have always been dirt poor. I expect he wanted more. Probably why he ran away from home."

"Sorry about this, Myrtle. I know it's been hard for you. Thinking you've lost your only child. Then your husband drowning in the well a few years later."

"I was glad he drowned. He was a terrible husband."

"Oh," said Jim, realizing he didn't know much about the Periwinkle family. Myrtle had been reclusive after her losses, living on a meager pension left by her husband from his job at the chair factory.

"If you don't have any more questions, I'd appreciate if you'd run those reporters off my property. I've got absolutely nothing to say to them." Sounding like her son Harry.

CHAPTER
EIGHT
Paying Their Respects

Nobody would ever accuse the Quilters Club of being busybodies, but they did have a certain reputation for nosing around. Thinking of themselves as detectives, they had solved a couple of crimes in the past two years. The police chief was none too pleased with them interfering with his job. But given their success rate, he kept his grumbling to himself.

If asked, the four women were merely "paying their respects" when they showed up on Maud Purdue's doorstep with an upside down watermelon cake in hand. It was Maud's favorite, so she invited them in.

"You didn't have to do this," Maud was saying as she put the cake in a glass cake dish on the kitchen counter. She tasted the frosting with a swipe of her finger before putting the glass cover in place.

"We were worried about you," said Maddy. "That scam that Harry Periwinkle tried to pull must have been very upsetting."

"I knew he wasn't my son," she grumbled. "Bobby Ray had blue eyes. But nobody would listen to me."

"Everybody's wondering how he fooled that DNA test," said Liz Ridenour, feeling a little guilty since her husband had helped arrange it.

"It's a mystery," Maud Purdue shook her head, still eyeing the upside down watermelon cake.

"Funny thing, Harry offering to sign back the chair factory in return for your quilt," said Bootsie.

"Harry Periwinkle is obviously crazy. Pretending to be my son and all. That old quilt ain't worth anything."

"Where is it?" Maddy asked casually. "I'd love to see it again."

"Packed away in the attic. In an old cedar trunk to keep the moths away. Ain't worth anything, but it has sentimental value. My husband's grandmother made that quilt by hand back in 1899. That was the year of the Big Fire."

"Yes," chimed in Cookie. "Burned down half the town. It started at the bank." She glanced at Liz as if by being the wife of a retired bank president she was somehow responsible.

"I've heard Edgar speak of it. The fire was set to cover up a robbery, as I recall. Don't think they ever caught the culprits. But that was more than a hundred years ago."

"Grandmother Purdue made the quilt to commemorate the Big Fire."

"Yes, the design was flames," Maddy recalled. "Yellows and reds and oranges."

"Faded a lot," sighed Maud Purdue. "But it's all I've got to remember her by. She asked me to give it to Bobby Ray when he grew up."

"It's a wonderful keepsake," Maddy assured her. "But puzzling why Harry Periwinkle would want it."

Maud shook her head. "Never did like that boy. Told Bobby Ray not to pal around with him, that he was trash.

But my son didn't listen. Him and Harry and that Watson boy were thick as thieves. Romping through the watermelon fields. Hiking on weekends. Camping out at Gruesome Gorge in the summer. Fishing in Edwin Baumgartner's pond. They caught a ten-pound bass there once."

Maddy could see that Maud Purdue wasn't going to fetch the quilt from the attic to show it to them, so she eased toward the door. "We'll go now. Just wanted to deliver that cake. And offer our condolences."

"No need for that. Bobby Ray's been dead for nearly thirty years now. Least that's what the bearded scallywag told me."

The visitors offered a chorus of goodbyes as they walked to Bootsie's Jeep Cherokee. Maud Purdue gave a final wave, then turned back to the kitchen where the upside down watermelon cake was waiting.

As Maddy eased into the backseat of the Cherokee, she glanced up at the eaves of the two-story house. Through the branches of the giant oak tree that dominated the front yard, she could see a small attic window. The mysterious quilt lay just beyond.

≈≈≈

Aggie was delighted to see Sprinkles the Clown again. Even there at the campground on the Bentley farm, he still wore his white greasepaint and red nose. He introduced them to a tall man with slicked-back hair and a walrus mustache. "This is Big Bill Haney," he said with a flourish. "He's the ring master, lion tamer, and strong man. What's more, he owns the circus."

Freddie Madison glanced at the side of the gaudy

circus wagon. The wording proclaimed: HANEY BROS. CIRCUS AND PETTING ZOO. He wasn't sure what there was to pet, the animals consisting of a lion, tiger, and other dangerous creatures.

Turns out, it was Happy the Elephant. A third guy – a leathery-skinned roustabout they referred to as Bombay – brought the dusty pachyderm around from behind the tent for Aggie to pet. Mr. Sprinkles gave her a pack of peanuts and showed her how to feed them to Happy.

"Ohhh, look at his long nose," she thrilled as he took peanuts from her hand.

"That's his trunk," said the elephant handler. He also doubled as a mind reader known as Swami Bombay. He claimed to be from India, but Freddie thought he looked Mexican. "He uses that trunk like a hand. He could thread a needle with it."

Freddie knew that was a slight exaggeration, but he merely smiled as the circus performers entertained his niece.

Mr. Sprinkles was also a gifted acrobat, which he demonstrated by walking on his hands.

To his surprise, Aggie emulated him. As the star pupil in her gymnastics class at Madison Elementary, she could walk on her hands, do back flips, and complete straddle vaults on a horizontal bar.

"Excellent," applauded Mr. Haney. "When you grow up we'll have a place for you here at the circus."

"Oh boy!"

"You too," joked the ringmaster-lion-tamer-owner. "We can bill you as the Alligator Man."

Freddie couldn't help but laugh at this reference to his

scarred and scaly skin. "I may need a job. Can't go back to firefighting."

"Lots of ways for a man to be productive," said Swami Bombay. Maybe he was a mind reader after all.

"When do you perform in Burpyville?" asked Aggie, remembering the itinerary outlined by the clown.

"Next week," said Haney. "We're putting on six shows at the Burpyville Shopping Center. Free passes if you two decide to drive over to see us."

"Thanks," said Freddie. "We just might do that."

≈ ≈ ≈

Bernard Warbuckle asked for a leave of absence from Burbyville Memorial, went straight home and packed his bags. An extended trip to Canada was in his immediate future.

Damn that Harry for getting caught like a kid with his hand in the cookie jar. The jerk should have stayed missing.

CHAPTER NINE

Lawyered Up

Harry Periwinkle was refusing to talk. Maybe he realized he's said too much already. He sat in the holding cell of the Caruthers Corners Police Department as silent as the statue of Jacob Caruthers in the town square across the street.

Maud Purdue had surprised him. He hadn't expected her to bring in the police when he asked her to meet him at the cemetery. He'd been posing as her son, but guess there's no fooling a mother. DNA results or not, she'd seen through him.

Now he –

His thoughts were interrupted when the deputy called his name. "Harry Periwinkle – you've got a visitor." The uniformed man unlocked the cell door to admit his attorney, Mark Tidemore.

"Hello, Bobby – uh, I mean Harry." He nodded toward the metal chair. "Mind if I have a seat?"

The prisoner shrugged. "Help yourself," he broke his silence. "But I don't need your services anymore. You're fired."

"I think you *do* need my services," said Mark the Shark. "And I hate to tell you, but you can't fire me – I was appointed by the court."

"Either way, I've got nothing to say." He turned his back, again looking out his cell window, staring vacantly at the bronze statue.

"Harry, you've committed a felony. They caught you with your pants down. You're probably looking at prison time. But maybe I can use your thirty missing years to get them to mitigate the sentence."

"Forget it. I've said all I'm going to say about that."

"All you've told them is that Bobby Ray drowned in a bog and that you became a pirate. Not much to go on."

"Bobby Ray fell in the quicksand. End of story."

"Maybe you could help them find the remains. Give closure to his mother. That might be looked on favorably."

"There's a zillion miles of Never Ending Swamp. I couldn't find my way back to that patch of quicksand even if I tried."

Mark the Shark shifted his weight, making the metal chair screech on the cement floor. "According to the US Park Service it's slightly over four hundred acres in size."

"That's a zillion acres to twelve-year-old boys," Harry waved the words away. "Bobby Ray's dead and gone. So I used his identity as a little joke, big deal."

"Not a very good joke. You gave his mother false hope."

"Didn't either. That old biddy never believed I was her son from the git-go."

True enough. "What about Jud Watson's mother. Can't you let her know what happened to her son?"

Harry looked out the cell window again, considering his words. "He's alive," he said at last. "But I can't help it if he doesn't choose to call his mama. He hates her, that old witch. Used to beat him with a belt when he was a boy. I've seen the strap marks on his back."

"So you know where he is?"

Harry chuckled. "Not at this precise moment. But I'd guess he's halfway to Canada."

≈≈≈

The Quilters Club was holding a meeting at the rec center, an emergency session. "We've got to come up with a plan to inspect Maud Purdue's quilt," Maddy Madison was insisting. She was a pretty woman, late '50s, wheat-blonde hair, maybe 10 pounds overweight – "more to hug," as her husband Beau liked to say.

Bootsie, being the police chief's wife, was more cautious. "We can't just break in and steal it," she shook her head. "Maybe we could just ask her to see it?"

"We tried that," Lizzie reminded her. "That's a dead end, f'sure."

"I agree," admitted Cookie. "But that doesn't justify burglary."

"We're not stealing the quilt," Maddy explained. "Merely looking at it."

"You're still talking B&E," said Bootsie, using the cop lingo she'd heard at home.

"What's that?" frowned Maddy.

"Breaking and entering – a serious crime."

"Not if we have permission."

"And how do you intend to get that?" Cookie raised her eyebrows. A slender brunette, she was quite attractive, keeping herself up now that she was married to Ben Bentley. Her first husband had died a few years back in a tractor accident.

"Watch," said Maddy, picking up her little flat iPhone and tapping in some numbers. "Hello, Maud. This is Maddy Madison. Following up on the other day, can we drop by and see your grandmother's quilt sometime? Yes? When? Oh, well, call me when it's convenient. Yes, I know you need time to grieve. Will there be a memorial service, now that you know what happened to your son? Well, let me know."

Bootsie wrinkled her forehead. "What was that?"

"Maud agreed we could see the quilt."

"When?"

"Never probably. But I'm going to take that as an invitation to drop by on our own schedule."

That schedule was 2 a.m. the next night.

CHAPTER TEN

Second Story Job

"Think you can do it?" Maddy asked her granddaughter. The Quilters Club, including Aggie, was gathered around the big oak tree in Maud Purdue's yard. They were eyeing the attic window.

"Of course, I can do it," replied the girl. "You ought to see me on the monkey bars at school."

Agnes Tidewell was spending the night at her grandparents' house. Her mom and dad had driven down to Indy for dinner and a show, celebrating their two-year anniversary of moving back to Caruthers Corners. At the time they had been on the verge of divorce, but the change of venue had worked wonders. No longer did Mark the Shark work the long hours he'd faced in Los Angeles. Milly had just announced she was expecting a third child, another reason to celebrate.

"Don't you go breaking your neck," admonished Lizzie, having second thoughts about this perilous mission. "You mother would never forgive us."

"Don't worry. A piece of cake," Aggie said, shimmying up the tree trunk. Climbing limb to limb, she reached her goal in minutes – the small attic window.

"Is it locked?" whispered Bootsie in a stage voice.

Aggie tried lifting it, nearly losing her balance.

"Watch out!" screamed Maddy, loud enough to wake Maud and all the Purdue family ghosts. But nobody seemed to be stirring inside the two-story Victorian structure.

"It's open," Aggie reported, lifting the sill high enough to crawl inside. The window was small, but so was Aggie, about 80 pound tops. She disappeared inside the Purdue attic in about three seconds flat.

"See? It's not breaking and entering if the window is unlocked," rationalized Maddy.

Bootsie merely rolled her eyes heavenward.

"It's packed in a cedar trunk," hissed Maddy, remembering the words of Maud Purdue.

Aggie's honey-blonde head appeared at the window. "Is it reds and oranges, but all faded?" she called down to her co-conspirators.

"Yes," nodded Cookie.

"Did you find it?" asked Maddy.

Aggie nodded. "Here it is," she said, pushing the armful of fabric out the narrow window.

"I've got it," huffed Bootsie, stepping under the falling quilt. A stocky woman, she'd excelled in volleyball at college and still had good reflexes.

The patchwork quilt landed on her head, draping over her like a tent. "*Mmft, hmpt,*" she said from under the thick cloth. It translated into words not meant for Aggie's ears.

"Okay, climb down very carefully," instructed Maddy, shaking a finger at her spunky granddaughter. "But close the window first."

Ten minutes later they were in Lizzie's Lexus heading

toward the Madison house on Melon Pickers Row.

"Good job," Maddy congratulated the team.

"Roger that," replied Aggie, a remark that struck everyone as funny. The four women and young girl all burst into fits of laughter as they pulled into the driveway at 3 a.m., purloined quilt stowed in the back.

≈≈≈

"Did you go out last night?" Beau Madison asked over breakfast. He liked a hearty Midwestern starter for his day – scrambled eggs, bacon, toast, OJ.

"Why do you ask?" his wife dodged the question.

"Someone forgot to close the garage door."

"That was when I was putting the garbage out," she said, shoveling another helping of eggs onto his plate. "City pickup this morning," she reminded him, not that he wouldn't know as mayor. Monday morning and Thursday morning, contracted out to Pete Turner, who had a dump on the west side of town. Turner's Trash Heap, it was called.

"Oh right," he mumbled, studying the *Burbyville Gazette*. He tried to stay up on local happenings. "I see Janey Baumgartner had twins," he added. "Bet her husband Errol didn't bargain for that windfall."

Maddy glanced up from the sink, where she was soaking the cast-iron skillet. "Errol? Isn't he Edwin Baumgartner's grandson?"

"You mean the old coot who owned the farm next to the Never Ending Swamp? Yeah, I think so."

"I wonder if the family knows more about what Edwin saw the day those boys disappeared."

Beau looked up from the paper. "I'm sure Jim

Purdue's already questioned them about it. Him or the State Police."

"Or the news media. There was quite a stir when everyone though Bobby Ray had returned from a soggy grave. Even you got interviewed by CNN."

"My fifteen minutes of fame," he chuckled. "Sure do wonder what happened to those boys."

"So do I," said Maddy.

≈≈≈

Being that school hadn't started yet, Aggie got to go to Burpyville to see the see the Haney Bros. Circus and Petting Zoo with her Uncle Freddie. Maddy and Amanda agreed that it was a good thing to encourage Freddie to go out in public. He couldn't hide away like the Elephant Man for the rest of his life.

A date had opened up at the Burpyville Mall, so the Haney Bros. Circus pulled up stakes. Another member of the circus – Big Bill Haney's brother William – showed up with a large truck and the caravan carrying elephant and lion and horses, etc. lumbered off toward the adjacent county.

Big Bill and Little William Haney stopped by the mayor's office on the way out of town to leave a handful of free passes. Although they claimed to be twins, they looked more like Arnold Schwarzenegger and Danny DeVito in that movie called *Twins*.

Aggie had mixed feeling about going to the circus. This was the day that the Quilters Club had set aside to examine Maud Purdue's lumpy old patchwork quilt for clues. They had waited a couple of days to see if the woman noticed that it was missing, then with a collective sigh agreed to meet today at 2 o'clock at the rec center.

Nonetheless, Aggie laughed and giggled as Sprinkles the Clown did a dance with Sneezy the Baboon. Big Bill Haney made the lion jump through a hoop and Little William led Sleepy the Bear around like a puppy on a lease – a fuzzy, 300-pound puppy that is. And best of all, Bombay gave her a ride atop Happy the Elephant.

Whoooo-ee!

CHAPTER ELEVEN
The Queen-Sized Quilt

The Quilters Club looked more like a witches' cabal at that moment, the four middle-aged women hunched over the faded red-orange-and-yellow quilt as if around a fire. The queen-sized quilt was spread across the big table in the rec room, its patchwork squares looking like lumpy little mattress pads. It gave off a faint odor of rotting leaves and compost.

"Not very elegant," observed Liz, a woman of style and taste. Even if it was evident her hair was dyed, you could tell it was an expensive styling job.

"Poor stitching," agreed Cookie, the most fastidious of the foursome.

"Smells," Bootsie wriggled her nose, remembering when the mephitic quilt had landed on her head. It took two showers to get rid of the fetid stench.

"What do you make of the design?" Maddy asked.

Cookie, being the most versed on historical quilt patterns, leaned closer to examine the flame-like image. The colors looked washed-out, the pigments deteriorated from sunlight and age. "Nothing special," she made her appraisal. "No museum would touch it. No collector would want it. A rag picker's dream."

"So why would Harry Periwinkle want it?" posited

Maddy.

"Badly enough to trade half of the E Z Seat chair factory for it," Bootsie mused out loud.

"Sentimental value?" tried Liz.

"No, it was a Purdue family heirloom," said Cookie, keeping the genealogy straight. "It had nothing to do with the Periwinkles."

"Maybe it's stuffed with money," joked the banker's wife. Poking it with her finger, you could hear a rustling sound.

"Sure, like Maud's husband's grandmother ever had any money," laughed Bootsie. "This quilt was made before the family started up the chair factory."

"So you didn't marry Jim for his family fortune," teased Maddy.

"I wish. His side of the family didn't even have a piece of the chair factory."

"Where did Amandine Purdue's husband get the capital to start a manufacturing business?" asked Lizzie. She was always interested in the money side of things.

"Good question," shrugged Bootsie. "One day they were poor, the next day rich. Ol' N.L. refuses to talk about it. Merely says his great grandfather managed his money well."

"So Abner Purdue started up the chair factory," Cookie traced the history. "He left it to his son Abe who left it to his son Amos – that's Maud's husband. And Amos left it to his two sons."

"Yes, but Bobby Ray never lived to claim his half," said Bootsie. "That's how Harry Periwinkle was able to hoodwink them into signing over those shares to him."

Marjory Sorrell Rockwell

"That will get reversed," Lizzie pointed out.

"Looks like we've hit a dead end," sighed Maddy. She stared morosely at the lumpy quilt. She'd been so sure it would reveal secrets, but it was just a smelly old family keepsake. "Now we have to figure out how to get it back in the attic."

"Aggie?" said Liz.

"I don't know," replied Maddy. "I was so afraid she would fall out of that tree. It was irresponsible of me to let her get involved in this."

"She wasn't in any danger," the redhead assured her. "That kid climbs like a monkey."

"Yes, but I want her to be around to see her new baby sister."

"Tilly's having a girl?"

"Has it been confirmed?"

Maddy smiled. "Yes, Tilly went to the doctor yesterday to get the results. A little girl. That will make three."

≈≈≈

Judge Horace Cramer refused to accept Mark the Shark's request to step down. "The man needs a defense, even if he is a scum-sucking no-good hornswoggler who tried to gyp the Purdues out of their family business. The Periwinkles were always shifty, little more than white trash."

"Are you sure you're not biased in this case, Judge?"

"No, I'm not. Else I wouldn't let them keep a sharp Los Angeles lawyer like you on the case."

"I grew up here," he reminded the judge.

"Course you did. I knew your daddy well. And you live here now. But you came out of a top-notch LA law firm, don't think I don't know it. If anybody can save Harry Periwinkle from twenty years in a state prison, it's you."

"Thank you," Mark said. "I appreciate the vote of confidence." Not sure he really meant those words.

≈≈≈

Edgar Ridenour got the phone call he was expecting from the director of Burbyville Memorial. As a board member of the hospital, Edgar was treated with proper deference. He had called for an investigation into how the DNA test on the Lost Boy had gone awry.

"We have a pretty good idea of what happened," said Virgil Hoffstedder. You could hear the nervousness in his voice. "The State Police are looking into it as we speak."

"And –?"

"We have an employee named Bernard Warbuckle, a lab technician. He ran the DNA test in question. Turns out, he's gone missing."

"Missing?"

"Warbuckle didn't show up for work today. He didn't answer his telephone when we called to check on him. The State Police says he's not at his apartment."

"You called them before alerting me?" grumbled Edgar Ridenour. He was head of the malpractice committee. And this was shaping up to be a big-ticket negligence lawsuit.

"When someone suggested Warbuckle might be guilty of switching the DNA sample, we immediately called the State Police. We didn't want to let him escape."

Edgar took a deep breath, then said, "What do we know about this Warbuckle guy?"

"According to his personnel file, he's forty-two, graduated from Ball State, has worked here for four years.

Clean record, no complaints about his work."

"Maybe he hasn't actually disappeared," Edgar said desperately. "Maybe he's just visiting his family."

"The file said he has no known relatives."

"Friends then ..."

"The State Police said his apartment's been cleaned out."

Edgar tried again. "Maybe he's been kidnapped ..."

"Not very likely. The State Police says the information in his personnel file is phony. That he never attended Ball State. And his Social Security number belongs to a man who got run over by a tank during Desert Storm."

The retired banker couldn't hold back his temper. "Don't you have any good news to report?" he shouted into the phone.

After a pause, Virgil Hoffstedder said, "I think he left without picking up his last paycheck."

CHAPTER TWELVE

The Sound of the Quilt

Maddy and the Quilters Club agreed that they would have to risk returning Maud Purdue's quilt the same way they got it: Aggie climbing in through the attic window.

"I can do it," Aggie assured her grandmother. "I got an A in gym last year."

"I'm sure you can. But I doubt your mother would approve."

"Maybe you'll forget to tell her. After all, you're getting old and forgetful." The girl winked to seal the secret.

"Thanks. I'm glad my age is helpful to this plan," said Maddy. But her granddaughter didn't catch the sarcasm.

"Lucky I'm two months younger than you," Lizzie joined the joke. "At least senility hasn't set in with me yet."

"Don't count on that," said Bootsie. "Remember how you lost your car keys last week?"

"That Lexus is a new car and I'm not used to that funny key. Whatever happened to the old-fashioned kind?"

"Time marches on," commented Cookie, ever the historian.

Maddy began folding the smelly old quilt in preparation for their late-night incursion. She had brought a Glad trash bag to carry it in.

"Why does the quilt make that sound?" asked Aggie, the curiosity of a tween girl.

"What sound?" replied Lizzie.

"Oh, you mean the crinkling sound?" said Maddy. "That's whatever it's stuffed with. Sounds like paper."

"That's an odd stuffing," said Bootsie.

"Perhaps it's old newspapers," offered Cookie. "That would be interesting, to find old newspapers from 1899."

"We'll never know," sighed Maddy as she continued to fold the quilt. "This unremarkable example of quiltmaking is going home tonight. Right, Aggie?"

"You bet. And I promise to be careful climbing that oak tree."

"Good girl."

Cookie fidgeted a tad. "Maybe we could clip a few threads and fish a scrap of newspaper out before taking it back."

"Cookie!" admonished her friend Bootsie. It was bad enough they had completed a burglary, but the idea of damaging the antique quilt was simply unacceptable.

"Oh, I know. But I am the town historian. So you can't blame me for being curious."

"Me too," admitted Lizzie.

"Why can't we take a peek?" Aggie weighed in.

Maddy held up her hands to silence them. "Okay, okay. Let's see if there's a loose thread."

Bootsie rolled her eyes, but joined the up-close examination of the quilt. "Here's a square that's kinda loose," she pointed.

"Hand me those tweezers," Maddy prompted her granddaughter. "Let's see if I can work it loose without breaking the thread."

"Pretty shoddy sewing," harrumphed Lizzie. "Looks like it was done in haste. No attention to the stitching."

"I agree," said Bootsie. "Surprising that Harry Periwinkle would want this ugly old thing. Poor needlecraft. Boring design. Stuffed with old newspapers. Can't be worth more than twenty dollars at yard sale."

"Not newspapers," said Maddy. Something in her voice got their attention. The women turned to stare at the quilt.

Maddy's tweezers had extracted a long green piece of paper ... US currency featuring the image of some stuffy looking man in formal military attire.

"T-that's a thousand dollar bill," stammered Lizzie. "Look it says so in big numbers on the backside."

"There no such thing as a thousand dollar bill," Bootsie stated flatly. "This must be counterfeit."

"No," corrected Cookie, calling on her encyclopedic memory. "Small-size Federal Reserve notes in the amount of one thousand dollars were first issued in 1890. They bore the portrait of General George Meade."

"He wasn't a president," said Aggie, having studied them in school last year.

"Neither was Ben Franklin or Alexander Hamilton," Maddy patted her granddaughter's hand. "And they're on hundreds and twenties."

Maddy fished out another $1000 bill.

"These are red seal bank notes." Cookie pointed to the circular red blob on the front of the bills. "They were known as Grand Watermelons because the zeros are shaped like large watermelons, oblong and dark green with black streaks."

"Watermelons," laughed the mayor's wife. The town was famous for its annual Watermelon Festival. "How appropriate."

"Are there more in there?" asked Lizzie.

"Let's find out," said Bootsie, ripping at the stiches she'd earlier tried to protect. "Holy cow! This quilt is filled with thousand dollar bills."

"N-no wonder Harry Periwinkle wanted it," stammered Maddy. "There must be a million dollars in here."

"But half interest in E Z Seat has got to be worth more than that," said Bootsie.

"This pile of money is worth much more than its face value," countered Cookie. "A $1000 Grand Watermelon is the most expensive US banknote ever sold at auction. One of them went for a world's record price of $2,255,000."

"One of them?" gasped the banker's wife. "There must be hundreds of them here."

Cookie nodded, dumbfounded by their discovery. "Before we opened this old quilt, only two red seal Grand Watermelons were known to still exist. The one that sold at auction and another that's in the museum at the Federal Reserve Bank of San Francisco."

"Amazing," muttered Liz. "We've just figured out what this Lost Boy charade was all about – a hidden fortune."

"Yes," said Maddy Madison. "But now the question is, where did Amos Purdue's grandmother get this much money?"

CHAPTER THIRTEEN

The Circus Comes to Town

The Haney Bros. Circus had returned to the Bentley farm on its way to a gig in Illinois. Ben was a sucker for helping out wayfarers in need of a place to camp out – whether stranded RV's, itinerant workers, gypsy troupes, or pocket-sized circuses.

Ben even helped the Haneys pitch their two tents. Big Bill and Little William slept in one, Bombay and Sprinkles the Clown shared the other.

Sneezy the Baboon had his own folding cot in the second tent. The horses were tethered out back. The elephant was chained to a stake. The lion and tiger had their own cages. And Sleepy the Bear slept in the back of the truck.

"We had a great run at the Burpyville Mall," crowed Big Bill, still dressed in his ringmaster's getup, a frayed red jacket and black top hat. His boots looked spit-shined.

"Indeed we did," confirmed Little William. While Bill was 6' 2" tall, William barely reached 5' even with thick-soled shoes. "It was worth waiting for a slot. Thank goodness that kiddy carnival got canceled because its Ferris wheel failed a safety check."

"You should have seen Big Bill put Grumpy and Bashful through their paces," the clown said to Ben. "He had those cats eating out of his hand – literally."

"Musta been quite a show," smiled Ben. "Little Aggie Tidemore talked about it for hours when she got back from Burpyville. It was nice of you to give Aggie and her uncle passes."

"Took a liking to the little girl," said Sprinkles. "I hope she'll come by to say goodbye before we pull up stakes and head to Peoria. We're playing a waterpark there."

"Dunno. She's caught up in some big excitement in town. My wife and some other women found about a zillion dollars stuffed inside a quilt sewed together by Amos Purdue's grandma. Somebody's gonna be rich, once they figure where all that cash came from."

"That's *my* money," blurted Sprinkles the Clown.

≈≈≈

Turns out, there were only five $1000 bills in the old patchwork quilt. But there was a plethora of other denominations: 1880 hundred dollar notes featuring Abraham Lincoln; 1882 twenty dollar gold certificates featuring James A. Garfield; 1891 five dollar silver certificates with Ulysses S. Grant; 1880 two dollar bank notes with Thomas Jefferson; and 1899 one-dollar silver certificate notes also with Abe Lincoln's portrait.

Some $73,512 in face value, but Daniel Sokolowski of Dan's Den of Antiquity estimated that all told it might be worth more than $100 million on the auction block.

Question was, to whom did it belong?

Police Chief Jim Purdue was boiling mad. His own wife involved in a third-rate burglary! Beau Madison was embarrassed by Maddy's actions. Ben Bentley was proud of his spunky wife. Edgar Ridenour was too distracted with that hospital business to notice. And little Agnes was grounded by her parents for about one hundred years.

Being that this involved prominent families, it was agreed to sweep the "theft" under the rug. The police chief released a story about how the women found the quilt in a trashcan, not that anyone believed it.

Maud Purdue said she wouldn't press charges if her rightful property was returned. She told her cousin Jim that it was none of his business how Grandma Purdue got the money – making the point that the quilt had been handed down to her husband's side of the family, not his.

She tried to hire Mark the Shark to represent her claim, but he pointed out that it would be a conflict of interest, him representing the miscreant who pretended to be her son in order to extort the quilt from her.

Maddy raised the question as to how Harry Periwinkle knew about the money being in the quilt, but it was the consensus that he'd learned about it from Bobby Ray Purdue sometime before his friend stepped into the quicksand.

Cookie had a theory about where the money came from, but she figured now was not the time to speak up. The town was filling with newspaper reporters and TV crews looking to cover this "hidden treasure" story. Everybody was abuzz. It wasn't until after midnight when Cookie finally got home that her husband mentioned the strange remark by the circus clown.

"Everybody wishes it was their money," she yawned. "Me too."

"Aw, we don't need the money," said Ben. "Farm's doing pretty good."

"Even so, having an extra hundred million dollars wouldn't hurt," Cookie smiled as she turned off the light.

CHAPTER FOURTEEN
The Property Dispute

Amanda Madison was worried about her husband. While the burns were healing nicely, his acceptance of his altered appearance wasn't going so well. He moped about his parents' house like one of those zombies in *Dawn of the Dead*. That used to be one of his favorite movies, but he hadn't even bothered to watch it when it came on TV the other night.

The adoption plans for the little girl he'd saved from the fire was going well, thanks to powerful friends in Atlanta. But she worried he might be too distracted with his own problems to take on the role of fatherhood.

"Maddy, do you think we need to talk Freddie into getting some therapy? The insurance would pay for it. But he doesn't seem interested."

"He'll work it out," her mother-in-law responded. "Freddie always had a good head on his shoulders. That fire may have burned off his skin, but it didn't reach the man inside."

"I hate seeing him like this. So despondent."

"He'll come around. His new face just takes some getting used to. By all of us."

≈ ≈ ≈

"I'm sooooo sorry," Aggie was telling her mother. "But

339

the Quilters Club was trying to solve a crime. We're detectives, you know."

Tilly Tidemore was still stewing. How dare her mother involve a child in illegal activities? The morning sickness had left her crabby lately. But this time her reaction was justified, she told herself.

"No trips to the Dairy Queen for a month," she pronounced the sentence. "And no more Quilters Club – ever!"

"That's not fair," said Aggie. "I'm going to appeal."

"You're going to do what?"

"Hire me a lawyer and appeal."

"Where are you going to find a lawyer, young lady?" her mother laughed at the idea."

"Daddy's a lawyer."

"He charges $300 an hour," Tilly countered.

"He does *pro Bruno* work," said her daughter.

"You mean *pro bono*."

"Doesn't matter. I'm going to appeal."

≈ ≈ ≈

Mark the Shark was having a meeting with his other client, Sad Sammy Hankins. That property dispute.

"My farm is north of town, next to the old Baumgartner place," the roly-poly man was saying. His skin was pale and puffy, like the Pillsbury Dough Boy. "There's a fence separating the Baumgartner pasture from my watermelon field." He laid two snapshots down on the table, there in a booth at Cozy Diner. "This first one was made twenty or thirty years ago, and here's one made only a month ago. See the difference?"

Mark leaned closer to study the images. He could see

that the position of the fence had shifted between the first snapshot and the second. A big elm tree was in front of the fence in one, behind it in the other. "Someone moved the fence," the lawyer stated the obvious.

"Exactly."

"Who do you think might be responsible?" asked Mark.

"Who else but Errol Baumgartner. He took over the farm when his grandpappy died."

"When was that?"

"Maybe ten years ago. Old Man Baumgartner lived to be ninety-three. Had the constitution of a horse."

Mark studied the pictures again. The newer photo was digital. The date it was taken was written by hand on the back – July 20, 2012. The older photo had been printed from a film negative. It had been time-stamped on the back by the photo processor – August 12, 1982.

The fence could have been moved anytime between those two dates. But it really didn't matter whether Errol Baumgartner or his grandfather moved the fence, it had clearly been moved.

"Do you have any surveys?"

"Right as rain, I do. Here's the plait survey from the courthouse. And here's the survey I paid for two weeks ago. Shows that the Baumgartner fence is setting twenty feet over on my property."

"Okay, this should be a slam-dunk," Mark concluded. "I'll need to keep theses photos and the surveys."

"No problem. Just kick Errol Baumgartner's butt. He's as weird as his grandpappy."

"Weird?"

"The Baumgartners never were very neighborly. I doubt anybody's been allowed to set foot on that farm in half a century. You'd think they're hiding Elvis out there."

CHAPTER FIFTEEN

Was It Murder?

That weekend the three families were having a backyard cookout at the Madisons' beautiful Victorian mansion on Melon Pickers Row. Ben was manning the barbeque grill, basking the steaks with his special watermelon sauce. Edgar was playing bartender. Beau and Jim were acting as tasters.

Their wives were taking it easy at the shaded patio table, happy to not be fixing dinner, the men waiting on them for a change. Not that they deserved any pampering after that misadventure involving Maud Purdue's quilt, Beau pointed out.

"But, dear," argued his wife, "if we hadn't bent the rules a little, no one – not even Maud – would have known about the money hidden in that ugly old quilt."

"A little," snorted Jim. "Breaking and entering is a criminal offence punishable by up to five years in prison."

"You'd miss me," teased Bootsie. Defiant as usual.

"Could I convince you to press charges against Lizzie," called Edgar from behind the Tiki bar. "Give me more free time for fishing if she was locked up in jail." He was enjoying his retirement, spending most weekends with a rod and reel in his hand.

"Oh poo," his wife responded. "Who would fix you

dinner?"

"Ben," he said, pointing toward the burly man at the stone grill. "He's a damn good cook. We'd eat steak every night."

"Not with his cholesterol levels," Cookie chimed in. "Red meat is off his diet, tonight being an exception."

"I have a theory about that guy at Burpyville Memorial," volunteered Maddy to no one in particular.

Being on the hospital's board, that got Edgar's attention. "What theory's that?" he asked while mixing a frothy gin fizz for his wife. Lizzie was fond of sweet alcoholic concoctions.

"I think he's really Jud Watson."

"You're saying Bernard Warbuckle is actually one of the Lost Boys?"

"Why else would he switch the DNA samples?" Maddy posited. "He was in on the swindle with his pal Harry."

"Doggone," said Jim. "That makes sense." You could almost see the lightbulb coming on over his slick head.

"But why would Jud Watson change his identity in the first place?" asked Beau, confused.

"So he could get a job at the hospital," speculated Cookie. "Pretend he was qualified as a lab technician."

"There might be another reason," suggested Maddy. "What if Harry Periwinkle and Jud Watson killed Bobby Ray Purdue? That would explain why they disappeared, changed their names."

"Why would they kill their childhood buddy?" asked Jim, switching back to cop mode.

"Maybe Bobby Ray told them about the money – and they killed him for it."

"And waited thirty years to go after it?"

"Who knows? Maybe they panicked, ran away. Only got up the courage in recent years."

"I'll float that idea with the state boys," said Jim after a moment's thought. "Might be something there."

≈ ≈ ≈

Daniel Sokolowski had been giving some thought to that money found in Amandine Gersbach Purdue's quilt. He'd spoken with several numismatists since his first appraisal and was coming to the conclusion it was worth even more than he originally thought.

In trying to figure out its provenance, he could pin it down to around 1899, the year Maud Purdue said her husband's grandmother made the quilt. The various bills were minted in 1880, 1882, 1891, and 1899 – nothing later.

Abner Purdue had started E Z Seat in 1899, according to public records. Did he come into an inheritance about then? Did he have secret investors? Or did this represent twenty years of scrupulous saving? It was anybody's guess.

Hiding money away was not an unusual practice back then. Simple country folk had a distrust of banks. Some buried it in their backyards. Others stuffed it in their mattress. Why not sew it into a padded quilt?

CHAPTER SIXTEEN

Connect the Dots

That Monday Cookie Bentley called a special meeting of the Quilters Club. Their regular room at the senior recreation center was booked, so they met at the Caruthers County Historical Society. The office was cramped but provided convenient access to Cookie's filing cabinets.

"I know where the money came from," she announced.

"What money?" said Lizzie, distracted by being late for an appointment with her hairdresser. Lee Ann would charge her whether she showed up or not.

"The money in the quilt. Pay attention, hon."

"Oh, right."

"So tell us," demanded Bootsie. A no-nonsense gal, she had little patience.

"What do you know about the Fire of 1899?" Cookie asked, as if she were a history teacher addressing a class.

"Not much," admitted Maddy. "Just that most of the town burned down."

"Half." Cookie spread a faded map across her desk. "The south end was completely engulfed in flames, all the buildings lost. The firemen made a stand, stopping the conflagration within a block of town hall."

"Didn't it start at the First Wabash National Bank?"

"That's right. Burned to the ground. Even melted the vault. Cleaned First Wabash out of some two million dollars, according to this report." She laid a yellowing newspaper atop the map. The headline read: FIRE LEVELS TOWN.

"What started it?" Bootsie wanted to know.

"No one knows for certain, but according to this account in the *Burpyville Gazette* it was thought to be 'spontaneous combustion of paint fumes.' Seems the bank had been painted the day before."

"You don't think so, do you?" Maddy was a quick study.

"No, I think the bank was set on fire to cover up a robbery. That's where the money in the quilt came from."

"Stolen by my husband's great grandfather?" gasped Bootsie.

"We know Abner Purdue came into money about then. Used it to start E Z Seat. His wife made that ugly old quilt the same year."

"And she left the quilt to her grandson's wife," Lizzie nodded. "Now I have to go. I can't keep Lee Ann waiting."

"Actually, to her son Bobby Ray," corrected Cookie.

"If you say so," shrugged Lizzie, gathering up her quilt squares.

"Just a minute," said Maddy, waving for her friend to sit back down. "We have to solve this mystery."

"Oh, okay. But the answer is as plain as the nose on your face. Bobby Ray told his two friends about the money in the quilt and they pushed him into a quicksand bog so the could steal it, right?"

"Something like that," beamed Cookie Bentley, proud

of her connect-the-dots theory.

≈ ≈ ≈

Police Chief Jim Purdue nodded his head. "Looks like the Quilters Club has solved another puzzle," he agreed. They were gathered in the mayor's office there in the Town Hall.

Beau was seated behind his desk. "I've gotta admit it all makes sense," he said. "A bank robbery. That money had to come from somewhere."

"Who's money is it now?" asked Jim.

"Beats me. Better call the state boys and let them sort it out."

"Before you do that," suggested Maddy, "why not confront Harry Periwinkle with this and see if he confesses. He might know where Jud Watson is hiding."

"Not a bad idea, but I'd have to have his lawyer present," the police chief pointed out.

"So call Mark," she said. "He should be at his office."

CHAPTER SEVENTEEN

A Pirate

Mark Tidemore met the entourage at the Caruthers Corners Police Department. "Sorry," he said to them, "but only the Chief gets to question Harry Periwinkle. The rest of you have to wait outside."

"But –"

"Those are the conditions," the attorney said, avoiding the stares of his in-laws.

"C'mon," said Beau Madison to the members of the Quilters Club. "Let's walk down the street to the DQ. I'll buy everybody a milkshake."

Mark looked at his shoes while everyone but Jim Purdue filed out of the room. The police department was a small brick building: Inside there was a reception area with a long counter, an inner office with two desks, two holding cells, Jim's own office, and a locked storage room where they kept weapons and ammunition and a battering ram they'd never used.

Harry Periwinkle was sitting forlornly in the holding cell on the left, as if waiting for something to happen. "Hi," his attorney greeted him, stepping close to the bars. "The Chief has a few questions for you. I'll be here to object if I don't think you should answer. Okay?"

The prisoner looked up, eyes blank. "Whatever."

Jim Purdue edged closer. "A great deal of money has been found inside that old guilt you tried to get your hands on. Do you know how it got there?"

"Bobby Ray's great grandmother made the quilt. I'd guess she put it in there."

"Where did an old country woman get her hands on that much money?" pressed Jim.

"Beats me. Bobby Ray never said."

"Do you and Jud Watson kill Bobby Ray?"

Mark interjected, "Don't answer that."

The prisoner shrugged and said, "Whatever."

Jim tried again. "Does Jud go by the name Bernard Warbuckle?"

"Maybe, maybe not."

"Did he jimmy that DNA test so you could pass as Bobby Ray Purdue?"

Mark spoke up again. "Harry wasn't there at the time. He can't know what Jud Watson did or didn't do."

Jim scowled in the attorney's direction. "But that was the plan, wasn't it?"

"Maybe, maybe not."

"Where have you been for the past thirty years?"

"I told you," said Harry Periwinkle. "I became a pirate."

CHAPTER EIGHTEEN
Photographic Analysis

Something about those photographs he'd gotten from Sad Sammy Hankins kept nagging at Mark Tidemore. What was it that danced just outside his recognition?

He fingered the two snapshots of the Baumgartner pasture. Fence. Elm tree. Grass. The dark tangle of the Never Ending Swamp in the background. Wait – what were those dots in one of the photos?

He reached in his desk drawer, fumbled around till he found the 6x magnifying glass, and held it over one of the photographs. The older one. There, climbing over the fence that separated the swamp from the pasture were four kids.

He turned the photo over to check the date – that was what had been nagging at his mind. August 12, 1982, the day those boys disappeared. Could this photograph taken by Sad Sammy have accidentally captured the Lost Boys?

No, something was wrong. There had been three Lost Boys – Harry Periwinkle, Jud Watson, and Bobby Ray Purdue. The snapshot pictured four tiny figures.

How silly of him to have thought this was a photograph of those missing boys ... it would have been too much to hope for.

≈ ≈ ≈

Freddie Madison drove out to the Bentley farm, hoping to say goodbye to the circus performers. They had been nice to him, a freakish fire-scarred ghoul. He appreciated their acceptance.

As he pulled his mother's Toyota SUV into the barnyard, he could see the two tents, trucks, and animal cages out there in the field. The elephant was getting a bath, Swami Bombay scrubbing him with a soapy brush on a long handle. Big Bill was brushing down the white horses. Little William was playing with Sneezy the Baboon. Mr. Sprinkles was nowhere to be seen.

He strolled toward the tents, waving a hand in greeting.

"Hey, where's your niece?" called Big Bill Haney.

"Grounded. Her mother is punishing her for some mischief."

"Too bad. I know Sprinkles was hoping to see her before we roll out. We're heading to Peoria first thing in the morning.'

"I'll pass along your goodbye to everyone. Things are pretty crazy in town today."

Big Bill stopped currying the horse. "Yeah, we heard. You mother and her friends found a lot of money in an old quilt."

"A local antique dealer estimated the loot might be worth a hundred million. Too bad my mom and her friends don't get to keep it."

"I'll say," laughed the tall ringmaster.

Freddie glanced around. "Where's Sprinkles?"

"In the tent," said Little William. "Took to his bed.

Seems upset about something. Maybe he wishes he'd found that money."

CHAPTER NINETEEN

Too Many Boys

First thing next morning, Mark Tidemore walked over to his mother-in-law's house on Melon Pickers Row. It was only a few blocks from where he and Tilly lived in one of those big houses facing the town square. He found her scrambling eggs for Beauregard. She gestured for him to sit down at the table and broke another three eggs into the hot cast-iron skillet.

"Something's bothering me," he said as she poured him a cup of coffee. Beau was dutifully ignoring them, reading the morning paper.

"What?" she responded. "The way you kicked us out of the police station yesterday?"

"No, I had to do that. Something else."

"I know you were only doing your job," she said, serving the eggs along with toast and two slices of bacon. "It's just frustrating to have loose ends."

"Seems the case against Harry's pretty air tight," he commented. "I'll deny saying it, but most I can hope to do is get him a reduced sentence. It would be easier if he'd cooperate a little."

"What brought you over here this time of morning? I know it wasn't my watermelon jam."

"That would be reason enough," he said, spreading the

pink jam onto his toast.

"But –?"

He produced the snapshot he'd got from Sad Sammy. "Do you have a magnifying glass?" he asked.

"There one over there in the junk drawer," Beau spoke up without lowering his newspaper.

Maddy pulled it out and handed it to her son-in-law. "What are we looking at?"

"A photograph of Baumgartner's farm on the day those boys went missing in 1982. I think they may be in this picture."

Maddy bent over the color snapshot, squinting through the magnifying glass. "Yes, I see them. That boy climbing over the fence looks like Bobby Ray. I remember him. His parents went to our church. The one in the middle might be Harry, judging from the way he's hanging his head. Reminds me of that hangdog look he had at the jail yesterday."

"Hm, you could be right."

"I assume one of the other two boys is Jud Watson. I don't remember him very well. But why are there four figures in this picture? There were only three Lost Boys."

"Yes," nodded her son-in-law. "That's the question of the day."

CHAPTER TWENTY

A Fugitive Captured

"**T**he ICE folks stopped Bernard Warbuckle as he was trying to cross into Canada at Windsor," Chief Jim Purdue told the mayor when they met for coffee at the Cozy Diner that afternoon.

"That a fact?" Beau was blowing on the hot liquid to cool it down enough to be drinkable.

"They picked him up about an hour ago. That ol' boy was hightailing it out of the country," the chief nodded. "Windsor's Ambassador Bridge is the southernmost US-Canada border crossing."

"They were watching for him, huh?"

"There was a BOLO on him. But the reason they caught him was because he tried to run the crossing gate. Must have panicked."

Beau Madison sipped at his coffee, careful not to burn his lips. "Have they been able to prove that he's Jud Watson?"

"Not yet. But the state boys are on their way out to Myrtle's place to take a swab to map her DNA. Just a matter of time."

"I take it, he's not talking."

"Said he's Bernard Warbuckle and that he's on his way to visit a cousin in Winnipeg."

Beau snorted. "How does he explain running the barrier?"

"Claims his accelerator pedal stuck."

"Good luck with that story."

"State's filing to bring him back to Indy. His goose is cooked."

"Like a Thanksgiving dinner," agreed Beau Madison.

≈≈≈

Maddy gathered up the Quilters Club and drove out to the Baumgartner farm that same afternoon. It was a pretty summer day with puffy white clouds filling the blue sky. The temperature was hovering at 98° when they pulled up to the wooden gate that blocked entrance to the farm. They could see the two-story house in the distance.

"Not very inviting," observed Maddy. There was a thick padlock on the gate. A handpainted sign said GO AWAY!

"Jim said Errol Baumgartner doesn't welcome visitors. Not even the FedEx man," said Bootsie, staring out the car window toward the forbidden citadel.

"We're here to see his wife," said Maddy. "At least that's the cover story."

"Okay," nodded Cookie. "Let's climb over the fence and hike up to the house."

Ten minutes later they were knocking on the door. "Hello," called Maddy. "Anybody home?"

The door swung open and a wild-eyed man said, "Didn't you see the sign on the gate?"

"We knew you didn't mean us," said Maddy. "We're the Caruthers Corners Quilters Club and we're here to see your wife Janey. We brought her some watermelon tarts.

We heard she just had twins, so we wanted to see if she needed anything."

"My wife is napping."

"Well, can you give her this basket of tarts?" Lizzie thrust the offering toward him. "They're quite tasty."

Errol Baumgartner looked at the basket suspiciously, but took it. "Thank you. Now if you'll excuse me –"

"Did you hear they found another of those Lost Boys?" Maddy continued as if she hadn't heard him. "You must've known them. They were about your age."

"Yes, I went to school with them," he admitted, eyeing the four women cautiously.

"You were with them the day they disappeared, weren't you?"

"Uh, what makes you say that?" A look of panic crossed his face. He was a slender man with dark hair and unshaven stubble on his chin. Handsome in a way.

"There's a photograph of you with them."

"That's impossible," he protested. "No one saw us go into the swamp." The blood drained from his face as he realized what he'd just said. "Uh, I mean –"

"What happened that day?" demanded Bootsie. Always a policeman's wife.

"Perhaps you'd better come in," said Errol Baumgartner, stepping aside to let his visitors enter the house. "But keep your voices down. We don't won't to wake up the babies."

≈≈≈

"Bobby Ray brought his friends over that day," Errol Baumgartner told the story. "They wanted me to take them into the swamp. Living out here, I'd explored some of it, knew a few trails that were safe. No quicksand."

They were sitting around the kitchen table, listening to Errol while his wife served coffee. Everybody was munching on the watermelon tarts.

"I've never told this to anybody other than Janey," he sighed. "I swore I'd keep their secret."

"What secret's that?" asked Cookie, fascinated with this untold history.

"That they were running away to join the circus. There was one camped on the other side of the swamp. They needed me to guide them across."

"Circus?" muttered Maud, reminded of her granddaughter's excited tales of Haney Bros. Circus and Petting Zoo. What kid wouldn't be tempted by the romantic idea of joining an entourage of lions and tigers and clowns?

"That's not so surprising," said Cookie, handy with her historical facts. "There were lots of circuses passing through. At one time Peru, Indiana, was known as the "Circus Capital of America.""

"Did those boys push Bobby Ray into a pool of quicksand?" asked Lizzie, looking for a sensational tale of murder.

"No," the man chuckled. "He fell into a marshy area and got his clothes wet. But last time I saw those boys – that was thirty years ago – all three were alive and well. They waved goodbye to me as the headed across the field toward those circus tents."

"Why didn't you tell anybody?" challenged Bootsie. "Their poor parents thought they were dead."

"The boys made me promise not to tell. Gave me a

pocketknife as payment. But I had another reason too. My grandpa would have beat the tar out of me if he found out I'd been in the swamp. It was off limits."

"Your grandfather has been dead for years," Cookie pointed out. "You could have come forward and put their parents' minds at ease."

"By then I was afraid I'd get into trouble with the law for not telling. I had a wife, this farm to take care of. I couldn't risk it."

"You're going to have to talk to my husband," said Bootsie. "He's the police chief."

"I know who he is, Miz Purdue. I may live out here like a hermit, but Janey and I go into town once or twice a month. Right, hon?"

The woman moved around the table refilling the coffee cups. "I told him it'd catch up with him one day," she said flatly. "Just be my luck that he goes off to jail leaving me stuck with twins to support."

"How are the babies?" inquired Maddy.

"The doctor says they're doing fine. I'm seeing a pediatrician over at Burpyville Memorial."

"Them two babies need a daddy. I don't know what we'll do if I go to jail," said Errol. He was a guy used to having bad luck.

"You needn't worry about that," offered Bootsie. "The statute of limitations has passed a long time ago."

"Then I'm willing to confess all. Especially since them boys have started turning up again. If I don't tell, they will."

CHAPTER TWENTY- ONE

Sprinkles the Clown

A week later, both Harry Periwinkle and Jud Watson were sitting in jail cells in Indianapolis, awaiting arraignment. They both refused to talk, not willing to further incriminate themselves in the identity scam.

Maud Purdue and her oldest son N.L. were meeting with the police chief to get an update.

"I demand that justice be done!" exclaimed N.L. "Those men deserve punishment, trying to bilk me out of half the chair factory. Not to mention trying to take my mother's life savings."

It was amazing, Jim Purdue thought, how that money hidden in the old quilt had morphed into a savings plan. Maud hadn't even known it was there till the Quilters Club got involved.

"They'll get some stiff prison time," predicted Chief Jim Purdue. "No question about it."

"Forget about them," snapped Maud Purdue. "What about my son Bobby Ray? According to Errol Baumgartner, he's alive."

"Those boys know where he is," the police chief

nodded. "Just be patient. Eventually they'll talk to cut a deal."

"I've waited thirty years," she sighed. "Guess I can wait a little bit longer."

"How can you be so sure they know where my brother is?" asked N.L. Purdue. He was a skinny man with bushy eyebrows and thinning hair. His black suit made him look more like an undertaker than a furniture maker.

"Because they had to get a DNA sample from Bobby Ray to substitute for Harry's."

"Are you saying he was in on the swindle?" frowned N.L.

"I doubt it. He could've stepped forward to claim ownership in E Z Seat, or retrieve his great-grandmother's quilt, without resorting to a scam that involved switching identities."

"My brother was declared legally dead more than twenty years ago. Don't see why I've gotta share ownership in the chair factory with a dead man – even if he comes back to claim it."

"That's a question for lawyers," said Jim Purdue.

≈ ≈ ≈

Tilly allowed her brother to come over that night to watch a Netflix movie with Agnes. She was still grounded.

With the Haney Bros. Circus lingering on Aggie's mind, she elected to watch a rerun of *The Greatest Show on Earth*, a story built around the Ringling Brothers Circus.

The big train wreck scene was exciting enough to make the Aggie squeal when the engine went off its tracks and wild animals broke from their cages.

She thought Charlton Heston with his leather jacket and fedora looked like Indiana Jones. "Where's his bullwhip?" she asked.

Freddie explained that the reason Jimmy Stewart never removed his clown makeup was because he was hiding from the law. "It's like a disguise," he said.

"Is that why Mr. Sprinkles never takes off *his* greasepaint?" she asked with childlike innocence.

That gave Freddie pause. Come to think of it, he'd never seen Sprinkles the Clown without his "face" on. Why was that?

"Sprinkles is like a Method Actor," he made up an explanation. "He likes to stay in character."

"Oh," she said, not really understanding the answer.

≈ ≈ ≈

That night when Freddie got home, he knocked on his parents' bedroom door. "Mom, are you asleep?" he called.

Maddy appeared at the door. "What is it? Has there been an accident?"

"No, no," the disfigured man assured his mother. "I just wanted to talk with you about something."

"You're all right?"

"Yes, of course."

"What do you want to tell me?" She stepped into the hallway so as not to wake Beau. She tightened the belt on her old blue bathrobe.

Freddie hesitated. "I'm not sure it means anything, but I've been thinking about the Lost Boys."

"And –?" His mother brushed her hair back, fingers combing through the blondish locks with little effect. It still looked like she'd stuck her finger in a light socket.

367

"Remember I told you about that little circus that was camping out at Ben Bentley's farm?"

"Yes, it's all Aggie could talk about for days."

"Well, Ben Bentley told me that when they heard about the Quilters Club finding all that money, the clown said it was *his* money."

"Oh? That's a strange thing to say."

"There's more. He never takes off his makeup, like he's hiding his face. Just like Jimmy Stewart in 'The Greatest Show on Earth'."

"What made you think of that old movie?"

"Aggie and I watched it tonight."

"Go to bed," sighed his mother. "You're just letting your imagination run away from you. Next you'll be seeing monsters in your closet like when you were five."

"Mom, Sprinkles the Clown fits into this somehow. Maybe he's really Bobby Ray Purdue."

"Go to bed," repeated his mother.

≈≈≈

Around 3 a.m. Maddy Madison came awake. She'd been having vivid dreams, something about the Phantom of the Opera swinging on a gigantic chandelier. When he reached up to remove his mask, she expected to see her son's scarred countenance underneath – but it morphed into a monstrous clown's face. She woke up with a start.

Maddy glanced around the darkened room, disoriented. She recalled the late-night conversation she'd had with Freddie, realizing that had been the basis for her nightmare.

Maybe she shouldn't have dismissed Freddie's comments about that clown. Could he have been Bobby

Ray Purdue? After all, hadn't the boys run off to join the circus? Had he recently been here in Caruthers Corners, right under their very noses?

No, surely not.

She rolled over and tried to sleep.

CHAPTER TWENTY-TWO

The Swamp Guide

"**N**o," said Chief Purdue, "I'm not going to try to extradite that clown from Illinois. There's not a shred of evidence that he has anything to do with this mess ... other than your overactive imagination."

"Not just mine," Maddy pointed out. "Freddie's too."

"Runs in the family."

"Okay, I guess we'll never know the full story of the Lost Boys," sighed his best friend's wife.

"Madelyn Agnes Madison, I've known you since grade school. You're not going to wheedle me into doing this. Judge Cramer would laugh me out of his office if I asked him to sign an extradition warrant for a clown who calls himself Sprinkles."

"Your loss."

"No, I'm confident Harry Periwinkle or Jud Watson will 'fess up. The state's attorney has offered to lessen the charges if they tell all. They'd be crazy not to take the deal."

"I think they were crazy to try to pull off this cockamamie impersonation in the first place," said Maddy

as she huffed out of the police department into the warm
August morning.

≈ ≈ ≈

Big Ben Bentley had been stacking bales of hay in the
barn. He kept a couple of milking cows on the farm.
Cookie liked fresh milk, not that over-priced pasteurized
homogenized vitamin-added fat-free white liquid you
found at Foley's Grocery.

Ben was hot and sweaty, his mile-wide shoulders on
display with no shirt. He only wore bib overalls, his usual
uniform for farm work. "Time to take a break," he told
himself, speaking out loud. There was a pitcher of cold
lemonade waiting in the fridge.

As he walked across the barnyard, he glanced toward
the open field behind the house. Only last week it had been
festooned with tents and banners proclaiming HANEY
BROS. CIRCUS & PETTING ZOO. Now it looked so
forlorn.

Big Bill Haney and his twin brother Little William
were getting long in the tooth. He'd guess they were in
their 70s. Big Bill had told him they were thinking of
retiring, the only thing keeping them from it was their
menagerie. Elephants live a long time. What would
happen to Happy and the other animals if they packed it
in?

For that matter, what would happen to Bombay and
Sprinkles, Ben wondered. "Circus performer" wasn't a big
draw on a resumé.

Swami Bombay looked to be in his mid-fifties.
Sprinkles might be younger, although it was hard to tell
under all that greasepaint.

Ben Bentley wondered if he could help them. He was a kind-hearted man.

≈ ≈ ≈

Chief Jim Purdue drove out to the Baumgartner farm, ignoring the GO AWAY sign at the gate. It was unlocked, so he drove up the dirt road and parked his cruiser in front of the two-story house. Walking around back, he found Errol working on his Ford RAM-150 pickup. "Hello there," he called to announce his presence.

Errol looked up with a start, not used to visitors. His face was streaked with grease. The carburetor in his hand looked like a mechanical heart from a failed transplant. "Guess nobody pays any attention to that sign on the gate," he groused, reclusive to the point of being rude.

"Knew it didn't apply to me," said Jim. "This badge on my chest is an Open Sesame."

"You're town police. Ain't got no jurisdiction out here."

"True, but I expect you'd rather talk to me than the state boys. They tend to arrest people who withhold evidence."

"Evidence? I ain't got no evidence. Unless you mean that Barlow knife Harry Periwinkle gave me to lead 'em across Never Ending Swamp. I still have it."

"No, I mean the info you kept to yourself."

Errol wiped his hands on a dirty rag and walked around the truck to where the police chief stood. "What info's that?"

"Like the name of that circus the boys joined. You saw it as you waved goodbye to them across the field. Circuses tend to put their name on the sides of their wagons and on big banners. You forgot to mention that detail."

"Hm, didn't pay much attention. And that's been thirty years ago. The memory's not as clear as if it happened yesterday."

≈≈≈

Cookie looked it up in the old newspapers she kept on file at the Historical Society. "Here we are," she told Jim Purdue. "The August 10, 1982 issue of the *Burpyville Gazette*."

He leaned forward to read the faded newsprint:

Haney Bros. Circus To Perform

The world-famous Haney Bros. Circus will give six shows this weekend at the Gruesome Gorge Campground north of Caruthers Corners. The small two-ring circus promises a great time for the kids, featuring a tightrope act and a magician this year. Highlight of the show is a lion tamer in a cage with two big jungle cats. Happy the Elephant returns with dozens of other exotic animals. Admission is $2.

"Well now," muttered the police chief, "maybe Maddy was on the right track after all."

"Hmph," said Cookie. "How many crimes does the Quilters Club have to solve to prove our detective skills to you?"

He laughed. "What do you gals want? Badges?"

"Aggie would like that," she grinned.

CHAPTER TWENTY-THREE

Off On a Road Trip

Police Chief Jim Purdue didn't like it, but he agreed to drive over to Illinois with the four women to confront Sprinkles the Clown. He explained that this was unofficial – he wasn't going as a lawman. "Since I can't talk you out of it, I'm just going along to keep you gals out of trouble."

Lizzie had offered to drive, her Lexus holding five comfortably. Jim sat in the back with his wife and Cookie, letting Maddy ride shotgun.

"Do you know where the circus is playing?" he asked as Lizzie barreled along at ten miles over the speed limit. It was going to be embarrassing for Jim if they got stopped by a state trooper.

"Peoria, they said," reported Cookie.

"Shouldn't be hard to find them once we get there," said Maddy. "A circus tends to stand out."

Jim leaned forward to make himself heard over the car radio, tuned to a Golden Oldie station. "Couldn't you have made a few phone calls in advance," he groused.

"My husband doesn't like flying blind," offered Bootsie. "He likes to have all the facts."

375

"That's exactly what this is," said Cookie, "a fact finding mission."

Jim Purdue didn't have much to say for the rest of the trip, cursing himself for letting his wife talk him into this foolhardy misadventure. But then again, he wasn't prepared to ask Judge Cramer for a warrant to extradite Sprinkles – or Bobby Ray – or whoever the heck he was – without more facts.

Maddy was wrong about the circus standing out. The small entourage played malls and grade schools and Lions Clubs – not countrywide assemblies. Finally, they got a tip at a gas station that led them to the Salvation Baptist Church where Haney Bros. had set up its tent for a weekend run, a portion of the proceeds promised to the church's Missionary Fund.

"Hello," Big Bill Haney greeted them. "Good to see you folks. But how come you didn't bring the little girl?"

"She's grounded," replied Maddy. "It's a long story."

"Well, Sprinkles is going to be sorry he missed you."

"Missed us?" gasped Maddy. "He's not here?"

"Alas, no. He left day before yesterday. Gave up the sawdust after thirty years as our clown."

"He quit?" said Lizzie, irked that she'd driven all the way to Peoria for naught. Her husband hadn't wanted her to put that many miles on the new Lexus in the first place.

"Had to happen. I didn't want the boy to wind up like me, old and washed up. This is going to be the last season for Haney Bros. But it's been a good run, forty-seven years under the Big Top." He glanced toward the sagging tent. "Well, little top," he amended.

"Do you know where Sprinkles went?" interjected Jim

Purdue, sounding like a cop, unofficial business or not.

"Didn't say. But he'll be in touch. He's a good son."

"He's your son?" muttered Jim, giving Maddy a glance that said the credibility of the Quilters Club as detectives had just hit a snag.

"That's right, the best of the bunch. Not counting Bobby Ray."

"Y-you mean Sprinkles isn't Bobby Ray Purdue?" sputtered Maddy Madison.

"Of course not," responded Big Bill Haney. "Bobby Ray is dead."

CHAPTER TWENTY-FOUR

A Man-Eating Lion

"**D**ead?" Maddy repeated. Her theory crumbling in front of Chief Jim Purdue and her fellow Quilters Club members.

"Sad story," nodded Big Bill Haney. "He got et by a lion. Back in '08 it was. Didn't you hear about it? Nearly ruined the circus."

"No," said Maddy.

"I vaguely remember hearing something about that," volunteered Lizzie Ridenour. "But I had no idea it was anyone we knew."

"Yeah, everything went downhill after that. Couldn't get bookings. Performers left for other gigs. We reduced the show down to one ring. Turned ourselves into a for-rent kiddy entertainment with a petting zoo."

Maddy was still trying to digest the news. "If Sprinkles isn't Bobby Ray Purdue, who is he?"

"Why he's Jud Watson, of course."

≈≈≈

Beau Madison had eschewed the trip to Peoria, choosing instead to go fishing with Edgar Ridenour. Since retiring from the bank, Lizzie's husband had devoted himself mainly to fishing and other outdoor pursuits. Serving on the Caruthers Corners Town Council and sitting on the board of Burpyville Memorial were the only two official duties he had left ... unless you counted trying to catch the fat catfish that lived in a bend in the Wabash just south of town.

Beau had joined him in that quest today. Even a mayor needs a day off now and again. "You sure he's in there?" he squinted at the dark water.

"As sure as the sun rises," Edgar assured him. "I've hooked that monster two or three times, but he's a Houdini when it comes to slipping off a line."

"Why didn't you join the girls on their trip to Peoria? Jim went with them."

The former bank president just shook his head and continued to bait his hook. Dough balls were today's tasty lure. No longer the immaculate businessman, Edgar had grown muttonchops and shoulder-length hair since retiring.

"C'mon," persisted Beau. "You've got a vested interest. Burpyville Memorial is being sued by N.L. Purdue over that false DNA report."

"That greedy ol' goat is asking for a million dollars in punitive damages. Claims that fiasco did irreparable harm to E Z Seat's reputation."

"Think he'll get it?"

"Who cares? It's not my money. Or the hospital's. It's in the hands of the insurance companies. Burpyville Memorial has malpractice policies up the wazoo."

"Has that guy Bernard Warbuckle confessed yet?"

"You mean Jud Watson? No, he's still not talking."

"Any question that he did it?"

"Not according to the investigators. They say they've got Jud Watson dead to rights."

≈≈≈

"Jud Watson?" said Maddy. "Are you sure?"

"I oughta be," nodded Big Bill Haney. "I raised him like a son since he was twelve years old."

"So he did run off and join the circus?" stated Cookie. She liked to get the facts straight.

"Him and Bobby Ray and Harry and Tom."

"Tom?"

"Yes, he came a few years later. But he and Harry hit it off. Developed a pirate act. I taught 'em to juggle swords."

"Harry said he became a pirate," the police chief remembered. "Guess he was telling the truth about that."

Big Bill nodded. "Tom and Harry were the jugglers. Jud became the clown. And Bobby Ray was supposed to be the lion trainer. But obviously he wasn't very good at it. I had to take over the act after his fatal encounter with Grumpy."

"Grumpy?" repeated Maddy. "My granddaughter said you had a lion named Grumpy."

"Same one. He's getting pretty long of tooth now."

"Didn't they make you destroy him after he killed someone?"

"We told the authorities we did, but we lied. Do you know what a draw it is to a circus to have a man-eating lion?"

381

CHAPTER TWENTY-FIVE

Bad Apples

"**L**et me get this straight," said the police chief. "You're admitting you kidnapped those boys?"

"No, no," Big Bill Haney waved away the accusation. "My wife and I took them in. They were runaways. They needed a home, even if it was a traveling circus."

"You have a wife?" said Maddy.

"Yes, Little William. Her name's really Willamina. She passes as my brother for the sake of the circus. We wanted to call it Haney Bros. – just like Ringling Bros."

Bootsie rolled her eyes. "He's a she?"

"Every inch of her. We've been married nearly fifty years. December will be our golden wedding anniversary."

"Congratulations," said Cookie. She considered wedding anniversaries to be significant historical events.

"Willamina was a good mother to them boys. Jud made us proud. Bobby Ray died too young. Too bad Tom and Harry turned out to be bad apples."

That got the police chief's attention. "Bad apples, you say?"

"About four years ago, they stole all the circus's money and run off. Haven't heard from them since."

"I'm pretty sure they're the two guys sitting in an Indianapolis jail cell at this very moment," said Jim Purdue. "Didn't you hear about them trying to embezzle money from the president of the E Z Seat Company?"

"I heard something about that, but I didn't realize it was my two boys." He shook his head sadly. "I told you they was bad apples. Willamina's going to be heartbroken."

≈ ≈ ≈

They were mostly silent on the drive home, contemplating the strange turn of events. All the mix-and-match identities had been confusing.

Harry Periwinkle had pretended to be Bobby Ray Purdue to get at the money in the quilt. Bernard Warbuckle was actually a guy called Tom Appleby, not Jud Watson. And Sprinkles the Clown was really Jud Watson, not Bobby Ray Purdue. And Bobby Ray Purdue ... well, he was dead ... but mauled to death by a lion, now drowned in a pool of quicksand.

Even Little William turned out to be Willamina.

You needed a scorecard.

CHAPTER TWENTY-SIX

A Day at the Circus

Haney Bros. Circus returned to Caruthers Corners, once more pitching its tents on the Bentley farm. It was a glorious end-of-summer afternoon, the sun glinting off the tin roof of Ben's big red barn. Happy the elephant seemed, well, happy to be "home," spraying water in the air with her trunk in celebration.

Maddy drove out with Freddie and Agnes. Aggie's curfew had been lifted, since she was being hailed as a hero among family and close friends for retrieving the treasure quilt from Maud Purdue's attic.

But with Bobbie Ray gone, there was a question of who might get all that money. Maud Purdue told a newspaper reporter it was hers to keep. However, her son N.L. had filed a claim as Bobby Ray next of kin. Brothers trumped mothers in the genetic sweepstakes.

"Thanks for coming out," Big Bill Haney greeted the Madisons. "I'm sorry Sprinkles is no longer with the Big Top. I know you liked him."

"I like clowns," Aggie smiled. "But I like elephants too."

"Happy will be pleased to see you. She will remember

you. Elephants never forget, y'know."

"Will you be getting another clown?" asked Freddie. He liked being here at the circus. Nobody seemed to pay any attention to his deformities.

"Are you applying for the job?" smiled the ringmaster.

"No, I can't travel. I have a wife ... and maybe a new daughter."

"Too bad. The Big Top's loss."

"Do you think I'd make a good clown?"

Big Bill studied him for a moment. "Yes, I do. All clown's are slightly sad."

Swami Bombay brought Happy the Elephant over to see the visitors. "She saw you from out in the field and insisted on coming to greet you," said the dark-skinned man.

"Look," said Aggie, holding out her hand. "I brought you peanuts, Happy."

The elephant trumpeted, then buried her snout in the girl's hand, scarfing up the peanuts.

"Happy likes them," nodded Bombay. "I knew she would. I saw it in a vision." Reminding them that he did a mind reading act.

"Thank you for helping clear up the mystery of the Lost Boys," Maddy said to Big Bill Haney.

"Lost Boys," he snorted. "They weren't lost because they had a home with us. Willamina and I loved those kids, even Tom and Harry. But I have to tell you we mourn the loss of Bobby Ray. Truth be told, he was our favorite. A good kid, a fine young man."

"I'm sorry how this turned out for you," Maddy said, extending a hand politely. "But it's over now. The Lost

Boys have been accounted for.

Swami Bombay closed his eyes and touched his temples with his fingertips, as if receiving a psychic message. "Ahh, my friends, I hate to tell you this," he wheezed, "but the story is not over."

CHAPTER TWENTY- SEVEN

The Real Lost Boy

"**E**xcuse me," said the slender man at the office door. "Are you Mayor Madison?"

Beau looked up from his paperwork, plans for a new gazebo in the town square. He was slightly irritated to be interrupted. How had this guy gotten past his secretary? Where was Martha? Probably taking another coffee break. She liked to hang out in the coffee room with that girl who worked for the city planner down the hall.

"Yes, may I help you?"

"Well, maybe. I am Bobby Ray Purdue."

The coffee cup in Beau hand dropped to the desk with a *crash!* spilling the brownish liquid onto the architectural drawings of the gazebo. "B-but you can't be," he stammered. "You're ... I mean Bobby Ray ... is dead."

"Not any longer," smiled the blue-eyed visitor.

≈≈≈

"I've convinced Judge Cramer to let me resign from representing Harry Periwinkle and Thomas Appleby," announced Mark the Shark. "After all, the court appointed me to represent Bobby Ray Purdue. Now that we've established who he really is, it would be a conflict for me to represent those pretenders."

"So this guy – the former Sprinkles the Clown – really is the third Lost Boy?" said the Police Chief, just to get it on the record. He'd called together the Town Council as well as the Quilters Club and assorted friends to help him unravel this ball of twine.

"That's correct," nodded Mark. "We just got the new DNA test back from Burpyville Memorial. And it conclusively proves that this gentleman before you is Bobby Ray Purdue."

"How do we know it's accurate? May I remind you, we've been through this once before," challenged Chief Purdue.

"You can bet the farm on this one," Edgar Ridenour spoke up. "I insisted that Virgil Hoffstedder, chief of Burpyville Memorial's lab division, conduct the analysis himself."

This informal gathering in the conference room at the town hall had no official status but Bobby Ray Purdue had agreed to meet with them and help straighten out this case of mistaken identities. As Man of the Hour, he sat quietly at the head of the table, listening to them talk about him like he wasn't even there.

"*Ahem,*" he interrupted the wrangling over his identity. "I *am* Bobby Ray Purdue and everybody may as well get used to it. I'm back to stay."

"Okay, let's say you are," conceded Jim Purdue. "But you've got lots of explaining to do."

"That's why I'm sitting here."

"So tell us the story from the beginning," said Maddy Madison. "I'd like to know how much we got right."

The slender man shifted uncomfortably in the wooden chair, feeling like he was on the witness stand, unofficial proceeding or not. "Well, I guess it goes back to when we ran away from home – me, Jud Watson, and Harry Periwinkle."

"Why did you boys do that?" asked Bootsie.

Bobby Ray seemed to think about that for a moment before responding. "We all had our reasons," he said slowly. "Harry hated his father, a man who belittled him and called him a bastard. You see, he wasn't really Harry's dad. Harry's mother had been a hippie, marched in Vietnam War protests, lived in a commune. She never knew who knocked her up. Willard Periwinkle married her, but he never did accept her son Harry."

He stopped to take a sip of water from the pitcher in the middle of the conference table, as if his throat were dry. But it may have been a delaying tactic, not eager to relive these memories.

"Go on," said Chief Purdue.

"Jud had to get away from home before his mother killed him. She used to whip him with a belt till his back was raw. He used to come to school with blood seeping through the cloth of his shirt. She was mean as a snake. Blamed him for her husband abandoning them. Left when Jud was still a baby, saying he didn't want no part of being a family."

"And you?" asked Maddy.

The man poured himself another cup of water, drank it slowly, his Adam's apple bobbing with each gulp. "Do I have to say?" he asked.

"No, you don't," his new attorney interjected. "This

conversation is entirely voluntary."

"But it would help us better understand," encouraged Maddy, at her motherly best.

"Well, okay. In for a dime, in for a dollar. It was because of my brother Newcomb."

"N.L.?" blurted Beau. As owner of the E Z Seat factory, Newcomb Lamont Purdue was the richest man in Caruthers Corners. And a big contributor to the mayor's political campaigns.

"That's right, my big brother. He used to beat the holy hell outta me when we were boys. He wasn't none too happy when mom had me. I think he resented not being the only child. Every time she turned her back he'd pinch me or kick me or smack the bejeebers outta me. I just couldn't take it any longer."

Beau was glad they hadn't invited the families of the Lost Boys to this meeting. It was like watching someone rip the scab off a painful sore. "So tell us about your running away," he shifted the conversation.

"We decided to join the circus. There was an announcement in the paper about one playing up at the Gruesome Gorge Campground. But that was a long hike, unless you cut through Never Ending Swamp. Errol Baumgartner claimed he knew a safe trail, so we talked him into taking us across the swamp. Gave him a Barlow knife I bought off Shorty Yosterman."

"So you boys really did join the circus?" said Cookie, mesmerized by the story.

"Yessum, we did. That is, Big Bill and his wife took us in. They trained us to do circus acts. Made us a part of their family."

"Circus acts?" uttered Lizzie, hoping he'd get to the juicy parts.

"Harry and another kid who joined up developed a juggling act. They dressed like pirates and tossed cutlasses back and forth. Those big knives couldn't cut butter, but it was dangerous enough to please an audience."

"And you?"

"Me, I was supposed to be a lion tamer, but Grumpy scared the tar outta me. I just didn't have what it takes."

"And Jud?" asked Bootsie. Trying to get them all straight in her mind.

"He became Sprinkles the Clown. I think he was hiding under that greasepaint in case his mother came looking for him. But she didn't."

"But Big Bill said *you* got killed by that lion," prompted the police chief.

"Wasn't me, it was Jud. He wanted to try his hand at lion taming, so I let him go into the cage. It turned out bad. That old lion practically tore his head off. You couldn't even recognize him, mangled as he was."

"That's when you decided to switch places with Jud," said Maddy, catching on.

"Right. I put on his clown makeup and pretended to be him. Couldn't believe I got away with it. I've been Sprinkles the Clown for over four years now."

"But why?" asked Bootsie.

"Partly cause I was afraid I'd get blamed for his death, letting him go into that lion's cage. But mainly because I was afraid of Harry and Tom."

"Why would you be afraid of them?" asked Lizzie. Her thickly mascaraed eyes were as wide as silver dollars as she listened to the story.

"Well, over the years I'd told them about that quilt my great-grandmother had left to me. How one day while playing in the attic, I'd discovered that it was stuffed with money. About a week before the lion got him, Jud overheard them talking about killing me and taking the treasure."

"Surely that was just talk," said Cookie, sometimes too naïve for her own good.

"Likely not," interjected Jim Purdue. "Four years later they did follow through with a plan to get their hands on the quilt. That shows some determination."

"Where was Harry Periwinkle and Tom Appleby during those four years?" Cookie wanted to know. Connecting the dots.

"Beats me," said Bobby Ray. "They robbed the circus of nearly ten thousand dollars and took off. I never heard of them again until Harry showed up here claiming to be me."

"As it happens, Harry was doing time in Oklahoma for killing a man in a bar fight," Mark Tidemore informed them. "So he did have a violent streak."

"How do you know this?" demanded the police chief. He hated being caught off-guard with someone knowing more facts than he did.

"Harry gave a statement to the State Police this week, trying to cut a deal."

Chief Purdue was clearly irked that the state boys hadn't informed him of this. "How did those two get your DNA if you weren't in on it?" he challenged.

"Hold on, Jim. My client isn't on trial here."

"Sorry, but it's a legitimate question."

Mark held up a hand to stop the argument. "I can answer that based on Harry Periwinkle's statement," he said. "Tom had been trying to go straight. He used his share of the stolen circus money to take a community college course that trained him to be a lab technician. He just happened to be working at the hospital when Harry got out of jail."

"But Bobby Ray's DNA –?"

"Harry still dreamed of getting his hands on that hidden treasure. He came up with this scheme of impersonating Bobby Ray after seeing a movie called *Sommersby* starring Richard Gere and Jody Foster. It's about a man who returns from the army, but people question his true identity."

"I remember that film," said Cookie. "It's based on a French film called *The Return of Martin Guerre*. It has the same imposter theme."

"So Harry saw his opportunity when he heard Haney Bros. Circus was camping in Ben Bentley's field. He enlisted Tom in his scheme and they slipped into the Haneys' tent one night. Seems Willamina kept locks of her boys' hair in a scrapbook. Tom was able to extract sample DNA from that."

"So Harry pretended to be Bobby Ray to get his hands on that quilt full of money and doing that finally flushed our Lost Boy out of hiding," Maddy summed it up.

"Hiding in plain sight," noted Freddie, who had decided to set in on this august gathering.

"Now I can go back to being Bobby Ray Purdue … and Sprinkles the Clown," nodded the subject in question. "But first my attorney here is going to help me claim that money. I plan to buy a circus."

EPILOGUE

Some people like a happy ending. And this latest adventure of the Quilters Club has one, as it turns out.

Thanks to Mark the Shark's persuasive argument, Judge Horace Cramer ruled that the money found in the quilt belonged to Bobby Ray Purdue. The quilt had been left to him by his great-grandmother and there was no way to prove where all those antique bank notes came from. The First Wabash National Bank had never reopened its doors after the Great Fire of 1899, so no one spoke up in its behalf.

Bobby Ray sold the rare bank notes at auction, many of them going to numismatists and other private collectors for undisclosed sums. Local antiques dealer Daniel Sokolowski upped his estimate to $200 million, but that was just an educated guess.

What is known is this: Bobby Ray bought his mother a new house on Field Hand Road and set up a $2 million annuity to provide for her. He sold his half of E Z Seat to his brother N.L. for the grand sum of $1. And he paid for the construction of the new gazebo in the town square. After all, his reappearance had caused the mayor to spill his coffee on those fine architectural drawings.

And more: He bought Rachel McGurty's old boarding house on Easy Chair Lane, turning it into a home for retired circus performers. Big Bill Haney and his wife

Willamina took the entire second floor. Bombay Martinez got a large room in back. There was even room for a couple of former Haney Bros. performers, now retired but eager to rejoin their comrades. Bobby Ray took the cottage out back for himself.

The big news: Ben Bentley donated that great field behind his house to the town (a referendum passed to annex the land into the city limits) to become a zoo.

Bobby Ray – the one-time Sprinkles the Clown – donated $100 million dollars to establish the Haney Bros. Zoo and Exotic Animal Refuge. The endowment would provide for the care of Happy, Sneezy, Doc, Grumpy, Dopey, Sleepy, and Bashful, as well as other animals that would join them in entertaining the children of Caruthers Corners and nearby towns. A giraffe and a hippopotamus had already been added. And Big Bill was negotiating with a traveling carnival for an old leopard that needed a good home.

On weekends, the retired circus performers put on shows at the zoo, free to the public. Bobby Ray would smear on his greasepaint and reprise Sprinkles the Clown. And he was joined by a second clown known as Sparkplug.

Sparkplug wore a fire chief's hat and rode around in a miniature red fire engine, squirting seltzer water into the air. Freddie Madison liked his newfound hobby – entertaining kids. Why not? He had a new addition to his own family, 2-year-old Donna Ann Madison. He and his wife had decided to stay in Caruthers Corners. Amanda had gone back to teaching and Freddie happily played Mr. Mom. But on weekends he covered up all those facial scars with white greasepaint and became Sparkplug the Clown.

He was having a ball.

Mayor Beauregard Hollingsworth Madison IV got credit for expanding the city limits and bringing in a town zoo. Maddy was so proud of her husband.

Aggie was happy to have a new cousin, mainly because it meant her Uncle Freddie would be sticking around. Next year she would be old enough to babysit. And she would have a second baby sister too. How cool was that?

But Bobby Ray Purdue was the real winner. Returned from the dead. Reunited with his mother. Remaining close to his foster parents and his circus friends. And richer than his avaricious brother N.L.

But forget about all that money. When you saw how happy he was entertaining kids as Sprinkles the Clown, you knew he was the wealthiest man in Caruthers Corners.

Hemmed In

A Quilters Club Mystery

4

"Our lives are like quilts – bits and pieces, joy and sorrow, stitched with love."

- Anonymous

CHAPTER ONE

The Mad Matilda Wilkins Quilt

Turns out that Maddy Madison missed Tuesday's gathering of the Quilters Club because she had to drive to Indianapolis to pick up her grandson, N'yen. Bill and Kathy had adopted the boy last year. Just turning nine, he'd asked to visit "Grammy and Grampy" as his birthday present. Which meant that he really wanted to see his favorite cousin, eleven-year-old Agnes.

Aggie was an honorary member of the Quilters Club and N'yen wanted to join too. The kids saw it as an undercover detective agency, being that its members – Maddy Madison, Lizzie Ridenour, Bootsie Purdue, and Cookie Bentley – had solved a couple of local crimes last year.

However, the four members of the Quilters Club saw it as ... well, a quilter's club. The crime solving had been incidental.

Aggie and her mom had joined Maddy for the drive to Indianapolis (a two-hour journey each way) to pick up the boy. As a result, they missed the biggest robbery that had ever taken place in Caruthers Corners – the theft of the Mad Matilda Wilkins quilt, a patchwork masterpiece that had hung in the lobby of the Town Hall for over one hundred years.

The quilt had been appraised at $100,000 ... but to the good folks of Caruthers Corners it was priceless.

Back in 1897, Matilda Wilkins had hand-stitched this wondrous patchwork creation, a scene that might have been conceived by Hieronymus Bosch. There on the fabric danced angels and demons, sinners and saints. The border was decorated with odd symbols that some thought might be a secret code, supposedly the language of Satan himself. You see, Mad Matilda was known to be a witch.

She had lived on Cloven Hoof Lane, so-named in deference to its only resident. Her cottage had been located at the end of the narrow dirt road. Once a stone structure with a slumping roof, the cottage has long since fallen to the ground. Nonetheless, visitors like to drive out to look at the scattered stones and the well where she is said to have died, refusing to float, as witches are wont to do.

The religious zealots who tossed Mad Matilda into the 80-foot well were never officially identified, but legend had it they were members of a snake-handling cult that maintained a house of worship over near the Never Ending Swamp. Other than the leader – Rev. Billingsley Royce – the identities of its members are a forgotten part of history. There's no sign of the church today, its exact location debated by old-timers.

Mad Matilda's patchwork quilt had been rescued from the crumbling cottage by a distant relative and donated to the Caruthers Corners Historical Society. Thereafter, the quilt has been displayed in the lobby of the Town Hall as a decorative wall hanging – its satanic history ignored, its craftsmanship admired.

Quilting Bee magazine once called it "the best example of allegorical quilt design extent in Indiana." Many museums had offered to buy it, but the Historical Society refused to sell this piece of the town's heritage.

For over five generations the 8' x 8' *objet d'art* had loomed over visitors to the Town Hall, accepted as an oddity, but nonetheless mesmerizing in its intricate design.

Then it was stolen.

There one day, gone the next – the very date that N'yen Madison had turned nine. Of course, there was no connection. Or was there?

CHAPTER TWO

The Quilters Club On the Case

Caruthers Corners had been founded in 1829 by three stranded fur trappers. One of them, a sour and dyspeptic man named Jacob Caruthers, had lent his name to the town that grew up on this very spot. The other had been a sneaky backstabber named Ferdinand Jinks. And the third had been a crusty old Indian fighter named Beauregard Madison. As it turns out, Col. Madison was the great-great grandfather of Beauregard Hollingsworth Madison IV, Maddy's husband – and the town's current mayor.

"This will be the ruination of me," groaned Beau as he sat at the kitchen table, head cradled in his arms. His wife had just returned from the airport in Indianapolis with young N'yen in tow. She was shocked by the news. The Wilkins Witch Quilt was one of the town's claims to fame, that and its annual watermelon festival.

With a population of only 2,577 (not counting N'yen's singular visit), the town got more recognition than you'd expect. Watermelon Days had been featured last year on *The Today Show*, with Al Roker entering the watermelon-eating contest. He came in 63 out of 87 contestants.

Beau had just finished reciting the known facts: The quilt had been in its place on the wall in the lobby when he locked the Town Hall last night. It was gone when he opened up this morning. The alarm had not been tripped.

Police Chief Jim Purdue was baffled. He was more used to handing out parking tickets along the town's two-block business district than solving art thefts. Jim was Beau Madison's best friend and the husband of Maddy's pal Bootsie. "I've called in the state boys," he said, patting Beau reassuringly on the shoulder.

The kitchen was crowded – Beau, Jim, Maddy, Bootsie, daughter Tilly and her husband Mark. Even Cookie and Lizzie. Plus the kids, Aggie and N'yen. The Vietnamese boy's parent's had entrusted him to the airlines for the trip, allowing the Chicago couple to enjoy a mid-week vacation at the Wisconsin Dells.

Tilly's hubby was also the town's attorney. Mark the Shark (as he was known to the family) had been a big-time Los Angeles lawyer before downsizing his life and moving back to the ol' hometown. "I spoke to the SBI this afternoon," he reported. "They're sending in an electronics expert first thing in the morning. Said they want to figure out how the perp bypassed the alarm system."

"Perp?" asked Tilly.

"Perpetrator," Jim Purdue explained the verbal shorthand.

"The SBI says –" Mark Tidemore continued.

"SBI?" interrupted Tilly.

"The State Bureau of Investigation," Jim translated.

Mark plowed on, "– says the alarm was still set, no signs of forced entry, no clues whatsoever. They can't figure out how the quilt was stolen."

"That makes two of us," sighed the police chief.

"Beats me too," nodded Beau. "That quilt disappeared as if by magic."

"Of course, it was magic," giggled little Aggie. "The woman who made it was a witch."

"Aggie!" scolded her mother.

"That's what my Sunday School teacher said."

"There is no such thing as a witch," her mother corrected.

"Didn't you say the lady who runs the Clothes Horse Boutique is a witch?" That was a small dress shop on Main Street owned by Missy Yager. Missy was a former Watermelon Days Queen (1998).

"That's because she said I was fat."

"Missy said that?" exclaimed Tilly's mother.

"Not exactly. She suggested I needed to go up a dress size."

"That was after the second baby," her husband pointed out. "You've lost all that extra weight."

"What? You think I'm fat too?"

Mark rolled his eyes, sensing a no-win conversation. "You look perfect, hon."

Maddy turned to her granddaughter. "Sometimes people call each other names when they get upset. But that doesn't mean Missy Yager is *actually* a witch on a broomstick."

"Like the ones at Halloween?" asked Aggie.

"That's just pretend," said Maddy. "Like ghosts and goblins."

"If there aren't real ghosts, how does a dead person float up to Heaven?"

"We'll talk about that later," grinned Maddy. "But as far as the quilt's disappearance is concerned, it has nothing to do with magic."

"That's right, honey," said Jim Purdue. "When I said 'magic' I was just exaggerating."

Aggie wrinkled her forehead. "Exaggerating?"

"Stretching the truth," explained Maddy.

"Well, yeah," grunted Jim.

Mark the Shark stated the obvious: "We still have to figure out how the thief managed to steal that quilt."

"Don't worry," said N'yen. "The Quilter's Club will solve this case."

CHAPTER THREE

An Inside Job

Police Chief Jim Purdue shook his head. "Sorry, young man, but your grandmother and her friends are sitting this one out."

"Why?" pouted N'yen. "The Quilters Club could help you find the burglar."

"It's bad enough when the Quilters Club meddles in one of my cases, but the state boys won't hesitate to arrest them for interfering with a police investigation."

Aggie Tidemore frowned. "But aren't you the police, Uncle Jim?"

"Well, yes. But these are state police. Higher up the ladder than me. They're taking over the investigation."

"Why can't you just deputize the Quilters Club?" argued N'yen. "Let them handle it."

Maddy was trying hard to conceal her smile. "It doesn't work that way, dear. We are *ex officio*. Not official detectives."

"That's right," nodded the girl's grandfather. "You gals are just pretend detectives."

"Gals?" challenged N'yen. "What about me? I wanna be a pretend detective too."

Chief Purdue laughed. "Oh? What could you tell us about this case?"

The boy raised his chin defiantly. "Well, if nobody broke *into* Town Hall, maybe they broke *out* instead."

That stopped everyone.

"Hm, if someone knew the code, he could reset the alarm system from inside the building, giving him time to get out without setting off the bells and whistles," admitted Beau Madison.

"But what about the locked door?" said Mark the Shark.

"The deadbolt has a knob inside. You could unlock it, step outside and let it snap back into place," replied Beau.

"But you'd have to be inside the building to begin with," argued the police chief.

Beau thought for a moment. "I suppose someone could have hidden in a restroom," he said. "Can't say that I checked them before leaving last night."

"An inside job," exclaimed Bootsie.

"Now don't go saying that," Jim Purdue warned his wife. "Anybody could have gone into the building during office hours and hidden out in the restroom."

"That's what I meant. Someone *inside* the building."

Beau thought about it. "If it really was an inside job, someone who works there, the list of suspects would be short – me, my secretary, the Town Clerk, and the Tax Assessor. The head of Building and Zoning was out sick, and the Director of Public Works is on vacation."

"What about the Town Planner?" asked Bootsie.

Beau shrugged. "We don't have one at the moment, not since Joe Johansson went to meet his maker last month."

"Oh, that's right," she nodded. "He's the fellow who stuck his finger in the light socket while changing a bulb. I don't think I ever met him."

"Joe was new to town," answered Beau. "I'd just hired him down from Gary. He was moving into his house on Rocking Chair Lane when it happened. Blew out the circuits on that side of town. They were without electricity for two whole days."

"I remember," said Maddy. "The funeral home is on that side of town so the refrigeration was out. They had to store his body at the ice plant till the electricity came back on."

"First, we need to establish alibis for all the town employees," said Mark. Liability insurance would kick in, if one of the officials were at fault.

"Me, I was here last night," said Beau.

Maddy nodded. "I can vouch for that. This isn't like the time Beau stole that statue of his great-great grandfather."

"That was different," muttered Beau. "It was a ploy to immortalize my forbearer."

Jim Purdue waved away their words. "You're not under suspicion, Beau. You're the mayor, for goodness sake."

"The last mayor was a crook," Beau pointed out. Not looking for any favoritism.

"But you're not," the police chief ended the discussion. "Besides, you have a reliable witness vouching for your whereabouts – your wife."

"That's right," said Maddy. "I barely slept last night, anticipating N'yen's arrival. I can attest you were in bed beside me – except for two trips to the bathroom. That nervous bladder of yours."

"We'd better clear the other town officials," Beau quickly changed the subject from his bladder, "so the state boys can focus on real suspects."

"And we need to make a list of everyone they can recall being in the building yesterday," added Jim Purdue. "I'd better interview them while memories are fresh."

"I can't believe the Wilkins Witch Quilt has been stolen," said Bootsie.

"Yes, it's an irreplaceable heirloom," nodded Cookie.

"Valuable too," added Lizzie.

"True," agreed Maddy. "A hundred thousand dollars is nothing to sneeze at."

"Point well taken," sighed Beau Madison. "Guess we'd better put surveillance cameras back into next year's budget."

CHAPTER FOUR

Rev. Royce and the
Church of Avenging Angels

In addition to being a member of the Quilters Club, Cookie Bentley served as head of the Caruthers Corners Historical Society. So it was no surprise to her friends that she knew all the sordid details about Mad Matilda Wilkins – the town's alleged witch.

The Quilters Club had gathered in the cramped quarters of the Historical Society to conspire. Despite last night's warning, they couldn't resist looking into the theft.

"Yes, Matilda Wilkins was certifiably mad," Cookie affirmed, sitting there behind her antique desk. "The old woman truly believed she was a witch. People came to her to buy love potions, have her to cast spells on their enemies, and predict their future. By all accounts these occult activities made her quite wealthy. But no money was found after her death. Everybody assumed that those fanatics who murdered her took it."

"Why didn't they take the quilt?" asked Liz Ridenour. Being a banker's wife, she always thought in monetary terms.

"We value it today, but back then it was just a fancy bedspread," explained Cookie. "Besides, all those symbols on the quilt may have scared them. It was said Mad Matilda used it in satanic ceremonies."

"Why didn't those people who murdered her get arrested?" asked Bootsie. As the wife of the police chief, she was curious about such details.

Cookie patted a stack of yellowed newspapers. "According to contemporary reports, all the members of the Church of Avenging Angels left the county in the dark of night. None were ever captured."

"Church of Avenging Angels?" repeated Maddy. "That sounds quite ominous."

"They were an extremist cult. Believed that violence against evil was justified. Hunted down witches." She pulled a faded photograph out a drawer. "This is Rev. Billingsley Royce, leader of the Avenging Angels. If anybody got Matilda Wilkins's money, it was this guy."

Maddy leaned forward to study the photo. The man had close-set eyes and spikey, unkempt hair. His pointed chin looked very defiant. A wine-stain birthmark covered half his forehead. He held a coiled snake in his hands. "Scary looking," she observed.

"Rev. Royce may have been crazier than Mad Matilda. It's said he slept in a bed of rattlesnakes. But I suspect that's just a tall tale," added Cookie.

"What does any of this have to do with the stolen quilt?" scowled Lizzie Ridenour. The redhead had a short attention span.

"Maybe nothing," admitted Cookie, pushing her wire-rimmed granny glasses back upon the bridge of her thin nose. "But knowing the quilt's history may be helpful in recovering it."

"We're going to recover it?"

"Don't you think we should?" responded Cookie.

"Of course," said Maddy. "After all, we know more about quilts than the State Bureau of Investigation."

"Jim's not going to like this," muttered the police chief's wife.

Maddy patted her friend's shoulder. "Then don't tell him. No need to worry your husband unnecessarily. That's my policy."

"One rumor had it that Matilda Wilkins's money was buried under the church's doorstep, awaiting Rev. Royce's return."

"Surely people have looked there," said Bootsie.

"Not really," Cookie shook her head. Her mousey brown hair glinted with gold from the overhead light. "You see, when the Avenging Angels pulled out, they burned their church to the ground. Or so it was claimed. It could be that the deputized posse looking for them burnt it. After all these years, nobody seems to remember exactly where it was located."

"How could you lose a church?"

"The town plats are pretty accurate, but no one paid much attention to the surrounding countryside back then. Old newspaper articles say it was on the far side of the Never Ending Swamp, but that's a lot of empty land. Mostly watermelon fields today."

"Okay, then let's concentrate on the quilt," decided Maddy. "Do you know if Mad Matilda make others?"

Cookie shook head. "Not as far as we know. 'The Battle Between Heaven and Hell' was the only one."

"Wow! That's a pretty dramatic name," exclaimed Bootsie.

"That's the official title given to the Wilkins quilt."

"I didn't know that," Lizzie admitted. "I've always heard it referred to as the Wilkins Witch Quilt."

"The official title is posted there on a little bronze plaque in the Town Hall," admonished Cookie. "Anyone could read it if they had a mind to do so."

"I hardly ever go to the Town Hall," rejoined the redhead, sounding a little defensive.

"The title comes from the design on the quilt, angels and demons fighting it out. An apocalyptic vision." Cookie pulled out a color photograph of the quilt, taken when it was still hanging on the Town Hall wall. "It's quite detailed."

The four women studied the picture. The orange-and-red quilt was dazzling to the eye. Each patchwork square was embroidered with tiny figures, some bearing wings, others displaying horns, with monsters scattered among them – like a scene from a Civil War battle, but being fought with otherworldly soldiers.

"Ooo-ee," said Lizzie. "I've never looked at the quilt up-close before. Reminds me of a nightmare I might have after eating too much pistachio ice cream."

"There's no such thing as too much pistachio ice cream," muttered Bootsie, a frequent visitor to the DQ on Main Street. She suffered a little weight problem from time to time.

Cookie described the scene: "Angels attacking devils with thunderbolts. Devils wielding pitchforks. Goblins and half-human monsters gnawing on angels' legs. Cauldrons boiling with witches' brew, fires burning, thunderclouds spewing lightning, the very earth splitting to swallow combatants, all hell breaking loose!"

"What an imagination," observed Maddy.

"Matilda Wilkins claimed it was a vision of things to come."

"Well, it's now more than a hundred years later and I haven't noticed any strangers with wings or horns hanging around the gazebo in the town square," smirked Lizzie. She and her husband Edgar owned a big Victorian house facing the grassy expanse of the square.

"Don't scoff," admonished Bootsie. It wasn't clear whether she was being superstitious or just overly reverent.

"What about these strange markings around the border?" Maddy pointed. "Do you know what they mean?"

Cookie pulled out a thick book titled *A History of Caruthers Corners and Surrounding Environs* by Martin J. Caruthers. He'd been the father of the former mayor, the scallywag that Beau had defeated in a landslide victory. "Let me read this. Old Martin Caruthers devoted a few paragraphs to the Wilkins quilt."

Fitting her reading glasses over the narrow bridge of her nose, Cookie continued:

"Whereupon an elderly crone named Matilda Elizabeth Wilkins lived on the outskirts of town, we come to a discussion of her subsequent murder and the patchwork prize she left behind. Said to be a sorcerer, Mrs. Wilkins sold magic potions to the lovelorn and vengefuyl. Thus, a

religious sect known as the Avenging Angels is thought to have kill't her. The followers scattered and were never tried for the heinous crime, drowning the old woman in her own water well.

"A relative rescued a wondrous quilt, purported to be a magical device, from her cottage and turned it over to one of the town fathers (that being my biological pater familias), who preserved it for all to see on display in the governmental building facing the square.

"This quilt was said to bestow the aspect of invisibility upon its owner. It is embroidered with scenes of the Armageddon, depicting the final battle between Good and Evil. Around the border are indecipherable symbols, thought to be a secret language known only to practitioners of the Dark Arts. Despite its frightening subject matter, the Matilda Wilkins Quilt is an example of superb needlework. It is deserving of preservation as an ignoble chapter in this town's history, as well as a record of the masterful craftsmanship of its inhabitants."

"Indecipherable,' the old man said." Bootsie looked frustrated. She liked things to be black and white.

"Those markings *must* have some meaning," insisted Lizzie. "Has anyone ever called in a language or code expert?"

Cookie pulled out a clipping. "Says here that back in the '40s a World War II code breaker took a look at the quit but was stymied."

"These markings look like they could be ancient runes or cuneiform writing," said Maddy. "Maybe it's not a code at all. Just some kind of little-known hieroglyphics."

Bootsie said, "Why not ask Daniel Sokolowski? He has lots of sources when it comes to things like this." Sokolowski was owner of Dan's Den of Antiquity, a crowded little shop on Main Street that displayed Tiffany lamps, Chippendale chairs, carousel horses, and a genuine Tlingit totem pole that came all way from Alaska.

"Surely someone would have recognized it by now," argued Cookie, not eager to gallop off on a wild goose chase. But when Maddy nodded her head at the suggestion, she knew the plan was approved. The mayor's wife was sort of the unofficial leader of the Quilters Club.

CHAPTER FIVE

An Accident in Wisconsin

The Quilters Club's plan to consult Daniel Sokolowski went astray when Maddy got the phone call from Wisconsin. Bill and Kathy had been in an automobile accident on the way back from the Dells. Her son had a broken leg, his wife a fractured hip. They were in the Aurora St. Luke's Medical Center, ranked #2 out of 153 hospitals in that state.

"No, don't fly up here, mom," Bill said firmly. "Kathy and I are getting good care. We just want to make sure you're okay with N'yen staying with you and dad for a few weeks. Give me and Kathy time to get back on our feet. So to speak." Her son had a way of laughing t adversity.

"Of course," Maddy replied. "You know how fond we are of N'yen. And he loves being here with Aggie. They're inseparable."

"Thanks, mom."

"Nonetheless, I think I should fly up there for a day, just to check on your medical care and help with anything you might need. N'yen can spend the night at Aggie's. Your sister Tilly won't mind."

"One day. No more. You know how fidgety dad gets when you leave him to fend for himself."

423

"I'll head to the airport in Indy this afternoon. You're sure you two are all right?"

"As they say, sticks and stone can break my bones. Apparently an eighteen-wheeler can do that too. My femur got cracked, my nose got bloodied, Kathy broke her hip, and the Subaru was totaled. Thank goodness for airbags – and Subaru's reinforced frame body structure!"

≈ ≈ ≈

Maddy was actually gone for three days. By the time she returned from Milwaukee, the Indiana State Bureau of Investigation had determined that the thief had hidden inside the Town Hall until after hours, removed the quilt from the wall using a step ladder stored in the janitor's closet, reset the alarm, then slipped out into the night.

A brilliant deduction.

Just as N'yen had said.

The SBI questioned the boy to determine how he knew the *modus operandi* of the thief, but gave up after he described the plot of a movie called *Flawless* in which a janitor robs a diamond distributor, an inside job.

They did, however, give Jasper Beanie a hard time. In addition to being the cemetery's caretaker, Jasper acted as the Town Hall's janitor. Fortunately for him, he only worked on Wednesdays and Fridays, so he wasn't there that Monday when a culprit had hidden inside the building to rob it.

Chief Purdue cleared all the town officials.

Like Beau Madison, the Town Clerk had been home with his wife ... and new baby. Being colicky, the tot had kept the couple up half the night.

The Tax Assessor had played poker with his cronies until 3 in the morning, then sacked out on his friend's couch. Divorced, he didn't have to report home to a wife.

Becky Marsch, Beau's new secretary, had spent the night with her boyfriend, though she'd been reluctant to admit the affair. After all, this was a small town.

Jim Purdue had also phoned Big Elk Lodge, the resort in Idaho where the director of Public Works was vacationing. Turns out, George Wilkerson had bagged an elk on Tuesday. Got his picture in the *Big Elk Gazette*.

And Doc Habegger confirmed that Ferdinand Gilmore, the Planning and Zoning guy, was in bed with a temperature of 102°. "If he's able to go out and steal quilts, it'd be a modern-day medical miracle," the doctor had said.

The list of people who had been in the Town Hall on Monday was lengthy. Even so, many visitors were likely overlooked. With property taxes coming due, Arthur Rutledge had processed 127 payments that day despite his usual hangover.

Rutledge printed out the list of people he'd processed, but he couldn't be sure who had accompanied them – wives, brothers, miscellaneous friends.

The Town Clerk added 32 names to the list. And Becky contributed 13 more from Beau's appointment book.

The SBI was studying all the names with the diligence of high school seniors cramming for their final exam.

"The state boy's will never catch the crook this way," Beau told his wife over supper. What with N'yen and Aggie joining them, watermelon à la mode was on the desert menu.

"Why not?" Maddy asked.

"Too many suspects. If the Wilkins Witch Quilt is ever recovered, it will likely be by some unscrupulous art fence turning in the seller for a fat reward."

≈ ≈ ≈

After dinner (the chili was great!), the phone rang. Aggie was first to pick it up. "Madison residence," she said with the aplomb of an experienced receptionist. "Whom may I say is calling?"

It was one of the state boys, a gruff agent known behind his back as The Nail. Lieutenant Neil Wannamaker was acting as lead investigator on the case. Aggie handed the phone to her grandfather, whispering, "It's a man named Wanna-something. He sounds scary."

Beau took the phone. "Yes, Lt. Wannamaker, I'd be happy to go over my appointments with you. But all the names on that list are leading citizens. I'd vouch for each and every one of the people I met with on Monday. First thing in the morning at my office? Fine."

"A waste of time," Beau grunted as he put the phone down. "But gotta go through the motions, I suppose."

"*Some*body stole that quilt," Maddy reminded him. "I just hope it's not anyone we know."

CHAPTER SIX

At the Ruins of the Wilkins Cottage

The next morning the Quilters Club – the four women and little Aggie – set out on a field trip to inspect the ruins of the Wilkins cottage. N'yen was at home pouting, seeing his exclusion as nothing short of sexism, girls ganging up against the lone boy.

About a half-hour north of Caruthers Corners, Maddy turned her big SUV onto a sandy road that cut through flat watermelon fields belonging to Aitkens Produce, the biggest farm in the county. About four miles in they came to an oasis in the farmland, a cluster of oak trees that shaded a stonewalled well. Someone – Boyd Aitkens most likely – had installed a pump to draw water up to a large cattle trough. Not that there were any cows in sight.

"Over there," Cookie pointed. "That clump of rocks must be where the house stood."

They strolled over to inspect the remains of Matilda Wilkins's cottage. Most of the foundation stones had been carried away, probably to build some other structure on the watermelon farm.

Lizzie paced it off. "Not a very big house," she assayed its diminutive size.

Bootsie was peering into the well. "I can't see the bottom," she said.

"Don't lean too far," advised Maddy. "That didn't work out too well for Mad Matilda."

"Did people really kill her?" asked Aggie, still learning about the inhumanity of fellow humans.

"Bad people," Lizzie told her, red hair blowing in the breeze that came off the surrounding fields.

"Church people?" The girl had heard them talking.

"A cult," corrected Cookie. "The Avenging Angels were more like a gang of murders and thieves hiding under the cloak of piety."

"And nobody knows where their hideout was?" asked Aggie.

"Well, they called it a house of worship, but that was certainly a misnomer."

"Miss who?"

"Misnamed."

"Oh," said Aggie. Her blonde locks brushed her shoulders, a tomboy look. "Why don't we go find it? Didn't you say they buried the treasure there?"

Cookie cracked a smile. "One newspaper article speculated they buried the money they stole from Mad Matilda at the church. But there's no basis for it, other than a local farmer who claimed Rev. Royce told him that."

"Why would Rev. Royce tell anyone where he hid the money?" scoffed Maddy. "What would keep that farmer from digging it up for himself?"

"Good point," nodded the bank president's wife.

"What's this?" said Bootsie, still staring into the well. "Looks like some markings on the inside."

The women gathered round the well. "Markings?" said Cookie, straining to see. Her eyes followed Bootsie's pointed finger. There on some of the stones about three feet down were scratches that might have been writing of some kind.

"Hard to make out," muttered Lizzie. Afraid to lean over the rim. "It's awfully dark down there."

"I've got a flashlight in the glove compartment," volunteered Maddy. "Hang on."

"Let me see the markings," begged Aggie, but her protective companions refused to let her near the open well.

"Better stand back," warned Lizzie. "It's dangerous." She stepped backward, away from the well, as if following her own advice."

"Awwww."

Maddy returned with a small penlight. It was more powerful than it looked. She aimed the beam at the scratches, tracing the indentions with the light. "Hm, could be the same kind of symbols that were on the quilt's border," she noted.

"Ruins?" said Aggie.

"I think you mean 'runes,' dear," Bootsie corrected.

"That reminds me," said Cookie. "We have an appointment this afternoon with Daniel Sokolowski. He's going to recommend someone who knows Old Norse writing."

"Why Norse?" asked Lizzie. "Didn't you say those markings could be Sumerian cuneiform writing or Egyptian hieroglyphics?"

Cookie glanced at the scratches before answering. "No, they're certainly not Egyptian hieroglyphics or Japanese kanji. Those forms of writing are more pictorial. As for cuneiforms, ancient Sumer was located a long way from Caruthers Corners. However, there is some evidence of Norsemen coming this way."

"Norsemen? You mean Vikings?"

Cookie nodded. Despite her plain-Jane hairstyle and spectacles, you could see she was a beauty underneath. "The Old Norse feminine noun *víking* refers to an expedition overseas. We know they came to Vinland – probably eastern Canada – around 1000 AD. And the Kensington Runestone was found in Douglas County, Minnesota, some seven hundred miles northeast of here."

Maddy looked skeptical. "You think Vikings carved these markings inside the well?"

"I doubt this well is that old. The Kensington Runestone dates back to 1362."

"Looks pretty old to me," muttered Lizzie.

"Maybe whoever dug this well picked up some runestones along with the other rocks when they built this wall," said Bootsie.

"Where did Mad Matilda get the markings on her quilt?" asked Aggie. Trying to piece if all together, without much luck.

"Maybe she copied them off these rocks," said Lizzie. Like Occam's Razor, always looking for the simplest explanation.

"We're all guessing," Cookie pointed out. "Let's wait to see what Daniel Sokolowski's expert has to say."

≈ ≈ ≈

Daniel Sokowloski rubbed his gray-streaked beard with one hand, as if petting a cat, while he thumbed through an old-fashioned carousel-style Rolodex with the other. "Here it is," he said. "Ezra Pudhomme. He's an expert on Runology. You may be familiar with his biography of Friedrich Bernhard Marby, the noted rune occultist."

"Must have missed that one," said Maddy.

Cookie spoke up. "Wasn't Marby the Germanic neopaganist who developed a set of occult exercises he called runic gymnastics?"

"Yes, the exercises were used as a means of channeling runic power. Or at least that was Marby's theory." Sokolowski grinned like a Cheshire cat, delighted to have found someone who shared his esoteric trivia.

"So where is this Ezra Pudhomme located?" asked Bootsie, eager to get them back on a subject she understood. Runic power – what the heck was that?

"Ah, it seems you ladies are in luck," said Sokolowski. "Professor Pudhomme happens to be doing a lecture series at ISU this semester."

"In Indy?" asked Lizzie. Her son Josh went to school there.

"Yes. A visiting professorship."

"Will you introduce us?" asked Maddy. "We could drive down for lunch tomorrow."

"Hold on and I'll phone him right now."

"Oh boy, a trip to Indianapolis," said Aggie.

"You'll have to ask your mother," her grandmother warned.

"What about N'yen? Can he come along? He's feeling left out."

Maddy was about to say he'd have to ask his mother, but caught herself. Kathy was still in the hospital – in traction, for goodness sake. N'yen was her responsibility for the next two weeks. "Alright, the two of you can come along," she acceded.

≈ ≈ ≈

Mayor Beauregard Hollingsworth Madison IV was unhappy about the meeting he'd had that morning with that pushy SBI agent. Lt. Neil Wannamaker was much too aggressive for Beau's taste. How dare he insinuate that one of Beau's office visitors might be a cat burglar capable of stealing the Wilkins Witch Quilt. All 13 names in his appointment book were leading citizens, the *crème de la crème* of Caruthers Corners society you might say. Not a shady character among them.

"Becky," he called to his secretary, "cancel my afternoon appointments. I'm going home. My stomach's acting up." In a small town like this, the term "administrative assistant" had not yet caught on.

"Okeydokey," she replied. All but snapping her chewing gun. Becky Marsch was fresh out of high school. This was her first job, according to the application. Beau wasn't sure she was going to work out. The girl daydreamed too much.

He wandered across the town square, pausing to watch the Poindexter twins play catch. Looked like Larry had a new catcher's mitt, while Lonny seemed content with his old glove.

As he turned onto Melon Pickers Row, the sidewalk got wider. One of the perks of having Public Works report to him. The street was lined with maple trees, tall and leafy. In autumn it looked as if the entire block was ablaze.

He noticed a black SUV, a Toyota, parked in his driveway. That was strange. Maddy was off with her Quilters Club cronies, so who would be at his house. Burglars didn't usually operate in broad daylight, he assured himself.

"Hello!" a tall man in a loose-fitting dark suit hailed Beau as he approached. The man had been standing behind the big leafy witch-hazel in the yard, having himself a smoke.

"Can I help you?"

"My card," the man brandished a sliver of paper that announced: *Maury Seiderman, Field Investigator, G.M.O.P.A.*

Beau stared at the card. "What's G.M.O.P.A.?" he said.

The man gave him a crooked smile. His face was thin, his eyebrows hooding purplish eyes (color contacts?), and he sported a pencil-thin moustache like a Lounge Lizard or silent movie star. "Greater Midwest Occult Phenomena Association. We're a non-profit organization out of Chicago."

"Never heard of it."

"We're an under-the-radar organization. Not seeking publicity."

Beau sized up the visitor. A beanpole, kids might've called him. Over 6' 5" but barely breaking 120 pounds. "Tell me how I can help you. We've got all the magazine subscriptions we need."

"Oh, we only publish a newsletter. And it's free to members."

"Well, my wife and me, we're not the joining type either."

The weird smile flickered, and then became fixed, like the face on a wax mannequin. "We're not recruiting right now."

"Then what do you want?"

"I'm here on official G.M.O.P.A. business. It has to do with that witch's quilt you lost."

CHAPTER SEVEN

Worrying About a Witch

Maddy Madison prepared duck à l'orange with dirty mashed potatoes, glazed carrots, and an arugula salad with watermelon dressing for dinner. N'yen's favorite. She was making up to the boy for leaving him in the care of Aggie's mother today. He was still pouty.

Beau piled a mound of potatoes onto N'yen's plate. The two had grown close. "Eat up, young man. You want to grow as tall as Grampy, don't you?"

Beau Madison was well over 6', a James Cromwell type. N'yen looked up at his grandfather with a twinkle in his brown eyes. "Not likely. We *Kinh* are usually short."

Aggie looked up. "What's a *Kinh*?"

"That's the kind of Vietnamese I am. I was born in Chicago, but my first parents came from the *ng□□i Kinh*."

"Do you remember your ... first parents?" Maddy asked.

"No, I was little when they died in a car crash. Now my new family has been in a car crash too."

"Your mommy and daddy are going to be all right. They broke some bones, but those will mend."

"You promise?"

"Yes, I do."

"Good. I like my new family."

"That's my boy," said Beau. A Viet Nam vet, he'd been reluctant to accept the boy at first. But that went out the window once the two met. Now they were fishing buddies, often accompanying Lizzie Ridenour's husband Edgar on hook-and-line forays along the Wabash.

"Want to go to Indianapolis tomorrow?" asked Maddy. "The Quilters Club is going to meet a man who might be able to read that writing on the quilt. You and Aggie can come along for the ride, if you like."

"Oh boy, we're going to play detective!"

Beau shook his head, the wispy white hair stirring with the effort. "Don't encourage this fantasy that you're the No. 1 Ladies Detective Agency."

"And why not?"

"Because you're not. You're a quilting society with nosey members."

"Same thing," said Maddy, nose in the air.

Beau rolled his blue eyes. "Heaven help me," he sighed.

About then, their son Freddie and his wife Amanda dropped by. "Is it too late for desert?" grinned Freddie. He was very fond of watermelon pie.

"Pull up a chair," said Maddy. "We are just about to cut the pie. But this is your sister Tilly's recipe, so it has strawberries mixed in."

"Strawberry-watermelon pie?" said Amanda. "That sounds interesting." She was followed into the dining room by their adopted daughter Donna Ann, the latest addition to the Madison clan (not counting Tilly's newest baby).

"I did say it was Tilly's recipe, didn't I?" Maddy grinned. Tilly was not known as a cook. "But I promise you'll like it."

"Whose black Toyota was parked in the driveway this afternoon?" asked Freddie. "I drove by on my way to clown practice." After being horribly scarred in an Atlanta fire, he'd returned to Caruthers Corners with his family to become a clown who entertained children at the Haney Bros. Zoo and Exotic Animal Refuge on the outskirts of town. The greasepaint may have covered his disfigured face, but it didn't disguise his pleasure in entertaining the local kids.

"A car in our driveway?" repeated Maddy.

"Well, I was going to mention that," said Beauregard Madison. "Just hadn't got around to it."

"Was it anybody we know, dad?" pressed Freddie. "I didn't recognize the car."

"No, no. It was just some quack. A field investigator for some witch-hunters organization. A real kook."

"Witch hunters?" said Aggie. "Is he hunting for Mad Matilda?"

"H-has she come back to haunt people?" stuttered N'yen. The Vietnamese boy fervently believed in witches and spirits of the dead. In Asia they were known as *vong h☐n, oan h☐n,* or *bách linh.*

"Beau, you're frightening the children," chastised his wife.

"No, he's not," protested Aggie.

"I'm not afraid of no ghosts," parroted N'yen. But there was a quaver in his voice. He still thought *Ghost Busters* was a horror film.

Beau Madison motioned everyone to calm down. "Take it easy," he said. "There's no ghost of Mad Matilda running around Caruthers Corners. Just this guy from the Greater Midwest Occult Phenomena Association looking for information about the missing quilt."

"What kind of information?" Maddy wanted to know. Her suspicions were easily aroused.

"Something about those symbols around the border of the quilt being a prophecy. Or a curse. Or something like that."

"A prophecy?" said Aggie. "What's that?"

"A prediction of the future," her Aunt Amanda offered. "But nobody can really predict the future."

Freddie laughed. "What about your Uncle Bernie? He's correctly predicted the Super Bowl winner for the last ten years."

"We don't talk about Uncle Bernie – he's a bookie. He handicaps sporting events based on stats and such. Nothing occult about that."

Maddy sliced the pie and served it on her special Blue Willow desert plates. She added a scoop of vanilla ice cream as she passed the pie around the table. "What kind of prophecy" she asked her husband.

"Didn't say. The guy was nuts. You could tell that just by looking at him. He could've been a character out of *Plan 9 From Outer Space*."

Amanda looked up from her strawberry-watermelon pie. "Isn't that supposed to be one of the worst movies ever made?"

"My point exactly," said Beau. "The guy was downright creepy."

"I've seen that movie," grinned N'yen. "There's a zombie and a vampire and invaders from another planet."

"Thank goodness we only have a witch to worry about," said Maddy, giving the boy another slice of pie.

CHAPTER EIGHT

The Visiting Professor of Runology

The drive to Indianapolis was uneventful. They only had to stop twice for N'yen to pee. Once at a service station, another time at a McDonald's. Ronald was still serving breakfast, so everybody but Bootsie had an Egg McMuffin; she ordered the oatmeal. This week she was dieting.

Visiting professor Ezra Pudhomme, the expert on Runology, met them at his on-campus office. He was a fat man, a human Jabba the Hutt. At a quick guess, he probably weighed in at 400 pounds. Two metal canes helped him waddle to his desk, where he deposited his bulk onto a couch that served as his office chair. "What's this question you have about runes?" he wheezed. "Dan Sokolowski didn't give me many details."

Cookie Bentley laid the color photograph of the Wilkins Witch Quilt onto the professor's desk blotter. "Are the symbols around the quilt's border runes or some other half-forgotten language?" she got straight to the point.

"Ahem, runes are *not* a language *per se*. They are a form of writing developed by Germanic people before the adoption of the Latin alphabet." You'd think he was teaching Communications History 101, one of his more popular freshman courses. "These are indeed runes, the

Scandinavian variant known as *Futhark*. The name comes from the first six letters in that alphabet – *Fehu, Uruz, Thurs, Ansuz, Ræið*, and *Kaun*. The symbols originally meant wealth, water, giant, god, journey, and fatal disease."

"That's fascinating," said Bootsie, barely able to hide her sarcasm. "But what has that to do with the price of ice in Iceland?"

Ezra Pudhomme sniffed haughtily, but refused to acknowledge her snide remark. "If you look at the photograph of your quilt, you will see some of those same runes. I'd say a loose translation might go like this –" He squinted over the image, using a magnifying glass because the inscriptions were small, even in this 8" x 10" color print. "*After a long journey, we are befallen by a fatal disease, so we hide our wealth in this deep water.*'"

"Wealth?"

"The rune also means cattle, that being a common source of wealth. But here I'd say it refers to some kind of money or treasure."

"Viking money?"

"Vikings did use this form of writing, so possibly."

"What kind of money did the Vikings use?" asked Liz Ridenour, ever the banker's wife. "Paper currency, metal coins, what exactly?"

"The Vikings did sometimes strike coins, but their basic exchange was what we call 'hack silver,' small bars that could be carried and easily cut – or hacked – to the size needed. The Norse did not place a face value on coins. Value was based entirely on the weight of the silver."

Maddy tried to pin the professor down. "So you think this writing around the edge of the quilt is talking about silver bars?"

"Well, yes. But of course, it's meaningless here."

"Meaningless?" huffed Cookie. She would not allow the quilt's authenticity to be challenged. There was an established chain of ownership – provenance, it's called – from Matilda Wilkins to her relative to the Historical Society.

"What I'm saying, the runes on this quilt are likely decorative, taken from somewhere else. Vikings never would've left a message on a flimsy quilt. They carved their messages onto runestones and other solid structures. Bells, bracelets, horns, buildings."

"This quilt was stitched in 1897," said Cookie. "Where would a turn-of-the-century witch woman learn how to write in – what did you call it? – *Futhark*?"

Pudhomme sat up, his body moving like a geological upheaval. "Witch, you say? That changes things. Perhaps the rune symbols were handed down as an occult tradition. Some people believed runes were not simply letters to spell words, that they also had deeper meanings ... magical or divinatory uses. The word *rune* itself means 'secret, something hidden.' Prior to their use as an alphabet, runes were used for different magical purposes, such as casting lots or casting spells."

Bootsie crossed herself. More out of superstition, for she wasn't even a Catholic. "Heaven help us," she said. "To think this witch's quilt has hung in our Town Hall for over a hundred years."

"Don't be silly," snapped Cookie Bentley. "We don't believe in witches. Matilda Wilkins was just a crazy old woman who made money selling love potions to hapless farmers – a snake oil salesman at best, a mad hatter at worst, but certainly not a woman with supernatural powers."

"Yes, I guess you're right," Bootsie acquiesced. "But it's downright spooky. We never suspected that those decorative symbols on the quilt contained a secret message."

≈ ≈ ≈

The Indiana State Police's lead investigator Neil Wannamaker had determined that the quilt theft had been pulled off by someone who knew the building's security code, allowing the burglar to escape by resetting it from the inside of the Town Hall after hours. An examination by the alarm company confirmed that someone reset the code at 1:03 a.m.

That hick police chief had pretty much exonerated all the city officials, Wannamaker told himself, but the janitor remained a loose end. Maybe Jasper Beanie didn't do the job himself, but he could have passed the alarm code on to a confederate. After all, Beanie was dirt poor, living in a shabby cottage provided by the Pleasant Glade Cemetery for its caretaker. And he had a history of drunkenness, often spending the night in jail in Burpyville. He drank over there because Caruthers Corners didn't have any bars.

Jasper Beanie was a weak man with financial needs. The perfect motivation for a crime.

Lt. Wannamaker crosschecked Jasper Beanie's telephone records against a list of his former cellmates, looking for any connection with a known criminal. Turns out, Beanie had been in regular contact with a petty shoplifter named Sam Stickley, A/K/A Sam Stickyfingers.

Aha!

≈ ≈ ≈

Liz Ridenour's husband had retired a couple of years ago as bank president. These days, he spent much of his time fishing. His scraggly hair, bushy gray beard, and grubby clothes belied his one-time executive appearance. Gone was the pinstriped suit and power tie, the wing-tipped shoes and $40 haircut. He could have easily passed as a hobo, a man without a penny in his pocket or a care in the world.

Edgar Ridenour was letting his aluminum flatboat drift with the current, his fishing line trolling behind. Fact was, he was snoozing in the afternoon sun, unconcerned that his boat was ten miles downstream from where it was supposed to be. He didn't have any board meetings or bank examiners to worry about. His pension was fully funded, more than enough for an ongoing life of leisure. And fishing.

Edgar came awake when he heard voices above his head. Opening one eye, he noted that he was under a bridge, caught up in a little eddy that kept his boat in place. Maybe it was the word he'd just overheard that caught his attention: *Witch*!

He'd heard enough at home about the Quilters Club looking into the disappearance of that old quilt from the

Town Hall. The one supposedly sewn by a witch. So what was this conversation coming from the bridge all about?

"Everybody thought those were some kinda magic symbols on that patchwork monstrosity. Little did they know it was a secret message."

"Secret message?"

"Yeah, like a treasure map. Giving the key to a hidden treasure."

"Ah, c'mon. That old rag has been on display forever. How come nobody ever figured out it was a secret message?"

"Beats me. Guess it hidden in plain sight. A message in some kinda foreign language nobody here spoke."

"How do *you* know about it then?"

"Some kid figured it out. A *Lord of the Rings* geek. He was visiting the Town Hall with his mama to pay her property taxes when he spotted it."

"*Lord of the Rings*, huh?"

"Yeah, there's been three or four movies, so it has a big following. Like Trekkies with *Star Trek*."

"So the message is like written in Klingon?"

"No, you idiot. Klingon's a made-up language. This is a real language that elves speak."

"Elves. Now I know you're bonkers. Ain't no such thing as elves and fairies and pixies."

"Well, there's Hobbits. That's a known fact. And they write in this secret language called runes."

"But how did you hear about this secret message?"

"My buddy's connected with the boy's mom. The kid told him. That gave my buddy the idea to steal the quilt."

"Because it's valuable?"

"No, 'cause it can lead to a Viking treasure worth zillions. That ol' witch knew where it's hidden."

"Dang."

"You can say that again, Bud."

"Dang."

Edgar thought he recognized one of the voices.

CHAPTER NINE

Jasper Beanie's Hard Year

Jasper Beanie was sweating it out in an interrogation room at the State Police office in Indianapolis. There were no windows, so he felt a tad claustrophobic. The State Police's Central District is located in the basement of the Indiana Statehouse, near War Memorial Plaza, a five-city-block memorial built to honor WWI veterans. Only Washington DC has more veterans' monuments than Indy. But Jasper couldn't see any of them from this cramped belowground dungeon.

"We're looking for your accomplice, a guy named Stickley," said Lt. Wannamaker, pointing an accusing finger at his prisoner. The tip was yellow with nicotine. The policeman had developed a three-pack-a-day habit. It was a stressful job, catching crooks.

"Sam Stickley? Yeah, I know 'im, but he ain't no accomplice of mine."

"Admit it," said Wannamaker. "You slipped ol' Stickyfingers the alarm code so he could steal the Wilkins Witch Quilt. How are you two splitting the money – fifty-fifty?"

"Hey, I told you before, that robbery happened on my day off. I wasn't even there. Matter of fact, I was sleeping one off in the Burpyville jail. They'll confirm it. I'm a regular there."

"You think that gives you an alibi? You're just as guilty as Sam Stickyfingers if you gave him the code. It's like one of those contests where you don't have to be present to win."

Jasper Beanie screwed up his face as if about to cry. "You got it all wrong. Sam couldn't have done it either. He was in jail that same night, arrested for shoplifting light bulbs at Home Depot."

"Light bulbs?"

"Said his apartment was too dark. Needed some 100-watt bulbs."

Wannamaker was at a loss for words. If Sam Stickley's alibi held up, he didn't have a suspect.

≈ ≈ ≈

Jasper Beanie had survived a hard year. His wife Nan had divorced him to run off with the former mayor of Caruthers Corners, an old crook named Henry Caruthers. His great-great grandfather had been one of the town's founding fathers, as had Beau's.

The kick in the pants came when Judge Cramer awarded Nan alimony. So in addition to his job as the cemetery's caretaker, he'd been moonlighting as the Town Hall janitor and as a pool man at the Hoosier State Senior Recreation Center. No wonder he drank, he told himself.

Now this, being accused of stealing the Wilkins Witch Quilt. He'd surely lose his job at the Town Hall over this. Maybe even be ousted from his cottage at the cemetery. This couldn't get any worse.

But it did.

≈ ≈ ≈

Sam "Stickyfingers" Stickley surrendered to the ISP and offered to turn state's evidence implicating Jasper Beanie in return for a suspended sentence. He claimed to know where Beanie had hidden the quilt.

Fact was, both Stickley and Beanie were innocent. But as a career criminal, Stickyfingers was used to playing snitch in return for favors. Truth be damned, this seemed like a good way to get the coppers off his back. And a good way to get back at Jasper for not loaning him the $50 he'd been phoning him about. He needed the money to buy a bus ticket to Des Moines to visit his daughter. His former cellmate had seemed like an easy touch, but no go. He'd be sorry.

"You're sure about this?" asked Lt. Wannamaker. He wanted to believe Stickyfingers in the worst way, a chance to wrap up this case. But the Burpyville police confirmed that one Samuel L. Stickley had been their guest on that Monday night in question. Hard to get around that.

"I swear on my mother's grave," the crook raised his hand as if taking an oath. "Me and Jasper did it. He has the quilt hidden in a crypt in the cemetery. Do we have a deal?"

"Not so fast. We gotta check it out. In the meantime you can bunk down in our holding cell. You'll find it more comfortable than Burpyville's accommodations."

Burpyville! That's when Sam Stickley realized his confession was going to be proven false. He wondered how much jail time he'd get for that.

≈ ≈ ≈

On the way back from visiting Professor Pudhomme, the Quilters Club was abuzz with new theories.

"I'll bet Mad Matilda belonged to a witches' coven that used runes as magical incantations," posited Bootsie. "Maybe those symbols came over from the Old Country and were passed down through the centuries."

"Matilda's maiden name was Süderdithmarschen," recalled Cookie. This info came from her research in the Historical Society's archive of *Burpyville Gazettes*. "That's a Germanic or Old Norse name."

Bootsie nodded. "Norway, they had witches over there, didn't they?"

"Dunno," shrugged Maddy, eyes on the road. Folks in Caruthers Corners spent more time studying the Bible than Scandinavian folklore.

"No, I don't think it was anything to do with magic," disagreed Lizzie. "I think she used that secret alphabet to mark where she hid a treasure."

"Where would Mad Matilda get a treasure?" argued Bootsie. "Her family had to be dirt poor, living in a tiny stone cottage in the middle of nowhere."

"Legend has it she became wealthy selling potions," Cookie reminded them.

"No, I mean Viking treasure," said Lizzie. "Silver bars."

"We don't *know* there was a Viking treasure," Maddy pointed out.

"That's what the runes say," insisted Lizzie. Buying into the theory of Norsemen hiding a treasure while camping near the old Wilkins place.

"Good point," Bootsie came around to that way of thinking. "The runes did say there was a treasure. Why would Matilda Wilkins put that message on the quilt if she wasn't leaving a clue?"

Cookie shook her head. "I think it's highly unlikely that an uneducated farmer's wife in the Midwest would know how to read or write an obscure runic alphabet like *Futhark.*"

"Then how did she manage to leave that message if she didn't know what the symbols meant?" argued Lizzie.

"Maybe she didn't know what the symbols meant," Aggie spoke up from the backseat. "What if she simply copied the markings she found inside the well onto her quilt?"

"Inside the well?"

"You said those markings in the well looked like those on the quilt."

"Kinda," said her grandmother. "But we didn't examine them closely."

Aggie gazed out the car window, watching the rolling green countryside slide by. "Like I said, maybe she simply copied the markings she found on those rocks."

"Why would she do that?" said Lizzie. Still not convinced, she was stuck on the treasure map scenario.

"Because they *looked* like magic markings."

"Actually, that makes sense," admitted Cookie. "Copying those runes inside the well without a clue what they meant."

Bootsie wrinkled her brow. "Okay, but how did rocks with Viking writing get inside that well in the first place?"

"There's credible documentation that Norsemen visited America 500 years before Columbus," replied Cookie. "And there's some evidence they made it this far west. The Kensington Runestone, for example. Also nineteen axes, seven halberds, four swords, twelve spears, five steel fire-strikers, and thirty-eight mooring-hole sites. Even rock carvings in Oklahoma have been attributed to Vikings. Who's to say these explorers didn't leave other runestones? Perhaps Mad Matilda's husband used some of them to build a wall around his well. It's not hard to imagine she copied the inscriptions onto her quilt because they looked magical."

Lizzie looked triumphant. "That would imply there's a Viking treasure buried near here – just like I said."

"Maybe there is," said Cookie. "People find pirate treasure all the time in the Caribbean. And sunken ships laden with gold bars and silver coins have been recovered off the Florida Keys. So why not Viking treasure just waiting to be found?"

"Here in Indiana?" scoffed Bootsie. "This is a long way from Norway."

"Maybe so," said Maddy. "But we all saw the markings inside that well."

≈ ≈ ≈

Edgar Ridenour caught the police chief at 5:15 p.m., just as he was punching out to go home. Jim Purdue and his four deputies kept track of their hours with a sputtering old time clock.

"Hold up, Jim," the retired banker called to his friend. "I've got some information you need to hear about."

"Can it wait till tomorrow? I promised Bootsie I'd be home on time. She's making watermelon stew."

"Hmm, I do love your wife's stew."

"Come home and join us for dinner. She'll have made a big pot of that nectar of the gods."

"Sorry, but I've been fishing all day. Need to get home, take a hot shower. I promised to take Lizzie to that new restaurant in Burpyville – Jack Splat's."

"Isn't that a health food restaurant?"

Edgar removed his baseball cap and ran his hand through his thinning hair. "Lizzie promises if I'll take her there, we can go to Big Bob's Steakhouse this coming weekend. I'm looking forward to chowing down on a 32-ounce Porterhouse, let me tell you that."

"So what's this news that won't keep?"

"You know Boyd Atkins's boy Charlie?"

"Know Boyd better. He was chairman of the Planning Committee for last year's Watermelon Days. I had the dubious pleasure of serving on it with that old tyrant."

"Well, I was out fishing today. My boat drifted under that bridge out on 101. I overheard Charlie Aitkens telling some fellow called Bud that he knew who stole the quilt."

"Probably just big talk."

"I don't think so. They didn't know I was under the bridge. Sounded pretty serious."

"Okay, I'll check it out. But not till in the morning. I'm going home for some of Bootsie's watermelon stew. It's her own recipe y'know."

CHAPTER TEN

A Picnic at Gruesome Gorge

Maddy got sidetracked again. Her son Bill called to say Kathy had taken a turn for the worse. Her fractured hip had become infected and there was talk of another operation. Maddy knew the couple didn't have any hospitalization insurance and the bills would be piling up. As inner city youth counselors they barely made minimum wage.

Bill's sister Tilly and Mark the Shark decided to drive up. Mark thought he might look into the insurance coverage of the trucking company whose rig had broadsided Bill and Kathy's Subaru.

That meant Maddy would be watching over Aggie and her younger siblings as well as N'yen. With four kids underfoot, it would be like running a Day Care. Quite a few years had passed since she'd cared for Bill, Freddie, and Tilly under one roof.

Thankfully, Freddie's wife Amanda had offered to help out. But that meant adding her daughter to the milieu.

"Don't worry," Beau assured his grandson. "Your mommy will be just fine. Doctors work miracles these days."

"You sure, Grampy?"

"My word of honor." He knew the boy was afraid of being orphaned again. "Your Uncle Mark is going up there to see to it."

"Can I go too? I want to see my mommy."

"Not yet. But soon. Meanwhile, you stay here and I'll take you fishing. I've got a few days of vacation saved up."

"Fishing? Oh boy."

"And your Uncle Freddie promises to take you out to Haney Bros. Circus. He and Sprinkles have worked up a new clown act."

"I like those clowns – even if I know one of them's Uncle Freddie under the makeup."

After being horrible scarred in that fire, Freddie had retired from Atlanta Fire Rescue Department and moved back to Caruthers Corners with his wife. His disability check allowed him to spend most of his time entertaining local kids as Sparkplug the Clown, his disfigurement hidden behind clown makeup.

"Meanwhile, your Uncle Mark and Aunt Tilly will check on your mommy and daddy, make sure they're all right."

"Okay. But I still miss them."

"I know you do," Beau Madison nodded. "I know you do."

≈ ≈ ≈

"I'm so worried," Maddy told her friends. She and her Quilters Club cronies phoned back and forth every morning. "Kathy has been such a good wife for Bill. He'd be devastated if her lost her. We all would."

"This second operation is not life threatening, is it?" asked Lizzie. Always trying to minimize life's worries, the result of a privileged upbringing.

"Supposedly not. But you never know what could go wrong."

"Nothing's going to go wrong. They'll just clean out the infection, pump her full of antibiotics, and send her home before you know it. That's the way these things work. I have a cousin who had a toenail infection –"

"Liz Ridenour, don't tell me that story. Your cousin lost her toe."

"Only one. She has nine others."

Bootsie was more sympathetic. "Little N'yen has really bonded with Kathy. I know he's worried about his mom."

The adopted Vietnamese boy had been with his new home for about a year, but other than his differing skin tone you would have thought he was born into it. His biological parents had survived the Vietnam War, only to come to America and have a bus hit their Honda Civic. N'yen was the only survivor of the crash, fastened safely in his car seat in the backseat. His folk and the drunken bus driver died. Fortunately, it had been 2 o'clock in the morning and the bus was empty, heading back to the garage. Windy City Transport's insurance company paid out two million – one mil per parent – to the orphaned infant. The money was tucked away in a college fund. But he'd spent nine years in foster homes before Bill and Kathy came along.

Cookie came through in a more practical way. With all the children under Maddy's care, she organized a day at Gruesome Gorge. Despite its name, Gruesome Gorge was a wonderful state park with a campground, hiking trails, and a waterfall that flowed into a lovely oval-shaped pond. There on the small sandy beach the Quilters Club had a picnic with the menagerie of kids. Aggie and N'yen splashed about under Bootsie's supervision in Bottomless Pond. (Contrary to its dread description, the pond was no deeper than three feet at any given point.)

"This was a good idea," Maddy told her friend Cookie. "Everybody seems to be having fun." She was cradling her daughter Tilly's youngest in her arms, the infant zonked out after a bottle of warm milk. Lizzie was watching the others.

The sun was bright in a cloudless sky, a perfect day for an outing. The mood belied the park's sordid history, hinted at in its name. Back in the early 1800's, Indian fighters slaughtered a tribe of Potawatomi, trapping them in the gorge like fish in a barrel. No one wrote of this shameful episode in the history books, merely implying that settlers pushed the indigenous natives off their lands.

The state's name actually means "Indian Land," an appellation that dates back to the 1760s. Then in 1800 Congress officially incorporated Indiana Territory, setting it off from the Northwest Territory.

Picnickers sometimes found arrowheads and pottery shards on the grounds of Gruesome Gorge, the only remnants of the Potawatomi. The 1838 removal of the Potawatomi in northern Indiana to designated areas west of the Mississippi was known as the "Trail of Death" (not to be confused with the Cherokee's "Trail of Tears" – although both were carried out under the Indian Removal Act signed into law by President Andrew Jackson).

"We need to go back to Mad Matilda's cottage and check out those runes in the well," Cookie was saying.

"Not really," argued Maddy. "The old woman copied them onto her quilt, and we have a picture of the quilt. Professor Pudhomme gave us a good enough translation. We know all that we're going to know about the location of the treasure."

"An excursion of thirty Norsemen could have carried quite a lot of silver. It would be a valuable find."

"More valuable than a hundred thousand dollar quilt?"

"Oh yes. Millions maybe."

"But anyone who knew runology could have translated the message without having to steal the quilt."

Cookie laughed. "True. But what a clever double crime, the thief got the quilt *and* the treasure map in one fell swoop."

Lizzie wandered over to join Maddy and Cookie in the shade of a leafy elm tree. "According to Edgar's story," she interjected, "it was a *Lord of the Rings* fan who spotted the runes. His mother's boyfriend stole it."

"Who do we know that's dating a single mom?" Bootsie called from the water's edge. Sound carried in this boxy canyon.

Maddy turned in her direction. "Good question. But we'll find out. The guy Edgar overheard was Boyd Atkins's son, Charlie. I imagine your husband is calling on him at this very moment to find out his buddy's name."

"Yes," said Bootsie. Her short dark hair was plastered against her head from standing under the waterfall. She looked like a plump little sausage in her black one-piece swimsuit. "I predict we'll have that quilt back on the wall of the Town Hall by the end of the week."

"Wouldn't that be nice," sighed Cookie. As secretary of the Historical Society, she felt responsible for the quilt.

"Don't worry," said little Aggie. "The Quilters Club will find it."

≈ ≈ ≈

Police Chief Jim Purdue and his deputy drove out to Aitkens Produce to interview Charlie. This was a delicate matter, considering his father was the biggest landholder in the county. The farmer pulled a lot of weight on the town council.

The main house reminded you of South Fork, that stately edifice you see on the opening credits of *Dallas*. Over to the west was a gigantic watermelon warehouse, a steel-framed building as big as a city block. Positioned between them was a two-story red barn. A blue Ram pickup was parked in front of the open barn door. The vanity plate – **Aitkens 3** – identified it as Charlie's. Boyd was **Aitkens 1** and his oldest boy Ralph was **Aitkens 2**.

Jim Purdue pulled his squad car next to the pickup. He wondered if Charlie might be inside the barn. "Let's peek inside before we try the house," he suggested to his deputy.

Pete Hitzer nodded as he unholstered his Glock.

"Hey," said Jim, "you're not going to need that."

"Don't be too sure. I know Charlie Aiken. Went to high school with him. He's a hothead. Got a mean streak."

"Keep it holstered."

"Yes, chief."

The interior of the barn was dark. Jim didn't like standing there silhouetted in the open door. Pete had spooked him, no doubt. "Hello," he called. "Anybody in here? It's Police Chief Jim Purdue."

No answer.

"Hello," he repeated.

Same lack of response.

"Must be over at the house," said Pete.

"Wait. Find a light switch." He had a feeling.

Click!

The barn was flooded with bluish light. There in the center of the floor was a body sprawled facedown. Jim Purdue recognized it as the Aitkens boy.

Talk about a dead end. Without Charlie Aitkens, they'd never be able to identify his buddy who stole the Witch Quilt.

"Looks like somebody konked him in the head with this rock." Pete Hitzer pointed to a fragment of stone laying on the dirt floor beside the body.

"Nothing we can do here. Charlie's dead as road kill. Let's see if any suspects are home."

"Gee, Jim. I've never worked a murder before."

"We don't get many of them around here," the police chief acknowledged. "I've not worked many myself."

Pete picked up the murder weapon, unmindful of fingerprints. But it was unlikely the limestone fragment would hold a latent print anyway. "Lookit this," the deputy said. "Some kind of chicken scratches on this rock."

Jim leaned forward to squint at the angular stone. Sort of a trapezoid shape, like it had been broken off a larger chunk. There were markings on it, sort of like stick figures.

Where had he seen that before? Then it came to him: These were like the decorative border on the Witch Quilt.

How did these markings get on a rock used to kill Charlie Aitkens?

CHAPTER ELEVEN

Cookie in the Witching Well

On the way back home from their picnic, Maddy and her entourage stopped off at Mad Matilda's cottage. Well, the ruins of the old farmplace. With all the kids under wing, there were two cars – Maddy's SUV and Amanda's hatchback. Maddy's car led the way down the narrow dirt road that dead-ended at the oasis of oak trees.

"There's the well with the funny rocks," Aggie pointed.

"Can I see them?" wheedled N'yen, nose pressed against the car window.

Maddy shook her head. "Too dangerous, young man. The writing's inside the well. If you slipped and fell your mom would be very upset. You're her treasure."

"I thought we're looking for silver treasure," said the boy. Disappointed that he wouldn't get to see the magic writing.

Maddy brought the car to a stop. "Everybody out," she called. "But keep the children away from the well. I'm surprised Boyd Aitkins hasn't had it topped off. An open hole like this could be a legal liability."

The Quilters Club and Aggie stood on one side of the SUV. Amanda and the other children were next to the car in back. "Why did we come back here?" she asked. "This place is kinda spooky, a few trees in the middle of a vast watermelon field. Must've been lonely for Matilda Wilkins out here."

"No doubt," said Lizzie. The redhead was feeling a little uneasy herself.

"Where did they bury Mad Matilda?" Freddie's wife asked.

"They didn't," replied Cookie. "According to the *Gazette* they left her body in the well. Too dangerous to retrieve it, 80-feet down."

"That's no big deal," huffed Bootsie. "They were probably just scared of going down there for a witch's corpse."

"Ooo," said N'yen. "I'm afraid that ol' witch's gonna get me."

"Don't worry, dear," his grandmother assured him. "Matilda wasn't really a witch. There's no such thing. Just a crazy old lady who fell in the well."

"Got thrown in," Aggie corrected her. "By those bad angels."

"Well, yes, but –"

"Don't sugarcoat it," said Cookie. "Aggie's smarter than the lot of us."

That may have been true. Her recent school test clocked the girl in with an IQ of 160. Genius level, to be sure.

"Got your digital camera?" Cookie addressed the redhead. "And do you have the flashlight?" she turned to Maddy.

"Camera," Lizzie replied, holding up a boxy little Vivitar.

"Flashlight," echoed Maddy, turning it on and off by way of proof. Like the winking of a firefly.

"I've got the rope," Bootsie volunteered, displaying a strand of nylon cord guaranteed at 200 lb. tensile strength.

Cookie set her jaw with grim determination. "Okay," he said, "let's get proof that these are the exact same runes as shown in the photo of the Wilkins Witch Quilt. Lower me down."

≈ ≈ ≈

Later, they would laugh about how Cookie nearly fell in the well. Being the lightest of the Quilters Club members (excluding Aggie), she was the one hanging by a rope over the lip of the well to get a digital shot of the runes. Lizzie says her hand slipped, but Cookie accused her of being worried about breaking a nail. Bootsie grabbed the rope just in time to prevent a disaster. Maddy dropped her flashlight in the well as she struggled to help Bootsie with the rope. Amanda fainted, although she later claimed to have tripped on the damp grass.

The kids thought it was grand fun.

One thing was settled: The comparison between Cookie's digital photo of the well stones and the Historical Society's photograph of the Wilkins Witch Quit was conclusive. Even though the markings on the rocks were hard to see, they clearly matched the quilt markings stroke for stroke.

"Okay," Maddy summed it up. "It's likely Mad Matilda copied the runes on the well stones onto her magical quilt."

"And somebody who could read runes finally saw the quilt and stole it," added Bootsie.

At this point the women were gathered around the patio table in Maddy's backyard. Amanda was riding herd on the little kids. Aggie and N'yen were sitting with the grownups, having appointed themselves as Quilters Club detectives.

"Couldn't someone have stolen the quilt for itself, not knowing about the secret message on it?" called Amanda from across the yard. Her daughter Donna had managed to turn on the garden hose, squirting one of Tilly's kids.

"No," Bootsie shook her head. "Based on what Lizzie's husband heard the Aitkens boy saying, the quilt *was* stolen because some kid translated the runes."

"That's right," confirmed Lizzie as she refilled her lemonade glass. "Edgar got it straight from the horse's mouth."

"Horse?" asked N'yen.

"Just an expression," his grandmother explained.

"I'd like to have a pony," said N'yen.

"I think you'd have trouble keeping one in your Chicago apartment," laughed his cousin Aggie.

"Uncle Freddie said I could keep a pony at the Haney Bros. Zoo."

"Hey, then I want to get a pony too," rejoined Aggie.

"Nobody is getting a pony today," shushed Maddy. "They cost too much money."

"Yes, but we can afford ponies after we find that Viking treasure," said Aggie.

"If we find that treasure, all of us can afford ponies," laughed Lizzie as she inspected her nail polish. She *had* chipped one out there at the well.

"First, let's think about who is dating a single mother with a nerdy son," Maddy suggested.

"Why bother," said Bootie. "Jim and his deputy went out this morning to talk with the Aitkens boy. He can tell us who he was talking about."

"That was hours ago. Hasn't Jim told you what he learned?"

"Lordy no. I haven't heard from Jim all day. I've been on a picnic with all of you."

"But you have a cellphone ..."

Bootsie shook her head. "Battery's run down. Forgot to charge it last night."

Lizzie held out her iPhone. "Here, use mine. We're all dying to hear what the Aitkens boy had to say."

≈ ≈ ≈

Beau Madison was the first person the police chief called after discovering the body of Charlie Aitkens. The second was Lt. Neil Wannamaker of the ISP.

Both had responded with the same word: "Dead?"

"That's right," Jim Purdue had told Wanamaker. "Head bashed in. Big rock laying nearby covered in blood and hair, clearly the murder weapon."

"Any witnesses?"

"Nobody has turned up. Boy's father was over in Burpyville buying a new Peterbilt to haul his watermelon crop. Hired hands were in the field. Charlie's bother Ralph is the foreman. He was out there supervising the pickers."

"Nobody else at the farmhouse?"

"Boyd's wife died about ten years ago. They have an Amish woman who keeps house, cleans and cooks, but this was her day off."

"Well, I can tell you Jasper Beanie and his pal Sam Stickley didn't do it. We've had them in lockup since yesterday."

Chief Purdue cleared his throat. "I could've told you ol' Jasper didn't have anything to do with this. He hasn't got the gumption to steal a paperclip. Beau Madison only keeps him on as janitor at the Town Hall out of pity. His wife used to be Beau's secretary before she ran off with the former mayor."

"Henry Caruthers? We've got a file on him six-inches thick."

"There you have it. Point is, we don't have a suspect."

"Sure we do," Wannamaker contradicted him. "The guy Edgar Ridenour overheard Charlie Aitkens talking about. The one he said stole the quilt. Probably killed the boy to shut him up."

Jim Purdue was frustrated. His hand gripped the phone as if he were choking it. "Yeah, but how are we gonna find that guy?"

"Figure out who Charlie Aitkens was talking to on the bridge and ask him."

"Isn't that your job? You're the state's lead investigator."

"Don't like to step on local toes."

"You don't say?" Was he being set up to take blame for a failed investigation? Those state boys were tricky like that.

Lt. Wannamaker wrapped it up. "I'll check in tomorrow and see how you're doing with your murder investigation. We'll keep looking for the quilt."

"Hey, aren't they the same case?" said Jim Purdue. But the phone clicked in chief Purdue's ear. Conversation ended.

≈ ≈ ≈

Beau Madison had already heard from Boyd Aitkens. Distraught over the death of his son, the powerful landowner wanted assurances that the villain who murdered Charlie would be brought to justice. Lynching's probably what ol' Boyd had in mind, but he had the smarts not to say it out loud.

"Beau, I backed you in your election campaigns. If you want to serve another term, you'd better kick Jim Purdue in the butt and get him to find the murderer. Somebody's gonna pay for this."

"Sorry about your boy, Boyd. He was a good kid. I feel for your loss."

The farmer's weathered face looked as sad as Iron Eyes Cody. "Who would've done such a thing? Charlie didn't have an enemy in the world. He was a little lazy, not a go-getter like his older brother. But everybody liked him, what you'd call a hail-fellow-well-met."

"Chief Purdue thinks it may have been the person who stole the Wilkins Witch Quilt. Edgar Ridenour overhead Charlie telling somebody that he knew who did it. Jim thinks the thief may have killed Charlie to shut him up."

"What would he know about that mangy old quilt? He never paid it no mind."

"Don't know. But you can be sure Jim will find out."

"Forget the police. Jim Purdue has got more experience directing traffic than solving murders. Put your wife on the case."

"M-my wife?"

"C'mon, Beau. Everybody know that her so-called Quilters Club is like an unofficial private detective agency."

"Whoa, hold on there, Boyd. You've got that all wrong—"

The watermelon farmer stood up, cutting off the conversation. "Let me put it this way, Beau. You get them gals to find the murderer of my son and I'll pony up a hundred grand toward your next election. Use it for radio advertising or take a vacation to Cancun, I don't care which."

CHAPTER TWELVE

Witchcraft in the Midwest

In the late 1600s New England was apparently infested with witches – as exemplified by the notorious Salem Witch Trials. And in the 1800s witching covens were scattered across the South, particularly around New Orleans (mostly Vodou cults). However, in the Midwest the history of witchcraft is scant.

Deep in the bowels of the Indiana State University Library, Cookie Bentley had found a rare volume titled *Occult Practices Among Early Settlers of Indiana and Illinois*. This had been a Master's Thesis by a long-forgotten student named Thaddeus Elmer Wapner.

"According to Thaddeus Wapner," Cookie told her comrades, "in 1882 a Master Warlock named Reginald Wentworth Evers settled near Burpyville. He was supposedly an outcast of Salem, Massachusetts, although records do not support this claim – nor does the timing. He established a small coven of eleven members who met on the full moon of each month. One of these was a woman named Elmira Süderdithmarschen."

"Mad Matilda's mother?"

"Exactly."

"So Matilda Wilkins learned witchcraft at her mother's knee."

"Apparently so."

Bootsie frowned. "Does that mean Matilda Süderdithmarschen Wilkins wasn't mad?"

"Who knows? But she came by her trade of selling love potions and spells honestly," said Cookie. "It was the family business."

"What does that tell us?" sighed Lizzie Ridenour. She was growing impatient with all this old history malarkey. Unlike her friend Cookie, Liz liked to live in the present. No dusty old books and yellowed newspaper clippings for her. She owned a Kindle, for goodness sakes! All the better to read the latest Nora Roberts on.

"Maybe it tells us nothing," Cookie admitted. "Other than that the woman who stitched the missing quilt believed in witchcraft."

"Yes, but did she know about the treasure or simply copy off those runes from the stones in her well?" pressed Lizzie.

"I think we should look into those Vikings," said little Aggie Tidemore, speaking with childlike insight. "It's their message on that witchy quilt. And they're the ones who hid the treasure."

Bootsie couldn't help but laugh. "Out of the mouth of babes," she said.

"Hey, I'm not a baby," she protested. "I'll be twelve soon!"

"Hm," Cookie thought it over. "I think Aggie might just be on the right trail."

"How do we investigate a group of people that even the archeologists can't prove where here?" grumbled Lizzie.

"Oh, we know they were here," said Maddy.

"How so?"

"Because we've seen their runestones in that old well."

≈ ≈ ≈

Lt. Neil "The Nail" Wannamaker may have told Chief Purdue to take over the Charlie Aitkens case, but he had his own men looking into it too. He sensed the murder was somehow connected to that missing quilt. Who would've thought an old rag like that could be worth a hundred G's?

The first clue his investigator picked up had to do with Charlie's circle of friends. His best pal was a guy named Tommy "Spud" Bodkins, an old football teammate from high school. That was probably who the fisherman – a retired banker – had overheard him speaking with on the bridge. Spud instead of Bud. According to Spud's mother, the two young men sometimes fished off that particular span of concrete and steel, convinced that there was a good catfish hole under it ... but they never caught much.

Unfortunately, Spud had gone off to Indy for the weekend to catch a Colts game. No one knew where he was staying, so Lt. Wannamaker issued an APB for a 5' 2" redhead with a potato-shaped birthmark on his left arm. Shouldn't be too hard to spot a guy of that description, he told himself.

He wondered if the birthmark was the source of Spud's country-bumpkin nickname?

≈ ≈ ≈

Maddy's son-in-law Mark the Shark phoned to say Bill and Kathy were on the mend. Bill was up and about; Kathy's infection had been stemmed with antibiotics. Little N'yen would be seeing his mommy and daddy soon.

While there, Mark had worked out a settlement with the trucking company. Bill and Kathy's medical expenses would be entirely covered. There was another $200,000 thrown in to cover their "inconvenience." That was quite a windfall for a couple of youth counselors who worked for an underfunded non-profit NGO.

Maddy's youngest son Freddie – A/K/A Sparkplug the Clown – decided to drive up to Wisconsin with his wife and daughter to check on brother Bill too. Maybe he'd put on a little show for the hospital's children's ward while he was up there. He liked his new job of entertaining kids as a member of the Haney Bros. Zoo and Exotic Animal Refuge.

"I was so worried about Bill and Kathy," Maddy told her husband that night after dinner. The grandchildren were in bed or she wouldn't have been so open about her concerns. Some people thought the Law of the Jungle was "Survival of the Fittest," but Maddy knew it was "Don't Scare the Animals." And these were cute little bunnies indeed.

Agnes and N'yen were her two favorite grandchildren, though she would never admit that out loud. Tilly's little ones – Taylor and Madison – were both too little to bond with. And Freddie's daughter Donna was just turning three. Besides, Aggie and her Vietnamese cousin were unofficial members of the Quilters Club. What's more, Aggie was getting quite good at stitching quilting square!

"Bill and Kathy are going to be just fine," Beau assured his wife. "That's what Mark said. And that boy's never wrong. He gets his facts right. That's what makes him such a good lawyer."

"That and his pit-bull personality. Once he clamps down, he never lets go."

"Determined, that he is."

Maddy leaned her head against her husband's boney shoulder. "I'm so glad he and Tilly worked through that bad patch a few years back."

"Me too. If they hadn't we'd be two grandchildren short."

"And they wouldn't be living a few blocks away from us here in Caruthers Corners." Mark and Tilly had bought the old Taylor House on the town square where Maddy had grown up. She was pleased that her old homeplace was staying in the family.

"Tilly and Freddie have returned to Caruthers Corners," she said. "I wish Bill would come home too."

"Maybe with that settlement Mark worked out with the trucking company, they can afford to quit their jobs and move back," speculated Beau.

"Not likely," said his wife. "Bill and Kathy are determined to save the world. And there's more of the world in Chicago than here in this flyspeck of a town."

"Hey, Caruthers Corners is a nice town," protested Beau, the mayor in him coming out.

"I know, dear. You and I have lived here all our life. There's nowhere else I'd want to be."

"Then Bill and Kathy –"

"– those two kids have lives of their own. They like Chicago. There are plenty of kids who need their help up there."

"Yeah, I suppose so."

"But we can still miss them," his wife said, patting him reassuringly on the arm. "That's allowed."

"Want to watch some television 'fore we turn in?" asked Beau. He liked to have a "little evening" before bedtime. Mindless TV was just the ticket, although he usually slept through the program. "A warm-up for a good night's sleep," he called it.

"That would be nice," nodded Maddy. "Maybe there's something interesting on the National Geographic Channel."

There was.

They tuned in just in time to catch a program titled *Severed Ways: The Norse Discovery of America*. The dramatization followed two Norse men struggling to survive in the wilds of North America when abandoned by the rest of their expedition.

Afterwards, there was an interview with filmmaker Tony Stone, where he explained what got him interested in these early explorers. "I wanted to know more about it when I heard brief mention of it back in the third grade. I wanted to know more about the Viking conquest in our own backyard ... "

Beau's snores were a soft rumble, but Maddy was leaning toward the TV, her senses on high alert. This was fascinating. Maybe there was more to this idea of Vikings reaching Indiana than traditional archeologists thought.

"The Norse site at L'Anse Aux Meadows in Newfoundland was discovered by sailing the geographical description written in the Vinland Sagas, which was Liefsbudir, the base camp Lief Ericson constructed around the year 1000," the filmmaker was saying. "Many of stories in the Sagas tell of other expeditions that set sail south from there and one expedition describes spending a winter at a location where it did not snow. They could have explored as far south as Virginia or beyond."

Severed Ways posited that a couple of scouts had been left behind during one of the Vikings' battles with "the Skraelings," as they called the North American Indians.

"Most historians agree that they probably traveled into the St. Lawrence and down the American coast," continued the filmmaker. "There just hasn't been any concrete evidence found yet. And it might never. Any archeological site has probably been trampled and plowed on the American coast. It's such a populated region. Plows or other modern machines probably have torn up any fire pit or building footprint that might remain. But you never know what we might stumble upon."

Like a stone well.

CHAPTER THIRTEEN

Runestone of Death

Bootsie Purdue was having breakfast with her hubby Jim before he went to work. It was a longtime ritual, a little one-on-one time, because the work of a law officer doesn't always conform to a 9-to-5 routine.

She'd just poured the watermelon juice, when he said, "I've gotta go down to Indy today and pick up Jasper Beanie. He doesn't have a ride home." Jim preferred watermelon juice over orange juice, a hometown foible. After all, Caruthers Corners was known as "the Watermelon Capital of Indiana."

"Now you're a taxi service?"

"I feel obligated. Jasper's being falsely accused has disrupted his life, which wasn't all that good to begin with."

Bootsie tasted her eggs, a little soft for her liking. She'd been distracted lately with that missing quilt. Her cooking was suffering. "Is Japer going to lose his job at the cemetery? That would make him homeless."

"No, Beau stepped in there. Told the town commissioners that Jasper was going to continue as caretaker at Pleasant Glade as well as keep his job at the Town Hall."

"Poor Jasper Beanie. He reminds me of that character in the *Li'l Abner* comic strip, the man with the perpetual storm cloud over his head."

"Joe Btfsplk."

"What?"

"Joe Btfsplk, that was the character's name." He pronounced it *Buf-spilk*.

"Oh, right."

"Jasper was always a loser, even in high school," he sighed. "When his wife ran off with Henry Caruthers, that was the final blow to his self-esteem. No wonder he drinks. That's why my deputies are instructed to take him home rather than arrest him when they catch him tying one on in the town square."

"I remember him in high school. He was the waterboy for the football team."

"Yeah, he tried out as a player, but didn't make the grade."

Bootsie sighed, remembering those halcyon days of their youth. "You and Beau and Edgar were the school's star athletes. You the star quarterback. Beau the winning scorer on the basketball team. Edgar still holder of the 100-yard dash record. Ben Bentley the wrestling champ. All of you on the baseball team the year it won the district series."

"And ol' Jasper always on the sidelines."

"This quilt theft is troubling you, isn't it?"

"Some. But it's Charlie Atkins's murder that has me losing sleep."

"Yes, you tossed and turned all last night."

Jim Purdue rubbed his balding dome. "I'm getting pressure on both sides. The state boys are giving me a hard time. And the Charlie's father thinks I'm incompetent. Wants Beau to turn the investigation over to the Quilters Club."

Bootsie almost spilled her watermelon juice. "To us? We're just a handful of busybodies who do needlework."

"You gals have developed quite a reputation as crime-solvers." He stood up and reached for his billed cap with a gold star that said CHIEF. He didn't feel much like a chief today. All told, he felt more kinship with Jasper Beanie than he'd care to admit. "Gotta go. A meeting with that jerk Wannamaker to report our lack of progress."

"He's that ISP lieutenant?"

"Yeah, the one they call The Nail. And with good reason. Every time I meet with him I feel like somebody has driven a sharp object straight into my brain."

"You have been taking a lot of aspirin lately." She'd noticed. Wives do that.

"He wants us to turn over any forensic evidence we have in the Aitkens case. But what kind of clues are you going to find on a rock."

"A rock?"

"That's right. The boy died of blunt force trauma. Somebody coldcocked him with a rock covered in marks."

That got his wife's attention. "What kind of marks?"

"Inscriptions. Engravings. Don't know what you'd call 'em. Probably a chunk that broke off a tombstone. I've assigned a deputy to go over to the cemetery and look for a broken grave marker."

"Were there letters? Words?"

"Naw. Just hen scratchings."

"Can I see it?"

"Hon, it's locked up in the safe down at the station. And Wannamaker's picking it up first thing this morning. Don't tell me the Quilters Club is actually going to poke into my murder investigation? Are you trying to put me outta work?"

She stood on her tiptoes to plant a kiss on his cheek. They were a cute couple, a middle-aged Mutt and Jeff, each maybe twenty pounds overweigh, a foot difference in height. "There, there, dear. I was just curious."

"Well, if you really want to see it, there's a photo of the murder weapon over there in my briefcase. Just picked up the pictures from the crime scene yesterday on the way home from work. Bob Tippey over at the *Burpyville Gazette* develops them on the side. Doesn't charge anything when I let him use one in the paper."

Tippey was a small-town newspaper editor who fancied himself a gonna-break-this-town-wide-open crusading journalist. His father had been editor of the paper before him, and his grandfather before that. A family business since the 1800s.

Before Jim Purdue had finished speaking, his wife had pulled the 8" x 10" color photograph from his battered leather briefcase and was examining it with the eyes of an eagle. "Dear, don't waste your deputy's time in the cemetery. This is not a chunk off a tombstone. It's a fragment from a runestone."

≈ ≈ ≈

By noon the Quilters Club was back at the university in Indianapolis, waiting outside the door of visiting professor

484

Ezra Pudhomme. He was running a few minutes late, having just delivered a lecture on Early Sumerian Cuneiform History in Lecture Hall 11-B.

Pudhomme seemed surprised to see them. "Ladies, to what do I owe this unexpected pleasure?" What he really meant was "unannounced visit." He preferred people to make appointments. This summer gig at ISU left his calendar with few free moments. His class load and scheduled lectures were quite arduous.

"Sorry, Professor Pudhomme," apologized Maddy. "We promise to take only a moment of your time. We need you to tell us what these runes say." She held out the color photograph that Jim Purdue had reluctantly let his wife borrow on the grounds she would get it translated for him.

"More runes? Wherever are you getting these? Did someone come back from a vacation in Scandinavia?"

"No, these are local," interjected Cookie. "We think it's proof of Viking incursions into the Midwest."

"Proof, you say?"

"Even better than the Kensington Runestone."

The fat professor smiled as if appreciating some private joke. "The Kensington Runestone has never truly been authenticated," he said. "Jansson, Moltke, Nielsen, Anderson, and Wahlgren, among others, have asserted that the stone is a forgery."

"What about Hall, Holland, Thalbitzer, and Hagen?" responded Cookie Bentley. "Those experts argued that it's real. And the Smithsonian displayed the Kensington Runestone in 1949, not an exactly institution known for supporting fakes."

"Hm, you've been doing your homework. Very well, let me see your photograph."

Pudhomme pulled out a 3x magnifying glass to help him inspect the image in the photo. His nose hovered inches from the glossy surface as he moved the glass from rune to rune, studying each letter like a Treasury Agent examining a counterfeit twenty.

"Well –?" said Lizzie. Impatient as usual.

"Don't rush me. This is interesting."

"What does it say?" asked Bootsie, antsy to get a translation. She'd promised Jim.

"This is only a fragment, so it is difficult to say. Something about digging a hole –"

"A hole?" said Lizzie, the banker's wife. "You mean like a place to bury treasure?"

"This fragment says nothing about money or treasure."

"But the runes on the Wilkins Witch Quilt mentioned a buried treasure," challenged Bootsie.

"Not exactly," corrected the professor. "The quilt inscription that you showed me contained the rune for *fehu*. That can mean either money or cattle."

"Cattle?" blurted Lizzie. Disappointed that this mystery could be about a herd of cows.

"The fragment in this photo does not contain the symbol *fehu*. Just something about digging a hole."

"You mean like a well?" asked Maddy.

"A water well, buried treasure – who knows?" exclaimed the professor. He was becoming exasperated with these ladies. What did they know of disciplined research and scientific method and responsible translations? Just a small-town coffee klatch sticking their nose where it didn't belong. If this was a photograph of an artifact found locally, it should be the province of archeologists and linguists like himself.

"Thank you for your time," said Maddy, sensing that they had overstayed their welcome. She was disappointed they hadn't learned more. Digging a hole indeed!

"Wait," grunted Professor Pudhomme. "Are you sure the stone in this picture was found in Indiana? That would be a remarkable discovery."

"Who can say," Bootsie interjected. "It was recovered at a crime scene."

"Oh my."

Maddy repeated, "Thanks for your time, professor. We've got to get home in time to fix dinners for our husbands. A housewife's job is never done."

He didn't pick up on her sarcasm.

≈ ≈ ≈

In the car on the way back, the women were trying to sort through the facts as they knew them. This was more difficult than those Sudoku puzzles in the *Indianapolis Star*.

"Fact One," said Maddy, keeping her eyes on the road as she drove. "Somebody stole the Wilkins Witch Quilt."

"And the Indiana State Police have determined it was an inside job," added Lizzie.

"Hey, Jim came to that same conclusion," Bootsie defended her husband.

Maddy didn't see any point of reminding them that her grandson N'yen had been first to put forth that theory.

"Fact Two, we determined that the markings on the quilt were runes, an ancient Norse language," said Cookie.

"And that Mad Matilda Wilkins copied those symbols off stones inside her well."

"Fact Three," added Lizzie, "the runes say there's a treasure hidden in a deep hole. Do you think it meant inside the well?"

"It *has* to be down there," said Bootsie. "The message was carved there at the top of a deep hole."

Lizzie continued that line of thought. "And the rock that killed Charlie Aitkens confirms that Vikings dug the well, not Matilda's husband."

Cookie nodded. "A Viking well."

"Now we're getting somewhere," said Maddy. "We may have located a Viking treasure. Bars of silver at the bottom of the well."

"Don't forget," warned Bootsie, "the bones of Mad Matilda are down there too."

"That's right," said Cookie. "The townspeople left her down there after the Avenging Angels drowned her."

"That's scary," shuddered Aggie in the back seat. "This is like a ghost tale."

"No ghosts," her grandmother assured her. "Just something bad that happened a long time ago."

"So who stole the quilt?" asked Bootsie, still a policeman's wife.

"A guy whose girlfriend has a teenage son," offered Lizzie. "That's what Edgar heard Charlie Aitkens say."

"Oh, that reminds me," said Bootsie. "Boyd Aitkens wants the Quilters Club to find out who killed his son."

CHAPTER FOURTEEN
A Well Digger's Nightmare

"**A**re you gals crazy?" shouted Beauregard Madison IV, not a man accustomed to raising his voice. "You want me to send someone down into the Wilkins well based on some cockamamie translation of the markings on a crazy quilt?"

"The markings are inside the well too," said Maddy. At her perky best. Trying to convince her husband. But Beau Madison was known to be as a stubborn as a mule.

"No way," he shook his head firmly. "I'd get laughed out of office, helping the Quilters Club search for a lost treasure."

"Dear, can't you just say a puppy fell in the well and that you're sending out the fire department to rescue it?"

The mayor rolled his eyes. "You're asking me to lower someone into an eighty-foot well ... not retrieve a kitten out of a tree."

"Beau Madison, this is an important piece of Caruthers Corners history," insisted Cookie Bentley. "We have an obligation to check it out." As secretary of the Historical Society, she wasn't going to let a major event like Norsemen visiting Indiana go unexplored.

"Heck, I'll do it," said Ben Bentley.

Cookie turned to her husband. "Do what?"

"Go down in the well. I've helped dig a lot of wells in this county. No big deal."

"You could keep this quiet?" asked Beau, showing a crack in his resistance. He had to live with Maddy. And she seemed determined.

"No biggie," grinned the bearded man. "I'll get a buddy to run the winch. We can do it first thing in the morning. By lunch these girls can be counting their Viking silver."

"Hm, there may be an ownership problem," mulled Beau, rubbing his chin. "That well's on Boyd Aitken's property. Wish Mark the Shark were here to sort this out."

"We have to find some treasure before that becomes an issue," Edgar Ridenour noted. He remained skeptical about Vikings burying silver in the Midwest. But he didn't want to say too much, for Lizzie was all a-twitter about the possibility of finding a cache of silver.

"Good point," grinned Ben.

"I'll call Boyd Aitkens and get his permission," sighed Beau. "Tell him the Historical Society is trying to recover Mad Matilda's bones."

"Perfect," said Maddy.

"Those bones would have a place in our little museum," Cookie nodded. "We'd create a display around them."

They were all seated around the Madisons' dining-room table – Beau and Maddy, Cookie and Ben, Lizzie and Edgar, Bootsie and Jim. The kids were in bed. Aggie would be irked that she'd missed this late-night powwow.

"Now that we've solved the treasure hunting issue, let's talk about who stole the quilt and who killed Charlie

Aitkens," said Jim Purdue. "May as well get it out on the table, seeing as Boyd's trying to drag you gals into this."

"We know the same thing as you, dear," said Bootsie. "That Edgar overheard Boyd's son telling someone he knew who stole the quilt."

"That was probably his friend Spud Bodkin," nodded Jim. "At least that's what the state boys tell me."

"Doesn't that make it simple?" said Maddy. "All we have to do is ask Spud who Charlie was talking about."

"Easier said than done," the police chief replied. "Spud's gone missing."

"Missing?" said Edgar.

"That's right. Nobody has seen him in two whole days. Went to Indy to see a Colts game and never came back."

"Maybe he's dead too," suggested Maddy as she poured coffee, refilling everyone's cups. The Madisons liked an inexpensive brand that contained chicory.

"You're saying the thief killed them both to shut them up?"

"That could explain him being missing," she replied.

Lizzie scowled at her coffee cup. She preferred a high-end coffee from Seattle. A Mucho Grande, with two lumps of sugar. "Charlie Aitkens said it was a guy whose girlfriend has a teenage son who's into *Lord of the Rings*. How many people in Caruthers Corners could that be?"

"Hmm," Maddy considered the question. "Mildred Gertner's son Stuart is into *Lord of the Rings*. She says he's read the book more than a hundred times. Thinks he's a Hobbit or something."

"His ears *are* big and he's barely five feet tall," Lizzie pointed out.

"Hobbits aren't real," snapped Cookie. A woman used to dealing in hard facts, she wasn't attuned to fantasy worlds populated by wizards and dwarfs and fire-demons.

"No ... but that's not the point. The boy's a devotee."

"Mildred can't be the thief's girlfriend," said Bootsie. "She and Frank have been married since high school. No boyfriend in the picture."

"Mildred isn't the woman Charlie was talking about," agreed Maddy. "But her son may know other boys who are hooked on those Tolkien books. I think Jim should question him to see if any of his friends have a single mother with a shifty boyfriend."

"*Ahem*," Beau cleared his throat. "That's not a bad idea, Jim."

The big moon-faced policeman nodded. "I'll put one of my deputies on it first thing in the morning. Got nothing to lose. We don't have any other leads."

Edgar sipped his coffee. He wasn't as fussy about his joe as his wife. Caffeine was caffeine to him. "At least we have a plan of action. Ben goes down in the well tomorrow morning. And Jim starts hunting for Hobbits."

"That about sums it up," said Beau Madison, finishing off his coffee in one gulp. He liked the taste of chicory.

≈ ≈ ≈

Aggie got up to go to the bathroom. It was just down the hall. As she passed her cousin N'yen's room, she heard sobbing.

Tapping on the door, she whispered, "Can I come in?"

"Y-yes," came a tiny quavering voice.

"What's the matter?"

The boy sat up in bed. Aggie could see his silhouette from the moonlight coming through the bedroom window. "I'm worried about my daddy and mommy," he said. "I don't want them to die."

"They're not going to die," the girl reassured him. "They just got banged up a little. That's what my daddy told me, and he never lies. After all, he's a lawyer."

"Honest?"

"Honest Injun. Don't worry so much."

"I'm afraid of being alone again, like after my first mommy and daddy died. They were in a car accident too."

"You won't ever be alone. You've got a family now. Forever."

"Really?"

"Yes, you've got me and grammy and grampy and my daddy and mommy and Uncle Freddie and Aunt Amanda and all your new cousins." She paused. "Besides, your own daddy and mommy will be getting out of the hospital real soon."

"Promise?"

"You know you can always trust me, your very favorite cousin."

≈ ≈ ≈

That same night Jasper Beanie heard a noise outside the caretaker's cottage. Could it be those prankish high-school boys again? They liked to initiate members into the Seniors Scalawag Society by sending unwary boys into the cemetery to retrieve a bone. Some of the crypts were in need of repair, access to skeletons being easier than the town commissioners would care to admit. Principal

Dorrety had banned such initiations, but they still went on behind his back.

As Jasper could attest.

Proper procedure was for the caretaker to phone the police and report any trespassers ... but after his week of confinement with the Indiana State Police he wasn't eager to see more lawmen. So he pulled on his trousers and hobbled out the backdoor, flashlight in hand.

"Yo, you boys! Get the heck outta the cemetery. It's closed to the public this time of night."

However, the voce that replied didn't belong to a student at Madison High School. "Hello, Mr. Beanie. Perhaps you could help us? We're looking for a tombstone with a piece broken off."

"There's lotsa tombstones like that. Pleasant Glades is better'n a hundred years old."

"Take a look at the picture," said the voice. "Maybe you'll recognize it as coming from one of your tombstones."

A light flashed on, revealing two men in suits, a photograph held out for him to inspect."

"Just who are you guys?"

"We're with the state police," said Neil the Nail.

CHAPTER FIFTEEN

Hunting for Hobbits

Deputy Pete Hitzer interviewed Harry "the Hobbit" Gertner that next morning. Harry's mother gave him permission to call her son out of First Year Algebra for the talk. Harry didn't mind getting out of the math class one little bit. He hated memorizing terms and coefficients. He'd rather be writing fantasy stories in an Elfin language on his online blog.

Principal Dorrety let them use his office. He had sent a teacher's aide to call the boy out of class so as not to upset students with a policeman's presence.

"Fare thee well, officer," said the chubby bespectacled nerd. "What wanteth thou of me?" He was dressed in a top hat, vest, and morning coat, despite the school's dress code.

"First off, let's speak the King's English," said Pete Hitzer. He only had a GED diploma, so he didn't like it when people flaunted their fancy education.

"Alas, these days the Crown is overseen by a Queen. So should we call it the Queen's English?"

The deputy put on his tough face, the one he used when arresting people. "I mean plain ol' American English. Got it, Harry?"

"Uh, yes sir."

"Good. Now here's my question –"

It took three minutes for Deputy Pete Hitzer to get two names of local *Lord of the Rings* aficionados who had single moms.

≈ ≈ ≈

Lt. Neil Wannamaker was on the phone with that hick police chief. "The rock used to kill the Aitkens boy didn't come off a tombstone at Pleasant Glades," he stated as if this were a major revelation.

"Why would you think it did?" replied Jim Purdue, determined not to show his cards.

"Because that's where Charlie's mother is buried. Thought it might have been a keepsake from her grave."

"Sounds pretty ghoulish, taking a piece of his mother's tombstone as a memento."

"Told you it wasn't that. His mother's tombstone is as pristine as the day it was placed there ten years ago."

Jim paused, debating whether to tell him it was a runestone. No, the ISP would never buy that theory. Vikings in Indiana? It was all too crazy. So instead he said, "There are several other cemeteries in the area. Family plots. Small churches. A big one over near Burpyville that's owned by a funeral home chain – Shady Meadows, it's called."

"We've checked them all. I had a dozen men poking around local graveyards yesterday. Went into overtime, up to midnight. That rock didn't come from any of them."

"So where did it come from?"

"Beats me. Maybe it's a souvenir Charlie brought back from Boy Scout camp in Michigan when he was sixteen years old. Maybe its origin isn't even important. But we try to run down every lead."

Jim screwed up his courage. He wasn't used to talking back to the state police. "I thought you said this was my case. What the dickens are your men doing checking out the murder weapon behind my back."

"Just lending a hand. I've got more resources than you do, so why not help you out?"

"Yeah, thanks," Jim said. But he didn't sound sincere.

≈ ≈ ≈

"No," said Cookie to the tall man with the thin moustache, "records of where the Church of Avenging Angels was located do not exist."

"Hey, I checked with the folks at Town Hall. They said to ask you."

"Wish I could help, but the church's location is lost to history. Old newspaper articles suggest it was on the far side of the Never Ending Swamp, but no one knows exactly where. *A Personal History of Caruthers Corners and Surrounding Environs* by Martin J. Caruthers tells us a little about the leader of the church, one Rev. Billingsley Royce. Caruthers claimed the good reverend was really a scalawag from St. Paul, Minnesota, named Billy Bob Rutherford."

"Is he the one who drowned that witch lady?"

"According to reports in an 1899 issue of the *Burpyville Gazette*, a local woman was drowned in her own well by a group of religious zealots. They thought she was a witch – and maybe she thought so too. The men were never identified, but rumor had it that Rev. Royce was the ringleader."

"And nobody ever found the money?"

"W-what money?" Cookie stammered. At this very moment her husband and his pal Bombay were down in the very well where Matilda Wilkins had died. It seemed highly suspect that this stranger would be asking about her murderers on this particular morning.

"Legend has it those religious zealots, as you call them, took Mrs. Wilkins's money and buried it under the doorstep of their church. Silver bars, it was said."

"S-silver bars? Why would an old farmer's wife have silver bars?" She was shocked he knew about the silver.

"Viking treasure she found in her well, the story goes."

"Where did you hear this?" Cookie could feel her hand shaking as she thumbed through the Caruthers book to the paragraph about the witch's death.

"My organization is called the Greater Midwest Occult Phenomena Association. G.M.O.P.A., for short. Or G-Mop-A if you like. We research occult phenomena. We've catalogued over fifty thousand strange happenings since 1800. Naturally, we pay attention to stories about witches. The tale about Rev. Royce and the witch woman's silver appeared in a book called *Angels of the Lord and the Silver Hoard*, supposedly written by one of Rev. Royce's congregation, a man named Simonton Poteet. It was published in 1937 by the Peoria University Press – now defunct."

"If you already know so much about Rev. Royce, why are you quizzing me?" She'd have to get her hands on that book, Cookie told herself.

"We try to be thorough. What's more, we know you and your quilting friends have been poking around the

Wilkins homestead. If you're after the silver bars too, you can forget it. I have a deal with Boyd Aitkens, the gent who owns that land."

"Matter of fact, so do we. But I thought you said the money was buried at the church ... or wherever the church used to be located."

"That's just it, we aren't sure. Legends are never totally accurate."

"Yes, I certainly agree."

"Then if you –"

"Sorry, but you'll have to excuse me. I'm behind in my filing."

"I thought you were going to show me the reference in that book. We don't have a copy of it in our library."

"Yes, it's a rare book. In fact, this may be the only copy existent. In 1913 Martin Caruthers paid to have it printed on the *Burbyville Gazette* press. Only 50 copies were pulled, according to the records."

"Does it say more about Rev. Royce?"

"Perhaps. But I'm too busy right now to look it up."

"Hey –"

"Go find the treasure on your own," snapped Cookie, closing the book with a *bang!* "I have work to do."

≈ ≈ ≈

At that very moment, Ben Bentley was 82-feet down inside the Wilkins well. Or if the Quilters Club was right, a well dug by Viking explorers.

Perhaps these Norsemen had spent a season here in Indiana, camping under this canopy of oak trees. That would have given them plenty of time to dig a well and carve messages on rocks that were later used by Benjamin Wilkins to build a protective wall around the well.

"How deep's the water?" Bombay Martinez called down to him. Bombay was a retired circus performer. He worked with the Haney Bros. (actually a man and wife rather than brothers) at the zoo next to the Bentley farm. Among other duties, he took care of the elephant.

"Not very deep at all. Water only comes up to my knees." Ben was wearing his hip-waders that he used for duck hunting.

"Found any silver bars yet?"

"Nope. Nor any witch's bones. There *is* an aluminum Coke can floating down here, but I suspect it's of a more modern origin."

"Dastardly picnickers!" huffed Bombay. He hated litterbugs.

"Wait a minute, there's something here in the muck," called Ben's disembodied voice from deep in the well. "A glass jar with something in it. I'll put it in the bucket and you haul it up."

"Got it," replied Bombay, putting the winch in motion.

That was the only find of the day, the glass jar.

≈ ≈ ≈

After his frustrating meeting with that Historical Society lady, Maury Seiderman drove out to the Wilkins cottage. He could see people milling about in the distance, so he parked his 1975 LeSabre convertible on a side road and pulled out his Bausch and Lomb field glasses to spy on them. He wasn't sure what to do if these interlopers had found silver down there in the well.

Seiderman wasn't a violent man, but his partners were. His cousin's boyfriend had killed that Aitkens boy in some kind of argument over the stolen quilt. Maybe he'd call his cuz and let her boyfriend handle this if these people discovered the treasure.

But it didn't come to that. No silver bars were hauled up from the well. Just a Mason jar and that stocky guy in hip waders.

CHAPTER SIXTEEN
A Magic Potion

That evening the Quilters Club and their mates gathered around the butcher-block counter in Cookie Bentley's kitchen to study the artifact from the Wilkins well. It was a sealed Mason jar, the name showing in bas-relief on the glass side. Some kind of bloated shape could be seen floating in the murky brown liquid that filled the container.

"A Mason jar. That must be from a picnicker, like the Coke can," Lizzie sighed. Obviously disappointed with the singular find.

"Not necessarily," said Cookie. "Mason jars were patented on November 30, 1858 by John Landis Mason, a Philadelphia tinsmith. See, there's the date embossed on the side of the jar along with the name."

"This jar was made in 1858?" marveled Aggie, standing on her tiptoes to see. She was still small for her age, practically the same height as her cousin N'yen.

"Probably not," Cookie shook her head. "Jars with that date on the side were manufactured well into the 1900s."

"But it has to be pretty old," said Ben. "Look how rusty that lid is."

"What's that blob inside?" asked N'yen. He squinted at the jar, the epicanthic folds making this eyes all the more narrow.

"Dunno," said his grandmother. "Maybe some old vegetable. A turnip or a cauliflower."

"Looks more like a chicken gizzard," Lizzie offered a guess. Not that she'd ever seen a chicken's gizzard in her life. She bought Tyson Farms roaster chickens, prepackaged and ready to slide into the oven. Cooking wasn't exactly her forte.

"I'd say it's a magic potion," guessed Cookie.

Beau Madison picked up the jar and shook it, just enough to stir up its contents. "Look, there's a lizard in there too."

"That looks like a tiny feather floating beside it."

Jim grimaced. "Hate to tell you, but that blob's not a turnip or a gizzard. It's an eyeball. See, it just shifted so it's looking at you."

"*Eek!*" cried Aggie.

"I don't mean that it's really looking at you," he amended his words. "It just seems like it is."

"Can we open the jar?" asked N'yen.

"No," said the police chief. "I'm going to send it over to the state boys to let them analyze it. Better we don't break the seal."

"*Ooo,* a pickled eyeball," said Aggie. "Mad Matilda must've been a *really* wicked witch."

CHAPTER
SEVENTEEN

The Greater Midwest
Occult Phenomena Association

Maury Seiderman hadn't been entirely honest with the town's mayor or the Historical Society lady. While it was true that he was a field investigator for G.M.O.P.A., he was also its president, its secretary, and its sergeant at arms. Matter of fact, he was the *only* member of the Greater Midwest Occult Phenomena Association.

Seiderman had grown up in Chicago, always a weird boy, perversely interested in the occult. The term comes from the Latin word *occultus*, meaning hidden or secret. For little Maury it included magic, mysticism, the paranormal, spiritualism, and theosophy. He subscribed to the Goodrick-Clarke thesis that occultism was "a strong desire to reconcile the findings of modern natural science with a religious view that could restore man to a position of centrality and dignity in the universe."

He was particularly fascinated by witchcraft and Satanism. The Feri Tradition founded by Victor Anderson and his wife Cora. Stregheria as popularized by Raven Grimassi. Raymond Bowers's Clan of the Tubal Cain. And especially the Order of the Trapezoid, led by Satan-worshiper Anton LaVey.

Perhaps this interest came from the fact he had a distant relative who'd claimed to be a witch – one Matilda Elizabeth Wilkins.

Seiderman had worked as a clerk at Borders, until the bookstore chain closed down. Now unemployed, he had nothing better to do than record stories of psychic phenomena he found online into the thick spiral-bound notebooks that lined the bookcases in his Irving Park apartment. This was the so-called database of G.M.O.P.A.

Even that was getting boring. So you can bet he was excited when his cousin called to ask if he'd help her and her boyfriend look for Viking silver that was described in runes embroidered on the Wilkins Witch Quilt. She knew he was good at research. All he had to do was follow the clues, like a scavenger hunt. She promised they would split the treasure equally, a third to each.

Seiderman had a plan. After he got his share of the treasure, he'd turn the other two in for the murder of that Aitkens boy. Maybe there was a reward. Or perhaps he could extract money from the boy's father. Everybody said Boyd Aitkens was richer than Croesus.

He'd have to go about it carefully. He didn't want to get arrested for extortion. Or as an accessory to murder. This called for a clever approach. But Maury's mother had always said he was a clever boy.

≈ ≈ ≈

Boyd Aitkens wasn't sure what to make of this odd-looking man who claimed to be an investigator for an Occult Phenomena Association. They were meeting in a back booth at the Cozy Café on South Main Street. The strange man obviously didn't want the two of them seen together.

"So what's this about?" demanded Aitkens. He was a large florid-faced farmer who had made a fortune growing watermelons. Normally, he didn't meet with nutcases, but this guy claimed he could tell Boyd who was responsible for his son's death.

"As you know, there are evil forces at large in this country," Maury Seiderman began his practiced spiel.

The farmer cut him off. "Look, Mr. Seiderman, I don't even go to church. So cut the crap about good and evil, and just tell me who killed my boy."

"It's not that simple."

"And why not?"

"Your land has been defiled. It was once the home of a witch." The man dug his fork into the slice of pie on the table before him. Cozy Café was known for its watermelon pie a la mode.

Boyd waved the words away. "Everybody knows about Mad Matilda. Around the turn of the century, she lived on a parcel of land that I now happen to own. She sold potions to gullible farmers. But what's that got to do with my son's murder?"

"Her bones lie at the bottom of that well next to the ruins of her cottage. So her spirit is not at rest. Her spirit entered a local man and enticed him to recover her quilt. Then it led this man to kill your son."

"Okay, I'll bite. Why?"

"Because your son disturbed her resting place by pumping water out of the well."

"If you say so. Now why did you ask for this meeting?"

"Because I can identify the man inhabited by Matilda Wilkins's spirit. The man who killed your son."

"You need to be talking to the police, not me."

The field investigator for G.M.O.P.A. finished off his pie, licked his lips, and said, "There are certain expenses involved in locating a wayward spirit. I hoped you might finance the exorcism."

"Finance? How much money are we talking here?"

"Forty thousand ought to do it."

Boyd Aitkens squinted his eyes, the muscles around his mouth tightening. "For forty G's you'll identify my son's murderer?"

"That is correct."

The watermelon farmer thought it over. "You bring me proof and the money's yours. But no proof, no payment."

Maury Seiderman frowned. "Might we discuss a small deposit?"

"No way, José." Boyd Aitkens stood up, towering over the occult investigator. "You don't get a thin dime till you identify the killer and I see proof of his guilt."

"You can count on it, sir." Maury stood up to shake the farmer's calloused hand. A deal struck. Now, after he located the silver, his cousin and her boyfriend were toast.

CHAPTER EIGHTEEN

A Pickled Pig's Eye

"**I**t was a pig's eye," Lt. Neil Wannamaker reported back to Chief Purdue. "Our forensic pathologist estimated it could be a hundred years old, pickled like that. Much of the tissue had deteriorated, but he had plenty for a DNA test. By the way, ISP will be invoicing your department for that test. Our budget's a little tight this year."

"Yours is tight? I don't even have one," carped Jim Purdue.

"So you think it was some kind of magical amulet?"

Jim sighed. "Something like that. Hard to say, but we're dealing with a self-professed witch."

"Any leads on that Aitkens boy's murder?"

"No," Jim lied. He had two very *good* leads from Harry the Hobbit. But he didn't feel like sharing with the guy who had just stuck him with a $1,000 DNA testing bill. The Nail indeed.

≈ ≈ ≈

Harry Gertner had given them two names, fellow Tolkien fans who lived with single moms. Pinkus "Pinky" Bjork and Gary "the Gollum" Goldberg.

Deputy Pete Hitzer had promised to put Harry in a "witness protection program," meaning the police wouldn't reveal him as the source of these names.

The police chief's wife knew both boys. Bootsie sometimes worked as a substitute teacher when needed, so she recognized a lot of the local kids. She'd met Gary's parents, one of the few Jewish families in Caruthers Corners. Mariam Goldberg was separated from her husband Haim, but no one had filed for divorce yet. "Just a rough patch," she told her friends. Bootsie was pretty sure Mariam wasn't seeing anyone, trying hard to put her marriage back together.

That made Jim and his deputies focus on Pinky Bjork. Pinky was a withdrawn 16-year-old geek, spending most of his time online with various *Lord of the Rings* role-playing games, living a second-hand life as an avatar. His mother was a frazzled middle-aged blonde named Wanda. She'd been divorced from Bern Bjork, manager at the DQ, for about ten years now. Word had it that she was living with a guy who worked at the chair factory, an upholsterer named Ted Something-or-Other. Nobody knew much about him, but he quickly moved to the top of Chief Purdue's "Persons of Interest" list.

"Why do you want to talk with me and my son?" demanded Wanda Bjork when Deputy Hitzer showed up at her front door. The small brick-front bungalow was located on Jinks Lane, a narrow dead-end street named after one of the town's founders.

"We think your son might be able to help us with the missing quilt. Somebody said he's able to read those markings on the border of the quilt."

"Pinky's already translated those old markings," she smirked. "He's a very smart kid. Learned how to read that rune writing by playing his video games. Elves or dwarfs or one of them magical characters communicate with that language."

"Great. I'm sure he'll be a lot of assistance to us."

She eyed the deputy suspiciously. "Why do I have to come along?" she asked, as if suspecting a trap.

"'Cause Pinky's underage. Gotta have a parent present when we interview him." True enough for the moment.

"Oh. That makes sense. Let me go get him. Can I ride up front, so the neighbors won't think I'm getting arrested?"

"No problem, ma'am. I'll wait here while you go fetch him." The deputy shifted his weight from foot to foot, a sign of impatience. But he displayed a polite smile, as fixed as the plastic face of a Halloween mask.

Three minutes later came a loud shriek.

Pete Hitzer dashed into the house and ran up the stairs. His 9mm Glock was in his hand. He encountered Wanda Bjorn standing in the narrow hallway, pointing into a bedroom.

"What?" he shouted.

"Pinky," she said. "He's gone."

≈ ≈ ≈

Chief Purdue personally picked up Ted Yost at the E-Z Chair factory. Wanda Bjorn confirmed that Yost was living with her, but denied any knowledge about the theft of the Wilkins Witch Quilt. A search of her house turned up nothing.

She dutifully filled out a missing person report, but there would be no 24-hour waiting period in this case. Pinky was a material witness in a felony. The police chief already had two deputies scouring the town looking for him.

Ted Yost sat in the holding cell, whistling to himself like a man who didn't have a care in the world. He wore faded blue jeans and a red flannel shirt, the appearance of a working-class man. He said he didn't steal the quilt, but took the Fifth when asked who killed Charlie Aitkens.

Jim was pretty sure he'd solved the murder.

Lt. Neil Wannamaker phoned to say he was on the way to Caruthers Corners. *Yeah, come get involved now so you can take all the credit*, thought Jim in a flash of anger. But he didn't say anything.

When told of Ted Yost's arrest, Mayor Beau Madison figured this wrapped up the town's crime wave. It was pretty clear this guy Ted also stole the quilt. Edgar Ridenour had overheard it straight from the Aitkens boy. All that remained was to figure out where ol' Ted had stashed it.

As far as finding any Viking silver, Beau considered that to be a wild goose chase. There was no real proof Norsemen ever came to the Midwest. This "treasure" was a just a fantasy fostered by his wife and her Quilters Club buddies.

Boyd Aitkens phoned Beau to thank him for the support in finding his son's killer. The watermelon farmer assured him he could count on generous financial support come next election.

Heck, that wasn't such a big deal, thought Beau. He had only spent $2,000 in his last campaign. Twenty posters and a few radio ads.

CHAPTER NINETEEN

Nothing Magic About Murder

Pinky Bjorn contacted his *Relic of the Runes* pal Harry the Hobbit. Little did he know Harry Gertner had given his name to the police in the first place.

As online gamers they used avatars, cyber characters that were fantastical improvements on their puny, dateless, real-life selves. Predictably, Pinky was an elf; Harry was a Hobbit. Both had magical powers, at least in the online world of *Relic of the Runes*.

"Are the cops looking for me?" Pinky typed into his laptop.

"Cops? What for?" replied the diminutive Hobbit on his screen.

"I know who killed Charlie Aitkens."

"Whoa, man. You better turn yourself in. That's serious stuff."

"No way. I'm responsible for the murder."

"How so?"

"I translated the runes on that witch quilt. If I hadn't done that, he wouldn't have stole it. And if he hadn't stole it he wouldn't have wound up killing Charlie over it."

"Who?"

"Can't say. But it's someone close to me."

"Your dad? Or Teddy Yost?"

"Can't say. Don't ask again or I will use fairy dust to immobilize you."

"Hobbits are immune to fairy dust."

"Says you."

≈ ≈ ≈

Meanwhile Ted Yost was refusing to talk. And Pinky Bjorn was still missing. Wanda Bjorn had been released for lack of evidence. Nothing tied her to either the missing quilt or the murder, not even Charlie Aitkens's own words.

With Charlie dead, the conversation overheard by Edgar Ridenour was being treated like a dying declaration. But Mark the Shark, now back from Milwaukee, told them it didn't meet the criteria for a deathbed confession, in that the boy's demise came days later.

Both Bill and Kathy had been released from the Aurora St. Luke's Medical Center and were now back at home in Chicago. Little N'yen was torn between his anxiousness to see his mommy and daddy and an eagerness to help the Quilters Club solve this case. He wanted to see that Viking treasure with his very own eyes.

Aggie told him not to worry, that tomorrow's picnic was really just a cover story for their treasure hunt. With a little luck, he'd get to see the treasure before heading back to Chicago.

But that was before Spud Bodkin turned up.

≈ ≈ ≈

Spud had been on the run, fearful that the same fate would befall him as happened to his friend Charlie. He'd been holed up in an Indianapolis flea trap when Lt. Wannamaker tracked him down. Spud had used his credit card to pay for the room, a mistake when the police are looking for you.

"Honest, I was gonna turn myself in," he lied to the state policeman.

"Sure you were," said Wannamaker.

"I didn't even know you wanted to talk with me till yesterday. Saw my picture on TV."

"Well, here you are – so talk."

"I didn't kill Charlie."

Wannamaker leaned back in his chair, one of two in the bare ISP Interrogation Room. Folding chairs, metal table, one-way glass on the wall – the room's total furnishings. "Didn't think you did," said the lieutenant.

Spud wrinkled his forehead. With his round face, thick glasses, and protruding ears, he did look a bit like Mr. Potato Head. "Then why were you looking for me?"

"Thought you could tell me who stole the Wilkins Witch Quilt. Valued at over a hundred grand, that makes it a felony."

"Wasn't me."

"But you know who did. Someone overheard you and Charlie Aitkens talking."

"Was that who killed Charlie, the eavesdropper?"

Wannamaker shook his head slowly, like the pendulum of a ticking clock. "Nope. We think it was the fellow who stole the quilt, trying to shut you guys up."

"That was my thought too. That's why I took off when I heard Charlie was dead."

"How'd you hear?"

"On the radio."

"So who is this fellow you're afraid of, the one who stole the quilt. We'll pick him up and then you'll be as safe as a babe in his mother's arms."

"Sure. I don't mind telling you – our ol' pal Bern."

"Who the fudge is that?"

≈ ≈ ≈

Chief Purdue was confused by the phone call he got from Neil the Nail. "What do you mean you've identified the quilt thief as Bern Bjorn? I've got the guilty party locked up right here in my holding cell, a guy named Theodore Yost. Works at the local chair factory."

"No," insisted the ISP lieutenant. "It's a fellow named Bern Bjork. Go pick him up. Me and my boys will be there in about two hours if the traffic's light."

"Can't be Bern Bjorn," insisted Jim Purdue. "Bern manages the local Dairy Queen. He gives me extra sprinkles every time I go in."

"You better have him in custody by the time we get there or I'll give you enough sprinkles to choke on."

"Hey, watch your tone. You said the murder was my case to solve. And I have – Ted Yost."

"Well, the art theft is *my* case and I just solved it – Bern Bjorn."

"But the same guy that stole the quilt killed Charlie Aitkens."

"Exactly," said the Nail, hanging up in the police chief's ear.

CHAPTER TWENTY

Searching for the Viking Treasure

With two separate suspects under arrest, the Quilters Club turned its attention back to the Viking treasure. Cookie was convinced it was buried at the site of the Church of Avenging Angels. Where else could it be, now that the well had proved to be a "dry hole."

"Dry?" laughed her husband Ben. "There was a good three feet of water in that old well. Came up to my hoo-ha."

"Your what?"

"Never mind. Let me just say my waders had a leak and that water was icy cold. Thought I'd freeze my –"

"Ben!"

"Like I said, never mind."

She smiled. They had married late in life. While she'd been a widow, he'd been an old bachelor. As such, Ben Bentley still got tongue-tied around his wife when risqué subjects came up.

"Point is, you found nothing down in that well. Not even the bones of Mad Matilda.

"There was that Mason jar," he reminded her.

She rolled her eyes. "A magic amulet of some kind. But nothing to do with a Viking treasure."

"True."

"So if the silver's not there in the well, the men who killed Matilda Wilkins must have taken it."

Ben was eating a bowl of cereal, his mouth full. "Tha iz gun."

"What's that you said?"

He swallowed, then repeated: "Then it's gone. You'll never find it if the old woman's killers took it. The law never found them."

"There's an old legend that says they buried the money under the steps of their church. All we have to do it find where it stood and look there."

"What church was that?" Ben knew the countryside around Caruthers Corners like the back of his hand. Having worked one summer as a surveyor of watermelon-growing allotments, he'd traveled every square inch of the county.

"The Church of Avenging Angels."

"Never heard of it." Ben refilled his bowl with puffed rice. He was fond of that snap-crackle-pop cereal.

"The church burned down in 1899. Nobody remembers where it stood."

"Like I said, the treasure's long gone."

"No, we just have to figure out where the church used to be."

"Ga tal t' Heni Guna."

"Don't talk with your mouth full, dear."

He swallowed. "Go talk to Howard Gunnar. He's the oldest man in town. Maybe he'll know."

≈ ≈ ≈

N'yen and his cousin Agnes were watching television, a movie called *The Black Pirate* starring Douglas

Somebody as a guy who pretends to be a pirate in order to rescue a princess. "Aw, they stole that plot from *The Princess Bride*. They just changed the name from 'the Dread Pirate Roberts' to 'the Black Pirate.'"

"I think *The Black Pirate* came first," said Aggie.

"When those pirates said, 'Dead men tell no tales,' it reminded me of the murder we're trying to solve."

"How so?" asked his cousin. Their grandmother had made them popcorn with lots of butter. AMC was running a day of buccaneer movies.

"Because the guy that stole the quilt killed that Charlie guy to keep him from telling tales."

"You're pretty smart for a boy," she complimented him.

"Thanks. Now all we gotta do is figure out which one is guilty, the man who works at the chair factory or the one who manages the Dairy Queen."

"Maybe they're both guilty."

"Naw, I think it's the frozen custard guy."

"Why's that?"

"That boy who translated the secret message would have told his dad. I know I would've."

"You're pretty fond of your dad, huh?"

"Don't remember my real dad. But Bill is about the best-est dad ever. I'd tell him anything. Sure hope he's okay."

"Don't worry. My daddy's up there making sure he's okay. Your mom too."

"Dads and moms are great, aren't they? I didn't have any for the longest time. Now I've got a whole family, including you."

"I like my grandmother a lot," admitted Aggie.

"And I like my grampy," N'yen added. "He doesn't care that I'm adoptated."

"Adopted, you mean."

"Yeah, that. It's kinda special when you think about it. Out of all the boys and girls in the world, Bill and Kathy picked me."

≈ ≈ ≈

It took Cookie all morning to round up the Quilters Club. Lizzie was already at the Garden Club Luncheon. Bootsie was baking a watermelon cake for Jim. And Maddy was working on her latest patchwork quilt while the kids watched movies on AMC.

In addition, Cookie had to contact Howard Gunnar's great-granddaughter to arrange for a visit. The old man tired easily, she was told, but would receive them following his afternoon nap.

"Howard Gunnar, that's a good idea," said Maddy. "If anyone remembers the location of that church, it would be him."

"Ben suggested it."

"You've got yourself a good man, Cookie. Going down in that well for you. Giving that land to Haney Bros. Circus to establish a town zoo. Supporting our misadventures."

"Don't I know it! He's my very own teddy bear." Although Ben Bentley had had a crush on Cookie since high school, it was only after her first husband died in a tractor accident that they got together.

"We're all lucky gals," said Maddy. "Finding good men to share our lives with."

"And we're lucky to have each other as friends," Cookie replied – meaning the Quilters Club.

≈ ≈ ≈

Howard Gunnar had celebrated his 100th birthday only last month. Mayor Beauregard Madison had declared the day as "The Howard Gunnar Centennial" and presented the old man with a bronze plaque to that effect. The *Burpyville Gazette* ran his picture on the front page. His great-granddaughter Roberta had accompanied Howard to the ceremony on the town square.

The Quilters Club arrived in mass at the Gunnar farm. Surrounded by the expanding town limits, the ten-acre farm was abutted on three sides by residential streets and new housing. No crops had been grown there in forty years, other than a few assorted vegetables in the small garden plot behind the weathered farmhouse.

"They're expecting us, right?" asked Maddy Madison. She believed in good manners.

Cookie nodded vigorously. "Yes, I spoke to Roberta Gunnar. She's Howard's caretaker as well as his only living relative."

"I brought watermelon cake," said Bootsie. "Jim told me the old man is fond of it."

"I wouldn't mind a slice myself," grumbled Lizzie. "I didn't have any lunch."

"Me either," Bootsie admitted, eyeing the cake platter in her hands.

"Behave yourself, you're on a diet," Maddy reminded her friend.

"I'm not," said Lizzie. Still as slender as when she was as a high-school cheerleader.

"What do you mean you didn't have lunch?" accused Cookie. "You were at the Garden Club bash."

"Nobody ever eats at those things. Rubber chicken and talk-talk-talk."

"Come along, girls," urged Maddy. "Maybe Mr. Gunnar will share a slice or two with you."

"He better," muttered Bootsie. "I actually baked it for Jim."

"We appreciate his sacrifice," said Maddy as she stepped onto the farmhouse porch.

Roberta Gunnar was a thirtysomething brunette with plump hips and generous thunder thighs. However, she had a radiant smile, all the more noticeable with her whitened teeth. "Come inside," she invited, holding the door wide. "Gramps is in the living room."

"We brought him cake," Bootsie announced, hold it up for all to see.

"Watermelon cake? That's his favorite."

"So we heard."

The old man looked something like a mummy, given his wrinkled gray skin and wispy hair. But his watery brown eyes twinkled with alertness. "Don't get many visitors anymore," he nodded his welcome. "Everybody I know is long dead – friends, children, even grandchildren. Nobody left but Roberta here. Guess I'll be joining them friends and relatives soon enough."

"Aw Gramps, you're gonna live forever," his great-granddaughter said.

"Sure looks like it, don't it. Never expected to see a hundred. They gave me a nice party last month."

Cookie broached the subject. "We wanted to ask you about an old landmark."

"Landmark? I've never traveled farther than Indianapolis."

"A local landmark. A church that's long gone," explained Maddy.

"Church, you say? Never was much of a churchgoer. Course I may regret that soon enough."

"We're trying to find out where the Church of Avenging Angels was located," said Bootsie, handing him a slice of watermelon cake. A bribe as it were.

"Avenging Angels? That was even before my time. I'm only a hundred years old. That church burned down 'fore I was born."

"But did anyone ever show you where it was located?" asked Lizzie, eying his cake with envy.

"Ever show me? No. But my daddy told me it was on the other side of Never Ending Swamp, over near Gruesome Gorge."

"Can you be more specific?" pleaded Cookie.

"Not really. My daddy didn't think much of them Avenging Angels. Said they was witch hunters from St. Paul. Told me they killed a local woman for being a witch."

"You mean Matilda Wilkins?" Bootsie coached.

"That's her, Mad Matilda. My daddy said she flew about on a broomstick. Changed people into frogs. Put curses on her enemies. Guess it didn't work with them Avenging Angels. They threw her down her own well."

"But their church –?"

"Told you, never seen it. Was burnt down 'fore I was born. I told you that, didn't I?"

"Gramps forgets what he says," Roberta explained in a stage whisper.

"I can hear you, girl," he admonished his great-granddaughter. "Lost my smell. But I still got my hearing."

"You say it was burnt?" Cookie pressed.

"To the ground. The posse that was looking for them did it, my daddy said. They was snake handlers. My daddy said rattlers came crawling outta the fire like creatures from hell."

"Snakes!" squeaked Lizzie. She had an aversion to snakes, mice, spiders, and bees.

"Rattlers fat as my forearm," the old man said. Enjoying having shocked his audience. "The preacher that led the Avenging Angels used to sleep with diamondbacks, according to my daddy. Said them snakes never bit him, like they were akin."

"Rev. Billingsley Royce, you mean?" prodded Cookie.

"Don't recall his name. Daddy said he had the mark of Cain on him."

"About the church –?"

"This sure is tasty cake," muttered the old man. "Can I have another slice?"

"Yes, of course. Now about the church –?"

"Pretty day, ain't it?"

≈ ≈ ≈

Another dead end. Cookie Bentley was pretty despondent. Excusing herself, saying she had work to do, she went back to her office. The Historical Society had recently moved into a small building on North Main Street. The town council thought it could become a tourist attraction, so the front room served as a museum with a permanent exhibit about the history of Caruthers Corners.

- A copy of Indiana's proclamation of statehood.

- A six-foot-tall wooden Indian in native costume.
- A first-rate collection of arrowheads and pottery.
- Bronze busts of the town's founders – Jacob Caruthers, Ferdinand Jinks, and Col. Beauregard Madison.
- A diorama of the Big Fire of 1899.
- Architectural drawings of the Town Hall.
- A 3-D model of the E-Z Chair factory.
- A video showing highlights from the annual Watermelon Days festival.
- A horticultural poster on growing watermelons.
- A display of prizewinning patchwork quilts.
- That rare copy of *A Personal History of Caruthers Corners and Surrounding Environs* by Marin Caruthers.
- Photos of local buildings.
- An antique bottle collection.
- A circus poster showing the Haney Bros. on each side of Happy the Elephant.
- Edwin the Enchanted Doll, basis of a local ghost story.
- A collection of carnival glass.
- An aerial photograph of Caruthers Corners.

The backroom was officially designated as the secretary's office, but it was more of a storeroom with a wooden desk in the center. File cabinets and stacks of newspapers lined the walls. Boxes of uncatalogued artifacts took one corner. Shelves of donated antiques occupied another corner. An ancient cuckoo ticked over the doorway.

Cookie was putting away the newspaper clippings about the death of Matilda Wilkins when she spotted the albumin photograph of Rev. Billingsley Royce. She paused to study the faded image. His slightly crossed eyes had a crazed look. That wine-stain could certainly be interpreted as a mark of Cain. He was frowning, a sign of his disapproval of the ungodly world around him.

Idly turning the photograph over, she discovered an inked notation on its backside: *Taken on the 12 August 1897 at the church at Steppin Rock.*

Hmm, where had she heard that name before? Wasn't Steppin' Rock an oddly shaped limestone formation out near Gruesome Gorge? Could that have been the location of the Church of Avenging Angels?

This called for another field trip for the Quilters Club. But they would have to call it a "picnic" for the benefit of their unsympathetic spouses. The boys considered the case closed. But Cookie knew better.

CHAPTER TWENTY-ONE

Steppin' Rock

Nobody seemed to recall where Steppin' Rock was located. Wasn't like it was a big tourist attraction. Just a colorful name given to a natural rock formation that didn't even appear on area maps.

Maddy used the picnic excuse to ask her husband. Beau didn't have a clue about it, though he'd lived all his life in Caruthers Corners. So had she. In fact, so had all the members of the Quilters Club and their husbands.

At Maddy's prodding, Beau checked with the Planning and Zoning Department, Public Works, and the Tax Assessor's Office ... but none of them knew where to find Steppin' Rock.

The Quilters Club may as well have been asking how to find the Church of Avenging Angels. Or maybe they were, in so many words.

Despite Ben Bentley's watermelon-allotment surveying, Edgar Ridenour's fishing excursions, or Chief Jim Purdue's patrols, no one had ever been to Steppin' Rock. Yet they all had heard the name, a local rock formation.

Young N'yen came through with the solution. He'd seen a movie where Osama ben Laden's hideout had been observed from satellite photos. *Zero Dark Thirty*, it was called. Maddy was aghast that the child had been allowed to see such a violent film. But Bill and Kathy were very liberal in their childrearing, as with most things.

"Satellite photos," laughed Lizzie. "Where would we get those?"

Maddy had the answer. "Not satellite images, but aerial plat maps for the entire county are stored in the Town Hall's basement."

"How would we ever find Steppin' Rock among all those rolls of aerial photographs. There must be a zillion of them down there," frowned Bootsie.

Cookie solved that one. "We don't have to look at all of them. Just the photos around Gruesome Gorge on the far side of Never Ending Swamp. That's where Howard Gunnar said it was located."

"That narrows it down some," Bootsie acquiesced.

≈ ≈ ≈

After two dusty hours in the Town Hall basement, they found it, Aerial Photo R-790-3. There it was – a rectangular rock slab. Even so, they would have likely missed it if someone hadn't written STEPPINGSTONE ROCK next to it with a red grease pencil.

"Steppingstone?" said Lizzie doubtfully. "That's not right."

Maddy squinted at the oversized photo. "That's got to be it."

"Um, I dunno."

"Well –"

"One way to find out," suggested precocious Aggie. "Let's go look."

CHAPTER TWENTY-TWO

Digging for the Viking Silver

The outcropping known locally as Steppin' Rock was located just inside the boundaries of Gruesome Gorge State Park. It was a flat sandstone boulder that looked like the foundation of a house. Supposedly, the rock had been the site of a Potawatomi sweat lodge.

A Personal History of Caruthers Corners and Surrounding Environs told how the Potawatomi had been members of the Council of Three Fires, along with the Ojibwe and the Ottawa. Although their tribal name translated as "keepers of the fire," they were considered younger brothers of the Council.

The leader of these Wabash Potawatomi was known as Winamac (meaning "Catfish"). He and his Fish Clan had sided with the British during the war of 1812. They were the ones who had attacked the wagon train led by Col. Beauregard Madison, Jacob Caruthers, and Ferdinand Jinks – the battle that led to the founding of Caruthers Corners.

Actually, there had been two Chief Winamacs, one an opponent of the US, the other an ally. The "bad" Winamac had made his camp at Gruesome Gorge.

Maddy Madison walked across the sandstone surface of Steppin' Rock, Aggie and N'yen following two steps behind. "So the Indians built a sweat lodge atop this outcropping?" she mused aloud.

"What's a sweat lodge?" asked Aggie.

"Kind of like a sauna."

"You mean this was an Indian health spa?"

"Not exactly." Maddy didn't want to tell her granddaughter how this settlement near Gruesome Gorge had proven quite unhealthy for the Native Americans who had died here in an ambush.

"Martin J. Caruthers wrote about the Potawatomi sweat lodge in his history book," Cookie noted. "But he didn't mention Steppin' Rock." She was standing on the sidelines, watching as Bootsie and Liz measured the boulder's squarish surface with a tape measure. Members of the Quilters Club always carried tape measures for checking out fabrics and quilting squares.

"Eighteen by twenty feet," Bootsie called out. "Plenty big for a sweat lodge."

"Eighteen and a half," Lizzie corrected.

"Eighteen and a half," Bootsie repeated to acknowledge the adjusted figure.

Maddy ran her hand across the reddish-brown surface, as smooth as if it had been planed and leveled. "This makes a natural foundation," she noted. "A perfect place to build a sweat lodge."

"What if Rev. Billingsley Royce and his followers built their church here too? Any remnants of a sweat lodge would have been long gone by the 1890s," Cookie posed the question. "After all, it *said* Steppin' Rock on the back of that photograph."

Maddy's gaze swept the outcropping. "If this were the site of a country church, where would the front door have been?"

"Over here, most likely," pointed Cookie. "The ground slopes. That makes the far side too high off the ground, I'd guess."

"Didn't the story say they buried the treasure under the church steps?" asked Lizzie, always an eye on the money.

"The steps would've been right here," said Bootsie, "if Cookie's right about the door." The ground looked undisturbed, the rock's shadow forming a triangle on the grass.

"That looks about right," nodded Maddy.

"Should we dig?" Bootsie asked. She sounded uneasy.

"Why wouldn't we?"

"Well, this *is* state park land."

"We're on a picnic," reasoned Maddy. "Wouldn't it be proper camping etiquette to dig a fire pit for our weenie roast? You know, to prevent forest fires and such."

"Oh boy," exclaimed little N'yen. "We're gonna have hot dogs!"

≈ ≈ ≈

Two hours later there was a pile of dirt the size of a Volkswagen next to the hole they'd dug, but no silver bars had been found.

535

"Guess we got this one wrong," sighed Cookie. In her enthusiasm, she'd done much of the digging. Tomorrow her back would be the devil to pay.

"Not necessarily," said Maddy. She'd been reassessing the situation. "Maybe the story got garbled. Instead of the treasure being buried under the church's steps, maybe it was buried under Steppin' Rock."

Bootsie laughed. "You mean under this giant slab of sandstone? No way."

"Maybe not under the entire rock, but under a corner of it," suggested Maddy. She studied the reddish-brown sandstone platform, looking for a likely entry point.

"We've dug four feet down and haven't come to the bottom of the rock," Cookie groused.

Bootsie rubbed her back. "Will Rogers said, 'If you find yourself in a hole, stop digging.'"

"Thanks for the helpful advice." Lizzie's tone meant just the opposite.

Maddy hadn't given up. "Perhaps we can get under it better on the other side. With the ground sloping, there's already four or five feet of rock showing over there."

Cookie acquiesced. "One small hole just to see how deep this rock goes."

Ten minutes later, Cookie said, "There it is, the bottom of this big slab of sandstone."

Steppin' Rock proved to be about six-feet thick. The remnant of a long-ago ice age, when glaciers moved boulders about like a game of marbles.

"Now dig under the edge," instructed Maddy.

"Hey, your turn."

"Oh, all right," said Maddy, stepping into the hole and taking the shovel.

Another ten minutes. "Anything yet?" asked Lizzie, trying to peer into the hole. Maddy had been tunneling under the bottom of the rock.

"Nothing. And my back's getting tired. Want to take over Lizzie?"

Lizzie grimaced. "No more digging for me. I've already broken a fingernail."

"Here, I'll dig for a while," volunteered Bootsie.

Ten minutes more. "The shovel just struck something solid," announced Bootsie. Sounding excited.

"Is it a silver bar?" Lizzie asked.

"Not sure."

"Brush away the dirt," ordered Maddy, taking charge as usual. "Let's see what you've found."

Bootsie bent down to scoop the dirt away with her hands. A rounded shape came into view. "Oh, shoot," she said. "Just another rock."

"Pull it out and keep digging," said Cookie. "Maybe there's something behind it."

"Your turn. I'm tired."

Cookie Bentley took the shovel. She'd borrowed it from her husband's toolshed this morning before setting out on this "picnic." Scraping away the loose dirt, the rock became more defined. An oblong chunk of limestone, about the size of a loaf of bread. "If there's another stone behind this one, I'm quitting. This was a stupid idea."

"Wasn't it your idea?" Lizzie asked with a false innocence.

"Rub it in," sighed Cookie. "I deserve it."

537

"Here," said Maddy, climbing into the hole with Cookie. "Let me help you pull it out."

The two women struggled with the rock, wiggling it side to side. It was starting to give. "On the count of three," said Maddy. "One ... two ... THREE!"

With a *pop!* the rock slid out, leaving a dark hole. "Okay," said Cookie, "unless there's a Viking sword and a bar of silver in there, I'm going home."

"Hey," wailed N'yen. "What about the hot dogs?"

≈ ≈ ≈

Maury Seiderman was lurking behind a large oak tree, a good vantage point for spying on those busybody women from Caruthers Corners. He recognized the one from the Historical Society. What were they doing out here?

He'd been scouting the area in his '75 LeSabre, looking for ruins of a church. Nothing. Just watermelon fields and grassy countryside. An occasional Amish farmhouse, identifiable by the lack of power lines. Then he'd spotted the SUV filled with women and kids. That Bentley woman from the Historic Society had been sitting there in the front seat, big as life. So he'd decided to follow them. They had led him down an unmarked cow path along the upper rim of Gruesome Gorge. Could they be looking for the treasure too?

Now he knew the answer.

They were pulling something out from under that big sandstone outcropping. Obviously, they had found the Viking silver.

CHAPTER TWENTY-THREE

Down to No Suspects

C hief Purdue didn't like it one bit, but he had to cut Ted Yost free. No evidence, other than he was dating the mother of a *Lord of the Rings* fanboy. No crime in that, Lt. Wannamaker pointed out.

The police chief had brought in Bern Bjorn, just as Neil the Nail had instructed. That meant no more free sprinkles for him. Bern was pretty irked.

In the end, he'd had to let Bern Bjorn go too. Came down to the word of Lt. Wannamaker's witness versus Bern's. No real evidence.

Quite a coincidence that Bern was the ex-husband of Ted's girlfriend. But this was a small town, a population of 2,577 give or take.

"Back to square one," grumbled Wannamaker, as if it were Jim's fault he'd taken the word of an unemployed ne'er-do-well over that of a local business owner.

"Yeah, I'll be in touch if I turn up anything new," said the police chief, his sarcasm as thick as watermelon jam.

"You do that."

"I'm not paying that invoice for the DNA testing. It was a clue."

"It was a hundred-year-old pig's eye, for goodness sake."

"We didn't know that till we tested it."

"You wasted the time of the state lab."

"That's what it's there for, to help us examine clues."

"Magic potions aren't clues."

"D'you think we'll ever find the Wilkins Witch Quilt?"

"Naw," admitted Wannamaker. "I've got a feeling that quilt's gone for good. Probably already in the hands of some private collector where it will never again see the light of day."

≈ ≈ ≈

Pinky Bjorn was hiding in Burpyville at the home of his cousin. He hadn't phoned his mother, afraid she'd tell the police where to find him. Somehow they had connected him with stealing that old quilt. Not that he'd had any active part in the burglary. But he knew who did. After all, he was the one who had translated those runes. Pretty simple when you'd spent the last two years playing *Relic of the Runes*, an online Tolkien-inspired game that required a basic knowledge of Scandinavian *Futhark* or its Anglo-Saxon variant called *Futhorc*.

The *Early Futhorc* was identical to the *Elder Futhark*, except for the split the a-rune into three variants, resulting in 26 runes. No harder to learn than the ABC alphabet, truth be known.

He'd been there in the Town Hall waiting for his mother to pay her property tax when he noticed that quilt hanging on the wall. He remembered being fascinated by its depiction of angels and devils fighting each other. Cool beans. Like a video game. Then he noticed the symbols around the quilt's border, clearly runes.

It took him less than fifteen minutes to decipher them. He was working from memory, without any reference books. But after two years of playing *Relic of the Runes* he was getting pretty good at it. He held the rank of Exalted Grand Wizard of the Elfin World.

The message went something like "After a long journey, we are hiding our money in deep water." He didn't know why anybody would put that on an old quilt, but it sounded like a clue on a treasure map. Money hidden in deep water ... you'd have to know something about the old woman who made the quilt to figure that out.

The bronze plaque on the wall said this Matilda Wilkins claimed to be a witch. She must have been nuts. He didn't believe in witches, although he *did* believe in wizards, elves, and Hobbits. He wondered if the old woman had lived around here? And did she have a pond or a well?

He'd have to ask somebody about that, he remembered thinking. Now he was sorry he'd ever seen that blasted quilt. Or told anybody about the message. How did he know that the person he'd confided in would steal it!

≈ ≈ ≈

Ted Yost went straight home, where Wanda was waiting for him. "Have you heard from Pinky?" he asked the boy's mother.

"Not a word."

"The police are still looking for him."

Wanda pressed her fingertips against her temples, as if suffering from a severe migraine. "W-what did you tell them?"

"Nothing. I clammed up, took the Fifth."

"Thank you for protecting Pinky."

"Your boy didn't have anything to do with stealing the quilt. We both know that."

"But he translated those symbols on the Wilkins Witch Quilt. They might arrest him as an accomplice."

"Nobody knows he broke the quilt's code. We've just gotta keep our mouths shut and he'll be all right. They can't prove anything."

"How do you know that?"

"Why else would they have let *me* go?"

CHAPTER TWENTY-FOUR

Another Pig's Eye

"**T**his is not a silver bar," said Maddy, holding up a dirt-encrusted Mason jar.

Cookie asked, "What's in it? Another pig's eye."

"I can't tell." She rubbed at the dirt off the glass. "There's something inside. Pebbles or something."

"Open it," urged Lizzie. Her red hair blazing in the noonday sun.

"No way," barked Bootsie, taking the shovel from Maddy. "It might be evidence that only the police should handle."

"Can't open it anyway," said Maddy, having tried. "The lid's rusted shut."

"I'll open it," said a strange voice. Everyone looked up to see an odd-looking man standing above them on the sandstone slab. He was as slender as Jack Skellington. A thin mustache crossed his upper lip. His raven-black hair was slicked back with a thick gel. In his hand he held an ugly-looking P-08 parabellum Luger. "Give that jar to me," he ordered, "or I'll shoot."

"Hey, who's that man?" asked little N'yen, confused by the intruder's sudden appearance.

"That's Maury Seiderman," answered Cookie Bentley. "He's with some paranormal research organization." She couldn't quite remember the name on his business card.

"The Greater Midwest Occult Phenomena Association," he reminded her haughtily. "By now you've probably figured out I'm on the same mission as you: To find the Viking silver that Rev. Billingsley Royce took from Matilda Wilkins."

"Well, it's certainly not in this jar," said Maddy, handing it up to him. "Last Mason jar we found contained spunk water, feathers, and a pig's eye."

"A witch's potion," he snorted.

"Exactly. This is probably something similar."

"Open it."

"Can't. It's rusted shut."

"Lemme take a look at it," he ordered. Tucking the pistol under his belt, he attempted to twist the lid but it refused to open. "*Umph!*" he grunted, face twisted with the exertion.

"Told you," said Maddy.

"Oh well," shrugged Maury Seiderman, then smashed the Mason jar against the unyielding surface of Steppin' Rock.

Kra-ack!

"You shouldn't've done that," admonished Aggie. "The jar didn't belong to you, Mr. Seiderman. We found it, so it was ours – fair and square."

"Too bad, so sad, little missy," he sneered. "Mine now because I've got the gun."

"Not for long," said Bootsie as she swung the shovel – *klang!* – knocking the Luger from his hand.

"Ow," he cried, stepping back.

Lizzie retrieved the gun, but in her hands it looked about as effective as a child holding a bazooka. She didn't even have her finger on the trigger. Probably afraid of smudging her nail polish, Cookie joked later. "Stop right there, buster!" barked Lizzie with enough authority to stop Maury Seiderman in his tracks.

"Look, ladies, this was just a joke," he pleaded. "I saw you digging down here and thought I might have some fun."

"With a gun?" retorted Bootsie. She often accompanied her husband to the shooting range out on Field Hand Road so she knew the damage a bullet could do. Sometimes they used watermelons as targets, making a big red splash when the 9mm slug hit its target.

"That pistol's not even loaded," he said.

"Then it will be okay if I point it at your head and pull the trigger," smiled Lizzie. She adjusted her aim, one eye squinted.

"No, wait. Don't do that. Gun safety and all."

"Right," said Lizzie, shifting her finger to pull the trigger.

Ka-bam!

The bullet zinged past Maury Seiderman's ear. "Holy rollers, you almost killed me," he shouted at her.

"I thought you said it wasn't loaded."

"Good thing you're a lousy shot," he muttered, a tremor in his voice.

"Right," said Lizzie. Not volunteering that she and Edgar often went to the shooting range with Jim and Bootsie. She was actually a very good shot.

Maddy spoke up: "Perhaps you don't mind telling us what you're doing out here waiving a gun around?"

"Looking for the treasure," he muttered. "I've got as much right to it as you have. Maybe more. I'm related to Matilda Wilkins on my mother's side. She was a Süderdithmarschen – although the family shortened it to Marsch generations ago."

"So you're not really an occult researcher?"

"Of course I am. That's why my cousin called me in to help locate the family treasure."

Bootsie had been talking on her cell phone. "Jim has a deputy on the way," she announced as she hung up.

"The police?" Seiderman offered a weak smile. "C'mon, we don't need to get them involved, do we?"

"When you start waving guns at the police chief's wife, the police get involved," stated Bootsie, an angry set to her jaw.

"Hey now –"

"Don't try to run away," warned Maddy. "Our friend Lizzie could have shot your ear off, if she'd wanted too."

"Okay, okay. But this is all a silly misunderstanding."

"I've got a question," said little Aggie. Hanging back, with a protective arm around her younger cousin.

"Yes, dear?" Maddy turned to her granddaughter.

"What was in the jar he broke?"

CHAPTER TWENTY-FIVE

The Shattered Mason Jar

Everybody circled the shattered Mason jar there on the sandstone surface of Steppin' Rock. The syrupy water formed a puddle, like a miniature pond with a couple of feathers and another eyeball floating in it.

"Aw shucks, another jar of goo," said Lizzie.

"A witch's potion," Cookie corrected her.

"Is that an eyeball?" squealed Aggie, pointing at the greasy orb. Yellowish from a century of slow pickling.

"Yes, dear," said Cookie, patting the girl's shoulder. "Probably another pig's eye."

"No silver?" grumbled their prisoner.

"Not an ounce," said Lizzie, sounding equally disappointed.

"Nothing to do but wait," sighed Bootsie, putting her cell phone back into her purse. "Deputy Hitzer will be here in another ten minutes."

≈ ≈ ≈

Beau Madison was sitting at his desk. Being mayor was quite an honor, but sometimes he didn't feel up to the task. Life had been much simpler when he ran the small Ace Hardware on South Main Street. Had he accepted the mayoral position out of fear of competing with the big Home Depot outside of town? Yes, probably.

Maybe he should just retire, take his Social Security, draw on his 401k, and spend more time with his grandkids. Little N'yen was fast becoming his favorite.

Let someone else worry about stolen quilts, witches, and Viking treasure ...

CHAPTER TWENTY-SIX

The Witch's Great-Great Granddaughter

That next day at 9 a.m. Cookie Bentley met her Quilters Club pals for coffee at the Cozy Diner. You could tell she was excited by the way she nervously batted her eyes, the lashes fluttering like twin butterflies. "Last night I was doing some more research," she gushed. "And I may have stumbled onto something important to the case."

"I thought the case was pretty much over," replied Maddy Madison. "The police have given up on finding the missing quilt. Charlie Aitkens's murderer may never be solved. Maury Seiderman is in jail for threatening us with a pistol. And as we've discovered, there's no Viking treasure."

"Maybe there's no treasure," said Cookie. "But I think the Quilters Club can still solve the theft and murder."

"Do tell," said Bootsie. A little defensive of her husband Jim's failed efforts.

Cookie mistakenly took that as a go-ahead. "I decided to do a little more digging on Matilda Elizabeth Wilkins to see if she has any living relatives."

"And −?"

"I found one," said the town's historian.

Maddy said, "You mean, Maury Seiderman?"

"No, someone else – his cousin."

"You're saying you were able to piece together the old woman's genealogy chart?" asked Lizzie, always impressed with lineage.

"Well, not me. I went online to YourAncestors.com and looked up Matilda Wilkins. The website taps into everything from birth records to wedding licenses."

Maddy sipped at her coffee. No chicory to her disappointment. "Surely they didn't have any of that stuff back in the mid 1800s when Mad Matilda was born..."

"Lots of people share Family Bible listings as well as their own genealogical research with the website. Happens, one of Matilda Wilkins's relatives had filled in the genealogy chart pretty well. And recently too."

"Who?" said Lizzie.

"Yes, who?" repeated Bootsie.

"Do we know this relative?" echoed Maddy.

Cookie paused to build up the suspense. "As a matter of fact, you do. The clue was in that history book by Martin Caruthers. He referred to her as Mrs. Wilkins. Matilda married one Benjamin Wilkins back in 1892. He died shortly after that. Her maiden name on the marriage certificate was Süderdithmarschen. That's a Germanic or Old Norse name."

"Maury Seiderman told us that yesterday," said Lizzie. "That's nothing new."

"Yes, but he said the name got shortened to Marsch. Remember?"

"Oh my," gasped Maddy. "Beau's new secretary is Becky Marsch."

"Bingo," said Cookie. "It was none other than Rebecca Matilda Marsch who posted the updated genealogical chart on YourAncestor.com. She's Mad Matilda's great-great granddaughter on the old witch's brother's side of the family. Maury Seiderman's first cousin."

"Are you suggesting Becky stole the quilt?" asked Bootsie, always looking for a culprit. A policeman's wife through and through.

"In a sense. I think she provided the Town Hall's alarm code to the actual thief. We always knew it was an inside job, but everybody kept focusing on that ol' reprobate, Jasper Beanie. He was just a red herring."

"Becky Marsch," Maddy repeated the name as if trying to get used to this new theory. Her husband's secretary of all people!

"Why did she do it?" asked Lizzie.

"The money?" said Bootsie. "The thrill? Because she didn't get a big enough raise?"

"Maybe Becky wanted to reclaim something she thought rightfully belonged to her family," speculated Maddy.

"I suppose I could understand that," said Bootsie. "But she certainly went about it the wrong way."

"Don't forget that somebody was her accomplice. And he may have killed Boyd's boy Charlie."

Lizzie sat down her coffee cup. "How can we find out who was in on it with Becky?"

"Why don't we just go ask her," said Aggie as she finished off her chocolate milk. "The Town Hall is only a block and a half away."

≈ ≈ ≈

They stopped by the police station on the way and picked up Bootsie's husband. He strapped on his gunbelt, pulled his cap over his balding head, and joined the parade up the sidewalk to the Town Hall.

Jim Purdue was thinking that the state boys were sure going to be irked if he solved both the murder and the theft. Jim had to admit he'd like that. Neil Wannamaker was just too darn pushy for his liking. The Nail indeed!

They found the pretty blonde at her desk, stationed just outside Beau Madison's inner sanctum. She looked up as the entourage entered and muttered, "Uh-oh."

"Becky Marsch," said Chief Purdue, "why didn't you tell me that you're related to the woman who created that missing quilt?"

"Uh, I'm only distantly related. Not enough to count."

"You must have thought it counted for something," interjected Cookie Bentley. "You updated her genealogy chart only last week."

"That doesn't mean I stole the quilt."

"Makes you our Number One suspect," countered the police chief. "I think the SBI's gonna want to talk with you, young lady."

"Okay, I did it," she gave in. "But I don't have the blasted thing."

"Who does?"

"Bern Bjorn. He took it."

"Bern?" said Chief Purdue. "We had him in custody only yesterday." It irked him that Bjorn had been Lt. Wannamaker's chief suspect. The Nail would never let him live this one down, letting Bjorn go for lack of evidence.

"Why would Bjorn do a fool thing like stealing the quilt?" asked Beau Madison. The mayor had come out of his office when he saw all the people gathered around his secretary's desk. "Bern's the manager of the Dairy Queen, for gosh sakes."

"Just got a confession," said the police chief. "Becky and Bern Bjorn did it."

"Y-you're sure?" sputtered the mayor. Bern Bjorn was a leading citizen. He'd been in Beau's office the day before the robbery for a meeting of the Town Square Beautification Committee.

Becky Marsch started to cry. "Bern's my boyfriend. I did it for him."

"Aha, your mystery man," said the police chief. Her alibi had been that she'd spent the night with her boyfriend. But she'd never named the man. And small-town decorum had kept Jim from asking.

"I've been seeing Bern off-and-on since he and Wanda split up," she sniveled.

"So you talked him into stealing the quilt?" said Maddy.

"No, the other way round. Stealing the quilt was *his* idea."

"Bern's idea?"

"Yes," she nodded firmly. "His son Pinky translated the symbols on that ratty old quilt. Told his dad what it said, that there was a treasure buried in my great-great grandmother's well. He took the quilt so nobody else would be able to figure out the secret message."

"We have lots of photographs of the Wilkins Witch Quilt," offered Cookie. "That's how we figured out what the runes said."

"Guess he didn't think of that. Bern's no genius, that's for sure. A miracle he has such a smart son."

"Pinky's a clever boy," agreed Bootsie. "I had him in a few classes last year."

Becky nodded. "True. But he needs to get out more. Always playing those stupid video games. Living off potato chips and Pepsi-Colas. The only friends he has are geeks just like him."

"Without those video games, he'd never have learned how to read runes," Cookie pointed out.

"Charlie Aitkens got it right," said Lizzie, whose husband had overheard the conversation while under the bridge. "A kid with a single mother figured out the message and told someone. But it turns out he told his dad, not his mom's boyfriend."

"It's only natural he'd confide in his dad," sniffled Becky. "Pinky doesn't particularly like Teddy Yost."

Chief Purdue pressed on with his questions. "You're saying you didn't want the quilt for yourself?"

"Why would I want that old rag?"

"Well, for one thing, it's worth a hundred thousand dollars. Some people might find that pretty tempting."

"Particularly a great-great granddaughter who thought the quilt rightfully belonged to her family," added Maddy.

"Poo," replied Becky. "That Viking treasure will be worth millions, so why worry about an old quilt?"

"There is no Viking Treasure," Maddy told her.

Becky Marsh turned to Cookie. "Mrs. Bentley, you're the town historian. Tell her she's wrong."

"Sorry, honey. There's no conclusive proof Norsemen ever made it to the Midwest."

"But my cousin Maury says –"

"So Maury Seiderman's in on this too?" said the police chief.

"Of course he is. I asked him to help Bern find the treasure. My cousin's a little nutty, but he's been chasing treasures all his life. He's fixated on witches and goblins and ghosts and buried treasures. He's a one-man paranoid organization."

"Don't you mean 'paranormal'?" corrected Maddy.

"No, I think she's got it right," said Chief Jim Purdue. "My night guy says Seiderman has been blathering about how Mad Matilda is gonna come save him from false imprisonment. False imprisonment ... in a pig's eye."

Aggie yelped, "What is it with pig's eyes?"

"Mad Matilda certainly seemed fond of using them in her potions," said Lizzie.

"I think I can answer that," grinned Cookie. "According to YourAncestors.com, Matilda Süderdithmarschen's family came from St. Paul, Minnesota. They were chased out of town for being witches. So those potions we found were actually curses on the people of St. Paul. Before its current name was established, the city of Saint Paul was known as Pig's Eye."

"You're making that up," accused Lizzie.

"No, really. It was nicknamed after a one-eyed tavern keeper, Pierre 'Pig's Eye' Parrant. Today there's even a Pig's Eye Brewing Company in St. Paul."

Bootsie was confused. "Then why would she bury one those curses under the foundation of the Church of Avenging Angels?"

"Simple. The Avenging Angels were witch hunters, a threat to Mad Matilda. So she put a curse on them. Rev. Billingsley Royce was originally from St. Paul."

"How do you know this?" challenged Bootsie.

"From *A Personal History of Caruthers Corners and Surrounding Environs.* It says Rev. Royce came from St. Paul. Page 321."

"That's true," admitted Becky Marsch. "My ancestors came here from St. Paul. They were run out of Minnesota by those witch hunters who called themselves the Avenging Angels. Those creeps even followed the Süderdithmarschens to Indiana."

"And they killed Mad Matilda?" asked Lizzie.

Becky nodded. "Matilda's mother and father died in the Great Tornado of 1889. And a few years later her husband was killed in a farming accident involving a mule. Kicked him in the head. So that left Matilda alone with her daughter to face those religious zealots. They killed my great-great grandmother for the Viking treasure she'd discovered in her well."

"I told you there's no Viking Treasure," Maddy said gently, patting the young woman's hand. "That was just a silly legend. We would have found it if there had been a hoard of hack silver around here. We've certainly looked."

"No, you're wrong. A family friend named Reggie Evers took Matilda's orphaned daughter Griselda – my great grandmother – and raised her as his own. Griselda recalled seeing the silver as a child. 'A dozen or more thin shiny bars that reflected the sun like a mirror,' she described them in her diary."

"Reginald Wentworth Evers was a Master Warlock who lived near Burpyville," remembered Cookie.

"Warlock, ha!" snorted Becky. "Reggie Evers and the Süderdithmarschens were members of *Seiðr*. That's an Old Norse religion based on Germanic paganism. You can find references to it in *Eiríks saga rauða*."

"In what?" said Beau.

"*The Saga of Erik the Red,* an account of Norse exploration of the Americas."

"You seem pretty up on all this stuff," observed Lizzie.

"Family tradition," Becky said modesty.

CHAPTER TWENTY-SEVEN

Crooks in the Can

After locking Becky Marsch in one of the police station's two holding cells, Deputy Pete Hitzer picked up Bern Bjorn and put him in the other one with Maury Seiderman. Lt. Neil Wannamaker was on his way down from Indy to pick them up.

"Gotcha, did they?" Seiderman greeted his cousin's boyfriend. He'd already claimed the top bunk, giving himself an on-high vantage point.

"Becky squealed on me," Bjorn spat out the words. He glanced angrily in her direction.

"No, honeybunch, I didn't," she called to him. "They had us dead to rights. They knew you killed Charlie Aitkens to shut him up about your stealing the quilt."

"Shut up, Becky! Don't say that in front of them."

"What? That you killed Charlie? You never should've told your buddies about stealing the quilt in the first place."

"Charlie was gonna help me sell it. Said he knew a guy in Cincinnati who fenced stolen goods."

Becky threw a shoe at him. It bounced off the cell's bars. "I thought you were only interested in finding the Viking treasure."

559

"That's true," he replied. "But I'm not going to turn away a hundred grand. The quilt had served its purpose."

Maury Seiderman slid off the top bunk, landing on the floor like a 6' 3" tomcat. "Hold on, chum. You didn't tell me about the hundred grand. I want my share. You promised me a third of whatever we got."

Bern Bjorn backed away from the threatening figure. "Your share, I was taking about the treasure."

"Well, there *is* no treasure, according to these old biddies."

"Who are you calling biddies?" protested Bootsie Purdue, standing next to her husband.

"You and your quilting pals," shouted Seiderman. "You've bollixed up this whole deal. Now I'm mixed up in a murder."

"Keep talking," grinned Chief Purdue. "We've got a station-full of witnesses." He gestured to the members of the Quilters Club. "No way you're walking away from this one. But it might go easier on you, if you tell us where to find the Wilkins Witch Quilt."

"I told you my great-great grandmother wasn't really a witch," shouted Becky. Angry about this turn of events. Being arrested. Her boyfriend turning against her. The treasure still out there unclaimed.

"Who cares whether the old hag was a witch or a Presbyterian," said Bern Bjorn. "I want to know where that silver is hidden."

"There is no silver," Seiderman repeated.

"There was," insisted Bjorn. "My son Pinky cracked the code of that message on the quilt."

"Your son has too much imagination," groused Seiderman. "Always playing those stupid video games. He probably made the whole thing up."

"No, Becky's great-grandmother saw the silver bars."

"That's true," she called from the next cell.

"Then where are they?" the skinny man challenged.

"I have a theory," said Cookie Bentley.

≈ ≈ ≈

All eyes turned to Cookie. She had everyone's attention. Even Lt. Wannamaker and the two burly state cops he'd brought with him.

"My theory is that a small band of Viking explorers made it here, having sailed across the Great Lakes from Newfoundland – or Vinland as they called it. They set up an encampment under the oak trees and dug a well so they'd have plentiful water. Or maybe it was simply meant to be a Money Pit like they'd dug on Oak Island in Nova Scotia."

"I've read about that," said the founder of the G.M.O.P.A. "It's been attributed to pirates, freemasons, and Norsemen. Some have speculated it holds a Viking treasure. Or even Marie Antoinette's jewels."

"Marie Antoinette wasn't a Viking," muttered Bjorn. He'd never liked Becky's know-it-all cousin. It had been her idea to bring him in on this treasure hunt.

Cookie continued doggedly. "Likely Mad Matilda's husband found the treasure while deepening the well. Word got out and Rev. Royce and his band of witch hunters saw it as their God-given right to confiscate the treasure from these spawns of Satan."

"*Seiðr* doesn't have anything to do with Satan," Becky objected. "Like I told you, it's based on Scandinavian mythology."

"Their religious beliefs must have got corrupted after a couple of generations in America," Lizzie pointed out. "The Wilkins Witch Quilts shows devils and angels doing battle."

"And she sold magic potions," added Bootsie.

The blonde had no response to that. So she sat down on her bunk to sulk.

"Old man Wilkins had been kicked in the head by a mule, so it was only Matilda and her daughter at the cottage. Stealing the silver was like taking candy from a baby. Rev. Royce and his followers dumped Matilda in the well and walked off with the loot."

"But legend has it they buried the silver under the doorstep of their church," said Maury Seiderman, his face pressed against the bars. "And you didn't find it when you dug around the foundation. I was there, remember?"

"That legend also said Rev. Royce planned to come back for it," remembered Maddy. "Perhaps he did."

"Exactly," chimed Cookie. "That Viking treasure is long gone."

"Damn," cursed Bern Bjorn. "All this for nothing."

"You've got the quilt," whined Seiderman. "I want my share of that."

"Nobody will be getting a share," snapped Lt. Wannamaker. "You can't profit from stolen goods."

Bjorn flashed a wicked grin. "Yeah, but I've got the quilt. You'll never see it again if you don't let us walk."

"Might cut some slack for little missy here and your weird friend from Chicago," said The Nail, "but no way you're going to walk on a murder charge."

"Wasn't murder," argued Bjorn. "It was an accident."

"Oh, that rock fell out of the sky and landed on Charlie Aitkens's head," scoffed Chief Purdue.

"No, Charlie was showing me this rock he'd found out in the field. Had some kind of writing on it. Like those markings on the witch's quilt. He was starting to figure out there might be more going on here than stealing a ratty old quilt."

"So you killed him," said Bootsie.

"Not just like that. He attacked me and I took the rock away from him and hit him with it. Didn't mean to kill him."

"That's your defense?" said The Nail. "Good luck with that."

"It's the truth."

"Tell it to the judge."

Bern Bjorn set his jaw stubbornly. "Then you'll never see that quilt again."

"I think I know where to find it," said little Aggie who'd been taking all this in.

Everyone turned to stare at the eleven-year-old girl. In the excitement they had forgotten she was there. "You do?" said her grandmother.

"Maybe. Mr. Bjorn said Charlie was going to help him sell the quilt. They had their fight in the Aikens Produce barn. Why not look for it there?"

"We searched the barn at the time of the murder," said Deputy Hitzer.

"But were you looking for a quilt?" asked Aggie.

"Well, no. I was looking for clues to the murder." This was the young policeman's first wrongful death case. His enthusiasm exceeded his experience, as Chief Purdue would later say.

"We'll take another look," said Jim Purdue, "with an eye to finding a missing quilt."

Bern Bjorn cursed again. "Damn, I may as well tell you. It's hidden in a stack of horse blankets in the tack room. The Aitkenses don't keep horses no more, so it could've sat there till Kingdom Come if this pint-sized Quilters Clubber hadn't stuck her nose in."

Aggie smiled, showing her missing tooth. Happy to be recognized as breaking the case for the Quilters Club. "Thank you, Mr. Bjorn. I hope to see you next time I come to the Dairy Queen for a custard parfait."

"You might have to wait thirty years to life for that," said Lt. Neil Wannamaker, his dry wit going over the young girl's head.

"*Hmmpt*, I might not be there," said Bern Bjorn, "but you tell Maisie the counter girl I said to give you extra sprinkles. You're smarter than the lot of these lawmen. You're the one who deserves a reward."

"Gee, thanks, Mr. Bjorn."

"No reward has been posted –" began Lt. Wannamaker.

"Sprinkles will do," said Aggie.

EPILOGUE

It Turns Out Well

The Wilkins Witch Quilt was eventually restored to the wall of the Town Hall. It had been found exactly where Bern Bjorn said, folded in a stack of horse blankets.

Bjorn was found innocent of negligent homicide, the jury buying his story about hitting Charlie Aitkens during a struggle over the rock. Nobody in Caruthers Corners believed that yarn, but juries in Indy don't get very indignant about small-town fisticuffs that end with tragic results.

Nonetheless, Bjorn and his girlfriend Becky Marsch left the area. Some said they went to live with her cousin Maury in Chicago. Becky and her cousin had received suspended sentences as accessories after the fact.

Rumor had it that Boyd Aitkens had hired a hitman to avenge his son's death, but that was never proven. Nor was there any reports of Bjorn's demise.

Aggie did get the extra sprinkles until the Dairy Queen closed down. Bjorn's ex-wife took over the franchise, but she let her boyfriend Ted Yost run it. He was not a very good businessman, as it turned out.

Maddy's son Bill and his wife made a full recovery. Kathy still walks with a slight limp. N'yen was excited to see them when they drove down from Chicago to take him home.

"It was a great visit," he exclaimed. "I got to join the Quilters Club and we solved a big murder case."

Kathy patted him on the head, convinced his imagination had gone wild. "That's nice, dearie," she said as he climbed into the car, a new Subaru courtesy of the trucker's insurance company.

Bill eyed his mother, suspecting there was more truth to the story than not. During their recovery they had not watched the news on TV, so they'd missed the frenzied coverage of the murder trial. The TV networks had had a field day with the witching angle. Nancy Grace did a segment from the Indianapolis courthouse steps. Piers Morgan had interviewed Christine O'Donnell about witchcraft, with her walking off his show for a second time. Anderson Cooper got an exclusive with Becky Marsch, talking about her great-great grandmother Mad Matilda Wilkins.

The story about the Viking silver never came out. The prosecutor had thought it too diverting a topic to introduce into the trial. Professor Ezra Pudhomme was disappointed, for he'd hoped to be interviewed about runology and how he'd helped crack the case.

Cookie Bentley did some more research on Rev. Billingsley Royce, leader of the Avenging Angels. He seemed to have disappeared from history after the 1899 murder of Matilda Wilkins. However, she did find a reference to the formation of a brewery in St. Paul at the turn of the century called Royce's Beverages. Its motto was "Beer Fit for the Angels." She wondered if it had been financed with Viking hack silver.

Royce's Beverages went bust in the 1920s, and records were lost in a fire. Particulars about its ownership were sketchy.

Freddie's daughter Donna was cast as Snow White in a kindergarten play. The Haney Bros. Zoo where Freddie worked part-time as a clown got a new elephant, this one named Rosie. She made a good mate for Happy, the circus's original pachyderm. An aging lion named Growly was also added to the menagerie. Bombay Martinez was happy with his new charges.

Tilly announced she was pregnant again. Mark the Shark was already handing out cigars. Aggie rolled her eyes at the thought of another sibling.

Boyd Aitkens was good as his word, offering to put up the campaign money for Beauregard Hollingsworth Madison IV's next mayoral campaign, but Beau surprised everybody by deciding not to run. Mark Tidemore announced his candidacy, and with Beau's endorsement was a shoo-in.

Lt. Neil Wannamaker nominated Aggie for an Honorary Lawman of the Year award. She was all giggly at the idea. She viewed it as validation of the Quilter's Club as *real* detectives.

The Nail also had offered to nominate the other Quilters Club members, but they didn't have time for such nonsense. Maddy, Cookie, Bootsie, and Lizzie were much too busy, already planning the quilting exhibit for the next Watermelon Day festival.

❀ ❀ ❀

Thank you for reading.
Please review this book. Reviews help others find
Absolutely Amazing eBooks and inspire us to keep
providing these marvelous tales.

If you would like to be put on our email list to receive
updates on new releases, contests, and promotions, please
go to AbsolutelyAmazingEbooks.com and sign up.

About the Author

Marjory Sorrell Rockwell says needlecraft arts – quilting, crocheting, knitting – are pastimes every woman can appreciate. And she particularly loves quiltmaking. "It's like painting with cloth," she says. But when not quilting she writes mysteries about a midwestern sleuth not unlike herself, a middle-aged lady with an unpredictable family and loyal friends. And she's a big fan of watermelon pie.

ABSOLUTELY AMA⚡ING eBOOKS

AbsolutelyAmazingeBooks.com
or AA-eBooks.com

19988121R00327

Made in the USA
San Bernardino, CA
23 March 2015